QUANTUM
KILL

Book 4

RON WICK

QUANTUM KILL
Ron Wick

a GlenEagle publication
Copyright ©2015 Ron Wick
Printed in the United States of America
All rights reserved.

* * * * *

* * * * *

Disclaimer
This is a work of fiction, a product of the author's imagination. Any resemblance or similarity to any actual events or persons, living or dead, is purely coincidental. Although the author and publisher have made every effort to ensure there are no errors, inaccuracies, omissions, or inconsistencies herein, any slights or people, places, or organizations are unintentional.

* * * * *

Credits
Author photo by Casey Wick Stewart Photography
Cover photo courtesy of Shutterstock Photo

Formatting and cover design by Debora Lewis
arenapublishing.org

* * * * *

ISBN-13: 978-1517289348
ISBN-10: 1517289343

DEDICATION

It is with great pleasure I dedicate *Quantum Kill* to Tony Cerasoli, a very special man for his unlimited encouragement. And with equal vigor to John "Z Man" Zuanich who first took a walk on the wild side with me in 1974 when we co-authored "1."

Acknowledgments

Many friends and writers have shared the various drafts of Quantum Kill. Each has made suggestions and shared input. I thank who have encouraged, read and provided feedback. My hat is off to Irene Coatta, Ed Harter, Nancy Hopkins, Mark Rodman, Darin Sicurello, and Don Stevens. Special thanks to Debora Lewis and Arena Publishing for her creative work in proofing, cover design and formatting Quantum Kill. I hope we work together again on Eyes of the Stalker.

I give special thanks to the two women in my life. My daughter Casey Wick Stewart provided new author photo. And always, my appreciation to soulmate Ruth Wick, forever "Jon" to me.

Thank you one and all.

Ron Wick

PROLOGUE
Washington, D.C.

Tony Mercedes stood smoking a cigarette in front of the Vietnam Veterans Memorial. He kept looking around and checking his watch. An unshaved older man with long gray hair wearing a threadbare oversized field jacket approached. Thirty yards behind him was a small cluster of older men in a variety of equally worn field dress.

Homeless veterans. Mercedes watched the man until he stopped in front of him.

The man looked at Mercedes's cigarette. "Can you spare one?"

"Take the pack," he said holding it out.

"Thanks. You serve?"

"Khafiji. You?"

The man nodded. "Qatar."

"Here." Mercedes handed the man $20.00. "Thanks for serving."

"You, too."

The man moved on. Mercedes checked his watch again, tossed the cigarette butt on the ground and crushed it. When he looked the up the man in the oversized field jacket had returned.

"I forgot something."

He pointed a .22 automatic with a silencer at Mercedes and squeezed the trigger. A small red circle appeared on Mercedes right temple. The shooter took hold of Mercedes overcoat lapel with one hand and slid the automatic back under his field jacket with the other. He lowered Mercedes to the ground in a sitting position, leaned him against the wall and turned his right cheek inward hiding a small stream of blood.

A woman walking past some twenty-five feet away called out, "Does he need assistance?"

The shooter was reaching into Mercedes's coat. "No. He's just tired. He's gonna rest for a few minutes while I get us some coffee."

The woman continued on her way.

The shooter stood, took Mercedes watch, sliding it and his wallet into a jacket pocket, and walked toward a small vendor cart in the direction of the Washington Monument. He took the oversized field jacket off and dropped it and the .22 in a trash container as he passed without slowing or looking back. He walked into the mainstream of mall visitors just another tourist wearing a green hoody, blue jeans, and tennis shoes with a camera hanging from his neck and a pair of gloves hanging out of a pants pocket.

A gray haired middle-aged woman watched the shooter walk away. She went to the trash and removed the field jacket. Another scruffy looking man ran up, grabbed the jacket and ran away. She looked in the trash can and saw the .22. She lifted it from the trash by the butt and hid it under her raincoat. She glanced around. Nobody approached her but a crowd began to gather by Mercedes. She walked away without looking back.

CHAPTER 1
Tuesday, July 8

Ray House, DataFlex Security Chief, stood in his Chandler, Arizona office listening to a cell phone. He looked around the office suite and out the window onto the main floor. Deep furrows creased his forehead when the call ended. He put the cell away and went to the adjoining office of Jessica Rodriguez, Security Chief Administrative Assistant.

"What's the matter, Ray? You have that stressed squinty-eyed look."

He gazed out at the main floor. "A mole, a damn mole. Somebody killed Tony Mercedes about twenty minutes ago in Washington."

"An accident?"

"Professional hit. Get a team in here to do another sweep of the building. I want everything checked including our offices. I'm going down to Mario's cubicle and have him go through the systems, see if we've been compromised. Get Mitch and Link in here now. And...," he said raising an eyebrow.

"Not a word to anyone, I know," she said.

He paused at the door. "All these years and never anything like this. Claude's always been proud of the fact only a few of our people have ever been seriously injured, none killed taking care of business; ours or the fed's."

"Does he know?"

"Not yet. I'll call him as soon as I'm done implementing our protocols. I have an idea to run by him."

"This feels like our days with the Agency," she said.

House stepped to the door. "Yes it does."

Mario Spears, a DataFlex under the radar master hacker computer tech was pounding his keyboard with the enthusiasm of a rock star when House walked into the cubicle.

"Mario."

Spears jumped in his seat and hit the exit key at the same time. "Mr. House, you surprised me."

"What are you working on?"

"The security code program for Spain."

"Put it on hold or pass it off. I have a special assignment for you."

Spear's looked at House. "Is this off the record?"

"Yes, I need to know if our systems have been compromised. One of our people was killed this morning at the National Mall."

"Who?"

"Tony Mercedes. His name hasn't been released yet, so nobody in the company knows."

"Understand. What do I tell my colleagues when I hand-off Spain?"

"Tell 'em you're working on one of my impulse projects. They're accustomed to it."

"They'll know we're being quiet about something.

"Yes, but they won't know what. Close your project."

Within the hour Michelle Santiago, Link Andrews, Jessica Rodriguez and Mario Spears sat in House's conference room waiting.

Andrews said, "I was two under on fourteen when my cell started vibrating." He started to laugh. "I came straight here. The new fellow on the gate thought I was looking for a golf course when I pulled up."

Santiago said, "He probably saw the clubs in the back of your truck. Maybe he caught a glimpse of your gaudy shorts and polo shirt."

Santiago and Andrews laughed. Rodriguez and Spears smiled at the interaction but said nothing.

Andrews looked at Santiago. "El Camino, Mitch, it's a classic and not a truck." He smirked. "And given the gym shorts and a tank top you're wearing I wouldn't think my attire is out of place or even noticeable."

"I was doing personal business just like you, a sketch on Mill. Jessica said it was an emergency."

House walked in, closed the door and went to the head of the table. "Mitch, Link, I'm sorry to tell you Tony Mercedes was murdered this morning. I know both of you have worked with him."

Santiago caught her breath. "What happened?"

"Long story. We got word somebody might be trying to gain access to a special project Maxwell Cyber Systems is doing for the government. We're a subcontractor on the project. It was Mercedes job to confirm the attempt if it existed."

Spears said, "Wouldn't that be something for the FBI?"

"Yes," said House, "but their inquiry found nothing. That's when we decided to look for ourselves, after you found those well hidden breaches of Maxwell's data files last month, Mario. Tony's murder confirms something is going on."

Santiago said, "And we can do things the Feds can't."

"That and we've also had a breach here. I suspect it's part of the same group. Mario has begun looking into data files and the entire building has been swept for bugs ahead of schedule. Five were found; one each in the staff room, my office, Jessica's office and the restrooms in this building. For now this is an internal matter since we can't tie the bugs to Mercedes's death as far as the government is concerned."

Santiago asked, "Have any bugs been found in the labs and other offices recently?"

"None. So far whoever placed the bugs is only probing our security operations, not research."

Andrews said, "The Feds could be investigating this without our knowing."

House nodded. "That's possible, even probable in light of our being breached. If they're working strictly by the book they don't comment on any ongoing investigation. If they suspect we've been compromised they'd want to keep us out of the loop anyway."

Andrews said, "So what is our plan of action?"

"Tony was probing weaknesses in Maxwell's security, with a focus on cyber espionage in the Barrier

Program. We know he was getting close to exposing a mole."

Santiago said, "What is the Barrier Program?"

"A classified research effort developing a hacker proof password process. Mario will brief us on it separately later today."

Andrews said, "How did they identify Tony?"

"He was highly visible, our liaison in their security department. DataFlex has invested heavily in the project. His last report hinted at something going on which could compromise Maxwell."

Spears said, "A few years ago a worm was embedded in the Iranians nuclear program which altered research data. It slowed the development by years. I'd think it would be more than a little advantageous for any number of groups or individuals to disrupt research on the Barrier."

Santiago said, "This sounds clandestine from the get go. With his background shouldn't Sam be here?"

House looked around the table. "He'll be brought on board later. For the time being we'll work independently, just this group."

Andrews said, "Sam's one of the most trusted people in this company and with an intelligence background."

"Precisely," said House, "and when he goes into Maxwell he'll be carefully watched by whoever was shadowing Tony. Maxwell does deep background on people assigned to them from other companies just as we do. There will be no connection between Sam and what goes on here today. As our replacement for Tony he'll go in clean. I'm sure they have some tools in place to evaluate his mission. If asked, he'll come across just as he should. He'll raise no doubts."

Santiago said, "Since the FBI is either not engaged at this time or leaving us out, how are the D. C. police handling Tony's murder?"

"They're treating it as a mugging gone badly. His watch and wallet were gone when he was found. The reason we were called was he had a DataFlex ID card on a lanyard. They wanted a family connection from us. That's the information Sam will have."

Andrews said, "So he was found almost immediately after he was killed?"

"Yes, Washington Mall is usually crowded."

Santiago said, "In other words, Sam can't suppress what he doesn't know."

House said, "Exactly. Since we know we have leaks of our own we'll have nothing about this inquiry in any company files, electronic or otherwise. Communications will be done in person and using pre-paid burn phones."

Andrews said, "Ray, do we know if the breach here is connected to the breach at Maxwell?"

"We don't and Tony never raised the issue either."

Santiago said, "But it could be, and until we know better we'll presume it?"

House said, "Yes, Maxwell's operational structure is similar to ours. They also work multiple secret projects. For now I'm thinking whatever Tony was dealing with was related to the Barrier. It's always possible he stumbled onto something different but we have no supporting evidence."

Andrews said, "It will be difficult to place any of us undercover at Maxwell. We've all worked with them in the past."

House said, "Claude and I have come up with a solution. I'm going to fire Mitch."

Santiago, Andrews and Spears looked at House then each other.

"In doing so I hope someone connected to the Maxwell operation contacts her; an ex-lover vengeful former consultant with an in-depth knowledge of DataFlex security. If the plan works Mitch has the dual tasks of finding Mercedes's contact and identifying the leak within their program, not necessarily the same person. We also know somebody at DataFlex is involved. We need to find out who."

Andrews said, "And who killed Tony."

House said, "If the authorities don't first."

Santiago glanced at Link and smirked. "You said ex-lover?"

"Everyone in the company knows you have a special relationship with our CEO and Nikki. It's common knowledge you visit their home often even when Nikki isn't there on confidential business with Claude. That's part of what makes this a believable cover."

Santiago said, "I'll have to watch my visiting habits in the future."

"Word will be all over DataFlex within the hour you've been fired for having an affair with him. Everyone knows Claude's reputation as a ladies man in years past. It's no big stretch of the imagination to think he'd be more than a little interested in a woman of your appeal even if you and his current wife are known to be best friends. It just makes the story juicier. And, it's Nikki Braun who insisted you be fired."

Santiago said, "Obviously Nikki is aware of the plan, too."

"Of course. In fact it was Claude's idea when we talked a few minutes ago just before this meeting. He calls it lover's revenge. He believes the plan will save us a great deal of time. He and Nikki will handle their parts of our little drama. You'll be ostracized. If anyone says anything to Nikki she'll paint you in ugly colors. Claude will pout."

Santiago said. "Do I stay in contact with you in any way other than the burn cell?"

"Link will be your conduit. Of course it will appear to be on the sly as far as DataFlex is concerned, a friendly romantic interest, not much of an exaggeration except for the Braun part."

Mitch and Link coughed simultaneously and cleared their throats.

"All employees will be told to have no further contact with you. Link's rogue behavior wouldn't be unusual for him."

Andrews said, "Independent behavior. Who all knows about the plan?"

"The five of us, Claude and Nikki, no one else. Mitch, when you leave this room you'll be angry, hostile. React like your best friend was sleeping with your father. Link, you and Mario are going to walk out of here in shock. The whole office knows the three of you are close knit."

Santiago said, "What about Sam Evans? He and I have worked very close. He's part of the team."

House smiled. "Whatever his reaction, it will be genuine. Our timeline is tight enough the firing should seem real, that and the fact Tony's murder isn't public knowledge yet."

Santiago said, "So I just leave here pissed off and wait for someone to call?"

"Pretty much. Do whatever you'd do if you weren't here. I know you've been taking art classes, sketching on Mill, working out with some local cops. You might even consider looking for another job since your big retainer client is gone. Get hold of your parents. Visit your cousin in Palm Springs. If someone wants to get in touch with you they'll find you, and we want you doing the sort of things you normally do when not working."

"You know my routines pretty well."

House looked around the room. "Link talks about you a lot when we take smoke breaks. Be convincing, people. When we leave everyone out there needs to believe Mitch has been canned. Then we'll let the rumors build. One more thing Mitch, you won't be receiving any deposits from DataFlex during this operation. I'll need your ID card. The purge must be real to everyone. Do you have sufficient resources for now?"

"I'm good."

Mario Spears grinned. "Who wouldn't be? Everyone here knows about the million dollar bonuses you and Sam got for saving Lindsey Braun."

House said, "That was for a job well done, Mario. Link, you'll be having clandestine meetings with Mitch. You two set that up before we leave here. When you call each other be careful, keep the conversations personal sounding. If you need to contact each other for something confidential that can't be talked about in public use the burn cells."

House handed Mitch and Andrews prepaid disposable cells. "We ready?"

Everyone stood. Andrews said, "Let's do it."

"Mitch," said House, "if for any reason you need to reach me and can't, Jessica is the one to contact. Use the burn cell for that, too."

"Of course," she said then turned toward Link Andrews.

*****

Rita Ramsey, head custodian at DataFlex, and assistant Marci Todd were cleaning the floor outside Ray House's office and conference room.

Rita said, "Marci, what do you think is going on in there?

"Haven't got a clue. They were all smiles when they went in. Then Mr. House shows up and now it all looks serious."

Rita said, "Not our problem. Everything Mr. House does is serious."

"I know and he's got the big guns in there. Something is happening."

Rita raised a brow. "Not Sam Evans."

"He isn't, is he?"

"Nope, and Mario gave someone else the project he was working on this morning, 'passing it off,' he calls it."

Marci glanced at the conference room again. "Really?"

"Said he was going to do something special for Mr. House."

Marci shrugged. "He always is."

"Even my new trainee, Christopher, thinks something's up."

"Could be. Last time we saw 'em all together was when the virus thing got so messy."

Rita looked at her hand and flexed her fingers. "Yeah, I remember. The Santiago woman almost got killed; was pinned to a table by an ice pick stuck through the back of her hand, and she's not even on staff."

Marci's eyes rolled. "I know she's Braun's special favorite; gets a big retainer, works when she wants, has been ever since she saved his daughter from that crazy old sniper nut last year."

"Well, she's a looker, too. Mr. Braun's never been bashful 'bout the ladies 'til she came along."

Marci looked around them in both directions. "Not only that, she always dresses like a model or a movie star showing a lot of skin."

Rita smiled. "Prostitute, she looks like a prostitute walkin' down Van Buren or one of those nasty ladies you see on T.V."

"Well the men in here sure like her. Link keeps real close and I think Mario drools every time she passes him."

"Just look at her today, wearin' those tiny shorts. She comes in here struttin' her stuff. It's not professional. We couldn't get away with that."

"Rita, relax. If we came in dressed like her everyone would just laugh. I don't think the packaging would look the same on us."

"There's no need to make this personal, Marci."

Christopher Reed approached. "Hi ladies. What's happening?"

Rita nodded toward the conference room. "I think you were right earlier when you said something was going on. Looks like a big pow wow."

"Um, so I see," he said, "and I just thought you two were gossiping."

Rita said, "Really?"

Marci nodded. "We call it networking."

Christopher said, "Whatever. Earlier I saw some people checking the lights and phones for dust, even the trash cans. Do we need to go back over our work before going to the lab building?"

"No," said Rita. "They do that all the time. They're a security team trained in finding listening devices, you know, bugs."

Marci said, "They don't call this the security building for nothing. You'll get used to it."

He nodded toward the conference room door. "Well, I best get back to work. It looks like they're getting ready to come out."

*****

Santiago and Andrews waited by the conference table as the others went out the door.

She said, "When will we get together for my briefing on this operation?"

He checked his watch. "My lunch is about an hour and half away. Ray is going to brief me on what he's gotten from Maxwell now. He rushed your termination to make it appear unrelated. Where do you want to eat at?"

"Tree House of Beans on Mill, if anyone is tuned in that fast we'll appear as a couple, at a loss on how to continue our relationship."

House poked his head into the conference room. "Mitch, on the way out remember, show a little invective. Your best friend got you fired because she thinks you've been sleeping with her husband."

She arched an eyebrow and smiled. "Not to worry, Ray. I'll give you both barrels just the way any self-respecting woman or mistress would."

Mario Spears stood near Jessica Rodriguez's desk between the conference room and the aisle to the exit. Santiago left the conference room in a rush, shoved him aside and stomped down the aisle toward the entry shouting, "Bastards! Outta my way!"

Christopher Reed pushed a janitorial cart past House's office suite. "What happened, man?"

Spears shook his head. "House just fired Mitch. Can you believe it?"

Reed said, "No shit."

"I don't believe it either, but he did."

Andrews came out of the conference room red faced. "You don't have to, Mario. If the wife of your boss thinks you're sleeping with him shit happens, even more so if you're like best friends."

Mitch neared the checkout exit.

Andrews watched Santiago's fast pace down the aisle. He moved toward the exit. "I better help the guard with this."

Reed said, "Mario, do you think she was bangin' Braun?"

"No way."

Reed smiled. "But if she was, holy crap, the lucky son-of-a-bitch."

Spears said, "I wouldn't let Link hear me say that if I were you."

"He and Mitch have something going?"

Spears smiled. "Oh yeah, but nothing official. Let's just say they're very close."

Both men watched her moving toward the exit; hips swinging, taking long strides, looking straight ahead, Link close behind her.

Reed grinned. "That's one pissed off beautiful woman."

Santiago approached the exit and shouted, "Open that damn door!"

The guard motioned her to the bulletproof glass window and pointed at the electronic clipboard. "Have to sign out, Mitch."

"Jesus, I don't even work here."

Another security guard appeared. "Please, Miss Santiago, I have to escort you off the property, company policy."

"Company policy, crap. You have no authority to stop me from leaving this phony black hole of happiness."

Andrews arrived at the exit. "I'll take care of this."

The guard said, "Thanks, Link."

Andrews signed the electronic clipboard and the door clicked. He held out an arm to Santiago. "Shall we?"

They went out the door as a few onlookers gathered in the aisle behind them whispering and watching. As soon as they cleared the door it automatically closed.

Andrews laughed. "Nice job. If I didn't know better I'd believe all this."

She touched the lanyard suspended from her neck. "I've still got my credential. I'm going to throw it at the gate guard as I drive out."

"I love it. Remind me to never piss you off."

She smiled. "Walk with me to my car. I'll see you at lunch, your lunch."

Santiago got in her red Mustang GT, fired up the 412 horsepower engine and leaned out the window. "Kiss me. We're being watched. It'll explain our clandestine meeting at lunch."

"And to think we've been so discreet 'til now."

Andrews bent down and kissed her then watched as she drove to the gate. She slowed approaching the guard shack. A man stepped out into the lane and held up a hand until she stopped. He heard inaudible shouts and saw the credential fly out the car window. The guard leaned over, picked it up, and the gate opened. The throaty rumble of the engine rolled across the parking lot as Santiago pulled onto Chandler Boulevard and disappeared in tire smoke. Andrews returned to the security building.

The building entry guard said, "I'm sorry, Link."

Andrews signed back into the building. "So am I, so am I. She was the best operative we had barring none. Just don't believe everything you're going to hear. Mitch is a good person."

"I know, but the rumors have already started to spread like a virus."

*****

The husky voiced woman stood on Pennsylvania Avenue looking at the White House and listened to a cell phone. "Yes."

A man with a high pitched voice said, "We've heard nothing here yet about the event this morning."

"It's early. The D.C. cops are classifying it as a mugging, but something has occurred out there or you wouldn't have called. What is it?"

The man said, "Two things. The entire security building has been swept again for bugs. They do that routinely, but yesterday was the regular day."

She said, "I know."

He said, "All five bugs I placed last night were found. That means they'll be looking more often."

"Replace them."

"They'll just find them again. They'll be looking daily, maybe even more often."

She said, "We'll miss a lot of intel."

"I have other ways that were more than useful last week."

The husky voiced woman took a deep breath. "You said two things. What is the other?"

"Ray House fired Michelle Santiago, the high profile security consultant that's been on retainer here for the past year. Word is she was sleeping with Claude Braun. His wife found out and demanded her dismissal."

The husky voiced woman smiled. "Interesting, knowing his reputation and her background it could be true."

The man said, "You know her?"

"Of her. It's my job to know about all of the main players at DataFlex."

He said, "Well, she created quite a scene when she left; slamming doors, cursing, shouting. She pulled out of the parking lot like a drag racer. She also kissed Link Andrews before she left the campus."

"How did her other colleagues react?"

"Four of the five she works with regularly attended a conference where she was fired at the end; House, Spears, Andrews and Rodriguez. The two men were surprised."

She said, "A public firing is unusual for Ray House. He had to have a briefing with Claude Braun before dropping the hammer. Public humiliation just isn't his style. I'm sure there was disbelief and sympathy for her from Andrews and Spears."

He said, "And some from other staff members, too."

She said, "You noted Sam Evans wasn't at the meeting?"

"He wasn't. I don't know why."

"Try to find out. Stay alert and keep an eye on Evans. DataFlex has lost two of its better operatives today. Someone will replace Mercedes, maybe Evans. I need to know who and when."

"Yes ma'am."

"Call again this evening, your time. I hope you have more news for me."

The connection broke. The lady in Washington punched in another number.

"The number you are calling is out of service."

"Damn it."

She tried another number.

"This is Xavier, talk to me."

She said, "Jerome?"

Xavier said in a harsh voice, "I'm here."

"Is Kohler in?"

"No, Canfield and the receptionist are out of the office."

"I have a task for you."

"I'm always available to you. Same arrangement as last time?"

"Of course, funds will be transferred to your account when we finish talking."

"Excellent."

"I tried calling Canfield, but your partner's cell is off and this is a rush job. I need you to shadow a woman named Michelle Santiago."

"I've heard of her. She's been in the press a few times. Works for DataFlex here in Chandler."

"Not any more. I want to know where she goes, who she talks to, who she calls if you can find out; everything."

"For how long?"

"Just a day or two."

"Am I looking for anything in particular?"

"No. I just want to know what she's doing. That's all the direction you need. I'll be contacting you for updates." She broke the connection.

Xavier checked the call number. "They're always different. I hate dealing with a mystery client. Better let Canfield know."

The woman walked to the center of the White House fence, stepped to the curb and flagged a cab.

*****

Michelle Santiago stepped to the lanai of her soft loft condo overlooking Tempe Town Lake facing north. She sipped a cup of rich black coffee and watched the traffic moving east and west on the 202. *I've got the better part of an hour before lunch with Link. No need to change.* She stepped around to corner of the lanai facing east. Five floors below, a silver colored Sienna pulled to the curb on Rio Salado Drive. The driver remained in the car. He appeared to be on a cell phone. "Smart motorist."

She went inside and called her parents on a cordless unit as she walked back to the deck. A lady answered.

Santiago said, "Hi, mom, how are you doing?"

"Had lunch today."

"What did you have?"

"Paper says rain, here of all places. I get pretty tired. It's not like our time in the Haight or Big Sur, rockin' all night and protesting all day. Think we'll ever get out of Nam?"

The image of Yancey Quarterman, an MIA turned mercenary psychopath she'd encountered finding Braun's daughter came to mind. "We did mom, a long time ago."

"Good, 'bout time we did. Got to do something 'bout LJB, too."

"He's been gone a long time, mom."

"There's a big bat with six-foot wings sittin' on the porch."

Tears flowed down Santiago's cheeks. She took a deep breath, gripped the phone tighter. "Is dad home?"

"Of course."

"Can I talk to him?"

"If he's here. I gotta find him. There's a strange man here."

She heard her mother calling her father then rustling sounds.

"Mitch?"

"Dad."

"It's always good to hear your voice."

"How often is mom like this now? She's really bad today."

"Almost daily, babe; it's getting a little harder to take care of her. Sometimes she doesn't know who I am, like just a minute ago. Then she'll snap back."

"Maybe it's time to find a nice place for her. I'll cover the cost. I worry about you, too. You need some relief and free time."

"I'm fine."

"I know, but she's 24/7. Everybody needs help sometime."

"I'm not so sure. We've been soul mates forever. You and your sister didn't even come along 'til later, kinda after our hippie days so to speak."

Santiago laughed. "That's not quite the way Jill and I remember growing up."

"Trust me, babe. The 70's were a lot different than the 80's when we became responsible parents. "So," he said changing the subject, "are you already at lunch, between assignments, taking the day off?"

"Fired, dad. Nikki thinks I've been sleeping with Claude."

"No."

"She demanded he fire me, end of story."

"That's not fair."

"No, but that's life, the bastards."

"You're angry."

"Damn right. I saved her step daughter's life, saved DataFlex's billion dollar virus project, did undercover work, all for this bullshit?"

"Calm down, Mitch. Braun made you a very wealthy young woman. You'll find a new position if you want. Your reputation is stellar. Things have a way of working out."

"This won't go away. Braun is a powerful man."

He said, "Nobody will believe it."

"Maybe. Right now I'd like to stick it to him and his precious company." She laughed. "Maybe I don't want to stick the company. I have a lot of DataFlex stock. It could be laughable that he's generating my income while I bury him personally."

"Vengeful doesn't sound like you, Mitch."

"Never been fired before. I don't like it."

"When did this happen?"

"This morning, maybe an hour ago. I got called in for a special meeting and dumped. I'm nobody's mistress."

"I know."

"Dad, I've got the time. I'm going to look into what's available that could help you and mom. I know you like the desert so I'll look first in the valley. If we don't find something really good here then I'll take a look in Palm Springs, even Yuma if you want. That way if you decide to move it would be to a place you've already lived."

"I don't want to move."

"I know. I don't want you to either. I just want something that's good for both you and mom; the right care and doctors."

"Well, you can look into it if you want, but not a word to your mother."

"Of course not, and dad, I would appreciate you keeping quiet about my being fired. Given how sensitive some of my work was, Braun could have someone checking to make sure I don't do something to hurt him. I signed a nondisclosure contract with DataFlex when I first started working for them. I don't want to get sued."

"Not a word, Mitch."

"I've got to go, dad. I have a lunch date. Love you."

"Love you, babe."

A smile crossed her face as she put the phone in its cradle. *It's a safe bet the whole clubhouse at dad's trailer park will know I've been fired, and I'm pissed off, within an hour.*

Going back to the deck she noticed the Sienna still parked with the man sitting in it. "I have company. You said this could go fast, Ray. This is fast."

Chapter 2

Kat Parsons had just returned to her desk in the DataFlex accounting office when her phone rang twice taking her away from a discussion with the lady in the next cubicle.

"Yes," she answered.

The receptionist said, "A Jerome Xavier on line three."

"Thank you." She punched line three. "This is Kat."

"It's me kid, Jerome."

She exhaled. "I know."

"Don't sound so enthusiastic, Kat. I need a favor."

"You always need a favor, usually something difficult."

"I know, but this one should be easy. Don't forget I did you a big favor once getting some records sealed, remember?"

"You'll never let me forget. What is it you need this time?"

"Information, of course."

"Who are you trying to collect from now?"

"Not that kind of info, Kat. This is about a person where you work. Do you know who Michelle Santiago is?"

"Everybody here does. Most of the women either admire her or are jealous. Some are both. Why?"

"Have you heard anything about her recently?"

"Funny you should ask. I just got back from coffee and everyone is talking about her being fired this morning."

"Really? Anyone say why?"

"Sleeping with old man Braun the way I heard it. Rumor has it the wife found out he was testing his dip stick and insisted he can her. What's even more outrageous is Mitch and Mrs. Braun were best friends."

"I've heard similar rumors this morning. Could you check her payroll records? I'd like to know if her status has been changed."

"Where can I reach you?"

"I'll hold."

"It'll take a few minutes."

"Okay."

Parsons went into to the accounts payable file and scanned Santiago. "The authorization to make monthly deposits based on her retainer has been canceled. Hold on a minute and I'll see if I have anything at her bank." A moment later she said, "Her bank account has been closed. She probably changed accounts this morning after getting the ax."

"That was fast."

"It doesn't take long and knowing this company, there's probably people that could access her banking information anyway if they wanted to."

"Check her benefits?"

"If your employment is terminated so are your bennies, Jerome."

"I know, but check anyway."

"She wasn't an employee. She was on retainer. However, it says here she received medical coverage as part of the company plan with special authorization. There's a notation from Jessica Rodriguez dated this morning saying the company will only cover her for the remainder of the month."

"You said she was on retainer?"

"Yes."

"How much?"

"$250,000 plus fees per assignment. That's a sweetheart deal if ever there was one."

Xavier said, "That's a lot of money just to be on call."

Parsons laughed. "I guess it depends on what you're being called for. Anything else?"

"Not right now, but thank you, Kat. I owe you."

Parsons voice cracked as she said, "You could stop calling me for favors. That would be nice."

"Until next time." Xavier hung up.

*****

Vladimir Clyburn, a tall blond Russian immigrant, worked in the cubicle next to Kat Parsons. When her conversation with Xavier ended Vladimir tapped his desk with a pencil and starred at his phone. *Why are you giving out confidential information, Kat? You could be fired just like Santiago.*

The faint sound of Kat whimpering bled into his cubicle. Clyburn stopped tapping the pencil. "Confidential, favors? Is someone blackmailing Kat?"

He got up and walked next door. "Kat?"

She ran a finger over the corner of her left eye. "Vladimir, come in. It must be dusty in here."

"You're crying."

"No, no, just dust."

"I heard you talking on the phone."

The cubicle became silent for a moment.

She said, "You were listening to my conversation?"

"You gave confidential information to someone."

She raised her head and blinked. Her eyes welled. "Yes, I did. I had to."

"You could get in a lot of trouble, Kat."

"If I didn't give him the information I'd be in more."

"How?"

"Last summer I did something bad, very bad. The man on the phone found out."

"Did you break the law?"

"No, well, yes."

"What did you do?"

"I was trying to get a collector to stop bugging my sister. I went to Xavier for help and told him I had accessed her bank records from here. Serious mistake."

"Tell the police you're being blackmailed."

"I can't for two good reasons; first no proof. It would be my word against his. Second and more important to me, I'd lose my job. I've given him information before."

"You'll lose your job anyway if security finds out about today and you haven't reported it to them or the police."

"They won't find out unless you report me."

"I wouldn't do that. You know I wouldn't."

"Yes, I know. I'm just afraid of him."

"Who is he?"

"Jerome Xavier, a private detective."

"I can go see him, tell him to leave you alone. What he's doing is against the law."

"Don't. He could hurt you, too."

"How? He has nothing on me."

"I mean hurt you. He's a violent man; short, strong, thuggish."

"Did he hurt you, Kat?"

She looked at Vladimir for a long moment. "Not physically."

"I know a lot of people. I'll think of something."

"Please don't. He doesn't bother me very often. You and I are friends, Vladimir. I want us to remain friends. This'll go away."

He shook his head. "I don't think so. Where I used live everybody was afraid. That was Russia."

She said, "Let's get together tonight when we can talk. In the meantime don't do anything, please."

"Okay, 'til tonight." He kissed her on the cheek. "I'll see you around 8:00."

*****

Link Andrews sat at an outdoor table and watched Michelle Santiago walk south on the east side of Mill Avenue, the hub of ASU social life; boutiques, coffee houses, clothing shops, book stores, music and head shops, fast food outlets and more lining each side of the street. A few panhandlers were already out; some roamed the sidewalk, a few sat on street benches or curbs – all hustling. A handful of musicians played guitars, fiddles or flutes with instrument cases or jars on the ground in front of them for donations.

Andrews watched her cross 4th Avenue with the light. A man rushed to make the crossing signal before traffic began. She stopped and spoke to a homeless woman sitting at a bench in the shade. A cart heavy with the woman's worldly belongings was beside her. The rushing man stopped to look in a shop window. Mitch gave the woman some money and moved on. The man followed about fifty feet behind her.

Andrews said, "Now I understand."

Andrews continued to watch and sipped his coffee.

She spotted him and waved. He waved back and took another sip. She crossed the street, approached him and kissed his cheek. "Hi."

"You have a tail."

"I know."

A young student waiter came to the table. "Ma'am?"

"May I have a medium Americano, please?"

He nodded and left.

"That's why I came down the east side, to give you a view if you were already here."

"Good idea. So how has the rest of your morning gone?"

"After being fired I went to the bank and changed accounts. It only took a few minutes and seemed prudent since I'm no longer retained by DataFlex. No direct deposit and less opportunity for someone checking into my business."

"You don't want to make it easy."

She smiled. "Never easy."

He glanced toward the tail now seated at an outside table next door at the Tea Shop. "When did you pick up your friend?"

"When I left the loft. He was parked around the corner. Had a good view of the building, Town Lake and the park. He'd see me coming or going."

The waiter arrived with the Americano. Andrews handed the young man a ten dollar bill. "Keep it."

The waiter left.

"You're generous today," she said.

"College kid, he needs the money."

She touched one of Andrews' hands. "So what have you got for me?"

"Do you know anything about cyber keys and quantum mechanics?"

"No. When I was with the Seattle Police Department I encountered an attorney who was always saying we had the least amount or quantum of evidence possible against his client. I took it to mean we had little or nothing, even the tiniest amount as my Captain once said, that and I thought he was in error by using the term."

"He probably was. Maxwell Cyber Systems, the Noble Group and DataFlex are working together on the Barrier Project. The purpose of their research is to develop a password structure or access code program that serves two purposes. First, the code can only be used once, then it must be replaced. Second, if a hacker tires to access the program and does not have the code the window crashes allowing no access until replaced."

"Yes. Think of it this way. There are two types of computer systems; classical and quantum. The classical system is in broad use today. The quantum system is primarily in research and development. Governments and business worldwide are working on it. The difference between to two systems is this: Classical programs require data to be encoded into binary bits which are always in one of two states, 0 or 1. Quantum computers use qubits which can be in what's called a superposition of the two states of 0 and 1, but setting one or the other only when used."

"For our purposes, two passwords."

"Yes, and given the randomness of quantum physics hackers have no way to figure out the cyber key's internal code. The quantum system uses qubits – the smallest measureable unit in a computer. Using a method called conjugate coding a qubit can only be read once. The passwords are encoded on the same string of qubits. When either one of the passwords is used the other crashes and cannot be used. If someone tries to hack into the program and enters the incorrect password the window crashes and can't be open again until the password is reset."

She chuckled. "Hacker proof. Link, you and I know there are several world class hacker's like Mario around the globe. While Maxwell Cyber Systems, the Noble Group and DataFlex are working on creating this unbreakable cyber key I'll bet on Mario and his peers finding a way into or around such a key by the time scientists have it perfected."

"Mario also pointed out since the quantum system is in conjugate coding, the process of entanglement used widely today in hacking cannot come into play. Maxwell's physicists are trying to entangle but have found it impossible."

"Stop," she said waving her hands, "entangle sounds like something that happens to hair. I'm a layman. From my point of view the long and short of it is a disrupted key equals no entry."

"Basically, yes."

She laughed. "Ray said this morning, my job is to find out who is trying to access the research, not what is the research."

He said, "Or who is trying to disrupt it, maybe both. Unbreakable codes are rare and I'm thinking all the way back to the Navaho code talkers in World Wars I and II."

"One thing is certain, whoever has the process would be a step up in the world of cyber warfare."

"Something else is in play, too. Mario says while the cyber key could be years away from implementation, we are in competition with others working on the same methodology."

"Competition serves as a motive for cyber espionage."

Andrews nodded. "Do tell."

Santiago smiled. "It still sounds like a world of possibilities for a creative hacker. Cybersecurity teams will love this someday."

"You mean the legal cybersecurity teams."

"Yes, Mario calls them 'white-hat hackers, the good guys.' He told me some of the best hackers are employed by governments and the business world just like he is here at DataFlex. We both know hacking has reached epidemic proportions. The government has even launched a hiring program for the best hackers, something the press refers to as this generations Manhattan Project. One of its biggest stumbling blocks is finding top hackers that trust the government and can gain the needed security clearances."

Andrews glanced at the Tea Shop. "Sounds specialized."

She shook her head. "It is. I won't even pretend to understand all of the quantum physics stuff. I'll just go find the bad guys."

"I'm with you, and I want to know who killed Tony. We may learn something to help the cops."

She said, "Yes, he was a good friend." Santiago paused for a moment then looked around. "This new Barrier lock could be a long time in coming."

"Perhaps, perhaps not as long as some think. Mario said the Germans are progressing faster than we are. Something else is on your mind, Mitch. What?"

"It just seems if someone wanted the research data they could put a worm in the program and gain feeds without detection for a period of time. To have contacts inside and outside of Maxwell, and someone murdered; this goes way beyond what we do."

"What are you saying?"

"There just seems to be more on the table than we know about."

Andrews smiled and snuffed out the cigarette. "Or maybe under the table."

"Does Ray have any idea who is after the research?"

Andrews said, "Several possibilities; everything from those we know don't like us such as China, Iran, and North Korea to our friends like Israel, Britain, and Japan plus various terrorist groups, organized crime, big business, and of course the competition."

"A lot of possibilities and we have not a clue who Tony's contact was. If it's not our competition trying to steal our data they could have the same type of problem we have. "

Andrews nodded.

Santiago said, "You know, Sam could find a group working both Barrier and the European's. Maybe having him go in clean to take Tony's place without knowing about me is best? I just don't like it."

Andrews smiled. "Ray said he'll be brought on board about your role but not until someone makes a contact with you and he's onboard at Maxwell."

She glanced at the man following her. "Contact appears to be more than a little imminent."

He checked the man at the Tea House again. "Doesn't seem beyond the realm of possibility given you already have a new friend. You just keep the chip on your shoulder. They'll bite."

"Assuming they do it becomes a matter of where they'll want me; Maxwell, DataFlex?"

He laughed. "Or maybe Berlin. Give me your hand."

She held one out. "What's our friend doing?"

Andrews kissed the back of her hand. "I think he just took a couple of pictures of us on his cell phone."

"So for now I just wait. You're my only DataFlex contact, and a romantic one at that as far as our new friend is concerned. I like this idea."

"Romantic. I like the sound of that, too, for a cover of course."

She smiled withdrawing her hand. "Now we play a part we've been living for the past year."

"Well, we're definitely in a public relationship now."

"I think the idea of us as a couple in the open is nice for a change, and it gives credibility to our meeting."

Andrews laughed. "There are dirtier jobs and I'm sure there has been some speculation because of our past assignments, House notwithstanding."

She sipped the coffee. "Obviously House already knew about us."

Andrews glanced at the man again then formed a steeple with his hands. "He just aimed a listening device at us."

Santiago nodded. "Honey, let's have dinner tonight at the loft. I can cook and curse DataFuck at the same time, those bastards."

The man watching and listening from the Tea Shop smiled.

"The company, your company, can't object to what they don't know."

Andrews laughed. "I like that, DataFuck, beautiful. You're abusing my favorite word, the one you keep telling me not to use. I'll bring the wine."

"No. I have enough wine, but we're out of your Captain Morgan. Seven o'clock okay?"

"Sure. I'm free as a bird as long as House doesn't know."

"Did you take your swim trunks home last time?"

"No, I took them home after our tubing date on the Salt River. You remember, the day you almost lost the top of that little tiny bikini as I recall."

She arched an eyebrow while watching Andrews face. "Really, I'd forgotten about that, but I do recall we were naked the last time we did the hot tub."

He laughed and lit another cigarette. "You may have forgotten the tube day, not me. I can bring my trunks back if you want."

"Bring 'em back. We can do the spa for dessert but with all the neighboring buildings so tall I don't think we want to go naked early in the evening."

"Trunks it is, but you'd like boxers better and naked wouldn't be bad. You know we could always go after dark."

"You have to be at work in the morning, remember?"

"Speaking of which, I better get out of here before House figures out why my lunch is taking so long."

They stood, embraced, and kissed.

"Things work out, Mitch. Until tonight."

They kissed again. Andrews walked south on Mill, Santiago headed back toward her loft. The man exited the Tea House and followed her.

*****

On her way home Santiago visited several shops on Mill Avenue. The tail kept close. *Either following someone is not your strongpoint or you want me to know you're there.*

On her way back to the loft she went into a courtyard on the west side of Mill just a short distance south of 4th Avenue. Stopping at a coffee bar she ordered ice tea and made a call while sitting at a table. The man followed and passed her table on his way to the men's restroom. She watched him without making eye contact while the phone rang.

"Peaceful Desert Care, this is Sara. How may I help you?"

"Doctor Grossman, please, Mitch Santiago calling in reference to John Abbott and a personal matter."

"One moment, please."

Doctor Grossman came on line a minute later with just the slightest hint of a German accent. "Hello, Miss Santiago. Thank you for being so patient. I assume you're calling for an update on John?"

"Two things. First, how's John doing?"

"His recovery is progressing with a few bumps along the way. When his former band mates visit I suspect he's receiving self-medication or alcohol from them but I can't prove it."

"Drugs? Have you tried getting a urine sample or perhaps blood?"

"He doesn't cooperate with our staff for a few days after they visit."

"He's probably purging. How about his speech, co-ordination?"

"His speech is slow, very articulate, much more controlled than normal."

"Movements?"

"Slow, sluggish, sometimes sloppy. He knows we suspect him of something. On the positive side he's done marvelous shows for the other guests."

"Really?"

"Yes. Two performances in the folk variety, quite a surprise knowing his rock history. He just beamed when performing."

"Has he been writing?"

"He told both audiences several of the compositions were original. They were excellent."

"Folk music, you say?"

"Just him with an acoustic guitar."

"That's a far cry from the stuff he did with Street Crud."

"He appears to enjoy performing and interacting with the audience. I believe the 'gigs' as he calls them are becoming a very positive part of his therapy and social life."

"John has a social life?"

Grossman laughed. "Some of the younger ladies here are quite attracted to him."

"Groupies, great."

"I beg your pardon?"

"Nothing," she said. "His old band isn't around when he performs are they?"

"No. On each occasion he's had no contact with them for a few weeks before the show and much to the joy of other clients he rehearses in the dining hall when it's not in use. My conclusion is keeping the old band members out of the picture helps his rehab."

"I'll see what I can do about their visits. When we finish here I'll need someone in the office to update my contact information. I'm no longer on retainer to DataFlex so they should be dropped as a work number."

"I'll take care of that, Miss Santiago. No need to be bounced around. Do you have a new employer we can add?"

"I'm retired. I'll continue to cover John's treatment. My resources are more than sufficient."

Grossman glanced at her financial statement attached to John Abbott's file. "Yes, so I see. You said you had two things to discuss?"

"Doctor Grossman, I may be in Palm Springs later this week. If so I'd like to come by for a visit with John."

"We would enjoy seeing you."

"The other item I want to discuss is do you have any contacts or recommendations for assisted living specializing in treatment for someone with dementia here in the valley, especially in Apache Junction?"

"I can make some inquiries. If not would you be interested in Palm Springs?"

"I would prefer the Apache Junction – Phoenix area or Yuma, but Palm Springs is a possibility. Quality is my primary consideration. I'm sure you have connections throughout the southwest."

"May I ask who the patient is?"

"My mom, and yes, I'll be responsible for her care also."

"Very well Miss Santiago. I'll be in touch."

She looked up as the man following her came out of the restroom. "Doctor, I can always be reached at my cell."

"I'll take care of this personally. It's the least I can do."

"Thank you."

"A pleasure."

"And doctor, please call me Mitch."

"So I shall, Mitch."

Chapter 3

Francis Dade, CEO of the Noble Group, watched the clouds floating below his Manhattan office windows. Fifty stories below, buried in gray, was Columbus Avenue. A small corner of Central Park peaked through the hazy cover. *It looks so lonely down there. I haven't had a close friend since my son was killed in the Gulf War.*

A cell phone rang inside a drawer of his massive executive desk. He took it out and checked the screen. It was blank. He answered and returned to the window and view below. "Hello."

"Mr. D., Andrea Nance."

"I recognize your voice, always throaty. We're secure?" She said, "Of course."

"What can you tell me about Miss Santiago?"

"She was fired this morning just as you heard, right around the time of the Mercedes incident. According to Xavier's contact in DataFlex accounting, her benefits were cancelled at the same time suggesting the decision was already made to terminate her services. Later, after leaving the DataFlex offices, she changed her personal account data as well."

Dade said, "What brought about her termination?"

"An affair between her and Claude Braun."

"Does she admit it?"

"Vehement denial. Her reaction appears to be more anger over betrayal, a lack of trust from those she believed in, and disrespect rather than guilt at being found out."

Dade said, "Good. The lack of loyalty is her source of anger. It means the killing of Mercedes and her firing are not related and will be our opening to secure her services."

Nance nodded. "My feeling, exactly. The rupture between Santiago and DataFlex is real. She made quite a scene leaving the premises."

Dade smiled. "Is she being followed?"

"After we talked this morning I contacted Jerome Xavier when Kohler could not be reached. They are handling surveillance for the next day or so. I'm sure Kohler will bug her loft while Xavier is following her. Xavier reports her only contact with a DataFlex staffer since the termination has been Link Andrews. They were already an item. Apparently Ray House issued a directive barring contact between staff and her."

"Do you think Mr. Andrews could become part of our plan, Andrea?"

"My gut feeling is no. He's one of their top operatives and has been for years. That's a risk we don't need to take right now."

"I agree. What was the nature of their contact today?"

"They had lunch together at a coffee house a few hours after the firing. According to Xavier they were kissing. He heard them planning an erotic dinner for this evening. They weren't chatting about work. She referred to the company as 'DataFuck,' her words."

Dade laughed. "So noted. An angry woman is a dangerous woman."

"Well, DataFlex pays well enough she has a high end soft loft in Tempe's version of Greenwich Village."

Dade said, "Perhaps our young lady is interested in the arts, too."

"We'll know soon enough."

"I'm going to have Kohler report directly to you and keep me out of his loop. His partner is too careless and this is a sensitive operation."

Nance paused for a moment. *I didn't know you knew Kohler. What else haven't you told me?* She said, "Kohler and Xavier know me only as an anonymous voice that transfers cash upfront when they are employed."

"He will. I've used him often over the years on some items. He's an old friend. I'll contact him as soon as we're finished. Jerome will be left out of this operation after today. Just give me ten minutes with Canfield after we're finished then call him."

Nance said, "Don't forget they're partners."

"In the next day or so we may be dealing with that, too. Xavier has been much too volatile in past dealings. Kohler is stable."

Nance said, "I believe he's been Canfield's muscle over the years."

A smile crossed Dade's face as a hole appeared in the clouds to the street. "I'm sure you're right. Canfield and I will deal with Xavier. You focus on Santiago. If you're convinced she's vulnerable we'll approach. She could be very valuable."

"We'll know shortly."

"Have you found anything out about Mr. Evans?"

"He was working on special assignment with an aircraft manufacturer DataFlex was developing operations programs for. He only returned yesterday. I can tell you he doesn't believe Miss Santiago was having an affair with Braun."

"What does he believe?"

"He thinks Mrs. Braun's dedication to alcohol and knowing her husband's reputation around beautiful women pushed her over the edge."

"Really?"

"The current Mrs. Braun was his mistress while he was still married to wife number two. She knows the routine."

"Has Evans tried to contact Santiago?"

"As I said, only Andrews so far."

Dade said, "He will. They've worked some sensitive operations together. Andrea, it would be interesting to hear what Mrs. Braun has to say about all this firsthand. Maybe even Claude's reactions. Fly out tonight. Use the Leer. Be subtle."

"Of course."

"We'll talk tomorrow."

Dade put the cell back in the desk drawer and turned back to the window. *Jeffrey, if you were here this problem wouldn't exist. How can a government be so blind as to put a genius in Harm's way on a desert road in some unknown country? They'll pay, Jeffrey, they'll pay dearly.*

*****

Link Andrews and Ray House stepped out of the DataFlex security building and walked to the shaded employee picnic – smoking table on the west side. Gold rays of late day sun washed Andrews's face when he looked up. "Sundown in a while. Been a hell of a day," he said and lit a Marlboro.

House took a long drag on a Pall Mall. "That it has."

"She's already picked up a shadow and he knows we're an item. He listened in on part of our conversation at lunch. He's been watching her all afternoon."

"Good."

"Think the staff will buy the story, Ray?"

"The male half likes the idea of Claude and her getting together. The ladies are definitely in Mitch's corner."

Andrews smiled.

House continued, "Beyond male admirers I'd bet most of the women look up to her and maybe have just a touch of jealously. Mario once referred to her as untouchable, probably because of her friendship with the Claude and Nikki."

Andrews exhaled. "I think the guys are fantasizing about Mitch having an affair with Claude, but many could see him having a new girlfriend. Just look at his past track record. A new girlfriend wouldn't be breaking news. Still, I'd bet most see firing Mitch as something in the line of get rid of her or we're done coming from Nikki."

House looked at the sky. "Nikki's probably taking most of the heat because anyone that's been around DataFlex can remember Claude's passion for younger women. One thing is for sure, everybody is talking and that is good."

Andrews said, "There's a couple of fantasies floating around."

House's eyes twinkled. "Probably."

Both men laughed.

"Hello Sam," said Andrews as Evans approached them.

He joined them at the table. "I must not have gotten the memo about the morning meeting. You guys know it's a bunch of bull. No way would Mitch have an affair with her best friend's husband. I think Nikki's still on the sauce."

House laughed. "Could be. It was obvious this morning Mitch was upset, angry."

Evans said, "I don't blame her. She had one of the best security jobs anywhere. Braun trusted her as much as any of us. She's been a big player here."

Andrews said, "I hope she doesn't do anything foolish."

Evans glared. "What's that supposed to mean? I've always thought you were more than a little interested in her."

Andrews nodded. "I am, but that doesn't alter the fact she was so upset. She knows a lot about this company and campus, too much to just be canned."

House flicked some ash which drifted toward Evans. "Right, unless it's the wife of the boss that wants you out of the game."

Evans said, "The trouble I have with all this is the loyalty issue. Mitch would never turn on this team. She was as loyal to Claude and this company as anyone. He cut her loose. All that says is screw you and anyone else that works here. Sure, we're well paid but it makes you wonder who could be next if Claude gets caught in another corner."

House said, "I see this as an aberration. It won't happen again."

Evans stood and looked at Andrews. "Well, I'll leave you smokers. Thanks for listening. This is just wrong."

Evans went back into the security building.

Andrews said, "Now that's a loyal guy. If he's got your back, you're covered."

House said, "He is. And he's feeling left out of the loop, hurt. Now tell me how you plan to go through the background data we have on our people. Time is tight and we have a large staff."

Andrews said, "I'm starting with a small group of new hires; the invisible people and new professionals. Fortunately we pay so well turnover is small. Most of the new hires come through retirement or death."

House looked confused. "Invisible people?"

"Support staff; custodians, cooks, maintenance. They come in and out of every area in the company. Nobody notices them yet they have unlimited access. They pick up the trash, change the light bulbs, empty the shredders, and clean the facilities. They're within hearing distance of many conversations, possibly comments on classified material because nobody notices them."

House lit another Pall Mall while nodding.

"I've pulled the applications of seven new staff hired in the last six months double-checking references, employment, education, criminal background, sources."

House said, "It's true, we don't go as far in depth with classified people as we do with techs. Not even close."

Andrews held up a hand, took out his cell phone and speed dialed Mario Spears. "Mario?"

"What can I do for you, Link?"

"I want you to dig deeply into the background of seven recent hires. Look for anything unusual; banking, family, links to other tech companies, labs or governments; information I wouldn't find on their applications."

Spears said, "That will take some time. You know I'm scanning our programs for possible breaches."

"I know, but isn't it possible to start this while the scan takes place?"

"Who are they?"

Andrews pulled out a list from a shirt pocket. "Norris Locklear, Ira Begay, Rupa Mudiraj, Francisco Gomez, Vladimir Clyburn, Priya Gupta, and Christopher Reed. I need this information ASAP."

Spears said, "People could be hurt."

"Only the two of us will be privy to the results. House doesn't even want the info except to identify the leaks, so keep the data out of our system."

"Hard copies?"

"Just for you and me."

"I'll start by looking for unusual bank activity, more in-depth criminal records than you accessed, medical histories, confidential and classified information. Just remember we can be in big trouble with the authorities if they catch wind of this."

"Mario, that's why you get the big bucks. Uncle Sam knows we can access almost anything. You've already done it for various government agencies. They presume you do it only for them. If the shit hits the fan our endeavors on their behalf could also become public."

"So," said Mario, "if we have a problem Homeland Security will help us cover it?"

Andrews ignored the question. "I'll be by in an hour to see what you have so far. Just remember, Mitch is in freefall. Move fast." He ended the call.

House said, "Back to our conversation. Your point about invisible people is well taken. I've had occasion to stop a meeting briefly because maintenance is called in to change a monitor or something."

"Don't get me wrong, Ray. Our staff is ninety-nine percent loyal and long term."

House laughed. "Claude always said, 'Hire the best, skip the rest.' Wages and stock options had a wonderful way of allowing all of our people to enjoy the highest standard of living, no second jobs. Made corrupting one of 'em harder, too."

Andrews looked at House with a smirk. "Speaking of benefits, don't you think Claude should build us a smoking lounge?"

"It'll never happen, my friend. You know as well as me he's into healthy living. He's always telling me I should quit."

"That's what Mitch tells me, too, that and to stop saying fuck."

"She's having a small effect on your language. Jessica's always telling me to cut down on the cigs like she has."

Both men laughed.

Andrews stood and dropped a butt in a can beside the table. "I've got a lot to do before I see Mitch and it's almost evening right now."

"You have a date?"

"Of course, dinner with Mitch. The shadow she's picked knows we're an item. He listened in on part of our conversation at lunch. He's been watching her all afternoon."

"Just be careful."

"Always. Tonight is dinner, hot-tubbing on her lanai and happiness while we chat."

House smiled. "Mitch in a spa."

"Don't go there, Ray. Think Jessica. You two have a good thing going."

"I know, but you with Mitch, Jesus, she's so... you know."

"It's called sexy and I won't be thinking about you and Jessica tonight either."

"You ought to head to her place now. We don't want to keep the tail waiting. I'll check with Mario and call you tonight. Damn, Mitch in a spa."

Andrews said, "Hold that thought. Jessica will be more than happy this evening, but Mario isn't expecting to hear from you."

"He'll handle it."

Both men returned to the building.

*****

The hallway was empty when Santiago stepped out of the elevator onto the fifth floor. When she turned toward her loft she stopped cold. The door was ajar. Sliding a Beretta 70 .22 automatic from her purse she stepped to the entry, listened for a moment. Not a sound. She stepped back from the door and raised her right foot while gripping the .22 with both hands. The door opened before she could kick it. A man came into the hallway and stopped dead in his tracks. His eyes bulged. He raised his hands automatically.

She took a quick step back out of reach. "Against the wall!"

The man moved away from the door turning to face the wall.

"Hands against the wall, one step back, lean." She patted him down. "Nice," she said removing a .38 revolver from a hip holster, "old but nice."

She pressed the .38 against his back and put her Baretta in her waist band. She took his wallet from a back pocket and thumbed through it. "Canfield Kohler, Private Investigations. So what's a local P.I. doing in my loft?" she said taking two items from the wallet and sliding them into her waistband without him seeing.

Kohler spun sweeping his right arm back at Santiago and the gun, hitting her arm. She spun and karate kicked the back of his knee. Kohler dipped to the floor while reaching for her gun hand but was off balance. She struck the side of his face with a backhand holding the gun. He fell on his butt and looked up as blood began to ooze from a small break in the skin.

He held up his hands. "Okay, okay."

"Get up. Guys in your business don't just break in. They're working for someone. Let's see, how about Nikki Braun?"

Kohler began to nod.

"No, she'd just nail old Claude. So who are you working for?"

"You know that's confidential."

"Well my confidential friend you must know a little about me or you wouldn't be in my loft. Does the name Thomas Grant mean anything to you?"

"Yes, you shot him between the eyes when he tried to kill you with an ice pick at the Quartzsite airport."

"Very good. Do you also know I shot his family jewels off first? Now, let's go inside."

Kohler did as directed. She tossed his wallet and .38 on a table by the door and waved her .22 toward the center of the area while pushing the door closed with a foot. "Sit over there in the middle of the floor."

"Are you calling the police?"

"Not just yet, but that is my plan if you don't talk to me."

"I'll be out in an hour."

"No, no. You don't know the whole plan. Let me explain. I come home to a burglary in progress. Burglar pulls a gun. Burglar is shot dead. Seems like a reasonable use of force to me."

Kohler watched Santiago's unblinking eyes, checked the steady gun in her hand. In a breaking voice he said,

"We do need to talk. It could be beneficial to both of us."

"Really? I'm listening."

"Look around, nothing is missing, not even disturbed. I didn't expect you to return so soon."

"Didn't expect me to return? You mean you're working with the fool tailing me on Mill?"

"You spotted him when you did lunch with your friend. He called me."

"Actually, I made him as soon as I left here for Mill Avenue. He's not a good tail." She laughed. "He should have called you again when I was coming back."

"I know."

"So, what were you looking for? What do you want? You were leaving, work done."

"Something, anything that would clarify your status with DataFlex."

"I'm an independent security consultant."

"Your current status with them."

"I don't work for them any longer."

"I've heard that rumor."

"Really? It's only been a few hours since I left there, maybe half a day."

"You mean fired?"

"Yes, fired."

"The people I represent are interested in DataFlex, a major competitor, much the same way your former employer is interested in other companies and people."

"You haven't answered my first question. I'm growing impatient."

"We have a few people working on the inside at DataFlex, our eyes and ears. Your sudden dismissal presents an opportunity that could be beneficial to you and us."

"My being fired means Nikki Braun is pissed-off and thinks I was bangin' her old man. She wanted me out, I'm out. DataFlex will get another consultant to replace me. Probably not as good and they probably won't get to hang out at the bosses pool."

"So you were having an affair with Braun."

"Only in his fantasies. It was always fun watching him ogle my French bikini. Until today I was Nikki Braun's best friend."

"You weren't having a relationship with Braun?"

"No, but it's water under the bridge now. I even tried calling him this morning when all this came up. He wouldn't take my call. His people cut me loose no questions asked."

"My employer wants to be assured you're no longer affiliated with DataFlex."

"They're history, but you broke into my home and that is current." She waved the automatic. "You still haven't answered my question; your employer?"

"You're a beautiful but cold woman. You'd do it wouldn't you?"

"Without a doubt."

"The Noble Group, I'm doing a background check on you. I'm sure you've had similar assignments."

"I've never been caught committing a burglary or any other felony if that's what you're implying. Being careless, getting caught, that's your problem. As for the Noble Group, I don't know much about them."

"They're a consortium involved with investments in cutting edge research technology, primarily security issues; the single biggest concern of the industry today. Companies and government's ability to guard against or participate in cyber warfare is a huge market. Data-Flex is involved with the same technology. As soon as Noble heard you may be available I was contacted to verify your dismissal and complete a background check."

Santiago smiled. "If you've been paying attention all you had to do was call."

"You know that's not how we work. May I get up now?"

"No."

"My job is to determine if you're a good fit for Noble."

She laughed. "Fit? I haven't adjusted to being fired yet."

"Are you angry enough with Claude Braun and DataFlex to want revenge? That is the question I must answer."

"No, I think your job is to tell Noble whether I'll rollover on DataFlex or not."

He shrugged. "Same thing, yes, well put."

She watched his eyes but said nothing.

Kohler shifted his weight. "So, are you interested? Obviously the background check is now altered, but it is clear you are a victim of in-house politics."

"I'll need a concrete offer, something better than you breaking into my loft, and an increase over what DataFlex was paying."

"Which was?"

She smiled. "My bet is you already know."

"Do tell. Do your research Miss Santiago. I'm sure you have your own sources. Noble's offer will be here tomorrow at this time."

"Who will present it?"

He looked at the gun Santiago still held on him. "Me, unless you shoot."

"Good, I thought it might be the downside of your office staff that was following me."

Kohler laughed.

She said, "Who do you report to at Noble?"

"I work freelance, they call me."

"Tell your contact I don't work for strangers, people without names. Someone other than you is going to have to contact me. Tell your friends at Noble I was very loyal to DataFlex. They violated my trust. Now I'm angry, but as I said earlier, I am expensive."

"Understood."

She stepped to the table by the door and tossed him his wallet. "Next time we talk call first."

"My gun?"

"Tomorrow. Mess with me and you'll pay."

Kohler stood, went to the door and left without another word.

Santiago closed and locked the door behind him and went to the lanai. She tossed Kohler's gun, driver's license, and credit card on the patio table. She checked the condo for listening devices using a handheld frequency detector. She found two bugs and disabled them, then retrieved the untraceable phone from her purse and called Ray House from the patio.

"Yes?"

"Ray?"

"Mitch, sorry for the bland answer, your untraceable phone doesn't provide caller ID."

"I was going to ask this morning how they work. All cells can be triangulated."

"Yes, but when you buy the type you have there is no personal information attached to it. Jessica went to one of the big box stores, bought a couple, paid cash, the store turns them on. She loaded minutes and was gone. No records or personal data."

"I've had a contact. I need background on Canfield Kohler and the Noble Group." She gave House the numbers off the driver's license and credit card.

"Good work."

"Yes, although it started as a botched burglary. I found two bugs after he left. He heard about my termination from an inside source."

"That's why this operation is so hush, hush. Mario will be on Kohler. The Noble Group is considered by some in the security field to be dangerous. A word of caution, the burglary may have been real or possibly a ruse."

"If Mario comes up with anything in the next hour get it to Link along with any Noble data you may have. He's coming for dinner tonight."

"Hm, a dinner of intrigue. He'll like that. Just be careful."

"Will do. Right now I'm going inside and take a closer look at what he was going through."

"Just make sure you and Link talk in a secure place."

"I'm thinking the hot tub."

House laughed. "That lucky bastard. He mentioned that just a little while ago."

*****

Jerome Xavier sat in the Sienna, this time in the Rio Salado Parking Lot waiting. Santiago was home. Link Andrews was coming to dinner but at 7:00. Xavier looked at the buildings surrounding the Tempe Town Lake. *Damn, I need my binoculars and telephoto lens. I'll be gone twenty minutes, thirty max. Canfield will never know.* His cell phone rang.

The husky voiced woman said, "Hello Jerome, has Miss Santiago had a busy day?"

"Things are moving fast. According to a source I have inside DataFlex accounting she's canceled her checking account used for direct deposit."

"Interesting. It would appear she's cut herself loose of DataFlex as far as the outside world is concerned."

"Yes, although she's made no move to liquidate her DataFlex stock. It's blue chip and she has quite a bit. Quite frankly if I was her I'd keep the stock just to make his company pay me."

"Possible. Check her benefits, health in particular."

"I already did. The company is carrying her health insurance until the end of this month then she's on her own. Something else you might be interested in. Her contract with DataFlex has a clause which says she can make no public negative comments about the company or personnel even after leaving for eighteen months. Apparently its part of a confidentially agreement all security personnel sign."

"In other words just let today die a natural death."

"As far as the public or press are concerned. According to some of the security people she's really pissed off."

"Did you talk to these people directly?"

"No, after Canfield visited the condo he hung out at the Nail Driver this afternoon, a favorite watering hole of the security folks."

"Did he learn anything special?"

"Sam Evans was heard saying he just didn't believe Santiago would have anything to do with Braun romantically. It wouldn't surprise him if Braun has a girlfriend or two on a string, nothing new there, but never Santiago. Most believe Mrs. Braun's thinking is off center because she doesn't trust her husband. Some say she has a drinking problem."

"Why not Santiago?"

Xavier laughed. "Given Braun's tastes she's too old for him. Braun likes 'em young, very early twenties. Someone in their late twenties would be too old for a notch in his jockstrap. Santiago and Mrs. Braun are the same age."

"Has she had contact with any of her workmates?"

"So far only Link Andrews. They're either close friends or an item. At lunch today they kissed, touched, and made a dinner date for this evening at her loft. I'm waiting for him to get here now. After their lunch meeting he was in a hurry to get back to the office before anyone missed him. If they actually stay here as planned I'll take up residence on a nearby rooftop and listen in."

"Good work. Continue the surveillance. We'll talk again tomorrow when I call. Meanwhile, I'd like you to find out from your source at DataFlex what Evans and Andrews are working on and if it is a joint task or two separate assignments. Until tomorrow."

*****

It was 7:04 when Link Andrews arrived at Michelle's loft. His eyes lit up like a video game when she opened the door. He studied her from head to toe. "Nice outfit."

"I thought you'd like it."

He shook a small backpack. "Trunks."

She stepped back. "Come in."

"If those shorts were any smaller I'd think we were doing the hot tub first."

She wet her lips. "We could. I prefer after dark."

He looked out the window. "After dark is better."

"I found two bugs. They're disabled."

"Your visitor will know."

"He'd expect me to find them since I caught him. He has a high opinion of my skills."

Link kept looking at the tiny shorts. "So do I."

"Not those skills."

"You know Mitch, this is ironic. We're pretending to fake a relationship we've had and downplayed for a year."

She smiled. "Mario and Sam know about us. Apparently Ray does, too. Some things you just leave alone."

"Like Ray and Jessica's relationship."

"Like our relationship. So what did you find out about Kohler?"

He nodded toward the kitchen area. "Coffee?"

"Of course."

They went to the bar built around the kitchen counter. She retrieved a large cup with a caricature of a golfer on it. "Let's see, half-a-cup of sugar, half-a-cup of coffee."

"Not quite, but close. Keeps me sweet."

He reached for a Marlboro. Santiago raised an eyebrow. He left the pack in his pocket.

She said, "I thought you quit."

"I'm a work in progress. Let me tell you about Kohler. He's a veteran PI; sophisticated and educated. His partner is Jerome Xavier. He's known more for muscle than mind. They work only the big dollar stuff."

"High-end clientele, no surprise there."

"The biggest. They don't care what the work is, just the size of the check. They'll do divorces, child custody, collections, intimidation, anything. If someone hired them to check you out consider it a compliment."

She thought of Tony Mercedes. "How about murder?"

"Never been charged. They've been involved in surveillance work for some big corporations in the States and Europe."

"How about Middle-eastern?"

"An oil cartel a few years ago. They dug up a lot of dirt on one of our government suits who could influence the cost per barrel and was keeping it down. Shortly after the discovery, which was never made public, we had another price hike per barrel and at the pumps."

"Terrorists?"

"Nothing I could find."

"You said they've never been charged with murder. Have they ever been tied to any?"

"A few rumors. Homeland Security was investigating an arms smuggling operation to Africa two years ago. One of the agents was killed in a gunfight on a New York dock. Xavier was rumored to be involved. He was doing inquiries on behalf of the exporter but no supporting evidence could be found. It was rumored Noble was involved in the financing but it couldn't be substantiated."

"Do they infiltrate companies?"

"Kohler and Xavier don't work like we do. They're old school, they'll try to buy or blackmail someone into working as a mole. The Noble Group is a different animal. They're big, sophisticated and do many of the same things DataFlex does and a lot more. They also recruit within companies, agencies, and organizations."

She said, "Ray told me Noble is considered dangerous in the security field."

"Yes, but like Kohler, nothing concrete."

"Well, we know I'm being recruited. Tomorrow I'll see how serious they are. Kohler is supposed to bring an offer. He anticipates my doing some background work on Noble, too."

"Did he give you any idea of what they want you to do?"

"None. I'm sure it involves rolling over on DataFlex, revealing secrets or procedures. He emphasized the opportunity for me to get even."

"When he brings the offer will you accept immediately?"

"If possible I'll wait maybe a day. I'm driving to Palm Springs on personal business. I learned working vice you don't want to be too eager."

"They'll probably follow you if they're still trying to satisfy any lingering doubts."

"If the opportunity presents itself I'll ask Kohler to make the drive with me. A round trip is a long run. Knowing how he and I view his partner I wouldn't make the same offer to Xavier."

Andrews drummed his fingers on the counter. "So what's in Palm Springs?"

"Personal. My cousin John is back in rehab."

"John the rocker?"

"That's the one."

"I thought he finished rehab several months ago in Mesa."

"He's relapsed, fell off the wagon or bandstand; something."

"I'd love to ride over with you but that won't work."

"Not this time. More coffee?"

He reached into his backpack and pulled out a bottle. "No, Captain Morgan is guarding my trunks."

"Imagine that. I'll get a couple of glasses."

She went to a cupboard on the far side of the kitchen area, stood on her tiptoes and stretched, reaching for a tumbler on the top shelf. His eyes never left her backside. "I like the way you stretch."

"You could help me get one down. I usually use wine glasses. They're on the middle shelf."

Andrews smirked. "I'm helping myself and enjoying the moment. Reach just a little higher."

She pulled a stool over to the counter and took a tumbler down. "I haven't put on a show like that since my college days."

They both laughed.

He said, "Lucky frat boys."

She mixed him a rum and Coke and poured herself a Chardonnay. "I just keep the tumblers on the top shelf for your entertainment."

He took a sip of his drink. "I know. It's appreciated. Gettin' back to the serious stuff, is being followed or watched going to be a problem?"

She looked around the loft. "No, this is home, the studio, a place where my artist friends and I hangout when we choose. If Xavier or somebody is monitoring who comes in and out they might even think they're in Greenwich Village."

"This assignment is dangerous, Mitch."

"I know. I'll be carrying my Glock 42, maybe with a thigh holster."

"You'll need a longer skirt, no shorts."

"I could use a purse, 42's are small," she said with a smile.

The doorbell rang.

He said, "Company?"

"No, I ordered pizza for around 8:00. It'll be dark by the time we're finished."

Link answered the door, paid the delivery boy and returned to the counter. "Pizza and the hot tub, my kind of dinner."

She flicked her teeth with the tip of her tongue. "He'll be watching from one of those buildings."

Link looked at the skyline. His face reddened. "I'm probably a little more modest than you, Mitch."

She leaned into his side and kissed a cheek. "Think so? To see us he has to watch from across the lake. He won't see much."

"You know, you really are a vamp."

She poked him in the ribs and laughed. "Really? Sometimes one's background helps. We'll just tease him, nothing too revealing, but we'll drive him crazy."

Link finished his drink. "Like in your college days, he'll see enough."

She laughed. "Stripper, it's alright to say. Come on, let's eat outside. We don't want to keep him waiting."

Link looked across the lake. "If he's there."

"He's there."

CHAPTER 4

Jerome Xavier was at his Ocotillo town house packing a camera and telephoto lens into a gym bag when the doorbell rang. "Damn, I've got to get going."

He ignored it. The bell rang again and again. He put a sack lunch and a thermos of coffee in the bag. "Okay, okay, I'm coming."

He crossed the room and jerked the door open. A young man with blond hair wearing white tennis shorts and a blue polo shirt faced him. He spoke with an eastern European accent.

"Mr. Xavier, I'm Vladimir Clyburn."

"I'm very busy right now, don't have time to talk. Call my office tomorrow."

Clyburn ignored the comment. "Kat's a friend of mine."

Xavier stepped back. "Come in."

Clyburn stepped through the door without a word. The two men stood in the entry.

"What do you want?"

"Leave Kat alone. I know you're blackmailing her. I heard the phone conversation you had today."

Xavier motioned Clyburn into the living room and followed. I don't know what you're talkin' about."

Clyburn said, "Just leave her alone, that's all I want."

"Does she know you're here?"

"No. I wanted to see you privately. She pleaded with me not to come."

Xavier reached behind his back and pulled a Glock 19 from the waistband. "But you're here," he said waving the gun.

Clyburn stepped away from Xavier. "I just want to talk to you."

Xavier moved around the man. "We're beyond talk. Down on your belly, arms and legs spread."

"I don't carry a gun, Mr. Xavier. I'm a computer technician."

Xavier waved his Glock. "This is Arizona, everybody carries. Down, now, and tell me exactly what you two talked about."

"You make her do things against the law. She doesn't want to go to jail."

"Did she tell you she'd be there now if it wasn't for me?"

Clyburn turned his head and looked up at Xavier. Their eyes met. "Yes."

Xavier noticed the wall clock in the kitchen behind Clyburn. *7:15, I've got to get out of here.* He waved the gun again. "Standup."

"I just want you to stop bothering her."

"Shut up. Down the hall."

"You're making a big mistake, Mr. Xavier."

"I said shut up. First door on the left."

They walked into the bathroom.

"Get in the tub."

"What the hell are you doing?"

Xavier stuck him on the back of the head with the Glock pushing him into the tub. Clyburn fell, unconscious. Xavier went to the kitchen and came back with plastic ties. He secured Clyburn's hands behind his back then his legs together and tethered them to the faucet. He stuffed a washrag in Clyburn's mouth securing it with tape from a first aid kit.

Xavier's nose began dripping. He wiped it on the back of his hand then wiped his hand on Clyburn's shirt while moving him flat onto his back.

Clyburn's eyes opened slowly as Xavier stood.

"You'll be here a while. Buttin' into other people's business ain't very smart."

Clyburn squirmed.

Xavier smiled at the squirming figure. "Gonna have to figure out what to do with you. We both know how this could end don't we, just not yet."

Clyburn made a muffled sound.

"I've got work to do."

He looked down at the victim and struck him again with the gun, this time on the side of the head. Clyburn's body became motionless. Blood seeped through his hair.

"Gotta go, fella. Have a nice rest."

*****

The Northlake Apartments are located directly across Tempe Town Lake from Santiago's condo and the park. Wearing coveralls like a maintenance man, Jerome Xavier had secured the roof with a "Closed" sign taken from a weight room. He looked at his watch. "7:50, nobody's sunning themselves now."

It was dark when he sat down on a lounge chair near the stairwell. The lights from Santiago's condo lit her lanai. His eyes never left her shorts as she crossed the room. "Thank God you're home. Probably goin' to a bedroom? Nice place, nice ass."

Link Andrews carried a small bag into another room. A moment later he came back out wearing swim trunks. Xavier said, "Must be workin' out."

Andrews walked to the kitchen, picked up a tumbler and sipped. Xavier shook his head. *A drink would be nice up here, too.*

Santiago returned. Xavier licked his lips. "Oh, sweet Jesus, look at that body. This is even better 'n the shorts. I love your blue bikini."

Xavier rubbed his belly and a thigh. "You could make a guy cum, easy."

She joined Andrews at the bar. They kissed lightly and touched each other's backs.

Sweat formed on Xavier's upper lip. "Damn lady, you're makin' my flesh jump."

The couple picked up their glasses and stepped onto the lanai. Xavier stretched his legs, took a deep breath. He dug a bottle of water out of the gym bag. "You must be drinkin' wine, honey. What's your boyfriend got other than a hard-on, whiskey?"

Stars sparkled, Xavier sipped tepid water, the lights from the surrounding buildings opened avenues to the private world of hundreds while the lights of Tempe

Town Lake reflected off the water's surface like a glowing foundation. "Anything else goin' on tonight?"

He scanned several surrounding windows with the binoculars. "You folks don't realize how visible you are."

A young man passed the slider of his apartment naked. "Hope you got a girlfriend in there, buddy."

A young woman ate something from a small cup licking the spoon with each bite. "Must be health food, yogurt, something. Great tongue action."

A young blond woman in shorts and a t-shirt talked on a cell phone. "Honey, when I was your age I couldn't afford an apartment like that. Daddy and mommy paying the bills or are you a workin' girl? On your back would pay well, especially downtown."

The blonde's free hand became more active; waving, pointing. The cell flew across the apartment. "Oops, must be pissed-off. If that was your boyfriend he ain't gettin' any tonight."

He swung the binoculars back toward Santiago and Andrews. They were standing at the rail looking toward the lake talking. "Saying sweet things, little lady? Turning him on? All you gotta do is nuzzle up against him. You've already got his attention and mine and anybody else watchin' you work."

He swung the glasses back to the window of the naked man's room. He was standing around, flaccid. "If you saw Santiago you'd be harder than a rock, boy."

He checked another building. A young Asian woman sat at a table working a laptop. Another was stretched out on a couch reading. Both were in shorts and halter tops. Xavier laughed. "College kids, business types, voyeurs; this is heaven for a P.I."

Returning the glasses to Santiago he watched Andrews step into the hot tub still holding a drink. He sat down slowly, turned, and said something to Santiago. She laughed and sipped from the wine glass then set it on the table and stepped into the tub. Andrews held out a hand. She took it. He kept looking up and smiling as she slid into the tub next to him.

"Betcha had a great crotch shot when she stepped in almost over your face. Shit, I'm in the wrong end of this business."

Xavier rubbed the inside of his thigh touching his groin then took another sip of the now warm water.

The condo below Santiago's also had a high ceiling. Xavier moved his attention to the middle-aged couple eating dinner on their lanai, a small lit candle on the center of the table. "Damn, that's fake. No flicker to the flame. I guess romance is goin' high tech."

Next door to the couple dining, a man with gray hair watched a flat screen television mounted on the wall.

Xavier shifted his gaze from Santiago's building back to student housing around the lake. "From the rich to the young. You kids don't know how lucky you are that a developer went broke building high-end condos and someone else bought the place in bankruptcy for a song. Luxury student living, for now."

He glanced back to Santiago's deck just as she stood with her back toward Xavier. She slipped the blue bikini top off and draped it over the edge of the tub.

"Damn, you've gotta turn around when you do that. Your boyfriend would like a tittie show and me too."

She slid back into the tub. They snuggled. Andrews took another sip from his tumbler. Santiago looked at her glass on the table, stood, leaned toward it. "Oh yes, what a rack. Damn."

Xavier took a deep breath and exhaled. He stood holding the field glasses on Santiago, smiling, his groin excited. "You should take the bottom off, too."

A laser beam shot from a student lanai to another building drawing his attention. As he scanned across the area he saw another man on an unlighted deck looking through a telescope. They looked at each other for a moment. The man waved without moving away from the eyepiece. "I wonder if that counts as eye contact."

Xavier laughed and continued to scan the building. Two young Hispanic men worked on opposite sides of a table. One floor down a Caucasian man and Hispanic woman read and typed. At another apartment a gorgeous middle-eastern woman walked about her apartment wearing a black string bikini then put on a robe and walked out the door with another young woman that just appeared. "Probably goin' to their pool."

Another floor down two middle-eastern men read in one apartment while right next door two Asian women sat, one at a desk with a lap top, the other on a couch texting.

He went back to Santiago's condo. All the lights were out; lanai and condo dark. He got out a pair of night vision goggles but could see nothing. "Too much light around here. Damn it."

He sat for several more minutes watching, waiting. "Did you get out and walk inside topless, maybe naked? Are you in there fucking right now? I just wanna see what's goin' on."

He waited. The darkness at Santiago's remained. "Son-of-a-bitch, where'd you go? I don't believe this."

He checked his watch. "9:37, security gonna be checkin' the doors, stairwells, and roof at 10:00." He gathered his stuff back into the gym bag and exited through the roof door the same way he came. On the way down the stairwell he passed a security guard on his way up.

The guard said, "Get everything fixed?"

"Yeah, checked a lot of stuff."

"I'm surprised you're not using the elevator."

"Closed spaces make me nervous. Bad 'nough workin' late in the dark up there."

"Any kids up there?"

"Not tonight. I made sure the roof was closed."

"I saw the closed sign, smart move."

Xavier continued down the stairs and out of the building. He looked back at the entry. "Didn't expect a guard on the stairs."

He approached his car. "Now I can deal with you, Mr. Clyburn. Canfield's gonna shit."

******

Canfield Kohler poured a shot of Jack Daniel's, walked to the second floor window and looked out at North Central in Phoenix. "Nice night." He returned to his desk. The Noble file was scattered across the top. A Maxwell document lay beside an open DataFlex folder. He studied the photo of Michelle Santiago and read her file. "You're good at what you do young lady, more lethal than most realize."

He sipped the bourbon and placed an envelope on top of the file imprinted with the gold letterhead of the Noble Group. "It's a generous offer young lady."

He heard the outer office door open. A moment later Jerome Xavier walked into his office and flopped down on an easy chair. "I lost her."

"You lost Santiago, how?"

Xavier explained the condo going dark and the guard doing his rounds.

"You weren't checking the other buildings were you?"

"Of course not. Mind if I have a drink?"

Kohler nodded toward the bar on one side of his office.

Xavier said, "Your office is a lot nicer than mine, very plush."

"I meet with most of our clients. You're more in the background, but you could upgrade your office anytime you choose."

Xavier emptied the tumbler of bourbon in one toss. "I'm good. I like being the guy doing the dirty work."

"Jerome, I brought you on board years ago. You have certain skills. I have certain skills. Together we've done rather well."

"True, you're the smooth operator, I'm the muscle. It works."

Kohler said, "Sometimes. Today you were to doing simple surveillance, no strong arming."

"Not quite accurate."

"Oh?"

"We've got a problem. A guy, I think a Russian that works with Kat at DataFlex knows about her and me."

"How did he find out?"

"He said he heard her talking with me. He came to my place just before I left for Santiago's loft tonight."

"Did you deny knowing what he was talking about?"

Xavier looked around the office. "Not really."

"What does that mean?"

"It means he's in my bathtub, tied and gagged."

"You took him prisoner?"

"I shut him up. What else could I do?"

"Denial would have been a good start, at least bought some time. You should have called me."

"He made me nervous so I knocked him out and dumped him in the tub 'til I get home."

"And then you plan to do what?"

"Thought I'd take him out in the west valley, leave him looking like a victim of the human smugglers. You know, a ransom deal gone wrong."

"In other words, you plan on killing him?"

"Well, yeah. I mean, he knows about Kat sharing information with me."

"Too bad you strong armed him. We may have been able to turn him in return for protecting Kat. It would have given us another contact."

"He's not dead, yet."

"No, but I doubt he'd make a reliable long term contact now."

"Well the good news is Kat doesn't know he came to see me. He'll just disappear. Even if she suspects something she'd have no proof." Xavier paused. "He did start to say something about his family but I smacked him."

Kohler sat for a moment and watched Xavier as he squirmed in his chair. "Family? What if he's associated with the Russian Mafia?"

"Kill him smuggler style. If he is in their family they'll think the Mexicans did it."

Kohler sipped his drink and watched Xavier quietly. *Family could be a problem.*

"Do you think the Russians would protect her?"

Kohler laughed. "If he is in the family and they know about her they wouldn't appreciate his veiled threat involving them. Hell, they'd probably take him out themselves just for drawing attention to them."

"That's a good point, Canfield, if he's related to them?"

Kohler said, "Let's find out," turned to his computer and began searching the Russian's name then moved to social media. "There you are," he said studying the screen.

"What have you found?"

"Vladimir Clyburn is well educated, born and raised in Moscow. His father and two brothers are alleged to have organized crime contacts, dad being high up the ladder. The good news is Vladimir is associated with Russian Mafia only through his family ties. No mention is made of criminal inquiries involving him personally."

Xavier looked confused. "How did he get in the country?"

"Green card, Jerome. What rock are you living under? It says here he has an M.A. in finance and relocated after receiving a job offer from DataFlex. They're known for hiring only the best."

Xavier said, "According to the press DataFlex is well connected."

"They are in many ways. It crosses my mind he may have been employed by DataFlex at the urging of the Fed. It's just a thought, but maybe he was brought into the company as a means to uncovering a link with the Russians. It is well known Braun's company has worked closely with the government for years."

"Do you think the Russians will buy the Mexicans making the hit?"

Kohler said, "I hope so. It's the best case scenario for us under the circumstances. You haven't left us much choice."

"Sorry about that."

"Have another drink, Jerome. We've a bit of a mess on our hands, nothing new. The trouble is this is our wealthiest client."

"No kidding, when that woman with the husky voice called today wanting me to watch Santiago she made an instant deposit of our fee. You know, that's only the second time I've ever dealt with her."

"I know, but I was not available when she called and her need was immediate. It's just too bad this other thing has surfaced. A little more thought, a little less thug."

"Well, I got him on ice, saved the day."

"Yes, yes you did. Tell me, how much does he know?"

"Just that Kat gives me information."

"Does he know about our agency?"

"No, he knows nothing about us, just me. But he could be dangerous."

"Yes, I'm pleased you came to me first. You say make his killing look like something the human smugglers would do, how so?"

"Tie his hands behind him, a bullet in the back of the head, leave the body out on the west side in the desert."

"Their victims are usually illegals."

"Mexicans, Hispanics, Russians; what difference does it make? They're all fighting with each other."

Kohler ran his finger around the rim of his tumbler. *Careless.* "Take the snub nose from the vault. It's untraceable."

"That's what I was thinkin' too."

I doubt you've had a whole thought in some time. "You'll have to be careful. You live in a very nice area. Good thing your garage is attached. Getting him out of your place would be difficult."

"It's late and we'll be in the garage."

"Even in your garage be quiet. Several people around you have dogs. Tell him the two of you are going to see Kat. Let him know she could be hurt if he doesn't cooperate."

"I think he knows I'm gonna kill him."

"He'll cooperate to save her and possibly himself. She's obviously important to him or he wouldn't have come to see you."

"I should boost a van, not move him in my car, no DNA."

"That would work. When you're done dumping the body torch the van like you did last year in San Francisco."

"You mean do it in a store parking lot?"

"Yes. Go to a parking lot near where you do the boost. Your car should be on the street within a few blocks. Burn and go. Just make sure to stay clear of the surveillance cameras. Keep your face hidden."

"I can get a nice van up at Chandler Mall."

"No, no, not in your area. Go to Mesa, and the van or SUV you get should be mundane, boring; no flash. You want something nobody notices."

"Of course. What do you think I am, an idiot?"

"Don't ask. Right now you wouldn't like the answer. Just make this go away. Tomorrow will be too late."

Jerome started to get up.

"Not yet. Tell me about the woman, Santiago."

"She's good lookin' and not too shy."

"What were they doing?"

"Havin' drinks, eating pizza, sittin' in the hot tub, her topless."

"And you lost her?"

"The lights went out. I figure they went inside to bed. I had to get off the roof anyway."

"Thank you for filling me in, Jerome. Take care of the Russian. I'll see you tomorrow."

After Xavier left Kohler called Andrea Nance.

"What have you got for me, Canfield?"

"Santiago is behaving the way you'd expect an angry former employee to behave. I believe she's been checking out the Noble Group. She had dinner and hot tubbed with her boyfriend, the same fellow she lunched with."

"You mean Link Andrews."

"Yes, they are definitely a couple. I found two charcoal sketches of him in her loft, a special golfers coffee cup, and some men's garments."

"Good."

"I suspect he's her background source, too. He's a DataFlex operative."

"I know. You have our offer?"

"I do. I'll see her tomorrow if you agree."

"Keep your appointment with her."

Kohler swallowed. "She'll want more information before she accepts, particularly who will be her supervisor, work location, that sort of thing."

"When you see her tell her I'll call an hour after you leave."

Kohler tapped his desk top. "Of course, but Andrea, we have an unexpected problem."

"Tell me."

"Jerome kidnapped a Russian that knows about his contact with Kat, the accountant at DataFlex. He's on his way to dispose of him as we speak, staging it like a human smuggler hit."

Nance took a deep breath. "Jesus Christ. Canfield, listen carefully. As soon as possible you must do something to permanently solve our problem with your crude partner. He's put this entire operation at risk."

Canfield emptied the tumbler. "He's very good at enforcement."

"So you say. I see him as a Neanderthal."

"I'll talk with him tomorrow. It won't happen again."

"No, Canfield, I want a permanent solution. Eliminate him. You've done it before."

Canfield was silent. He looked at the empty tumbler. "I'll take care of it."

"Until tomorrow, then."

*****

When Santiago and Andrews left the hot tub they retreated to the dark interior of the loft. Andrews watched the faded light play off Santiago's near nude bikini bottomed body in the shadows. She stepped to a closet and slid on a men's dress shirt over her shoulders.

He smiled. "Shall we play or get dressed?"

She said, "First we have work. If he's up there somewhere do you think we can spot him?"

"Possibly, but it could be hard to do in the shadows."

"Let's take a look. I've got a pair of binoculars. Maybe we can catch a silhouette. At least we'd know he was out there, something I can share with Kohler tomorrow."

Andrews smiled. "You just happen to have a pair of binoculars. Mitch, do you spy on your neighbors?"

She went to a cabinet, retrieved the binoculars and walked to the windows. "I'll never tell." She scanned the edges of the overlooking roof tops. "There, take a look."

Andrews took the field glasses. "There's someone up there. He's hard to see, mostly shadows. I can't tell if it's our guy or someone else. He's looking at a different building."

"I'd bet it's him."

"Damn," said Andrews, "he moved. I can't see him in the shadow anymore."

"His being there tells us Kohler is still doing my background work."

Andrews continued to look at the shadowed roof edge. "Just as we're doing them." He laughed. "I'll bet he got more than he bargained for when he spotted your swim suit. He can linger up there but the rest of the evening is ours."

"So it is and I doubt he could see anything in here."

"True."

Santiago's burn phone rang. "Hold on, it's got to be Ray," she said reaching for it.

"Hello, Mitch. Is Link still there?"

"Of course."

"This is for both of you. Our personnel office received an inquiry late this afternoon from Maxwell Cyber Systems. They wanted to know if you were free to work for them or under some restrictions because of a severance agreement. That's good for us. Obviously the word is out on you."

"Given the questions raised about Noble's reputation I'm inclined to think Maxwell could be a legitimate job inquiry."

House said, "My thinking exactly."

"I'll see what kind of offer Noble brings tomorrow, but if it's good and I get to know who I answer to I'll accept. Otherwise I'll stall them. I have to go to Palm Springs anyway."

"Palm Springs?"

"It's personal, Ray, but a good cover unless Noble puts on the pressure to come aboard immediately."

"They will. Be careful, Mitch."

"Careful and not too easy. I'll let you know when I accept."

"Fair enough. You and Link have a good evening." The connection broke.

Link smiled and said, "I'm thinking night."

She rubbed his flat belly. "Me too."

He said, "I thought we'd spend a little more time in the bubbly water."

"I don't think it was the bubbles that had your attention," she said with a laugh.

"I have to admit I almost lost my cookies when you took the halter off."

"I doubt it was your cookies."

"I just don't want to share you."

"Link, other than awaken his fantasy world he got nothing, not even a boob shot, just the halter laying there. Too many plants and we were more than cozy."

"It's been a few days. I'm glad we're both home," he said squeezing her shoulders. "Sometimes the quick trips make me question my career choice."

"Only briefly, big guy, but now I have more time than you; more sun, fun, and always being available."

"Until tomorrow, you mean. And we're actually working right now."

"I know, don't you love your work? I do." She kissed him and rubbed his belly again.

He said, "I need another drink."

"Let me get it. I can stand straighter than you right now."

"Can you pour a drink in the dark?"

She licked her lips. "I can do anything in the dark, but I'm thinking of turning on a soft light so he can watch me cross the room in your sexy shirt. After I get our drinks we can go back to sitting in the dark or go in there." She pointed at the bedroom door.

"You're bad, you know that."

"I have plans on how we debrief that don't include Mr. Kohler or his roof-top partner."

Andrews turned a lamp on low and watched her cross the room, refill their glasses and saunter back. She never looked toward the window. She sat down and he turned the light off.

"So, what have you found out about DataFlex's leaks?"

He said, "We have seven new hires we're looking at first; some are invisible people. All but one are from different cultures. Two are in low level positions."

"What do you mean, invisible?"

"Staff in positions like custodial, maintenance, kitchen; they are there but seldom noticed."

She said, "I see."

Andrews cleared his throat. "On maintenance we have Chris Reed. He's a trainee working with Rita Ramsey, our head custodian. He has access to all of our buildings including security. A graduate of ASU in facilities management he's in his current role to gain what Claude calls 'real work experience.' Like many new graduates he's financially buried in student loans. He comes from Montana and has a juvenile record. During the interview he said he'd been busted for possession."

She nodded. "I'm not sure I like calling support staff invisible people."

"I don't think Ray did either." He swallowed. "Moving along, Marci Todd is an assistant custodian in security. She has given off a negative vibe to most of our people on the floor except the guards. She refers to most of us as rich bastards to her peers, that sort of thing."

Santiago said, "She sounds angry."

"She is. We also have Norris Locklear, a Native American from the Gila Tribe. He's thirty-two, a graduate of Stanford Law School, obviously bright, well liked and does some pro bono for the tribe. The Gila's gave him a scholarship. Now he's in legal. He's also a sci-fi fan, books and movies. His car of choice is the popular Escalade."

"I'll bet the ladies like him."

Andrews said, "Yes. Then we have Ira Begay, a Navaho gentleman from the Four Corners area. He's a recent graduate from ASU in marketing and is learning the ropes in the business office."

She laughed. "That's hardly an invisible place, Link."

"We have Priya Gupta, a programmer born in India, raised in the states. She's a naturalized U.S. citizen, gorgeous, westernized, talented and smart. She is at odds with her family about refusing to proceed in an arranged marriage. Her attire is very western most of the time, not unlike yours. Ray says you dress provocatively. Personally I like sexy. Anyway, Priya does wear traditional attire when attending some Indian ceremonies. She graduated from the University of Arizona with honors. She is now working as part of the DataFlex White Hat Team. She's twenty-seven, and worked her way through school as a bartender."

Santiago laughed. "A lady after my own heart and a beautiful class hacker. She sounds pretty high profile to me. You noticed a lot of her for someone so 'invisible.'"

Andrews laughed. "She's not invisible, just ask Mario. Sometimes she reminds me of you. Now," he cleared his throat, "we have Saanvi Madira. Her family is of Indian origin, Bombay. She was born in New York, Manhattan to be exact. She's a 4.0 intern from ASU, and works with Mario on some projects. He describes her 'more than hot.' She is shy sometimes, usually around older people, but also a flirt. She is just beginning to experience the coming out most young woman experience as a teen."

Santiago chuckled. "Your list of invisible people seems to be noticeable, very noticeable."

Andrews said, "An interesting thing about Saanvi is how she is shunned by many other Indian staff members. In India her family was untouchable. However, she has no problem relating to non-Indians."

She said, "If Mario calls her 'hot' it's a given most of the crew in security like her. Anyone else?"

"A Russian fellow, Vladimir Clyburn. He was raised in Moscow and has very little verifiable history prior to his attending the Leningrad State University. He's a whiz in accounting and plays chess almost as good as a master. He's somewhat arrogant but enthusiastic about becoming a U.S. citizen. He doesn't have many close friends although he gets on well with another accountant, Kat Parsons. He does have an unusual educational history for an account."

"Really?' she said.

"While being a scholar in accounting Vladimir also was a scholar at Moscow State University Institute of Nuclear Physics but did not complete his studies. Apparently his family wanted him to study business."

Santiago said, "Why?"

"Not much is known about his family. I'll have to do more research on him. There is some suggestion his family is involved with organized crime. I haven't confirmed it yet."

Santiago said, "Sounds like an interesting man."

Andrews nodded. "Mario also discovered our head custodian, Rita Ramsay, is dealing with some personal issues within her family. Apparently her husband is a drunk. She is attending counseling but he won't go. It's got to be stressful at best."

Santiago said, "It could be rehab or marriage counseling."

He leaned toward her and kissed her cheek. "That's all I have to report so far." He kissed her again.

"So far? You've found quite a bit in a short time. From the sounds of it the boys in security have a couple of hotties with Priya and Saanvi in the building. No wonder Mario is always so happy."

He said, "Now can we relax?"

"No, now we can play," she said running a hand across his bare chest. "Got any ideas?"

"Oh yes," he said snuggling close to her.

She said in a soft voice, "Bedroom?"

"Bedroom, Mitch, I have a plan."

"You have the same plan I have." She leaned toward the nightstand and turned on the soft light and laughed. "He can watch us go into the bedroom if he's still there, but that's all."

Chapter 5

Xavier left their offices, went to a mom and pop hardware store and purchased a gallon of paint thinner and rags. He followed Highway 60 east to Alma School Road, then north a few blocks and pulled into the Fiesta Mall parking lot. He cruised several parking lanes looking for the perfect van to use in transporting Clyburn.

Jesus, I thought this area was economically depressed. There's nothing but late model cars, trucks, SUV's and vans.

On the eighth aisle he spotted an old moss green Ford Aerostar.

"Perfect; dinged, old, dirty and tinted windows."

He drove his car back to the Alma School exit, crossed the intersection and parked in a crowded restaurant lot. Taking the paint thinner, rags and a screw driver he returned to the intersection. He re-crossed Alma School returning to the Aerostar as he mumbled, "I hate walking."

A shopper backing out of a parking place almost hit him. "Asshole."

He reached the aisle with the Aerostar. "Good, it's still here."

Xavier went to the driver's door and looked around. *No foot traffic.* He broke the window, opened the door, brushed the glass from the seat and quickly climbed in tossing the paint thinner and rags on to the passenger seat.

He bent over the steering column while taking a quick look around the parking lot. "I haven't done this in a while." He removed the plastic cover from the column pulling out the bundle separating the battery, ignition and starter wires. Using a pocket knife he stripped the insulation from the battery wires and twisted them together. "Damn, no tape, but the engine will run when I start it."

He made another quick glance around the van. "Now, let's hook this to this," he said connecting the ignition on/off and battery wires.

He stripped a half-inch of insulation from the starter wire and touched it to the battery wire. "Yes," he said revving the engine.

He cranked the steering wheel firmly left then right hearing a snap as the pins broke and the wheel went free.

He backed out of the parking space and drove toward the Alma Road exit. Before reaching the road he pulled into a parking place, got out and checked the lights.

"Everything works, gas is good."

He drove back to his house following Highway 60 to Arizona Highway and then going south to Ocotillo. He pulled into the garage after punching in a code on a door panel. "A beater, no one will pay any attention to this van until it burns."

Once inside the townhouse he went straight to the bathroom. Clyburn was still in the tub, hands and feet bound. "Good, you're awake."

Clyburn glared at Xavier.

"We're going for a ride."

Xavier cut the ties on Clyburn's ankles. "Get up," he said taking Clyburn's arm.

Clyburn tried to speak but could only make muffled noises with the tape on his mouth.

They went to the garage. Clyburn got in the van through the sliding door and was buckled into the center of the middle bench seat, his hands still bound behind him.

Xavier chuckled. "It's probably a little uncomfortable but I can't have any distractions driving." He closed the slider, opened the garage door and backed out. "Have to close it with the keyboard, damn clicker's in my car."

He started to open the driver's door but the interior light flashed on. He looked up then smashed it with the handle of the screwdriver. "Damn things a distraction." He got out of the van, closed the garage door, looked back at Clyburn then got in and slammed the driver's door. He reached back and pulled the tape from Clyburn's mouth. "Let's talk."

"About what," Clyburn said in a soft raspy voice.

"Let's talk about Kat. She works for me, has for a long time. She's good at what she does."

"You're blackmailing her."

"I like to think we work together. I'm thinking you and I could work together, too."

"Don't kid yourself. We both know you're going to kill me. That's the plan, but you're making a big mistake."

"You're a smart Russian, so how is this a mistake?"

"My people, my family will find you."

"Your people?"

"I'm an accountant at DataFlex, my father and brothers are more closely associated with your line of work."

"You mean the Russian mafia? That's good for me. The cartels already know the Russians are moving into their turf. When you end up dead in the desert it will look like a cartel hit. The cops, the Russian's and the warring cartels will all think it's a business related hit. I'm home free."

"I wouldn't bet on that. My people aren't stupid."

"Enough is enough," said Xavier getting out of the driver's seat, reaching back and striking Clyburn on the side of his head with the gun butt again. "No one will see you on the seat."

He moved back into the driver's seat, buckled up, and glanced into the rearview mirror. "We'll just drive quietly out to the west valley."

*****

Francis Dade stood at his dark office window sipping bourbon and watched the lights of Columbus Avenue fifty floors below, barely visible through the late New York clouds. The phone on his desk rang.

"Finally," he said picking up.

Andrea Nance said, "Good evening, Francis."

"I've been expecting to hear from you. How has the day gone?"

"Mostly the way we planned. The only real glitch is Kohler's partner. He's taken a Russian prisoner and is executing him as we speak somewhere out in the west valley of Phoenix. I've told Canfield he must solve the problem of Xavier permanently."

"That could be difficult for Canfield. They've worked together a long time."

"He'll take care of it. I think he's more concerned right now that the Russian is connected to organized crime."

"As in Russian Mafia, Andrea?"

"One and the same. Otherwise all is well. Canfield is supposed to meet Santiago at 2:00 p.m. tomorrow with our offer. I'm now on my way across country and expect to meet Mrs. Braun tomorrow at her gym in Paradise Valley. Tom Logan is picking me up at Sky Harbor when I get in."

"Tom Logan? Have you involved him in this activity?"

"No, but he has a directors meeting with our Phoenix branch office scheduled late tomorrow afternoon. If for any reason he learns I was in Phoenix and didn't contact him he'd have suspicions of his own."

Dade said, "Yes, that's a quarterly session he does with his people, but usually in the morning as I recall."

"I was fortunate enough to get six of his people into a cyber-hacking workshop with the city governments and the FBI at the last minute. The meeting is a good cover for my visit as Noble's lead lobbyist in the area."

"I won't even ask how you got the FBI to invite six of our people."

"Good. Now moving forward, Santiago is definitely out of DataFlex from all observations and inside information we've collected. Tomorrow after I encounter Nikki Braun at her gym if all goes as expected, I'll meet with Santiago at 2:00 rather than Canfield."

"Good, you're always on top of what's going on, Andrea. I like that."

"Thank you. We'll talk again tomorrow, probably after I have Santiago on board. I don't want her slipping through our fingers and I'm sure other firms are learning of her availability."

"You're right about that. She should prove to be a long term asset not only for this project but in Washington with you for some time to come. If you're sure make the offer. It ought to be generous enough."

"Your offer is more than generous. I expect to have her signed and on her way to New Orleans by tomorrow evening."

"Excellent, Andrea, until tomorrow."

*****

Xavier followed Interstate 10 west staying in the middle lane at the speed limit. Traffic moved easily in the late night hour. "You're out cold, the windows are tinted and no one will see you or notice us."

A Camaro passed them at a high rate of speed.

He chuckled. "That's good for us. Give the cops a little business and a big distraction."

Clyburn moaned. Xavier glanced back but saw him lying on the seat. "You make much noise or try to sit up I'll pull off and smack you again."

Clyburn remained quiet but Xavier could hear him wiggling.

"Patience, Clyburn. We'll be there soon enough. You'll never get those ties loose. You should know that. I'm sure your father and brother have used them on occasion."

Xavier watched the rearview mirror. "Here comes a state cop. They can go any speed they want," he said with a laugh. A moment later a semi passed. "He's got enough lights to be in a parade."

Clyburn moaned again.

"Just sharing what you're missing. If things had been different you could've made a deal, worked with us. Dumb mistake."

They passed a truck stop at Exit 137 on the south side of I-10.

Xavier said, "Too bad. I'd like to stop and get a bite to eat on the way. Of course I would be eating alone." He laughed.

Traffic slowed as they approached the Loop 303 construction zone. Bright lights illuminated the entire area. Xavier pulled off the freeway to a mall parking lot, shifted into park and climbed out of his seat. He leaned toward Clyburn.

"Sorry, pal. But I can't have you try to sit up right now." He hit him on the side of the head again with his gun knocking him out. "If you lived through tonight you'd probably have brain damage. Too bad, fool."

Climbing back into the driver's seat he glanced at the dash clock. "Only took two minutes. Not bad."

After driving another half-mile on I-10 traffic came to a complete halt. Even with the tinted windows one could see into the Aerostar. A semi pulled up and stopped on Xavier's left. A Chevy was on the right.

"Come on guys. It's too bright out here." He glanced back at Clyburn. "Keep sleepin' comrade."

Up ahead Xavier saw a road grader move off the freeway. A flagman motioned traffic forward.

"About time."

The next mile was slow. Even more light came into the van. The semi merged into his lane ahead of him. "Snails could go faster," he said watching for the lights of the car behind him lost below the rear window.

Finally the lights began to fade, the freeway darkened, and the truck returned to its original lane. Headlights reappeared in the rear window and the pace picked up to the speed limit.

Xavier wiped his brow. "Only a few more miles, Clyburn, then you'll really sleep."

Exit 98: Wintersberg Road/Palo Verde Nuclear Plant loomed out of the dark. Xavier took the exit and turned right leaving the lights of Palo Verde in his rear view mirror. A few miles north of I-10 he saw a dirt road leading into the desert on his left. He slowed and turned off. No cars were around as he drove a few miles followed by a huge cloud of dust. He pulled off the road onto the desert which was rock hard and drove a few hundred feet to a small mound.

Xavier parked on the far side of the mound, doused the lights but left the engine running. He got out the driver's door and whistled as he walked around the van to the slider and opened it.

He reached into the van and began pulling Clyburn out. "Come on big guy, time to get up." He held both of Clyburn's arms and walked behind him, directing the wobbly Russian to a spot only a few feet from the van but hidden from any view south toward I-10.

Xavier shoved him to his knees. "End of the line, Clyburn."

Clyburn turned and looked at Xavier. Even in the dimly lit moonlight sky the Russian's eyes seemed to burn and sparkle. Sweat covered his face. He made no sound.

Xavier went back to the van and got his jacket. He returned and placed it over Clyburn's head. He held it away from the back of Clyburn's head with one hand and aimed the .38 with the other.

He said, "No flash. I love it," and squeezed the trigger.

Clyburn fell forward in the sand, the top half of his head a bloody mass. Xavier reached Clyburn's mouth and tore the tape loose. "No clues, punk. Death by cartel."

Xavier returned to the van and drove back along the side road to I-10, then to Highway 60 and the Fiesta Mall. He parked in a dark corner near the sidewalk on University. Before getting out of the van he spilled the paint thinner around the interior and onto the jacket. He soaked the rolled paint towel then exited the van. He lit a cigarette and placed it on the towel so it would burn onto the thinner. He closed the door and walked to the sidewalk. He was almost to the corner of University and Alma School when the van burst into flames.

"Kohler will like this" he said crossing with the light. He walked south down Alma School to the restaurant parking lot, now almost empty. Fire trucks raced down Alma School and University into the mall parking lot. Xavier yielded to them waiting to pull into traffic.

"Now to dump the gun."

Xavier drove to Tempe and parked on side road just off Mill Avenue. He walked the now sparsely populated street to the Mill Avenue Bridge. A few couples were huddled along the sidewalk watching the water and half hidden moon on one side. He walked to the center of the bridge on the opposite side and looked back. The couples were now walking back to Mill Avenue. No cars were coming. He took the .38 from a pocket, wiped it clean and dropped it into the lake.

He looked across the lake toward Santiago's loft. "Damn, the lights are on. Enjoy the night beautiful lady."

*****

The flight attendant tapped Andrea Nance on the shoulder.

Nance opened her eyes. "Yes?"

"We'll be landing at Scottsdale Airport in a few minutes, Miss Nance. You asked me to wake you when we approached."

"Thank you."

Nance yawned and looked out the small window near her seat. *Always strange at night coming into a smaller field; bright clusters of city lights, some highway street lighting and then deep blackness.*

She took out her cell phone and speed dialed Tom Logan.

A sharp male answered, "Hello."

"Good evening, Tom. Sorry for the late hour but I am just now landing."

"Andrea, sorry for my tone of voice. I was napping. You said you were coming in tonight. I just didn't expect to hear from you until morning."

"Not to worry. I'll be busy in the morning while your people are at the workshop. Tomorrow afternoon I'll visit the meeting but stay only for my presentation. I have to go to New Orleans and then get back to the capitol ASAP. We have several irons in the fire as Mr. Dade likes to say."

"Would you like me to come and pick you up? I'm only twenty minutes away."

"I'll be in my hotel in twenty minutes; in the bathtub with a martini, alone."

"I won't go near that statement."

"Don't. It's been a long day."

"Where are you staying?"

"The Scottsdale Royal Spa."

He said, "Nice place."

"So I've heard but I'm only there for a few hours of sleep then back on the treadmill. I'll see you at the meeting." She broke the connection.

The attendant approached again. "Miss Nance, your limousine is waiting."

"Excellent," she said and started for the car. "Oh, when we leave tomorrow afternoon I'll have a passenger with me."

"We'll be ready. The pilot already told me we'll be going to New Orleans. I like to let my husband know where I'm heading next as soon as possible."

"It's always good to keep your other half informed," said Nance looking at the attendant's tag, "Gail."

*****

At 10:45 p.m. Canfield Kohler sat at his desk drumming the fingers of his right hand. He took another deep breath. *Why this, why now?*

He picked up his phone and punched in a number.

A man with a Jamaican accent answered. "Yes."

"Thelonious, its Canfield. Can you make a set of new identification papers for me by tomorrow?"

"What all do you need?"

"Everything; birth certificate, Social Security card, driver's license, passport, maybe even a little background on a character."

"You're asking for a lot. The background part could be a little dicey on such short notice, the other stuff is possible but I'll have to pull an overnighter and call in some favors, probably Thursday morning."

"Okay, it's necessary for Jerome to permanently disappear. I want him somewhere he can enjoy the rest of his life without looking over his shoulder."

Thelonious said, "Jerome?"

"Long story. Someone wants him gone, out of the way; someone big."

"You mean he fucked up the wrong people this time, don't you."

"You have a classy way of explaining my partner."

"He's my friend, too, in a business way." Thelonious paused for a moment. "Canfield, you're smooth, articulate, and educated. Jerome is pretty much a thug; muscle."

Kohler said, "He's a little rough around the edges, always has been. But he did graduate pre-law."

Thelonious laughed. "He musta been a linebacker. He has no polish."

Kohler said, "Just get us the papers Thursday morning."

"I already said you'll get 'em Thursday morning, but it'll cost you."

"Of course."

"$25K on delivery."

"What time?"

"10:00 a.m."

Kohler said, "Done."

Thelonious said, "Where will he go?"

"I don't know, someplace nobody knows him."

"This is really serious, isn't it?"

"Beyond serious. There can be no records of this transaction anywhere. He must disappear with no way to be traced."

"I understand."

"Good, anybody finds him he's dead. I can't let that happen."

Thelonious said, "Will he be careful?"

"Jerome's tough, rough around the edges, but he'll do what's necessary to survive."

Thelonious laughed. "He likes the west coast. I hear Coronado, Mission Bay, Redondo, and Manhattan Beach are nice."

"They always are, Thelonious, until Thursday." He broke the connection. *Were you just chatting or trying to find out where Jerome would go?*

Kohler next accessed their offshore account. "$1.5 million ain't bad," he said while creating a new account and transferring half the funds into it. "That should take care of you for a while, partner."

He got up and paced the office. The wall clock was at 11:18. "Good thing Thelonious works odd hours."

He went to the bar and poured a tumbler of bourbon-water. He noticed a photo of Xavier landing a fish on a charter trip. "Thelonious wants to know where you're going. He'll cut a deal with someone, sell you out, Jerome. I can feel it."

Kohler looked at a photo of him and Xavier on the wall beside the bar. "Tomorrow we'll talk about your future. It's time to leave; no packing, no goodbyes, just disappear and live my friend. If they find you we're both dead, Andrea will see to that." He finished the bourbon. *Still, three-quarter of a million dollars is a lot of money, partner.*

He refilled the tumbler and returned to the desk.

"Mistakes, Jerome, always those damned little mistakes; ten years of mistakes." He took another sip. "Thelonious was right. You were a football player in college."

Kohler stood and walked slowly to Xavier's office carrying his drink.

"Jesus, what a mess; papers everywhere, maps, snapshots, cup rings on the coffee table. Damn good thing I've always been the front man for us. This is worse than usual."

He stepped toward Jerome's desk. "Talk about a fire hazard, that ashtray is a mini-mountain. Risky, risky."

He returned to his office carrying the now empty tumbler and turned on the news then poured another drink.

"Ten years, Jerome; hundreds of cases, a few little mistakes, careless errors." He took another sip. "Three unnecessary homicides, then the stunt in New York. Jesus, you almost brought the NSA down on us. Now the Russian."

He glanced at the television screen shaking his head. A bright eyed blond in a very short tight skirt was pointing at a weather map.

"Honey, who cares about blue skies, all I see are hot, hot thighs," he said smacking his lips. He finished the drink.

He sat looking around his office. "What to do, Jerome? Maybe fake a suicide; disappear leaving a note behind. How will I ever get you to do that?"

Kohler sat back in his desk chair. "Suicide, something tomorrow, a lot of money moving. I gotta rest my eyes."

Chapter 6
Wednesday, July 9

Andrea Nance pulled into the visitor section of the Mummy Mountain Country Club parking lot at 7:30 a.m. after a short night's sleep. *Thank you Mr. Receptionist. I'd never guess Nikki Braun was such an early riser when I called this morning trying to catch up with an old school mate.*

She went into the woman's locker room after checking in on the guest register. *Francis, you make access so easy.*

Walking down two rows of lockers she finally found one with the name plate of Nikki Braun. The padlock was attached to the door.

"Good, you're here."

Nance went to the guest lockers and dressed for a morning of exercise; gym shorts, sweat pants, sports bra and a blouse. She laced her running shoes and headed for the workout room. Only three people were there; two men and a woman.

Nance went to a stationary bike next to the woman and began riding. After a few minutes she looked at the other woman.

Nance said, "You do this often?"

The other woman answered, "Three times a week. I like to ride a little. I swim at home."

Nance held out a hand. "I'm Andrea Nance. I'm just visiting, taking advantage of the guest privileges of my companion for the week."

"Nikki Braun. I hope your companion for the week isn't named Claude."

"No. Why?"

"Nothing," said Nikki Braun shaking her head, "it's just so many wealthy men seem to take advantage of their position. A good friend of mine found out her husband was screwing her best friend. Can you imagine that, her best friend? She worked for him at one of the tech companies in Chandler."

"Worked for him?"

"Yes, I, I mean she told him to dump the bitch and can her ass or say goodbye to his big house and made over reputation."

"And he did it?"

"You bet your ass he did it. Worthless bitch."

"Well, I'm happy for your friend. I had a similar experience but I was the one hitting the road. You know the story; prenuptials and big appetites."

"You come out okay?"

"Got a tidy sum and my freedom. What kind of woman would take such advantage of her friend I wonder?"

"One that works and does secret stuff with her best friend's husband. God, I have to stop talking about this. My blood pressure is going through the ceiling. I can feel it rushing."

"Look, we've been peddling for half an hour. I've got to get going. I don't want any surprises like your best friend."

Braun said, "No, no surprises."

Nance said, "And I've got to keep this firm." She patted her backside. "Nice meeting you, Nikki."

"Same here, Andrea," she said with a smile and turned around facing the wall mirror and peddling. When Nance cleared the gym Nikki Braun speed dialed her husband.

"Hi," he said, "a little early for a call isn't it?"

"We have had a contact, Claude. She bought the story on Mitch hook, line and sinker."

"Good. I'll call Ray. What was the woman's name?"

"She introduced herself as Andrea Nance."

"Thanks, Nikki. Have a good workout. I've got a task to take care of," he said breaking the connection.

*****

Link Andrews sat up in the king size bed, twisted his neck and blinked. He smiled at Michelle Santiago as she walked out of the master suite bath wrapped in a large blue towel.

"Morning, Mitch, sleep well?"

She raised an eyebrow. "Apparently not as good as you but we have time for breakfast before you go."

"You mean coffee."

"The way you use sugar it's almost liquid cereal," she said with a laugh. "Come on lazy bones, up and out. I'll make the coffee while you shower and shave."

He climbed out of the bed and grabbed for a package of cigarettes on the nightstand.

"Hey," she said, "naked guys shouldn't smoke until they're completely awake. You might burn something just hanging loose."

He ran a hand over his flat tan belly and looked at the bed. "We could skip the coffee."

"No we can't. I have some family business to take care of and get ready for this afternoon. Kohler's bringing an offer from Noble."

He said, "The offer should be interesting."

"I'm sure it will be, but Kohler is just a freelancer. I need to know about the particulars on the inside of Noble."

Andrews said, "Mario will be on it."

"I know. Now, don't you think you should do something about showering?" She waved a hand. "Naked works for me but I doubt Ray would see it the same way."

He held out a hand. "Towel?"

She rolled her eyes. "Yours is hanging in there, dry," she said nodding toward the bath. "I'll be at the counter."

Santiago went to the kitchen area and put on a pot of coffee. Then she returned to the bedroom and dressed in shorts and a t-shirt. The burn cell began to ring out on the kitchen counter. She caught it on the third one.

"Good morning, Mitch."

"Good morning, Ray."

"You sound chipper. I thought maybe I'd be waking you at this hour since you're not working."

She smiled. "Been working all night, but what's up?"

"The Noble Group has sent an email inquiring about your work at DataFlex sans the rumors."

"So they are checking me out to the last minute."

"So it would seem. How about last night?"

"Link and I spotted a man on the roof of a student apartment building. I'm betting it was either Kohler or Xavier."

Ray said, "He could have been a voyeur."

"Possible, but what you're telling me reinforces my thinking."

"Well, there's more. Noble has an office in Washington headed up by Andrea Nance, a registered lobbyist."

Santiago said, "Where Tony was killed."

Ray said, "Yes. Washington is a city of many connections above and below board. What makes the inquiry more unique today is Nikki just called Claude from her gym a few minutes ago. A woman named Andrea Nance showed up this morning at her workout."

"Interesting, Ray, why a lobbyist from D.C. out here?"

House said, "She's also in charge of Noble's security in D.C. Be careful when you meet Kohler this afternoon."

"Of course," she said. "Have you responded to Noble's inquiry?"

"I sent a response noting you're one of the best security operatives we've had and noted rumors are just that, rumors. More interesting, Andrea Nance then called representing Francis Dade, Noble CEO. I spoke with her regarding your investigative skills and integrity. The important thing is we know who we're dealing with. Noble is big time, well connected with a questionable reputation."

"Nice recommendation. Thank you."

House laughed. "Truthful."

"It would be interesting to know if Miss Nance has an investigative background. Link says Mario is looking into her. Let me know if something important comes up. I feel this operation is about to speed up."

*****

Canfield Kohler looked at his partner. "Long night? You look like crap."

"I popped the Russian out by Palo Verde on the north side of Interstate 10. It was pretty late when I got home."

"How far north of the highway?"

"A mile or two."

"You said van."

"An old Aerostar. I found it at Fiesta Mall."

Kohler smiled. "Good job. I saw the late news with the fire off of University."

Xavier said, "It got a lot of coverage. The news guys were close but not accurate."

"The gun?"

"I dropped it off the bridge at Town Lake."

"I don't believe you walked that far."

"Didn't have much choice. You can't park on the bridge. It was funny, too. I could see the side windows of Santiago's loft. Of course they were dark. It's a small world."

Kohler forced a laugh. "It is."

Xavier stood quietly for a moment then said, "Something is bothering you."

"Yes."

"What?"

"The woman you talked with yesterday."

"What about her?"

Kohler went to his coffee bar. "You want a cup?"

"I want to know what is bothering you."

Kohler poured himself a cup of coffee, walked back to the desk and sat down. "Damn it!" he shouted as coffee spilled in his lap.

Xavier went to the bar and grabbed a towel. "Here," he said tossing it.

Kohler wiped his lap. "They want you out of the game, Jerome."

"They?"

"The woman and her boss."

"They fired us?"

"Not exactly. They think you are too careless, make too many mistakes."

"Me?"

"For example, you didn't call me when Santiago was returning to her loft."

"An accident. It won't happen again."

"Then you took the Russian prisoner and we had to solve that problem."

"Exactly, dead Russian, problem solved. If anyone finds him they'll think the Mexicans did it. What else do they want?"

"You out of the picture."

"Okay, I'll work our other clients if that's what you want."

"It's not what they want."

Xavier took a deep breath. "What do they want?"

Kohler looked across the desk but said nothing. He pressed his lips tightly and narrowed his eyes.

Xavier said, "You can't be serious."

Kohler said in a soft voice, "They want you eliminated."

"They're putting a contract out on me?"

"No."

"What then?"

"Jerome, we've been partners for a decade."

"They want you to pop me?"

"It's not going to happen. I have a plan."

Jerome shifted in the chair, glanced around the office then back to Kohler. "I don't believe it. You told 'em to get screwed, right?"

"Wrong. They'd kill both of us. I agreed to eliminate you so we could make you disappear without them knowing you're alive."

"I don't even know these people. How am I goin' to disappear?"

"We'll do it the same way the Feds do, a fresh start with a new identity, new location, preferably some place you've never been."

Xavier said, "You think I should do this?"

"Yes, we have no choice."

"What about the business? It will cost a lot for me to start over."

"We have over a million-five in the offshore account. We'll create a new account moving $750,000 into it for you."

"Where will I go? I've never travelled much?"

"At our age I would suggest Florida, maybe the Caribbean. Move to a retirement community, rent or buy a condo or house; retire. After your house here sells I'll put that money in your account, too."

"$750K won't last a lifetime."

"Jerome, each month I'll deposit funds into your account just as we do now offshore. Money is not the problem, keeping you alive is."

"You mean both of us."

"Yes."

"This is so strange."

"Jerome, we're closer than brothers. I told them I'd do you so they wouldn't send someone. Now we need to move quickly."

"Will we ever see each other again?"

"That's something in the future, I don't know."

"Shit, Canfield, we're a good team."

"Yes, we have been, but people bigger than us, stronger than us are in control."

"Just for the sake of argument, if I do the disappearing act, what happens to you?"

"Assuming I can convince them of your death I'll continue the business, hire someone on a contract rather than getting another partner. He'll work our normal clients."

"You plan on keeping the people that want me dead?"

Kohler smiled. "To do otherwise would tip our hand."

"You know, Canfield, they will eventually come after you. You're a loose end."

"I don't think so. We've built a strong intelligence network. I believe they will continue to pay top dollar, and that my friend is your retirement."

Xavier smiled. "And yours, we hope."

"Yes, in a few years when our accounts will support both of us, but today we need to take care of you; new name, ID, disappearance, everything."

"What about my stuff? I can drive to Florida."

"No, leave your car. Fly down using your new ID. Thelonious can get you everything you need including a passport. When the police find it abandoned your disappearance will be reinforced."

Xavier said, "Thelonious is expensive."

"Yes my friend, but he's the best."

"What will you tell the bitch on the phone?"

"That you've been taken care of out in the desert, maybe southwest of Gila Bend in the Maricopa Mountains."

"You think she'll believe it?"

"She and her cohorts have little choice. People are killed out there all the time. Bodies are often found, some even partially eaten by animals."

"My DNA won't match."

"Jerome, for every body found there's probably another five out there some place."

"In other words, if I'm not found you did a good job. If someone spots me in Florida the plan will go under fast."

Kohler emptied his cup. "Yes. I was thinking some plastic surgery, a new look you."

"Good idea, Canfield, I could open an agency in Florida."

"That would be another mistake, Jerome. You'd never pass the licensing background with its fingerprint check. If you go into any business it would be have to be something completely different and without a criminal background check. Your body is the problem."

Both men laughed.

Xavier said, "How about this. You don't front killing me, I do a suicide note. You know, depressed because I'm such a fuck-up, no friends, alone. I leave a note like the one we did on that guy in Tucson a few years ago."

"That is a good idea, but don't tell them where you're going to do it, just disappear. It would make the papers, probably back page. Now what name do you want to adopt for the rest of your life? We've got to let Thelonious know."

Xavier sat quietly for a moment, rubbing his chin and shuffling his feet. "Wyatt, I like the name Wyatt."

"Why?"

"Wyatt Earp, my boyhood hero."

Koehler said, "You can't be Earp."

"I know, but I could be Wyatt Henderson. I like that."

"Done," said Kohler. "I'll call Thelonious in a minute, but first, who do you admire with the name Henderson? It's new to me."

"The City of Henderson, Canfield, next to Vegas."

"Really, a city?"

Kohler dialed Thelonious.

"What have you got for me, Canfield?"

"Jerome wants to be Wyatt Henderson. When will the papers be ready?"

"Tomorrow morning. I'll come by your office."

"Good. You said $25K?"

Thelonious said, "Right," and the connection broke.

Xavier looked Kohler in the eyes and said, "Thank you, I think most of the people we know would just kill me."

"Go home, Jerome. Write your note and but don't pack anything. I'll come by when I get the papers and the money is transferred. We can have a drink, say our goodbyes. Don't be too specific in the note."

"I won't. See you later."

Xavier left the office.

Kohler sat quietly. *Suicide, what a brilliant idea, and to think you thought of it with just a little guidance.*

*****

Kat Parsons sat in her DataFlex cubical sipping coffee. "9:05, Vladimir, you're an hour late."

She went to his cubical. Nothing on the desk was disturbed. "Always the neat freak," she mumbled, returned to her cubical and called the security desk at the entry to the building.

The man at the security desk entry answered, "Yes, Miss Parsons. How may I help you?"

"Did Vladimir call in sick today?"

"No ma'am, but he hasn't arrived yet."

"Thank you," she said and hung-up. She called his cell. The recording told her to leave a message. "Hi, it's Kat. Please give me a ring."

You said you wouldn't look up Xavier until after we talked last night. Then you didn't come over. You didn't answer your cell last night, either.

She dialed Xavier's cell.

"Good morning, Kat. Do you have something new for me?"

"No, I am calling because a friend of mine didn't come to work today."

"People get sick every day, Kat. Why call me?"

She felt a surge in her body. She pursed her lips for a moment then took a deep breath. "I made a mistake, yesterday."

"What did you do?"

"A workmate came into my space yesterday after you and I talked. I was crying. He wanted to know why."

"What did you tell him?"

She gulped. "The truth. It was wrong, I know, but he said he wouldn't report me. He wanted to visit you and have you stop bothering me."

"You were very foolish, Kat."

"I know, but he promised not to see you until I talked with him last evening."

Xavier said, "So what is the problem?"

"Vladimir didn't come over. Did he come to see you last night after work?"

"Who? Vladimir. Sounds Russian. No, nobody visited me last night. Why?"

"He didn't come to work today. He doesn't answer his phone or return his calls. I just thought, you know, maybe he looked you up."

"No, Kat, no Russians looked me up last night or any other night," Xavier said with a smirk. "I'm sure he will talk to you first and I'll never see him. We don't want any trouble, do we Kat?"

"No, no trouble. I just don't want him hurt."

"Of course not. I'm sure your friend will surface. People miss work for many reasons. Don't bother me with your personal problems. I'm a busy man," he said breaking the connection.

Kat shuffled some papers on her desk and began to work. *Maybe he'll be here by lunch and we can talk.*

*****

Canfield Kohler sat in his office reading an old press clipping about Michelle Santiago. "You're a well-trained detective Miss Santiago. Everything appears to be correct, almost too correct." His desk top phone rang.

"Yes, Teresa."

"Andrea Nance on line one, Mr. Kohler."

"Thank you."

He punched the line. "Good morning, Andrea. I'm pleased you called."

She said, "I've had a busy morning, Canfield. I did a workout with Nikki Braun at her country club."

"Really? You're here in Phoenix? Did you discover anything of interest?"

She laughed. "Don't sleep with your best friend's husband."

Kohler smiled. "She verified they had an affair? Interesting."

"Why?"

Kohler said, "Miss Santiago denies the affair. She thinks her friend may be a bit delusional and drinks too much."

Nance said, "True or not, Nikki Braun believes it and is quite proud of getting Santiago fired."

"That's good to know. I've been thinking everything about this firing is too good to be true. You're meeting with Mrs. Braun explains Santiago's anger."

Nance said, "It also bodes well for us. Revenge is a powerful tool in the right hands."

"Yes it is, Andrea, and you know how to use tools."

"I have made one change in plans, Canfield. I will come by and pick up the offer for Santiago."

"You know she's expecting me at 2:00."

"I'll surprise her, and I believe you have another piece of unfinished business. Did Jerome deal with the Russian problem?"

"Yes. I suspect someone to discover him within the next few days."

"Good. It's 12:15. I'll be at your office around 1:00. I would rather Jerome not be there when I arrive."

"Of course," said Kohler. "He's still tailing Santiago."

"That's a good way to keep him engaged."

Kohler smiled. "My initial plan was to deal with our mutual problem later this afternoon, after I finished with Santiago."

"Enough, Canfield. I don't want the details."

And I won't share them. "I'll see you this afternoon," he said and broke the connection.

*****

Francis Dade stretched and answered the phone in his desk drawer. "Hello, Andrea, what do you have for me?"

"Nikki Braun confirms Santiago was terminated because of an affair with Claude Braun."

"I wonder if it was real or imagined."

"It was real as far as Nikki Braun is concerned. No question about it, Michelle is gone because of her."

Dade said, "That should put Michelle fully in our camp."

"It should," said Nance, "but I wouldn't let her know what we are really doing at Maxwell, just what she needs to know."

Dade nodded. "Good thought. For cover assign her to an onsite lobbying team. That should get her access to most of the staff; whoever she needs to find the individual who was going to talk with Mercedes."

Nance said, "Speaking of Mercedes, I'm sure DataFlex will be assigning someone to take his place. My feeling is it will be Sam Evans."

"Yes," said Dade, "Ray House will send in the best. Evans and Santiago worked together before she joined the company. That could explain why he wasn't at her firing."

Nance said, "If you're right it'll be interesting to see how they work around each other."

"They're professionals, Andrea, on opposite teams. My bet would be they try to squeeze information from each other – all in the spirit of collegiality."

She laughed.

"Tell me, Andrea, has our problem been dealt with?"

"Yes. Canfield assures me it was taken care of last night. He is confident the Russian will be found in the next few days."

He said, "Excellent. What about Xavier?"

"Kohler is taking care of that problem as we speak."

"Good. I'm thinking we may want to deal with Canfield, too. No loose ends."

"I'll make the arrangements before I go to New Orleans with Santiago. I have an appointment with Senator DuBois or I'd take care of it personally."

"Good. I liked the way your people dealt with the Washington problem."

Nance smiled. "Accidents happen."

"So they do," said Dade breaking the connection.

Nance punched in another number.

"Wolfe," answered a man.

"I have another task needing resolution. Are you available?"

"Of course."

"Fly to Phoenix. After you get here call this number. I'll give you the details."

Wolfe said, "I'll be there late tonight. Any particular script to follow?"

She said, "An accident."

"We'll talk tonight." The cell clicked.

*****

Santiago was at the counter by the kitchen area sipping a cappuccino when she heard the door knocker. As she opened the door an attractive woman in her 40's smiled. She wore a tailored skirt cut just a few inches above the knee, four inch black heels, black mesh nylons with a pattern, a white blouse opened to the second button, a colorful scarf around her throat and an open waist jacket matching the skirt. Her green eyes stood out against her fair complexion and brown hair with a red tint.

Santiago stood quietly for a moment. *You're not Canfield. You look more like a professional cougar.*

The woman held out her hand. "Miss Santiago, I'm Andrea Nance from the Noble Group. We've had a change of plans. Mr. Kohler won't be coming today. You asked who your supervisor would be. If you join the company it will be me."

"Come in. Shall we sit on the lanai?" said Santiago walking toward the sliders.

Nance followed Santiago. "A loft. I like it."

"Thank you."

"Obviously you're also an artist."

Santiago laughed as they looked around the loft. "Self-styled student is probably a more accurate description. But you already know about my background; the loft, painting, current circumstances, even my male friend."

"I do, all the way back to your college days at the University of Washington including your time as a stripper, and then homicide cop. In our business we need to know as much as possible about the people we wish to employ. I'm sure you've looked into the Noble Group as well."

Nance took an envelope from a folder she carried and handed it to her.

Santiago removed a single sheet from the envelope and glanced at it. "$300,000.00, this is very generous. Not bad for a U-Dub stripper."

Nance chuckled. "Except for an increase of the retainer the offer covers everything you had previously with DataFlex."

"Yes. Obviously you have good resources." *Someone inside the business office.*

Nance said, "We try."

"Miss Nance, what will be my responsibilities with Noble?"

"The same type of work you were doing at DataFlex; deep cover background research. I'm sure our methods are similar to those of your former employer."

Santiago laughed. "DataFlex never had anyone caught committing a burglary."

Nance smiled. "That was unfortunate. Kohler's partner forgot to call him before you got into the building."

"You're referring to the incompetent tail he had on me. Not a good professional."

"No, he isn't. Kohler and his partner are contract people. I didn't have time to put my own people into play. As I'm sure you know, Noble is based in New York."

Santiago nodded. *You knew of my firing immediately. That means you have someone in the DataFlex security office.* "I discovered Noble also has an office in Washington."

"I am the lead in their lobbying group. As I said, background, background, background."

"So I could be involved with politicians?"

Nance nodded. "They are the reason I'm there – power brokers. Like you, my team is smart, young, and sassy. They're professional lobbyists that know their way around power brokers and how to appeal to their every need while always keeping an upper hand."

Santiago said, "So my job is to find what you can use."

Nance said, "That is the game and where the government is involved millions, even billions are at stake?"

"You're talking about the east coast. I'm not sure I want to make that move."

Nance laughed. "Michelle, you don't need to move. You could be assigned to one of our projects anywhere in the country or even overseas just as you've done with DataFlex. None of those assignments would be long term. While working security you'll always be part of my team based in Washington regardless of assignment. Being a registered lobbyist opens many doors and secrets."

Santiago smiled. "If we're going to work together you'll have to call me Mitch."

"Mitch it is."

"When do you want me to start?"

"Now, we'll be leaving for New Orleans in two hours. I have a senator I want you to meet and a project for you."

Santiago said, "New Orleans?"

"We're sending you to Maxwell Cyber Systems."

"DataFlex is part of a project at Maxwell. I've never been involved with it but an associate of mine is."

Nance said, "We're both large investors in a project with Maxwell and need to guard our interests. Who is your associate in the Big Easy?"

"Tony Mercedes. I haven't heard from him in months. Knowing him, he's busy chasing the ladies in his spare time. He went to Maxwell when the project started."

"Mitch, I know you're out of the DataFlex loop but something happened yesterday you need to know."

"Really?"

"Tony Mercedes was killed in Washington."

"Oh no," said Santiago. Her eyes welled. She covered her mouth and looked out at Town Lake. "What happened?"

"I saw on the news he was killed by a mugger."

Santiago said, "Did you know Tony?"

Nance said, "I knew of him. I knew he was assigned to Maxwell by DataFlex. That's what caught my attention when I heard the name. I'm surprised your friend Link Andrews didn't tell you about Tony."

"He's very careful about company business, always by the book. But if Link knew about Tony he would've told me. Someone getting mugged isn't the sort of thing that crosses his desk. I'd bet he knows about it now. If he doesn't he will when I tell him."

"Doesn't DataFlex have a ban on their people talking with you?"

"You know Link and I are way beyond talking."

Nance ignored the comment. "You're cautious, a woman of your word. I like that."

Santiago said, "How so?"

"The project you refer to is 'Barrier.' You're bound not to speak about DataFlex's involvement per se. Noble is also participating in the project."

Santiago said, "Maxwell does a lot of research and development."

Nance nodded. "Not unlike DataFlex, but Noble is more of an investor."

Santiago sat quietly and wiped an eye. "I noticed this morning your man Xavier was still following me."

"Not any more. My background work is done. Have you done enough checking on Noble?"

"Link found some interesting things, shadows surrounding some of Noble's dealings. One was the implication of their involvement with arms dealings and a shootout in New York. He also found rumors of some under the table trade with nations under UN sanction."

"Allegations, Mitch, just allegations spread by some of our competitors."

Santiago waved the offer sheet. "So what flight and terminal do we leave from?"

"Scottsdale Airport, Trapper Aviation. They take care of Noble's Leer jet."

Santiago said, "Are we travelling together?"

"I'll brief you on the plane."

"How long will I be in New Orleans?"

"I'm not sure. I'll only be with you for a day. I'm needed back in Washington."

"I need to make a few personal calls."

Nance said, "While I think of it keep in mind we'll be communicating by burn cells. Fewer records are left to be subpoenaed or demanded by full disclosure demands."

Santiago said, "Smart move. Right now I need to call my dad and Doctor Grossman in Palm Springs."

Nance said, "Don't forget Link."

"Never."

"Well, I best be on my way, too. I have a meeting date to break. I'm sure he won't feel badly about that."

Santiago said, "In an hour, then. Oh, you may want to return these to Mr. Kohler." She handed Nance a small plastic grocery bag holding Kohler's gun, driver's license, and credit card.

Nance took the bag and stepped into the doorway. "I like your style Mitch."

CHAPTER 7

Andrea Nance called the man with the high pitched voice at Dataflex as soon as she got to her car. The man with the high pitched voice answered in a whisper. "You know you're not supposed to call me here."

Nance said, "Are you alone?"

"Yes, but I'm in the security building. Let me call you back from the men's room."

"No, you never know who's in the stall next to you. All I have is a quick question or two."

"Okay."

"Who is taking Tony Mercedes place at Maxwell Cyber Systems?"

"Sam Evans for a while."

"Have you heard anything else about Santiago?"

"No, just that she's persona non grata to all Data-Flex employees."

"Good. What's Link Andrews behavior been like since Santiago was terminated?"

"Pouting."

Nance laughed. "From now on you're my only source inside DataFlex. Be careful."

"I thought you had a secondary source. What happened?"

"Past history. We'll talk tomorrow."

After cutting off the call to the man with the high pitched voice Nance called Tom Logan on her personal cell phone.

"Hello Andrea, the meeting is just getting started. I'll put you on the program whenever you get here."

"Not to worry, Tom. Thank you for the change of schedule allowing your staff to attend the FBI Cybersecurity Workshop this morning, but now Mr. Dade has summoned me back to Washington immediately."

Logan pressed his lips together for a moment. "He's the boss, but it's not very efficient to fly you out here and then have you leave without doing something."

She laughed. "No, but as you said, he's the boss. I'll see you next trip."

"Have a safe flight. I have to go," he said breaking the connection.

Nance sat for a moment after the calls. *It would've been nice to know who Xavier's contact was. Maybe Canfield knows.*

Nance looked up as a car parked only two places away. "Well, well, Sam Evans is visiting. Not a surprise.

*****

Santiago was crossing the loft to the bedroom when the door knocker sounded. She crossed the room mumbling to herself, "What did you forget, Andrea?" When she opened the door Sam Evans greeted her.

"Mitch."

They embraced. "Come in. What a pleasant surprise."

As he came through the door he said, "I don't believe the crap circulating about you and Claude."

"You shouldn't. Coffee?"

"Love some."

They went to the kitchen area counter and she poured two cups.

"How could Nikki think this, you know the rumors, for even a minute?"

Santiago shook her head. "Hard to say, sometimes people are just insecure, Sam. I guess that's Nikki's Achilles heel."

"I think she's back on the sauce."

Santiago sipped her coffee. "Booze, pills, whatever; I'm the victim here. Claude just didn't have the stones to stand up to her."

Evans squinted. "No he didn't, and that's unusual for him. He's a man known for callin' the shots, all the shots."

She said, "Except this time."

"So," he said, "what are you goin' to do now?"

"I've just signed on with the Noble Group. In an hour or so I'm leaving for New Orleans. I've been assigned to Maxwell Cyber Systems as a lobbyist."

"Lobbyist, Christ that's a waste,"

"It's a job and pays well."

He laughed. "Yeah, well it's a small world."

"How so?"

"I'm goin' to New Orleans in Tony Mercedes's place until they decide who to fill it with permanently."

She chuckled. "We'll be seeing each other. How are you going to handle Claude's ban on contact with me?"

"The same way I am now, not well. I'm sure Link isn't too good at following directions either." He shrugged. "Ray can fire me but I doubt he would."

"Me too."

"The one that's goin' nuts is Mario. He spends more time with Ray than any of us do. This mess has left him walkin' on eggshells."

She said, "Mario is a survivor. He'll do just fine."

Evans laughed. "I expect you'll hear from him. You've gone from heartthrob to big sister lust job in his world in the last two years."

Santiago stood. "It's good to see you, Sam, but I have to finish getting ready for my flight."

Evans stood and laughed. "And I'm not supposed to be here."

"I'll see you in New Orleans, Sam."

"Lookin' forward to it. I'll be coming in sometime tomorrow."

*****

After Sam Evans left her condo Michelle Santiago went to the bedroom to pack. *Travel light.* She took four skirts; two minis and two just slightly longer. *I may need something for a thigh gun.* Blouses, underwear, two pairs of stilettos, and makeup filled her suitcase. A sketchpad, Glock 42, thigh holster, electronic notebook, and $5,000.00 in cash went in her flight bag. *Good thing I have an Arizona carry permit even though it's not needed at home. Louisiana honors it.*

She punched in the number of Link Andrews's burn cell.

"Hi Mitch, shall we go out tonight and make it easier for your tail?"

"Only if you pick me up on Bourbon Street."

"New Orleans?"

"Where else? I'm being picked up in less than an hour and heading for Scottsdale Air Park. From there it's off to Maxwell. But before I go here's a little input for you and Ray. Noble has someone inside our security. Andrea Nance knew about my being fired almost immediately."

"Really? Andrea Nance?"

"Yes. She is the registered head of Noble's lobbying team in Washington, but in reality is their head of security. She also knew everything about my DataFlex contract and Tony's 'mugging' as she put it."

Andrews said, "Ray was right, we've got some work to do here."

"There's more. She wants me to meet a senator along with Maxwell's people. I'm being assigned to Maxwell. And you'll like this; my job is to find out who was leaking information to Tony. Apparently it's not one of their people."

Andrews chuckled. "That'll make it easier to concentrate on the task at hand."

"Link, I need to know more about her. She knows my history inside and out."

"I'll get you everything we can find. I can tell you she did a workout with Nikki this morning."

Santiago bit her lip. "That's what brought about the change of plans."

"What change?"

"She cancelled Canfield's 2 o'clock appointment with me and came in person."

"What was she like?"

"Cold, smart, efficient, and cougar easy on the eyes."

Andrews laughed. "In other words, an older Mitch."

She shook her head. "No, no, I'm not cold. And when we talked about Kohler and Xavier she referred to them as a problem she's dealt with, over and done."

"I must say Mitch, you've had an interesting afternoon."

"Well, the next step is her briefing me on the flight to Louis Armstrong International. Right now I've got to get going. We'll talk later."

He said, "Be careful. Love you, babe."

Santiago next called Doctor Grossman on her cell.

"Yes, Miss Santiago, you're a pleasant surprise two days in a row. How may I help you today?"

"I'm going to be out of town for several days. I know it's only been a day, but have you had the opportunity to give any thought to my parent's situation?"

"Yes, I sent out a few inquiries after we spoke yesterday but thus far I've received no feedback. Usually such inquiries take up to a week to gain a response."

She said, "So you would expect to have something in hand next week?"

"Yes, will I be able to reach you?"

"Of course, just call my cell. You'll probably have to leave a message. I'll be working some odd hours."

Doctor Grossman laughed. "It didn't take you long to find a new employer."

"I'm in a unique profession. If I don't hear from you within a week I'll call."

He said, "Very good."

"Do you have anything new on my cousin, John?"

"One moment, I'll bring up his file," he said as he accessed John Abbott's file. "Miss Santiago, he had a good night's rest. I've nothing else new on him since our conversation yesterday."

"I understand."

"Tell me, who are you now working for?"

"The Noble Group. I'll email the information to update my file. Right now I must fulfill another commitment. Have a good day."

After breaking the connection she speed dialed her father.

"Santiago residence."

"Hi, dad, how's mom today?"

"Same as always. How's unemployment?"

"In the past. I have a new position with the Noble Group."

"It's not one of those off-beat societies we read about is it?"

"No, it's a company similar to DataFlex. The only difference is Noble is an investor in technical research. DataFlex did research, product development and investing."

"Well, Mitch, don't get too close to the boss this time."

"Dad, I didn't get too close at DataFlex, just caught in the middle of something I didn't create."

"I know, but folks talk." He laughed. "Didn't take very long to get hired."

"They came to me once they knew I was available."

"Word travels fast now days."

"Indeed. I called Doctor Grossman. He's sent out some inquiries for you and mom. He's looking first in the east Mesa, Apache Junction area. He said he probably won't have anything for a week or so."

"Don't worry about it, Mitch. It's been years. A week won't mean much. But let's go back to this Noble Group for a minute. What will you be doing for them?"

"I'm becoming a registered lobbyist. I'll be working currently out of New Orleans although I'm assigned to a team in Washington D.C. I'll be moving around the country a lot dealing with other lobbyists, business people, city governments...."

"And politicians."

"Yes, them too.

"God, Mitch, I remember the days; North Beach, Monterey, Big Sur, the Haight. We spent a lot of time with politicians; them and cops."

"Mine is a different role, not protesting, making money."

"Money's good, Mitch, it's always good, especially if you're in New Orleans. I understand you can buy anything."

"I have to go, dad. I'll call. Love you."

"Love you, babe."

She checked her watch. Her ride was due in ten minutes. The burn cell rang.

"Hello," she said cautiously.

"Hi, Mitch."

"Link, what have you found?"

"Your Miss Nance is a graduate of the University of Virginia, has spent a lot of time working with politicians since she was in high school when she did her first internship."

Santiago said, "A busy girl."

Andrews laughed. "When she was an undergraduate she kidded her sorority sisters she was going to need knee pads to work with some of the good old boys."

"So she knows her way around the track."

"Oh yes. She's also worked on various security details for a couple of senators. Apparently she was good at getting confidential information out of the opposition."

Santiago smiled. "I think I have an idea how she works that angle."

"Well, Mario found some photos of her early career – not too shabby looking."

She laughed. "She's not too shabby now, think Shari Stiletto; an old flame of yours and hot operative – professionally speaking. How long has Nance been with Noble?"

"That's somewhat hidden, Mitch. It appears she was with Noble even when working for the senators early on. She's definitely a lady who's played at industrial deep cover."

"Any social connections?"

"None of record. She's well off and has been the subject of a few inquiries, usually from other parties such as DataFlex. Otherwise she is a very private person."

Santiago smiled. "D.C. is alive and well. I've got to get going. A limo is due any minute."

"Be careful, be safe Mitch. Love you."

She smiled. "Love you, too. By the way, you told me once you like sailing."

"I do."

"I'm thinking of making love on a deck under blue skies on a sexy vacation."

"I'll hold that thought while you're in New Orleans." He chuckled. "We should do the Big Easy sometime."

"Limo's here, gotta go."

*****

Xavier and Kohler arrived at Giovanni's Spaghetti House and Wine Cellar in downtown Chandler around 2:30. The hostess seated them at the back of the dining room at a table Kohler used often. She said, "Joseph will be your waiter."

Kohler said, "Thank you, Sophia, he's the best."

Joseph approached out of the heavily shaded background almost instantly. "Good afternoon gentlemen. Are you here for a late lunch or early dinner?"

Kohler said, "Dinner, we plan on a leisurely meal beginning with a bottle of your best Chianti, something from Tuscany."

"We have an excellent Ruffino Chianti Classico Reserva Ducale, '08."

Kohler nodded. "An outstanding selection."

Xavier said, "And I'll have a Jack Daniel's double on the rocks."

Kohler looked across the table and Xavier. "I thought we'd have a good wine with dinner."

"We will, but I would like a taste of bourbon, too, this being our last supper so to speak."

Kohler laughed. "That's a good one."

Joseph brought the wine and bourbon. He opened the bottle and poured a sample for Kohler to taste.

Kohler smiled. "Leave the bottle, Joseph. I've never been served anything but the best by you."

"Thank you, sir."

Xavier said, "I'm kinda hungry. Let's order now."

Kohler said, "Of course. You first, Jerome."

"Tonight I'll have the filet, medium rare, with spaghetti and meat sauce. I'd like the house salad with extra salami and olives. And I want an appetizer of steamed clams. I love those little beggars."

Kohler sipped the Chianti as Xavier ordered.

Joseph said, "And for you this evening?"

"I would like the ribeye and pasta with Alfredo. May I also have some sautéed mushrooms, the house salad and I'll need extra breadsticks."

Joseph said, "I'll have your salad in a moment. Would you like the family bowl or individual servings?"

Xavier said, "The family bowl with Italian dressing and I need another JD."

Joseph left the table.

Jerome looked Kohler in the eyes. "So tell me, Canfield, how are you going to describe killing me to the bitch?"

"I've given it some thought. Unlike the Russian, no smuggler tales. I'll tell her we drove into the Maricopa Mountains to a deserted place at the top of a cliff, I shot you in the head, then pushed your body over the side."

"No, no, you shot me in the head and I tumbled over the edge. You got in your Jeep and drove away. End of story."

Kohler nodded. "Yes, the Jeep, of course."

"Canfield, how do we reconnect when this blows over?"

Kohler handed Xavier a piece of paper. "This is the address to my postal box. You can send me a note, but remember, it will be using your new name."

"So how do you reach me?"

"You get a postal box wherever you land at and send me the address, but don't send anything for at least six months. It's quite possible someone will be watching for you. Always remember, there will be no body."

When the food arrived Kohler watched Joseph set the table. Xavier waved his empty tumbler and asked for another drink. Joseph nodded and left the table.

"You're pounding those down pretty fast, Jerome."

"Not a problem," he said with a thick tongue while looking at his plate.

Kohler watched Xavier waving the tumbler. *I was right last night – a fake suicide. No suspicion, just guilt on your part. You drink too much. One slip and we're both dead.* He sat up straight. "Your glass is almost empty. Have another."

"Don't mind if I do."

"And while we enjoy this evening let's speculate on another way to have you die, like just disappear."

"That bitch would never buy into that, I'd still be alive in her book."

Kohler said, "True...."

Xavier smiled as another drink arrived. "How 'bout I commit suicide. Ya know, leave a note and say what an ass I've been, that sort of thing. I could say I'm going to the mountains and do myself in. Hell, it's like you said, there's lots of bodies out there that never get found."

"What a brilliant idea. You could leave a note and just go away. Why didn't I think of that?"

"Because I handle this sort of thing better'n you. All you need to do is report me missing and have the cops find a suicide note."

"Jerome, I love your idea."

"Good. When we leave here come on down to the house about fifteen minutes after me and we'll put together s note. I'm not a very good writer, especially tonight."

Joseph brought the bill and Kohler paid. As they stood Xavier kicked a floor pot over and grabbed at the table.

Kohler looked at him. "Are you alright to drive?"

"Sure, I'm only a few miles away. I'm good."

Kohler looked closer at him. "Did you piss your pants?"

"Just a little. I'd have tried for the flower pot if I'd seen it."

Kohler said, "Let's go. I'll walk out to your car with you."

"You do that. I need a smoke, too."

They left Giovanni's while many diners turned their eyes away avoiding any contact with Xavier.

"Drive carefully, Jerome. We want your suicide to be fictitious, not a drunken accident."

"I'm good. See you at my place. We can have a drink and write a note."

Kohler watched Xavier drive out of the parking lot. *Fifteen minutes and you're a dead man.*

*****

It was three hours later in New York. Francis Dade walked across the living room of the fourteen room eastside apartment thirty-nine floors up also on Columbus Avenue. He stopped beside of his wife, Ishtar, and glanced out the large windows at Central Park. "We have a better view than the Noble offices two blocks up the street."

"Yes we do. I'm sure father planned it that way when he purchased the apartment forty years ago. That is why we have so many rooms; to accommodate us and the domestics."

"Speaking of which, I see Carl has the table set. It is almost the dinner hour, dear, and I must say you are beautifully dressed."

"It is appropriate, Francis, but I do wish you'd get another white dinner jacket. The one you're wearing just looks outdated."

"As you wish, dear, but it was tailored only six months ago."

"Get a new one," she said holding out her hand. "Walk me to dinner."

Dade escorted his sixty year old youthful appearing wife to the formal dining room and seated her at the dark wood twelve foot table. He stroked the glistening surface. "Each night I believe this is the most beautiful table on earth."

"It is. When father had it made African Blackwood still came from Ethiopia. Today it comes from Tanzania or northern Mozambique."

Dade smiled. "I wonder how many clarinets could have been made from the wood used for this table."

"Obviously none," she said. "It's our table."

At exactly 7:00 Carl served dinner, never speaking unless spoken to. Ishtar and Francis were seated across from each other at the table's center this evening rather than opposite ends.

"Ishtar, why the change in seating this evening?"

"We need to talk, not shout back and forth. Have you employed the woman we spoke of last evening?"

"Yes, as a contract employee."

"Did you talk with her personally?"

"No."

"I trust your Mr. Deaver did not hire her. Every woman he employs looks like a slut, but why not, they usually are."

"Deaver did not hire Miss Santiago, Andrea did."

"Good, she selects smart, handsome people; male and female. Her people always look like film stars, have the brains of Einstein, and achieve whatever goal is set. However, I do have a concern. Last night you called her Mitch. Is she a lesbian?"

"No, her parents were hippies. Her father wanted a boy as a first born just as your father did. Since their first child was a daughter and both he and his wife were huge fans of Mitch Ryder the child was named Michelle, forever Mitch within the family and a nickname that has remained to this day."

"Hippies, how I remember the days. I wanted desperately to go to San Francisco but father would never allow it. Is Santiago a modern woman?"

"What do you mean by modern?"

"Is she a strong independent woman not afraid to articulate her own thoughts, sees women as the unquestionable equals of men... I could go on, Francis."

"Yes, she is a modern woman and I might add brutal when necessary."

"Brutal?"

"Perhaps strong is better word. Last year she killed a man in a gunfight at Quartzite, Arizona."

"Good. Does she sleep around?"

"She is currently in a relationship with a man named Link Andrews, one of the top security operatives at DataFlex."

"Do you believe she will discover who it is that threatens our special project?"

"That's why Andrea recruited her as soon as she became available. The fact her male friend is involved with DataFlex security also bodes well. She may gain insights into their thinking and find out what if anything Tony Mercedes knew about Reaper's guidance system and the identity of the mole."

Ishtar smiled. "That would be very nice. Do we know who is replacing Mr. Mercedes at Barrier?"

"No, but Andrea speculates it may be a man named Sam Evans, a former CIA operative and another of Claude Braun's top investigators."

She laughed. "Interesting that we both want the identity of the mole, but for different reasons."

"I'm sure we will prevail."

"I trust we shall, Francis. I want our program made to be so much a part of the Reaper's new guidance system it won't be discovered until we use it." She shook her head. "I just cannot understand how our leaders can take a gifted genius, a scientist, away from his work to tramp around a dirt road and be killed."

"Neither do I, but Jeffrey insisted on going with his National Guard unit. He said it was a way to demonstrate he was one of the people and a patriot, brave and willing to serve. When his unit was called he told me, 'Father, I need to do this for my public service record and the people.' He was quite sincere."

Ishtar laughed. "Sincere? Machiavellian is more like it. We wanted him to pursue science and be recognized as a brilliant physicist. He wanted to be president. What a waste of a gift for the ages. That idiotic senator and General Lube will never realize the error of their ways. Jeffrey would have changed directions if given time. They must be punished and the government needs to realize we cannot just waste the best and brightest. They are the future."

Francis applauded. "Perhaps you should run for office."

"Not in your lifetime." She rang the servant bell.

"Yes, madam," said Carl entering the dining room.

"My dinner is cold."

"Would you like another?"

"No, bring our coffee into the sitting room."

"Yes, madam."

Francis Dade watched the butler take his dinner away, too.

Ishtar looked at her husband. "Francis, did you earn a reward for tonight?"

"Yes, dear."

"Good, father always wanted you to be a strong assertive leader at the office; the man in charge, even if you are following my directions on all big matters."

She rang again for Carl.

"Yes, madam."

"Mr. Dade will be having a guest this evening. Please handle the arrangements."

"As you wish."

"Francis, shall we go to the sitting room while you wait? I love looking at the skyline of light."

He stood and rounded the table. "Shall we?"

Chapter 8

After takeoff from the Scottsdale Airport the flight attendant asked Nance and Santiago if they would like something to drink.

Nance said, "Gin and tonic."

Santiago was watching the landscape pass under the wings of Noble's Leer jet. "A Corona would be nice."

Nance was seated facing Santiago. "It's certainly a different landscape than one gets at Dulles or Reagan."

Santiago smiled. "This is the first time I've viewed the course for the Phoenix Open." She chuckled. "Its real name is the Waste Management Open, but purists have a hard time changing."

"Oh," said Nance," you mean the golf tournament. I've heard it's more like spring break with golf clubs in January than the more traditional tournaments."

"I haven't heard that one but Link says it's the only course aerated by hooker heels."

"On a golf course?"

"A large number of the patrons come to be seen; dressed for the club scene, and especially the Bird's Nest."

"Bird's Nest?"

"It's a nightclub located on the course site. In the evenings they have some very big names entertaining into the early morning. My sister Jill calls the tourney a party on grass, the 16th Hole in particular."

The drinks arrived.

Santiago pressed the wedge of lime into the bottle. "So tell me, Andrea, what exactly am I doing for Noble. First you said something about Maxwell, then a senator?"

"You already know. Someone is leaking information to outside sources. Mr. Dade wants to know who it is and get them out of the project."

"How do you know there is a leak?"

"A few reporters have come close to revealing secrets about ongoing research."

"How far along is Barrier? I thought you said it was years away."

"It is."

"Good, you're confirming what I found out in a few journals. Their articles were more concerned with validating the initial research. Many scientists were interested in a Doctor Yeager's results but need to verify his findings."

Nance took a sip of her drink. "True, but the Barrier is classified."

"Andrea, you know DataFlex has a team working with Maxwell."

"I do and keep in mind all three companies have access to Barrier. That's why one of the things you'll be doing initially is to become familiar with all personnel working the both Barrier and Reaper."

"Will I have support people with me?"

"Not on site. You'll transmit data to me via the burn cell and occasionally an email if it's something routine on the PR line such as a request for interviews which come to my office. The projects are not for public consumption. Regarding Reaper, nobody outside of the necessary government staff, Maxwell people and Noble are familiar with the project. It is Top Secret."

"You do realize the security people at Noble and DataFlex are going to conclude I'm doing security work."

"I'm sure you're right but they'll guard your cover. None of the companies want the public involved at this point. That's why the mole is such an issue at Barrier. It compromised security." *We'll get to Reaper later.*

Santiago finished her Corona. "I do have some information you want. Sam Evans will replace Tony for the time being. He told me himself just before I left my condo."

Nance laughed. "Another admirer breaks Claude's rules."

"I wouldn't go that far, just a good friend which you already know."

Nance laughed. "I would have known sooner if you hadn't found Kohler's bugs."

"You wouldn't hire me if I missed them. Something about incompetence would bother you."

"True."

"Actually, Sam and I are planning on going to dinner on Bourbon Street and sample the nightlife. But know ahead he won't be sharing any inside information any more than I would."

Nance raised an eyebrow. "I hear a 'but' in that statement."

"I'm sure we'll both be probing in a professional way while we patter on."

"Mutual respect, I like that. Now, when we first arrive in New Orleans I have another task. I want you to meet Senator DuBois. He's Chairman of the Senate Appropriations Committee. Noble has spent a lot of time and money on him. Unfortunately he's beginning to show signs of not always agreeing with us. He's in New Orleans on a fact finding trip but mostly recreating without his wife."

"In other words big money and power are going hand-in-hand with a Teflon zipper."

"We need to provide him with an escort and...."

"Andrea, I'm an investigator, not a call girl. I won't sleep with your senator."

"Not to worry. We have professionals. Your job tomorrow is to steer him to a rendezvous with one of our ladies."

"Like a pimp."

"No, I think of pimps as street people. We book girls through a classy agency at a fee as high as $5K for a hedonistic night."

"My job is to gather information on the visit?"

"No, just keep him away from the public and especially the press. We have other people gathering facts on him."

"So we're building a dossier to correct his thinking."

"Exactly, Mitch, then we're off to Maxwell."

The flight attendant brought Nance another drink. "Another Corona, Mitch?"

"No thank you. I'm going to get some rest. It sounds like tomorrow is going to be busy." She sat back. "Where will I be staying?"

"Noble has four condos at Jackson Square. We'll be going there as soon as we arrive. Right now a nap sounds good to me, too." She set the fresh drink on a tray. Tomorrow you'll see many different sides of the Big Easy."

*****

Xavier sat quietly on the couch in his living room waiting for Kohler. *What the hell are you thinking, Canfield? Get me drunk, a suicide note, new ID. What a great cover for killing me. It won't happen.*

The doorbell rang. Xavier answered. "Canfield, buddy, you got here earlier than anticipated. Let's get to work."

Kohler said, "This is so strange, Jerome, but necessary for your survival."

"Yours, too. Wanna a drink? I do."

"Yes, a little bourbon sounds good. I'll pour," he said heading for the kitchen.

"Okay, I'm gonna start my note, you know, *the note.*"

Kohler called back from the kitchen, "Where are you going to place the note?"

"I haven't decided, yet. Hell, I haven't even started to write the thing."

Kohler returned with the drinks and held one out.

Xavier was seated at his computer. He took the tumbler. "Yours looks a little weak."

"I prefer some water. I'm just not a hardcore bourbon man." Kohler took a sip. "If you do the note by hand it will be more believable."

"Yeah, it would," he said reaching for a writing pad. He held up the tumbler. "Here's to us." He pointed to a water glass full of pencils on a buffet. "Would you give me one of those?"

Kohler turned toward the buffet and took out a pencil. Xavier emptied the tumbler on the dining room rug under the table. Kohler turned back to Xavier and handed him the pencil.

"Thank you," said Xavier holding up the empty tumbler. "How 'bout 'nother drink?"

"Sure, I'll just bring the bottle in here. Who are you addressing it to?" he called back from the kitchen.

"You, of course."

Kohler returned with the bourbon bottle and refilled Xavier's glass. "Make it personal."

"I haven't got a clue what to write."

"Just write Canfield."

Xavier did so.

"Now just scribble a note, something about being lonely, feeling guilty about people you've hurt and killed...."

"Maybe I should put somethin' 'bout bein' depressed. That'd be good."

"Keep it simple, no details. Maybe something like, 'I've decided to end the madness surrounding me. Sorry to leave you, Canfield, but I can't face you or life any longer,' and don't worry about the spelling. You've had a few drinks."

Xavier wrote the note in large messy cursive letters and nodded. "There."

"Now sign it."

"I think I'll tape it on the mirror in the bathroom."

"That'll work. Are you ready for a refill?"

"Oh yeah. Just a minute."

Xavier took the note and tape down the hallway. He went to the mirror and began taping the note to one side. He caught the reflection of a shadow in the corner of the mirror. Suddenly a hand holding a wash cloth drenched with chloroform covered his face. He held his breath and struck with a powerful downward fist behind him. Kohler groaned and bent from the blow to his groin. His grip on the rag weakened. Xavier pulled Kohler's hand away from his face, gasped, turned, and faced his bent over partner. He hit Kohler on the side of his head and shouted, "You stupid bastard!"

Kohler fell sideways to the floor, rolled and tried to stand. He looked at Xavier and said, "I, I had to protect myself."

"You think you could take me down with a washrag? Damn fool."

Sweat covered Kohler's face. His breathing was forced. He looked up at Xavier but said nothing.

Xavier laughed and grabbed Kohler by the shirtfront and pulled him to his feet. "You always said I was the muscle." He smashed Kohler's jaw knocking him back to the floor.

Kohler's eyes welled.

"You really thought I was buying all the brother shit, moving money? Damn, you're naïve," he said kicking Kohler in the belly.

"I have to admit it was a good set up 'til you got to the part about the suicide. Really? I mean $25K for Thelonious to provide instant new ID – that's a good move."

Kohler said in a whisper, "Jerome, I beg you...."

"You're begging now you weasel. A few minutes ago you were trying to kill me."

Kohler's lips moved but he made no sound.

"Well, Canfield, my brother, I'll tell you what, someone is going to die today but isn't going to be me."

Xavier kneeled beside Kohler. "Tell me, how you were going to do me, make it look like a suicide?"

Kohler didn't answer.

Xavier jammed a thumb into his right eye. "I can't hear you."

"The car, in the garage, motor running."

"I'm a big guy. It would have been a lot of work gettin' me into the car while I was out. Tell you what, I'll do you in the car. It won't be much effort and you won't miss a thing."

Tears filled Kohler's eyes. "Jerome, please...."

"Please? You sleazy swine. You lose and I win. You're a dead man, totally dead."

Xavier pulled him up from the floor again and held onto his shirtfront. Kohler looked him in the eyes. Xavier smashed a fist into his face rapidly three more times. Kohler went limp. "Damn, I want you to feel the pain."

Xavier picked Kohler up and slung him over a shoulder. "You'll never wakeup asshole. You can die in my car."

When Xavier got Kohler into the garage he dropped his unconscious body on the floor, got in his car and started the engine. He picked Kohler up and slid him into the driver's seat and closed the door.

"Sweet dreams, partner."

Xavier stepped into the house and looked back at the car as exhaust began to fill the garage. "At one time I did love you like a brother, but you just never gave me any respect. You can only dis a man so long, then you got to pay. Tomorrow I'll see Thelonious. I'll get the ID."

*****

Santiago and Nance arrived at Louis Armstrong International at 10:35 Arizona time. A limousine took them to the Frenchman Condominiums at Jackson Square. As they approached the entry a building security doorman welcomed them.

"Good evening Miss Nance," he said nodding at both ladies.

Nance said, "Tony Joe, nice to see you this evening. This is Mitch Santiago, the newest member of my lobbyist team. She'll be staying in 402 for the next week or so."

Tony Joe tipped his hat. "Miss Santiago, welcome to the Frenchman."

"It's my pleasure."

Nance said, "Let's get you put away for the night. We have a big day tomorrow and it starts early for you, 8:00 a.m. New Orleans time. You've lost two hours."

The women took the elevator to the fourth floor. Santiago looked across the hall at dark wood double doors. The brass number read 402. She laughed. "This is very nice on the outside."

"It gets better. Let's take a look and get you settled. I'm in 403."

"Good, I want to call Link before he crashes for the night."

They went in, Nance showed Santiago around then left. Santiago went over the room for listening devices and cameras, closed the curtains, and called Link Andrews.

He answered on the first ring. "Hi, Mitch, how was the flight?"

"Very nice."

"Where are you staying?"

"The Frenchman Condos at Jackson Square."

"Noble must own one. That's a nice area."

"I think Noble owns all four units on the top floor."

"Sounds like DataFlex."

She chuckled. "A bit."

"Wait 'til tomorrow. You'll have street musicians, artists, and hustlers of every variety all over the place. The Square is a creative center, one of many."

"Hm, the voice of experience?"

"Very little. How's the condo?"

"Great, two master suites, sitting room, beautiful patio overlooking the square, and bug free."

"Speaking of bugs, how's the humidity?"

"It's not a dry heat. If you were here it could be a sexy heat, all sweaty and sticky."

"Sweaty sounds good, even nasty, but fun. Did Nance comment on the cemeteries?" He paused. "You sound very sexy tonight. Does that mean your room-mate has gone to bed?"

"My boss has her own condo, 403, so we're good to chat here. I've cleared the room. In answer to your question, no, but the pilot mentioned if we were want-ing to see the above ground crypts we should go in the daylight hours with a group. He said at dark those loca-tions are often dangerous for tourists; muggings, rob-bery, murder. I doubt I'll be doing much sightseeing anyway. Andrea has me booked pretty tight."

"Speaking of your boss, I have some new data. She often travels, almost always using one of Nobles jets. When she does go on one of her junkets it's usually to a fantastic location and a big player sans their spouse. The trips are usually for a few days, occasionally a week."

"How fantastic?"

"The most popular is Las Vegas, then Cape Cod, San Francisco, Honolulu and Whistler. St. Tropez and Barbados make the list occasionally."

"I'm from the northwest but don't get the draw of Whistler."

"Babe, it's a world class ski resort, hosted the Win-ter Olympics once, and is a summer playground for the children of the worldwide rich and famous."

"That's funny. I was there once in the summer while attending the U-Dub. We all had a great time but I never picked up on its reputation."

He laughed. "I'm sure you were busy with other things."

She smiled and glanced at Jackson Square's lights. "Could be."

"Probably not too different than some of Nance's trips. As I said, her guests were always solo, usually stayed at her hotel in separate rooms but had visitors – sometime Nance, sometimes a lady or group of ladies." He chuckled. "Sounds kinky, interesting."

"We're not going there, Link."

"Of course not. I've never met your new boss. Even though she was a hottie in some photos when she was younger I imagine her as an easy on the eyes cougar anal power lady, pin striped in a 'wish-I-were-male-suit type.'"

"Link, she is smart, seductive and worldly."

"I know, you said, 'a Shari Stiletto type.' I know how she works."

"We both know how Shari works. She has a lot of fun with many friends."

"That's exactly what I was thinking, too." He swallowed. "Your smart seductive boss visited Nikki this morning before seeing you. You'll be happy to know Nikki painted you as a dark sex crazed immoral ex-friend."

"Good, I suspect Andrea is still checking me out. I'll leave my cell here and expect it to be bugged or checked for calls."

"Be careful. The other important thing is Sam's on his way to New Orleans. He'll be coming by commercial carrier unlike the Noble people."

"Does he know our plan yet?"

"Ray says, 'Not until he clears the security procedures at Maxwell.' I'm sure the only way that will change is if something unique occurs."

"Good enough. I'm about beat between the trip and humidity. Tomorrow is a long day."

"Get a good night's rest babe."

"Right after a nice shower."

"It's sticky down there, do you have cotton pajamas?"

"You know I wear my favorite scent. Why change now?"

"I know, now I won't sleep."

"Of course you will, Link. Just keep thinking about the hot tub and last night."

"Mitch, those thoughts do not encourage sleep."

"I know, love you."

Someone knocked on Santiago's door. When she opened it Nance was standing there.

"Mitch, can I use your phone, my battery is dead."

"It's on the coffee table. When you're done I need to recharge it."

"Did you get to talk to Link?"

"Oh yes. Now he's going to try and sleep – alone. I'm going to get ready for bed while you talk."

"Not a problem. When I finish if you're not out I'll just leave."

Santiago went to her master suite. *Check the phone Andrea. See who I called. Then I'll look for bugs again.*

*****

Xavier returned to the living room and poured a drink. He could barely hear the car engine running. "Here's to you Canfield." He raised the tumbler and faced the hallway.

"I'll give you an hour. That ought to do you in. When you're gone I'll shutoff the engine and raise the door a little. Tomorrow morning I'll restage it just before I leave."

Xavier turned on the television set. "Damn, too late for the late news. No Russian yet." He flipped through several stations but only found late night talk shows beginning, half-hour advertisements, a few signed off stations, sports networks and movies. "I don't want any of that shit."

He turned off the television and poured another drink. He looked at the tumbler. "Christ even throwing booze in the flower pot and on the rug I'm probably legally drunk."

He went out the back door and sat on the deck of his house watching the stars. "I wonder if there are any spacemen out there from other planets or solar systems. Could be." He chuckled and faced the house. "Hey, Kohler, you may be meeting some new friends now that you're leaving us."

He checked his watch. "One hour. You ought to be dead."

He walked back to the garage. Exhaust was even seeping under the door into the house. He coughed several times while opening the garage door and then shutting off the car engine. Without turning on the garage lights he checked Kohler slumped behind the steering wheel. Even with the interior light he knew Kohler was dead. He felt for a pulse. "You've been smoked, partner."

He let the garage clear and fill with fresh air then locked it up for the night. He returned to the house and did the same thing. He went to his bedroom and stretched out. Sleep wouldn't come.

He watched the ceiling as light reflected off the blades of a fan. "Tomorrow Thelonious. Then I gotta know who wants me dead. Once they know Canfield is gone they'll be sending someone."

Xavier dug out an address book he hadn't used in years and looked up Ned Beam. "Damn I hope this number is good." He punched in the number.

A man answered in a groggy voice. "Yeah, it's late. Call tomorrow."

"Ned, it's me, Jerome."

"Jerome who?"

"Xavier, you made a complete set of ID for me once."

"Really? What is the name of your secretary?"

"Linda Drake, Linda Great Legs Drake."

"Okay, Jerome, what do you want?"

"Is the ID you made me six years ago still useable?"

"Yes."

"Can you fix me up with some new credit cards using the same ID?"

"Yes."

"How much?"

"5G's."

"I'll be in Wichita tomorrow. I'll call you from the airport so we can meet."

"Good enough, but bring cash."

"Of course. Just a reminder, the name we used was Sydney Loomis."

"Got it."

Chapter 9
Thursday, July 10

It was 6:00 a.m. Phoenix time when Wolfe took a cab to the offices of Kohler and Xavier. He was rested even after his late arrival. When he entered the lobby he passed a coffee shop busy with business types; mostly attorneys, private investigators, a few plain clothes detectives, and some uniforms.

The hostess greeted many of the early arrivals by name. As Wolfe passed she said, "Good morning, party of one?"

He said, "Perhaps. Could you tell me if Canfield Kohler has come in yet?"

"No, Mr. Kohler doesn't usually arrive until around 9:00 a.m. but Mr. Xavier usually gets in between 6:30 and 7:00."

Wolfe checked his watch. "I'll have breakfast and wait for Mr. Kohler."

The hostess led Wolfe to a small table with a view of the lobby. "You'll see Mr. Kohler when he comes in."

"Thank you."

"Lola will be your waitress this morning."

When Lola arrived he ordered coffee, looked at the menu, and listened to the hostess greet passersby.

At 6:59 she said, "Good morning, Mr. Xavier."

Wolfe looked up. Xavier nodded at the young lady as he passed.

Wolfe took out his cell phone.

Andrea Nance answered in a thick voice, "Hello."

"And a good morning to you, Andrea."

"Is it done?"

"No. I'm sitting here in the lobby of the building where their offices are located waiting for Mr. Kohler. His partner, Jerome Xavier just walked in."

"What?"

"His partner, Jerome. Didn't you say Kohler was solving that problem?"

"Xavier is there, alive?"

Wolfe pursed his lips and glanced at the lobby. "The hostess greeted him by name."

"Damn, Kohler said he took him out yesterday."

"So, do I have two jobs now?"

"Yes. Do you know what time Kohler is due in?"

"The hostess told me around 9:00, but I'm sure Xavier can tell me. You know, Andrea, two accidental deaths will look very suspicious."

"You'll think of something. Of course I'll double the fee in your Cayman account as soon as we hang up. Contact me when you're finished." She broke the connection.

Wolfe left money on the table and went to the second floor office of Kohler & Xavier Investigations. He tried the door. It was locked. He knocked. The shadows of a figure moving passed through the frosted glass of the office suite, then the door opened.

Xavier said, "We're not open yet," and studied Wolfe's face. "Do I know you?"

"I'm Josh Shepherd. Mr. Kohler is handling a very delicate matter for me."

"Strange, I'm his partner, Jerome Xavier, and he never mentioned it to me." He stepped back. "Come in. Canfield usually comes in later."

"Thank you. How much later?"

Xavier's hand brushed his side against a .38 Special in his waistband. "Usually around 9:00."

"He told me he was busy today and to see him early. He wanted to talk about a few options available for me."

"He's probably in another meeting that's running late."

"There's a coffee shop downstairs. I can wait there a little while and brace myself until he shows. I have a court date at 9:00."

"Does your attorney know you're here? I mean, you could call him or something. I don't mean to pry."

"Yes, but he knows I'll be in court after a brief meeting with Mr. Kohler."

"Right, you'll see him when he comes through the lobby." Xavier laughed. "Too bad he's so busy today. He usually has breakfast downstairs before starting his day."

Wolfe stepped towards the door. "Good meeting you, Mr. Xavier. Have a pleasant day. You've increased my belief in the integrity of private investigators."

"How so?"

"Mr. Kohler told me my divorce would be handled discreetly. Obviously he's a man of his word. Have a good day."

*****

Michelle Santiago and Andrea Nance walked across the street to the corner of Chartres and Peter, a half block from the Frenchman Condominium to the Voodoo Coffee Shop.

Nance said, "One of the things I like about the Quarter is early morning. The artists and musicians setting up for the day."

Santiago chuckled. "I see a few early birds already arriving."

"Tourists come from everywhere. Their body clocks need to adjust, some just like the early hours before it gets crazy."

As they crossed Chartres Nance said, "That's Senator Broderick DuBois seated comfortably at the outside patio chatting with a waitress."

"There are several men chatting up the waitresses."

He's the one in gray slacks, short sleeved white dress shirt, no tie or coat and wearing the big aviator sunglasses."

"Good thing you mentioned the glasses. Most of those guys look the same except the senator is more athletic in appearance."

Nance laughed. "Trust me, Mitch, he's getting a lot more than most men his age, especially when you consider he's mid-sixties. He likes to rock 'n roll, a man of many various needs."

"You know him well."

Nance chuckled. "Well enough. We had a brief fling two years ago. Today it's strictly business, but sleeping with a senator is a power trip."

"He looks quite comfortable."

"Mitch, hitting on attractive women is his hobby. You'll find that out soon enough." She checked the yellow mini-skirt and cotton blouse Santiago was wearing with hooker heels. "I told you to dress sexy and you didn't disappoint. He's probably already spotted you as we cross the street."

"He's not unlike most of the men I know. It can play to our advantage."

Nance said, "He's a hound dog."

The two women approached DuBois's table. He stood and smiled. "Good morning, Andrea. Please join me."

"Always a pleasure, Broderick. May I introduce a new colleague, Michelle Santiago?"

"Miss Santiago, please have a seat," he said pulling out a chair and waving a hand. "It's always a pleasure meeting new colleagues of Andrea. Are you from New Orleans?"

"No, Chandler, Arizona."

Nance said, "Mitch was originally a Seattle Homicide Detective before joining the DataFlex Corporation, and now Noble."

"Oh, you were in Claude Braun's company."

Santiago smiled and nodded. "One and the same."

Nance said, "Broderick, are your accommodations comfortable?"

"Oh yes, and the Cajun Queen Boutique is so full of history. It's an excellent place to, ah, relax on this fact finding trip."

Nance laughed. "Broderick, Mitch knows why you're here. She knows about the services you enjoy at Noble's expense."

DuBois looked at Santiago, smiled, and tilted his head as he checked the open top two buttons on her blouse.

Santiago said, "Sorry senator, I'm not the toy. I'm a Noble lobbyist."

He said, "Andrea, why does lobbyist sound like security when she says it?"

"It's her job to keep you and your visitor away from the press and public while you're fact finding."

"Good, I'll probably see you around Washington, too. It's a marvelous place."

Santiago said, "It's a possibility."

The waitress approached. "Ladies, may I get you something?"

Santiago said, "A double Voodoo Espresso would be nice."

"No, no," said DuBois. "Lisa, this lady is new to New Orleans, a serious coffee drinker from Seattle. Please, get her a cup of our famous chicory coffee and beignets." He looked at Santiago. "It makes a delicious southern breakfast."

She flicked her front teeth with her tongue. "Really?"

He smiled. "The best. So tell me Miss Santiago, are you staying at the Frenchman?"

She nodded. "We are."

"We?"

"Andrea and I, separate suites of course."

"Wonderful, maybe we can have dinner tomorrow evening on the patio at Charles Bistro over on Royal. They have the finest roast chicken in the city. It's the least I can do – southern hospitality."

Nance said, "You never can tell, Broderick, by tomorrow we could both be gone. You know how fast things can change."

"I do know," he said with a laugh. "It's so very sad, Andrea. You bring me here to unwind and you two ladies are so tense."

"It comes with the territory."

He smiled looking at Nance. "But wouldn't it be relaxing, fun for the three of us to have dinner and socialize just a little. You know, take the edge off our busy lives." He glanced at Santiago again. "Michelle and I could become friends."

Nance said, "Anything is possible."

DuBois checked his watch and flagged the waitress. As she approached he held out a business card. "I may be back tomorrow, Lisa. If so maybe we can chat. I like to know what the people think."

She looked at the card and a huge smile crossed her face. "I hope so."

He handed her a fifty dollar bill. "I'm sure this covers our tab. Keep the change."

"Thank you, Senator DuBois."

Nance said, "An appointment has been made with your special friend for tonight. I'll see you at the Old Absinthe House around 1:00 with details."

He smiled. "I like the way you make my appointments so hard to track. I'll see you after my public meeting at the Rosa Keller Library and Community Center." He stood. "Ladies."

Santiago watched him leave. "Nice fit."

Nance smiled. "Size matters."

Santiago looked across Jackson Square. A train passed following the river's edge. Tourists were beginning to fill the area.

Nance said, "I know you sketch and paint a little. This looks like your kind of place."

"It does but back to business. Now what? Do I just follow the senator around?"

"He'll be at the Old Absinthe House around 1:00. You'll be there, too. He expects me, but he won't mind. You'll give him the key to a suite at the Augustine Bayou Suites and background him on your role there. Let's take a cab to the Augustine. It's further down Chartres, then we'll head out to Maxwell just long enough to meet their CEO and head of security, Lilith Towne. We'll be back to the Quarter by 11:30."

"Why the rush?"

"Maxwell security needs to get the necessary prints and eye-scan for your clearance tomorrow. The other data they use is coming from the government. We'll do a final sweep of the hotel room before you meet DuBois at Absinthe House."

Santiago stood. "Let's do it."

*****

When Wolfe left Xavier's office he returned to the lobby coffee shop to wait for Kohler. By 8:30 the lobby was full of early morning people coming through the doors. Some hurried to the elevators, others were meeting and greeting each other. Some came into the coffee shop. A man in a white Panama hat, purple slacks and a loose fitting Hawaiian shirt crossed the lobby passing the coffee shop entry. A large diamond decorated his left earlobe. He carried a small package.

Wolfe watched him. *Pimp*.

The hostess smiled. "Good morning, Thelonious. Breakfast?"

He answered with a slight Jamaican, accent, "Not yet beautiful lady." He waved a small package. "First I have business with Mr. Kohler. Then we'll see."

She said, "I haven't seen him yet today."

Thelonious smiled. "He'll be in."

He walked to the elevators and went to the second floor. When he entered the outer office door the lights were off. Xavier was standing in the doorway of Kohler's office.

"Good morning, Thelonious. Come in."

"Where's Canfield?"

Xavier smiled. "Business, but thanks for coming earlier than originally planned. My travel schedule is getting jammed."

"You got the money?"

Xavier held out a thick envelope. "Of course, twenty-five big ones just as Canfield said. The ID?"

Thelonious held out the package and took the envelope.

"Aren't you goin' to count it?"

"No need, man, if it be short Canfield will pay it. Check my work. Its good stuff for a rush job, really good stuff."

Xavier took out the driver's license. "Wyatt Henderson, I like that."

"There's a second license."

"Why?"

"Because Truman Greene fits the profile you want for new ID. Check the passport."

"Excellent."

"There's two credit cards in there. You see 'em?"

Xavier held them up. "Got 'em."

"And read the two pages in there. That's background on the new Mr. Greene. Become familiar with it and you can talk about Greene, easy man."

Xavier looked at the pages. "What the hell is this?" He held up a wallet sized picture.

"It makes your backstory more believable, a wife and kids."

"Good idea. I'd never thought of it."

Thelonious tucked the envelope under his arm. "So where you goin'?

Xavier laughed. "Man can't tell what he don't know."

"That's smart. I should never have asked. Remember dis though, go to places not like anything you do before. You like big cities, go to towns. You like big houses, think small. You like boats and coast, go inland."

"Good advice. Been nice working with you these past few years."

They shook hands and Thelonious left the office. A few minutes later he crossed the lobby of the office building.

Wolfe looked up. "Here comes purple pants, can Xavier be far behind?"

The hostess said, "Breakfast now, Thelonious?"

"Not right now pretty lady, got important business. Maybe tomorrow."

He crossed the lobby and was out the door with the envelope gripped in one hand.

*****

Santiago and Nance were driven out to Maxwell Cyber Systems following Almonaster Avenue to where it merges to become Gentilly Road at the I-510 intersection. When their limousine dropped them at the administrative building they were shown to Maxwell Cyber Systems CEO James Trainer's office.

The receptionist greeted them. "Miss Nance, Mr. Trainer is expecting you and your associate. He said to go right in."

Nance said, "Thank you. Shall we, Mitch."

As they came through the double door to his executive office Trainer stood and came around to the front of his desk. "Andrea, how are things in Washington?"

"Fluid as always. Jim, allow me to introduce our new PR staff member, Michelle Santiago. She joins us after leaving DataFlex and will represent Noble on both Barrier and the Reaper Guidance Modification Project."

"Excellent. Miss Santiago," he said with a lingering look at the yellow mini and five inch spiked pumps, "it's a pleasure."

"It's a pleasure to be here."

He said, "Andrea, will you be here for a few days while Michelle gets acquainted with our staff?"

"Only for today. I have some pressing business in Washington, but Mitch is more than equipped to deal with anything that may come up."

Trainer said, "Let's sit down," and walked to a couch and chairs surrounding a large square granite topped coffee table. The women went to the couch. Trainer watched Santiago take her place, his eyes focused on her legs and mini-skirt then took the chair directly across from her.

Santiago crossed her legs at the knee. "Beautiful office, Mr. Trainer."

"Yes, it is." He looked at Nance, who was smirking, and cleared his throat. "Andrea, have you briefed Michelle on the projects?"

"No, I thought it would be best if you and your people completed the orientation, perhaps have someone show her briefly around the facility today where the two projects are located."

"I agree. Michelle, we'll also be taking your fingerprints and eye scan to be used in our security system. I'm sure DataFlex has similar practices."

Santiago said in a soft voice, "Yes, and Mr. Trainer, would you please call me Mitch? All my friends do."

He sat up straight. "Mitch it is. Maxwell is working on two projects with Noble; Barrier and Reaper. Data-Flex is also involved with Barrier."

"I received some background on Barrier before leaving DataFlex."

Trainer said, "Good, Barrier is a superb concept to stop hacking. Doctor Yeager and his team know what they're doing. When the research is complete and the program ready for public consumption the market will be huge, a wonderful investment opportunity for all three companies."

Santiago smiled. "So I understand. Also, a former associate of mine is coming in to replace Tony Mercedes."

Trainer shook his head. "Yes, Mr. Mercedes death was a tragedy. It demonstrates how vulnerable we really are to the unexpected. Who will be taking his place?"

"Sam Evans."

"I'm not familiar him."

Nance said, "He's a top security officer for DataFlex with a background in the Agency."

Trainer laughed. "Braun and House always go top of the line."

Santiago said, "What is the timeline for Barrier?"

Trainer shook his head. "I wish I could tell you. When you meet Doctor Yeager, the lead of Barrier, he'll explain the project."

She said, "And Reaper?"

"It is a 'Top Secret' project. No offense, but until our security team has cleared you with the Fed's no briefing can take place even though we know you've had the needed clearance previously at DataFelx."

Nance said, "We understand, Jim. Beyond lobbying for federal funding I'm not sure how much detail Mitch needs. She worked in security at DataFlex which you know, Noble hired her for her expertise in other arenas."

Santiago just nodded. *Top Secret*

Trainer looked Santiago in the yes. "Tell me, Mitch, do you still have contact with anyone working in the DataFlex organization?"

"Yes."

Nance said, "It's complicated, but Braun has forbidden his people from contacting Mitch."

Trainer laughed. "I've heard the rumors about the firing, Mitch. Maxwell inquired to contact you but we found out Noble beat us to the punch."

Santiago said, "I'm in a relationship with Link Andrews. He is a security operative for DataFlex and yes, we are in constant contact, but not involving company business. Link and I are personal."

Trainer said, "I understand, but that puts your friend at risk, yes?"

"Link's always been independent. Ray House knows about us. If he chose to fire Link he could. If they give Link a bad time about me he'd quit. Link's one of the best at what he does. He's also loyal. I think they'll leave us alone."

Nance said, "Jim, would it be possible for you to personally introduce Mitch to Lilith and the leads, Alfred and Acadia? It would establish her credibility here as Noble's representative. Mitch will run our operation here."

"Ladies, I would be pleased to do so. Lord knows we put a lot of money into gaining positive congressional action. When would you like to meet them?"

Santiago said, "A brief introduction this morning would be most helpful. Andrea is returning to Washington shortly and it would be useful for all of us if the other players understand my role, especially since I have a security background. They need to know I'm now a public relations specialist, something I'm also well versed in."

Trainer said, "Well put."

Nance smiled at Trainer. "I told you, she's good."

He said, "I'll clear my calendar for an hour. Shall we ladies."

Ten minutes later Santiago, Nance and Jim Trainer were in the general office area of the Maxwell Developmental Building with laboratory and work station facilities. Trainer had taken them to a secured viewing area where one could observe Yeager's team working. "Unfortunately Lilith Towne, our Director of Security is in a Homeland Security briefing at the moment so we'll focus on the project leads."

Trainer pointed at a figure moving about the laboratory. "See the small elderly man? He's Alfred Yeager, head of the Barrier Project."

Santiago watched Yeager. He moved quickly around the lab watching his associates perform specific tasks. He stopped often and spoke with an individual team member while flipping through pages on a clipboard. He never smiled. The only time she saw his whole face his eyes were piercing.

Trainer said, "Yeager is a renowned physicist and has often been a candidate for a Nobel Prize."

Santiago said, "He seems to be a nervous little man."

Trainer laughed. "He's always on the move. He also drums his fingers against the back of the clipboard while reading and flipping pages. He does the same thing with his iPad and sometimes loses the image being studied. Then he goes off the deep end."

Nance laughed.

Santiago said, "The turning of pages I can understand; quick reads for details. Even the drumming of his fingers is not that unusual to me. It's the feet. He constantly is shuffling his feet."

Trainer said, "The guy is wound tight, no question about that. He's uptight about everything, especially the scientists around the world verifying his initial research findings. The people you see here are all brains and egos. They can achieve wonderful things but sometimes they're more concerned with the recognition received than the achievement. It's odd."

Santiago said, "Any filings, patents pending?"

Trainer nodded. "Yes, we've got to guard the research."

When they returned to the general office area of the building Santiago noticed the gray painted steel double doors on the far side and removed by a short hallway. Two armed guards at a desk were beside the doors. "Reaper?"

He smiled. "Yes, Top Secret. If I tell you anymore I'll have to kill you."

They all laughed.

Nance's cell rang. After looking at a message she checked her watch. "I'm sorry, Jim, but we're going to have to cut this visit short. We have another pressing matter. Mitch will have to finish her tour de force tomorrow."

"Not a problem, we've used most of the hour. Let's head back."

Santiago said, "Thank you for the abbreviated tour. I look forward to tomorrow."

Trainer smiled. "So do I."

He walked the ladies back to the front entry of the office building where the limousine met them.

"Mitch, if you call ahead I can meet you here and finish the tour without interruption."

"Thank you, Jim, I'll see you tomorrow."

On the way back to the French Quarter Nance laughed. "I thought you'd only have to beware of DuBois. Jesus, I think Jim had an orgasm walking you around. I don't know if it was the heels or the mini."

"He's a pretty handsome hunk. As far as my outfit goes, I think it was the skin that got him."

"Endless legs can be dynamite. What happened to Link?"

"Nothing, but I do notice other men, don't you?"

"Oh yes, don't we all, God bless 'em."

*****

Jerome Xavier waited for ten minutes after Thelonious left the office. He took the papers, $50,000 cash from Kohler's wall safe, put it all in a portfolio, and stepped to door. He passed a mirror and the thick gold chain around his neck stood out like a beacon. "Chain," he mumbled, took it off, tossed it on the shelf by the door, and stepped into the reception area.

Linda Drake, their receptionist had arrived. "Good morning, Jerome. Are you leaving? Don't forget you have a 1 o'clock appointment today with someone from Florida."

"I haven't forgotten, Linda. Have you heard from Canfield, yet?"

"No, he hasn't called in but that's not unusual and it's still early for him. If he's even out yet he's probably meeting with some attorney over breakfast."

"True, he does that all the time. I'll be back by 11:00. At least we're not on daylight savings like the rest of the country."

He left the office and went to the lobby. On his way through the café receptionist said, "Breakfast or brunch, Mr. Xavier?"

"Not this morning. I have an appointment in east Mesa."

Wolfe watched Xavier leave the building and followed. Xavier flagged a cab. Wolfe jogged to his rental parked only two spaces down from the door. *No car! You're on the run.*

Wolfe followed Xavier's cab. It pulled into a small used car lot on Country Club and Main in Mesa. Wolfe pulled off on the side of Country Club into a closed gas station and watched. Xavier paid the cabbie and walked onto the car lot. He started to look at cars.

Wolfe waited. *A new ride. Smart move.*

Xavier walked around the cars carrying the portfolio and finally stopped. A salesman quickly approached from the small office at the back of the lot. They talked, laughed, and went to the office. The salesman gave a thumbs-up to two other salesman on the office steps as they passed.

Wolfe walked onto the lot as he watched through the office window, stood by a Honda and waved. Another salesman quickly approached. He asked, "Is this car low mileage?"

"Yes, sir, about 51,000."

"Runs good?"

"Still under warranty."

"Is the tank full?"

"No, too much theft when we're closed, damn kids."

Wolfe saw Xavier stand-up and shake hands with the salesman. "Let me go grab my checkbook. I'll be back in a minute." He turned and jogged back to his rental car and got in just as Xavier came out the door.

Xavier drove off the lot and pulled into the outside northbound traffic lane on Country Club then turned right onto Main. Wolfe followed as his salesman watched him drive by. They drove east a little over five miles and going through downtown Mesa. After passing several businesses and strip malls Xavier pulled into a small older restaurant parking lot, the Dusty Spur, on the south side of Main, and went in with his portfolio.

Wolfe pulled into a crowded lot next to the Dusty Spur. "I'll give you five minutes. Then I come in. If you're eating so much the better. When you come out you're mine."

Five minutes passed. Wolfe went into the restaurant. He looked around. Clean wooden furniture, a ten stool coffee counter, country music, and a full house, but no Xavier.

Wolfe went to the men's room. "Empty. Damn!"

He stepped into the hallway leading to the back of the restaurant. "Damn, damn, damn," he said stepping out the back exit. A dirt parking lot was full of cars and trucks.

Wolfe returned to the restaurant as the music blared. *Christ, it's even louder.*

He went back to his rental and fired up the engine. "You son-of-a-bitch, I'll find you and kill you. How did you make me? Maybe you saw me in the lot. That's a possibility."

A late model yellow Lexus convertible pulled into the Dusty Spur parking lot with the top down. The tall driver in the Hawaiian shirt got out of the car and put on his white Panama hat. He glanced at Xavier's car then walked into the Dusty Spur. A moment later he was back out the door and in the Lexus.

Wolfe got out of his car and approached Thelonious. He leaned into the car and pressed the blade of a stiletto against his neck. In a soft voice he said, "Purple Pants, why are you here?"

"Breakfast, man. Take my money, the car. Just don't hurt me."

Wolfe pressed the blade harder and pierced the skin. Thelonious touched his fingers to the blood, a thin trickle running down his neck.

"Let's start again, Thelonious. You followed Xavier here, why?"

Thelonious didn't respond fast enough. Wolfe pressed harder.

"Okay, okay! I sold Jerome some Meth. He owes me 5K. I think he's skipped. I wanted to get my money or product before he was gone."

"Why would you think he was running?"

"He was in trouble with his partner. He said Canfield wanted to get rid of him, make him disappear."

"You had a package with you this morning."

"Man that was the Meth."

"You left with an envelope."

"It was short, never happened before. That's when I knew he was running. You want 'im, too?"

Wolfe pulled the knife back. "Yeah, business. If you find him tell him a man named Wolfe is looking for him."

"I can go?"

"Yeah, get out of here. I'm feeling generous today."

Wolfe went back to his rental. "Cops are going to be all over this. I better let Nance know what's happening."

Wolfe got back in his car, fired up the engine and turned on the radio. He was punching in Nance's cell number when the light jazz station was interrupted by a news flash, "...of an unidentified man was found this morning inside a car parked in a garage of an Ocotillo home. Neighbors in the high end area identified the house as belonging to Jerome Xavier, a private investigator. No further details are available at this time. Police are still...."

Wolfe hit the steering wheel. "That's got to be Kohler. You son-of-a-bitch. You're weren't dodging me. You were losing Purple Pants but it's not over money. He knows something; maybe where you're going, a new name, something. This isn't about any 5K."

He glanced out onto Main Street. A quarter mile down the road was the yellow Lexus at a stop light. Wolfe pulled out and followed the Lexus down Main, slowly catching up to it. "We've got to talk again, Thelonious. Just make a stop."

Chapter 10

Michele Santiago stood outside the front of the Augustine Bayou Hotel looking at the aged building. Andrea Nance noted her interest and said, "It's a beautiful building."

"Yes, and it seems loaded with character. I bet it could tell some stories."

Nance laughed. "You're in the Big Easy. I'm sure it can. Let's go in. We have a lot to do and then the Augustine will have another story to tell."

As they walked through the lobby to the elevator Santiago enjoyed looking over the interior of the hotel. "It's just so unique. I've never seen anything quite like it."

"We use their meeting room for small conferences from time to time."

They stepped to the elevator. Nance selected the fourth floor as the doors closed. "He'll be using 407 this afternoon, tonight, or whenever."

"This is where the senator meets the prostitute?"

"No, Mitch, this is where he'll spend his time with the escort. We're paying his pleasure toy $5,000. That's way beyond the price of a prostitute. But she's worth the money. He'll remain agreeable."

"You said he's a player."

"He is, just not in the public's eyes. To the voters he's the dedicated family man, super dad. But he knows women are drawn to him. He picks and chooses when and where, especially in Washington. But on a venture like this it's all behind the scenes."

"So why are we here if he knows the rules?"

"Senator DuBois is a big investment. We don't want him compromised and given his sometimes unique appetites we're going to do everything possible to protect him and us."

Santiago smiled. *Unique appetites. Don't go there.* She said, "In other words, keep him locked in for the night."

"Exactly. Right now we're going to check for bugs, cameras, anything that can be used to compromise him, just in case there's been a leak."

"Smart move."

"I'm sure DataFlex watches over a few select power-brokers. They seem to have a great deal of expertise and connections when it comes to government contacts."

Santiago shook her head. "It's possible. I never worked that type of assignment."

"No, but you did gather sensitive information on selected individuals. The two go hand in hand."

The two women stood at the door of 407.

Santiago said, "When we go in keep the conversation casual while we work."

Nance gave a nod. "You know the business."

"I found Kohler's bugs in my loft."

"So you did," said Nance opening the door. "Shall we."

They checked everything in the suite while chatting about New Orleans.

Nance used a compact RF detector and lens locator covering parts of the suite rapidly. Santiago spent time searching areas of the suite Nance seemed to ignore or missed.

After moving through the area around a dresser, wall painting, and ventilation opening Santiago waved while placing her index finger over her lips. Nance looked across the room as Santiago held up a mini keychain digital recorder and pointed to the vent.

Nance said, "It's clean."

Santiago looked at the voice recorder.

"It's ours. So is the camera in the vent. There's nothing else here so we're good."

Santiago said nothing. *You're making a porno film, this is getting sleazy.*

Someone knocked at the door.

Nance said, "That'll be the champagne and fruit bowl. DuBois likes to enjoy his evenings of sex."

When she opened the door a bellman rolled in a cart, placed a fruit bowel on a table and set a large bucket of ice in a stand beside it. He wrapped a magnum of champagne in a towel and placed it in the bucket, accepted a tip from Nance and left without a word.

Santiago said, "The ice will melt before DuBois gets here."

"Valentine will ice it again. It just needs to be chilled when Broderick arrives. He likes a glass to get in the mood."

"My meeting him at Absinthe House, is that part of a routine?"

"Yes, if I have any last minute changes I tell him personally, no phone or texts."

"Smart, no record."

"Exactly, and I can't control him on the outside."

"Do you have any last minute changes?"

"No, you being there is my way of saying everything is good to go. He'll know it. Just give him the key and tell him where he's meeting Valentine."

"You gave him a number to call at coffee. How do you know it will be Valentine?"

"In New Orleans it's always Valentine. If he changed I would know immediately and the plan would still work smoothly."

"You have great trust in the escort service."

"Why not, Noble owns it." She went to her purse and brought out a small brass card case. "Take this, your new business cards."

"Very fancy."

"One of the traditions at the Old Absinthe House is to place one of your business card on the wall. You'll see what I mean when you're there. You'll be playing the role of tourist. DuBois will meet you casually by accident, not a preplanned encounter as far as anyone on site is concerned."

"Got it. You think of everything."

"That's my job."

"And you're filming the senator today."

"Only for his pleasure if he behaves. Trust me, he'd never want this one to hit the internet or anywhere else."

When they got outside Santiago walked toward the limousine with Nance.

"Mitch, I want you to take a carriage to the Old Absinthe House, the tourist all the way. Later, when you return take a position allowing you to keep track of the first floor hallway and elevators. I suggest down the hall toward the rear. The security cameras are being disabled as we speak. I'll already be in room 106 when you return, hopefully not too long. When I leave we don't know each other. A tech will be in sometime after I leave to get a laptop and some other equipment. The equipment in 407 will be picked up later.

"I understand. This whole event sounds like something out of a spy movie."

"It could make for an interesting scene, or two."

Nance spoke to her driver and they left the curb. Santiago flagged a carriage.

*****

Wolfe followed Thelonious and talked with Andrea Nance on his cell. "Xavier is on the run. I lost him in a double-car switch. He's running from the cops and a man named Thelonious that I'm following right now."

She said, "I want Xavier dead, ASAP."

"Will do, but first I need to have another chat with Purple Pants."

"Who?"

"Thelonious."

"Do whatever you need, just extract the information you need and kill him."

Wolfe smiled as Thelonious pulled into a parking lot on Alma School and Warner. "As always, no strings attached."

She said, "Keep me posted," and broke the connection.

He waited half an hour in his car until Thelonious returned. Wolfe got out of the rental and stepped to the passenger door of the yellow Lexus. Thelonious saw him and pressed the up button closing the passenger window.

Wolfe laughed, smiled through the window and waved a .38. "Shit, you're an idiot. Drop the keys on the floor." Wolfe smashed the window with the gun and laughed even more. Glass fell all over the passenger seat. "Jesus, the top is down you fool. Now, we need to have another conversation."

Thelonious looked Wolfe in the eyes. Sweat covered his forehead. His left leg began to shake. He gripped the steering wheel and swallowed, then looked at the building. "I already told ya, Xavier owes me 5K."

"That may be but I want to know where he is."

"I don't know."

"Slide over here."

"These are bucket seat, man. Glass is everywhere."

Wolfe waved the gun again. "I'm not sittin' in it, you are Purple Pants."

Thelonious moved to the passenger seat struggling to get over the center console and shifter. Wolfe walked around to the driver's side and got in. "Remember, click it or ticket." He started the car.

As Wolfe drove north to East Main in Mesa again Thelonious asked, "How'd ya know my name?"

"The hostess this morning."

"I already told ya, I don't know where Xavier went. He gave both of us the slip at the Dusty Spur."

"Thelonious, let me make this clear. I can shoot you now or later if you don't tell me what I want to know. If I don't get what I want you're going to suffer and die from my trying, understand?"

Thelonious nodded.

"Good, now help me here, how do I get to Tortilla Flats?"

Thelonious gave Wolfe directions. "You're goin' to kill me either way aren't ya?"

Wolfe chuckled, "Maybe, maybe not. I didn't cut your throat earlier."

They passed Canyon Lake and a marina, Tortilla Flats, and followed a washboard road toward Roosevelt Damn. A few miles down the dirt road they found a pullout and stopped.

Wolfe said, "Get out of the car." He motioned Thelonious toward a large boulder. "Let's go over there."

Thelonious squinted and stared at Wolfe, opened the door and got out slowly. He brushed the glass shards off his shirt and pants cutting his hinds. He walked to the boulder, turned and waited. Wolfe placed the gun barrel under his chin. Thelonious raised his head but said nothing. Wolfe kneed him in the groin and he fell to the ground.

Thelonious looked up at Wolfe. His nose was running and tears filled his eyes. "Please, man, I don't know nothing."

"Get up. I want you on the boulder face down, spread-eagled."

Thelonious put his hands flat on the ground and pushed himself into a sitting position. "I can't get up, man."

Wolfe stomped on his groin. "I told you, if I don't get what I want you suffer. Now get on the damn boulder."

Thelonious rolled onto his knees and clawed his way up onto the boulder, threw up and then spread-eagled himself face down as tears ran down his face. "Please, please, you don't understand. I don't know where Xavier went."

Wolfe picked up a large rock and crushed the left hand of Thelonious.

He screeched in pain, crying out, the sound echoing off the canyon walls. "Kohler hired me to get a new identity for Xavier, that's all."

Wolfe tossed the rock over the edge of the canyon. "Now that's a better way to start. What name did you give him?"

Thelonious looked at Wolfe but said nothing.

Wolfe picked up another rock.

"No, no, please," he said hold out a hand defensively. "The name is Truman Greene with an 'e.'"

"Good, now where was he going?"

"I don't know. He wouldn't tell me."

"But you picked Truman Greene?"

"Greene had the right profile."

"So false ID's are your business?"

Thelonious wiped his brow and nose. Mucus covered the back of his right hand. "Yes."

"But you were trying to find out?"

"Yes, that's why I followed him. I knew someone would pay a lot of money for the information."

"Where do you think he'd go?"

Thelonious wiped his face again. "He likes big cities, destinations, crowds and action. If he's smart and wants to stay alive he'll stay away from the high life."

"Does he have money?"

"Kohler and Xavier made a lot of money. I'm sure they had an offshore account. Everyone in the business does."

Wolfe nodded. "You didn't know it, Thelonious, but I'm missing a family event because of Xavier and Kohler, and, oh yes, you. Get in the car."

"What are you gonna do? I told you everything I know."

"I'll make it fast."

Thelonious stood, his legs shaking. He swallowed and swayed, held out his good hand and arm and tried to step toward the car. "Please, don't do this."

Wolfe stopped him after a few steps and pointed at the ground. "Sit and stay put."

Thelonious did as directed after almost falling several times trying to cradle his crushed hand. "Thank you."

Wolfe got in the car and moved it to the edge of the road facing the canyon. He got out leaving the engine running. "Now, get up and get in the car."

"No, no, please. Why don't you just shoot me?"

"Car accident won't explain a bullet hole. If you don't get in I'll smash a knee, an elbow, something," he said bending over to pick up another large rock. "You know it's hard to tell which rock did what to a body going over a two or three hundred foot cliff in a car. Right now the question is pain. How much more would you like to experience?"

Thelonious got up and moved toward the car. He lunged at Wolfe but fell to the earth on his crushed hand crying out in pain. Wolfe walked to his side and kicked him squarely in the ribs. "It's gonna take longer to die asshole. Now get in the car or get a little more. You're trying my patience."

Thelonious struggled but couldn't stand. Blood flowed over his lips. He crawled to the Lexus, his breath short. He climbed behind the steering wheel then passed out. Wolfe reached across him and slid the shifter into drive. The Lexus rolled over the edge. The doors flew off. Thelonious came out of the car and bounced off boulders as he and the car plummeted to the canyon floor.

Wolfe tossed the rock he was holding over the edge and rubbed his gloved hands together then peeled them off. "Driving gloves in the desert, who'd believe this?"

He checked his watch. *Damn, it'll be late by the time I get to the marina. I'll call Xavier's office from the restaurant in Tortilla Flats. I want to talk to their secretary again. She can identify me.*

*****

It was just past 10:00 a.m. in Chandler, Arizona, at Ray House's DataFlex Security office. Link Andrews came through the door and House motioned him to sit down.

Andrews said, "What's up?"

"Sam Evans is on his way to New Orleans to take Tony Mercedes place as we planned. He'll get in around 7:00 tonight our time. Hear anything from Mitch today?"

Andrews laughed and looked at his watch. "She's probably at lunch at the Old Absinthe House by now. We talked last night and she gave me a heads up. This morning Mario and I have been doing some deep background on Senator Broderick DuBois, Chairman of Senate Appropriations. It seems Noble has a big interest in a bill coming up that authorizes spending for work on Unmanned Aerial Vehicles."

House said, "Drones, Maxwell is working with the Space and Naval Warfare System Center at the New Orleans Research Technology Park, a facility owned by the University of New Orleans. Noble is an investor in that project."

"What are they working on?"

"Link, it's like some of our work, Top Secret, off limits to anyone without a need to know. I do know they have employed two UAV specialists on programming ground control, and all the work is totally isolated from everything at Maxwell."

Andrews smiled. "Tony would follow leads wherever the trail led, even if it wasn't part of Barrier. According to Mitch, she and Andrea Nance have come to the conclusion the leak is in the other program. All of us want to know who the leak is and where."

"That ought to help Mitch but I'd bet we want to know the leak's identity for different reasons. The senator's interest in a UAV program is equally interesting. Our people in PR have been telling us for years DuBois is the lapdog of Noble, bought and paid for."

"Mitch will find out what the other project is. She's going to be Noble's lobbyist, read that security on site until they find the leak."

"Link, we protect our research and investments such as Barrier; security, patents, contracts – sound business practices. Barrier is classified but still in early research stages. We have no guarantee it will even be successful or competitive with a European program. Its impact on computer security if successful would be tremendous. But that is a long ways away."

Andrews squinted and looked at House. "At this point it doesn't seem like something one would kill for."

"Not at this point. Someone wanting the outcome would wait until we had something to steal. I agree with Mitch, Tony was working something outside of Barrier's Quantum world."

"Ray, do you believe Noble was involved in Tony's murder."

"Without a doubt. Why else the cloak and dagger approach in snatching up Mitch as soon as she became a free agent so to speak."

"I reached the same conclusion early on but then Maxwell was interested in her, too."

"Link, in the last twenty-four hours we've had six requests for references on Mitch. She's good at what she does. Her reputation is well known. Don't forget Noble knew she was available instantly and upped the ante with a very lucrative contract."

"I have another idea. I've got vacation coming. Everybody knows Mitch and I are tight. So why don't I officially take a week off and visit her, see how she's doing, all that 'I'm missing my lady jazz,' and leave here with a smile on my face?"

"You want to go to New Orleans?"

"Yes, I think I'd be more useful there than faking another task here."

House's phone rang. He listened for a moment then hung up. He rubbed his forehead.

"Something wrong, Ray?"

"Jessica just told me Kohler's body was found at Xavier's house. His death makes your idea brilliant. We'll arrange your vacation through accounting. It'll get leaked. And it wouldn't seem out of the ordinary if you had some contact with Sam while you're visiting Mitch."

Andrews smiled. "Why don't we chat about this at lunch in the cafeteria? Someone will be listening. I'm betting Noble will know I'm coming before Mitch, certainly before I make it to Louis Armstrong International."

House reached for his phone. "Make your reservation now while I call Spears extension."

A moment later Spear's answered.

House said, "Mario, come by my office before you leave for lunch."

Spears said, "I'll be there in a minute."

House went next door to the office of Jessica Rodriguez. "Can you join Link and I for a moment, and bring another burn cell."

When they returned to his office Spears was already there and Andrews had made his travel reservations. House reviewed Link's vacation plan. "Mario, Jessica has a burn cell for you. With Link out of town you become an intricate part of our communication as well as our researcher. Until Link talks with Mitch only the three of us know about this latest move."

Spears said, "Why the change?"

House said, "Kohler is dead. Just a reminder, no talking about what we're up to. Now Link, let's go to the staff lounge for an early lunch and talk about your vacation. I'm curious to know how long it takes for word to reach Noble."

*****

Santiago paid the carriage driver and went into the Old Absinthe House. It was 12:10. She saw DuBois at a small table by a wall covered with business cards. "I'm fashionably late."

DuBois stood. "At last we're alone."

She laughed. "Right, in a bar full of people."

"You know what I mean."

She sat down as the mini hiked. "I do, Senator."

"Mitch, please, we're friends, workmates."

She smiled and looked into his eyes. "You bond very fast. I'll bet Valentine is really close."

He closed his eyes and laughed. "We can look beyond a triste can't we?"

She ignored the question. "How did Andrea recruit you?"

"Andrea is very much the professional lobbyist, Mitch, but she didn't. I met her at a barbecue at Nelson and Rosemary Noble's home overlooking the Hudson River. Ishtar invited me as an old school chum. We both attended Harvard. Andrea was also at the gathering of a few hundred casual friends and business associates. Ishtar made the suggestion to Andrea that Noble may want to work with me in furthering certain legislative bills beneficial to everyone."

"So you and the Mrs. Dade were old college pals back in the 70's."

"It seems so long ago now, but yes. We were good friends in school but never an item. We dated only occasionally. Her parents had greater plans for her than a budding Louisiana lawyer."

She laughed. "Funny how times change isn't it."

"It is." He looked at the wall beside them. "Do you have a business card?"

She took out the brass card holder. "I do."

"Pin it to the wall. It's an old tradition."

She pinned the card. "There are hundreds of them."

"Yes," he said taking another pin and placing his card next to hers. "And now there's two more. Shall we have a drink?"

"I'd like a Chardonnay."

He flagged a waiter, ordered two Chardonnays, and held out a hand. "I think you have something for me."

Santiago gave him the Augustine Bayou Suites key to room 407.

"I love that place," he said waving the key.

"Miss Valentine will be waiting. I'll be downstairs in the hallway. You two stay in the suite and everything will be fine. Use room service, but have Valentine make the calls. My orders are to keep you under wrap."

"I'm sure she will."

"And your security man? What do you do with him?"

"We've worked out a nice arrangement for my moments. He will be available if I call him, otherwise he is having a little sport of his own."

"So much for protocol and security."

"We all need flexible people around us, it's not all work. You'll see when you're in Washington. Perhaps then we can get together for a drink, socially. You'll love DC."

"I've been there." She checked her watch. "I think you best be on your way. We'll arrive separately, of course."

He stood. "I assume the drinks are on Noble. I'm off to a night of pure pleasure." He smiled and gave the slightest bow and whispered, "See you at the hotel."

Santiago watched him go out the door and laughed. *No cute waitress, no chit chat, no fifty dollar tip.*

*****

Xavier had met up with his cab behind the Dusty Spur. The cabbie took him to a second-hand store where he purchased worn pants, shoes, a lightweight jacket and an old backpack. After shopping he put the portfolio in the backpack and took a different cab. At Interstate 10, Exit 137 the cab got off, pulled into a truck stop and dropped off Xavier. Once inside he had gone to the men's room, changed into the older clothes then went to the counter for lunch. In his now clean but homeless appearance a waitress brought him coffee and bowl of soup.

"That'll be $3.81 with tax."

He dug a few dollars and change from his pocket and paid before she'd leave the food. He mumbled, "Bitch, I'm not a bum, yet."

A big trucker seated two stools down laughed. "Don't mind Mable, she's a good ol' gal but burned more than once."

"Yeah, I understand."

The trucker slid over a stool. "You look a little down, fella. We've all had our moments."

"Mine must be today. The old lady kicks me out. I've got hardly any money, gotta get to Tucson so I can crash at my brother's place." He kicked the backpack.

"Your brother can't come pick you up?"

"Doesn't have the money for gas. I'll try hitchin' but the odds aren't good at gettin' picked up the way I look."

"Tell ya what, I'm headed for Mirana. I can take you that far. If I see one of my pals there we can get you a ride into Tucson, at least closer to your brother."

"Damn, that'd be great. Lord knows I'm in a bind here."

"Soon as I'm done we'll be outta here," said the trucker. "Hey, Mable, how 'bout a burger for my friend. I'll pay."

"Fair enough," she shouted, "but you don't know him."

"Mable, folks helped me when I was down. Time to give back. Just bring the burger, please."

*****

Michelle Santiago arrived at the Augustine Bayou just after DuBois. He went in and headed straight to the elevators, she went to the back ally entry on the first floor. She took a seat by a small table with magazines and waited. Forty-five minutes later Andrea Nance left room 106, passed a housekeeping cart parked between 104 and 106, walked down the hall, through the lobby and out the door.

Santiago laughed. *A quickie, that didn't take long.* She went down the hall to 106. "I've got to get that laptop." A fire alarm box was directly across the hall. Stepping to the housekeeping cart she took one of the complimentary hotel robes, put it on then went to the alarm. *Nobody watching.* She pulled the alarm.

As guests began streaming into the hall she knocked on the door of 106. Nobody responded. She removed a set of picks from her handbag, stood with her back to the door and picked the lock as a few guests rushed past her. It took only a moment to open. She stepped inside and closed the door. "Just like the senator's suite, nice." On a table by the window was a laptop. She took the unit, tucked it under the robe and left.

Santiago headed toward the ally entrance. She slid the robe off, wrapped it around the laptop, and hid it behind the chair she'd used earlier. A few guests came down the stairs and rushed past her. She went up the stairs toward the second floor. Some guests were slow in moving, reluctant to leave.

She saw a house phone on the wall by the stairwell in a seating area same as on the first floor. She dialed the front desk. When the operator answered she said, "Ha, ha, false alarm," hung up and ran up the last two flights. She banged on 407's door. A blond woman covered by a towel answered.

"Valentine, where's DuBois?"

The woman said nothing. He came out of the bedroom naked. I'm here, Mitch," he called waving a bottle of champagne.

In all your glory. Santiago said, "Stay put, both of you."

The room phone rang.

"Valentine, you answer. We don't want him on the phone."

Valentine picked up the receiver. "Yes."

"Sorry for the inconvenience, Miss Smith, false alarm. You may stay in your room."

She said, "Thank you," and hung up.

Santiago looked at her. "False alarm?"

"Yes."

"Good, you two can go back to whatever. Do not go out until tomorrow. The police, fire department and reporters will be around here for hours."

DuBois said, "You could stay with us. We could...."

"No, no. But I'll nail you if you stick your head out."

Valentine laughed. "I don't think he could make it to the lobby. He already drank all of that one and another was ordered just before the excitement."

Santiago stepped to the door. "Then I best leave."

She went back to the first floor and retrieved the robe and laptop. As people began to return to the building she stepped into the ally, went the opposite direction to Decatur. Flagging a cab she went to the bus depot on Loyola Avenue, placed the laptop in a locker then returned to the Augustine Bayou.

Santiago checked her watch and went back to the rear entry seating area so she could see 106. *That took about half-an-hour. I'll wait and see if anyone shows up for the equipment. The fire alarm and crowd may have slowed the pickup, maybe not. I'd like to know who the contact is if possible.*

As evening approached nobody came except house-keeping. "That's got to be the pickup, no hotel cleans rooms at this hour."

When the housekeeping person came back out of the room 106 a minute later she was dressed in street clothes and went down the hall and out the front door carrying a small suitcase. Santiago smiled. *Mission accomplished.*

Santiago called Nance. "Andrea, I believe your pickup person just left the hotel. She came dressed like housekeeping and left as a tourist."

"Thank you. And the senator?"

"Still in his room, probably asleep. We had a fire alarm several hours ago, right after you left. I went up and made sure they didn't come out unless necessary. He was naked as a baby and drunk as a skunk. The alarm was false."

"Mitch, with DuBois out of commission, call it a night. Valentine will take care of him."

*****

It was nearing dinner hour for the Dade's in New York. Ishtar and Francis were in there sitting room enjoying their before dinner cocktail.

Ishtar said, "Has our new associate found any useful information?"

"Andrea reports she has been keeping track of your friend, Broderick."

"He's not involved with Maxwell."

"Not directly, dear, but through the coming appropriation, and he's been difficult of late."

"And he's in New Orleans?"

"Yes, one of those junkets he likes so well."

"Really, he's becoming an expensive bore."

"Necessary, Ishtar, but Andrea has a way to make him even more cooperative than in the past and cost less."

"That sounds interesting."

"I thought you'd like that."

"Will her methods be effective?"

"Without doubt."

She laughed. "Knowing Broderick it involves women."

"It does."

"Hm, sounds juicy."

"It could be most scandalous."

"Then we'd lose him."

"That's not likely, dear. He wouldn't lose his senate seat unless the immediate disgrace is too much for him and he resigned."

She sipped her cocktail. "Politicians have behaved scandalously for years."

"They have, but most didn't have to deal with the media coverage of today."

"When will the new woman...."

"Santiago, Michelle Santiago."

"Yes, when will she finally get to Maxwell?"

"She already did. Andrea had her there this morning. She met Jim Trainer and had the opportunity to observe Alfred Yeager briefly before heading back to the DuBois assignment. She'll be back at Maxwell in the morning."

"I did some checking on my own. I've found only good things about Miss Santiago, including loyalty."

"Andrea says she's top flight. But, Ishtar, we have had a setback."

"What?"

"Your friend Canfield Kohler has been murdered."

"Wasn't he Andrea's primary contact in Arizona?"

"Yes, although Andrea was reevaluating his value to us."

"Who killed him?"

"His partner, Jerome Xavier, is a person of interest."

"Suspect, Francis, he's a suspect. I don't care what terminology the police use."

"Mr. Xavier has disappeared. He was last seen by one of Andrea's associates sent to clean up loose ends."

"Does Xavier know about us?"

"No, he doesn't even know Andrea's identity, only Kohler knew about us."

"Unless, my dear Francis, Mr. Kohler told him before his demise."

"That is a possibility, dear. We still have our other contact inside DataFlex."

She finished her cocktail. "Good, I want results at Maxwell and I want Braun under a microscope. I've never trusted him."

"We both want results. Santiago will find the leak feeding Mr. Mercedes information. I have no doubt."

"Well, Francis, we'll see how long it takes. I see your Miss Santiago as one with possible lingering loyalties to DataFlex."

"I know, but Andrea has checked and rechecked. Santiago is the real thing. Andrea will have her heading up the New Orleans operation until we find the leak."

"She passed all of Andrea's tests?"

"With flying colors."

"Good. Tell me, Francis, did you enjoy your reward last night."

He smiled. "I did."

"Good, because you won't get another until we have some results from the new woman."

He nodded.

"Walk me to dinner, Francis." As they moved toward the dining room she said, "Do you believe the authorities will find Mr. Xavier?"

"No, I believe Andrea has a most professional friend that will find him."

"Excellent."

Chapter 11

After leaving the Augustine Bayou for the night Santiago returned to the Jackson Square condominium and called Ray House on the DataFlex burn cell.

He answered on the second ring. "Hi, Mitch, what have you got?"

"More questions than answers, but it has been an interesting day."

He said, "Let me share my news first. Sam should be coming in about now. I don't know his exact time. He'll be in touch after he gets settled, I'd expect tonight."

"I've been anticipating his arrival. Any change in his status?"

"Yes, I want you to fill him in on the operation. Instead of blind innocence he'll be depending on his acting skills tomorrow. It shouldn't be a problem and truthfully won't make any difference. He's our man in New Orleans."

"I'll update him."

"Next, Link will be calling in the next few hours. He's also on his way down in the role of lonely lover."

"What's happened?"

"I tried to reach you earlier but your cell was off."

"I didn't have my burn cell with me, just a small compact with a Glock 42, lock picks, and some money. I was with Andrea most of the day and I surely didn't want it going off then."

"The body of Canfield Kohler was found this morning in the car and garage of Jerome Xavier. Police also found a suicide note written by Jerome. Right now he is missing, is a person of interest, maybe a victim by his own hand, nobody knows."

So police think he killed Kohler?"

"Yes."

She said, "It could be staged, Ray."

"I know. Either way things are looking dangerous. Link had suggested coming down to work with you. We were talking about it when I got notified about Kohler. End of discussion but we kept his covers in place."

"Good."

"There's more, Mitch. The body of one of our accountants, Vladimir Clyburn was found today in the west valley by some hikers. The press is reporting it as a cartel hit; bound hands, bullet in the back of the head."

"What about the authorities?"

They think a cartel is involved. Clyburn's family has some relationship to the Russian Mafia although he was clean. But keep in mind, we have or had a leak in accounting, too."

"Does Link know about this?"

"No, neither does Sam, yet. While the body was found earlier today confirmation can take some time as you well know."

"I'll fill them in. God, no wonder whoever we're looking for is hiding. They're totally at risk."

"I agree, but so are you, Mitch. Who the hell can be trusted has to be their biggest issue and ours. But enough about my end. What's happening on your turf?"

"I spent the day babysitting the senator. I met him this morning for coffee, then went to Maxwell for a visit. Jim Trainer, CEO, showed us around. I was supposed to meet Lilith Towne, their security head, and the two project leaders, Alfred Yeager – Barrier, and Acadia Sigmund – Reaper Guidance Modification. Instead Andrea and I got a brief tour, and I watched Yeager in the lab. The visit was cut short when Andrea got a call. I've no idea what it was but we left immediately."

"Busy morning. The call could have been one of her contacts with the news about Kohler."

"Certainly a possibility. But I have more to share. In the afternoon Nance made a porno video of the senator and his escort. She left the hotel with a flash drive. I purloined the laptop before her media people showed up. It's stashed in a bus depot locker. Andrea said she'd delete the video when she was finished. I'm sure she knows about the theft but I haven't talked with her since her people came for the equipment."

"You will. She's probably trying to verify your whereabouts first. You're still the new kid on the block."

"Ray, I don't have the skills to recover the deleted files. I'm thinking I should send the laptop to Mario, but we'll lose a couple of days in transport."

"Give it to Sam. He has contacts down there that can handle the recovery and save us time."

"Excellent, Andrea said they need the senator's vote on an upcoming appropriations bill. It's only a few days away. If we need to take action it must be soon."

House said, "Maybe we have some people that can slow it down until we have a clear plan. None of us want a corrupt senator."

"Can you send a second investigator? If Sam gets involved with what is going on in the Mercedes activity Barrier will be left pretty much open ground."

"Do you have a suggestion?"

"Dash Varga. She's smart, new, and good with people, a team player, and works well with minimal direction. If not, try to free-up Desiree Larsson. She'd be good."

"You're comfortable with Desiree. I haven't forgotten our last big operation, Killer Disc, when she and Paxton became a separate item."

"Past history. They had to work that out. He left me out of the picture and I've long since moved on to better things as if you hadn't noticed."

He laughed. "Mitch, we've all noticed. And speaking of being noticed, do you think the senator could be distracted by Shari Stiletto?"

"She could distract most men, Broderick for sure. Why?"

"I'm just toying with an idea. She may be coming through New Orleans on a brief layover."

"Sounds like the whole team is coming down here. Keep me posted."

*****

When Sam Evans arrived at Louis Armstrong International he picked up his luggage, rented a car, and drove to the New Orleans Sanctuary Hotel on Chantilly near Maxwell Cyber Systems. After checking in he tried Michelle Santiago's cell phone. It was out of service.

"Damn, I know you're here, but where?" He checked his watch and set it ahead two hours to 9:10.

He went to the dining room for dinner. Reading the menu he shook his head. *Cajun this, Cajun that. There's got to be a steak in here somewhere.*

When Evans finished dinner he drove to the French Quarter using the built in GPS of the rental. He parked on Canal Street, walked to the Frenchman Condominiums and rode to the fourth floor. At 402 he knocked.

A moment later Santiago opened the door. "Sam, what a nice surprise. Ray told me you were flying in today. Come in."

He looked around the living room. "Nice place. I didn't know if you were in or not. Your cell is out of service."

"Yes it is. Ice tea?"

"Please."

"Have you talked with Ray since arriving?"

"No."

"I have some news for you. First, I am still employed by DataFlex."

He raised an eyebrow and watched her face. "I knew something was up."

"I'm doing an undercover assignment. We think Noble was involved in Tony's death."

"So firing you was a con?"

"Yes."

"And I wasn't told."

"Ray said he wanted you to go through Maxwell's screening clean."

"I haven't done that yet. What's changed?"

She updated him about Clyburn's murder, Kohler's death, Xavier's status, and the details as she knew them about Tony Mercedes.

"You've been busy, Mitch."

She laughed. "Today I was babysitting a senator have a fling. I acquired a laptop with an incriminating video."

"How did you do that?"

"You don't want to know, but I did use a skill you taught me."

"Really?"

"Lock picking."

"What's on the video?"

"I don't know. It was deleted before I acquired the lap top. I thought I should send it to Mario but Ray says you have connections down here that can do the recovery job."

"Is the lap top here?"

"Bus depot."

"Give me the address and key." He looked at his watch again. "I have some people that will begin work on it immediately."

"Great, that'll save time. As I understand it your cover is Barrier. You'll be dealing with an egocentric scientist named Alfred Yeager. I won't know any more until tomorrow when I meet him. I'll be doing that in the morning while you go through clearance screening with Lilith Towne, Maxwell's version of Ray House."

Evans almost spit ice tea. "God, there's two of him?"

"Could be, she's very sharp, very plugged in, but then so is my boss."

"What can you tell me about the other project? Ray briefed me on Barrier."

"Nothing beyond it's top secret. I'll know more to-morrow."

Santiago's cell phone rang. She looked at caller ID and smiled.

"Hello, Link."

"Hi, Babe, I'll be at Louis Armstrong in about an hour."

"I'll pick you up."

"You already have. I'll take a cab. You can surprise me when I get there or we can go for a walk."

Santiago licked her lips. "Or both."

"My imagination is already starting to race."

"Good, I like it when your motor is running."

Sam Evans took the last sip of his iced tea, put the glass on the table and pointed to the door.

"Santiago waved as he went out with the bus depot locker key and quietly closed the door."

"Sam was here. He just left."

"That's why I'm here. This is a dangerous assignment. I'll fill you in when you get here."

*****

Adrian Nance called Santiago at 8:01.

"Mitch, how long were you at the back entrance of the Augustine Bayou?"

"Up until a few minutes after you left. We had a fire alarm and the building was being evacuated. I went upstairs to 407. After the alarm I was back in position until we talked."

"Did DuBois and Valentine evacuate?"

"No. Valentine answered the door draped in a bath towel. DuBois came out of the bedroom stark naked carrying a champagne bottle after he heard my voice."

"What happened?"

"First he invited me to join them. I in turn told them to stay put for a few minutes. We had no smoke or flames showing. I was working on how to get our drunk leader out, probably with a robe over his head, hopefully all of him. Before I decided a hotel operator called and told Valentine we could remain in the room, that it had been a false alarm."

"Thank God, a naked senator wandering the streets of the French Quarter would be a newsworthy trash piece with or without Valentine."

Santiago laughed. "It would've been a PR disaster. All turned out well, they're staying the night."

"Not exactly all good."

"How so?"

"I believe the false alarm was a cover for a burglary and to get you out of the way. Someone broke into 106 and stole the laptop. The theft was discovered when my associate came to pick up the unit later."

"You have the video don't you?"

"Yes, on a flash drive, but the data is still on the computer. I deleted everything before leaving, but a good tech could recover it."

"What about the cameras in 407?"

"After the senator and Valentine vacate."

"I'm assuming no police report."

"None."

"Who knew your plan?"

"You, me, the lady retrieving the computer and the tech doing the equipment tomorrow – just the four of us."

"Valentine?"

"Sorry, the five of us."

"And all the surveillance cameras were off line?"

"Yes, by my request."

"Anything else taken?"

"Nothing, the hotel furnishings were intact, just the laptop."

"Did your associate see anyone or thing?"

"She came late and saw you at the back entry but no one else."

"Before your retriever I only saw a few people in the hall. None stopped or even looked at 106 as they walked the hallway."

"Contact his security man and tell him to take the senator back to the Cajun Lady Boutique when he leaves the Augustine tomorrow. I'll book a flight for them back to Washington."

Nance gave Santiago the security man's cell number and name.

"I didn't think you knew him beyond name."

"He works for me on the side."

"And the senator is flying commercial?"

"Yes, part of his, 'I'm one of the people,' campaign pledges."

"Andrea, sorry to keep coming back to it but his security man knew of the visit with Valentine, too."

"Yes he did, and now that I think about it maybe one or two in my Washington office, all trusted, were aware of the plan. I don't believe it. Crap, I've got a leak."

"I'm sorry now I didn't stay on the first floor during the alarm."

"No, you did exactly what you should've done. Damn!"

"What's next?"

"Back on plan. If someone else is dogging DuBois I'll know soon enough. Tomorrow you're at Maxwell. That is your priority. But thank you for the insight. I would never have included his man in my list, nor anybody he may have had contact with."

"Will do."

"Oh, Mitch, are you expecting company tonight?"

"No."

"I'd get a bottle of Captain Morgan if I were you."

"Really? I like the sound of that." *Link won't.*

"Really, and heh, good job with the senator. His being out there in his skin would have been unbelievable."

*****

Santiago opened her condo door at 9:51 p.m. to a gentle knock and peeked out. Only her face was visible. "Hi handsome, looking for a good time?"

Link Andrews stared her in the eyes and smiled. "Are you accepting guests?"

She opened the door wide. "Only one."

The background light displayed her silhouette in a green chiffon peignoir as he stepped through the door.

He looked her over from head to toe. "Good thing it's me. If I was Sam you'd be dealing with a heart attack victim."

She pushed the door closed and embraced him. "Sam was here an hour ago when you called. All he got was a laptop." She licked her lower lip. "And I was in my street clothes."

"I know about your street threads." He glanced briefly around. "Nice place."

"For a few days."

"What's next?"

"For us or Noble?"

"Both."

She kissed him again. "For us pleasure, for them I don't know."

He waved his suitcase.

She pointed toward her master suite. "In there. I'll fix you a drink. I just happen to have some Captain Morgan on hand."

"You went shopping after my call," he said stepping out of the bedroom. "Nice touch."

"I knew I had to go shopping when Andrea asked if I expected company and shared I ought to get a bottle of your choice."

"Damn it, when?"

"A few hours ago. Her DataFlex connection is alive and well. But I'll make you feel better. Ray told me you were coming, too, and speaking of him, business first."

Andrews laughed. "It always comes first, but some-day...."

"You know about Clyburn, Kohler and Xavier. I've filled in Sam."

"Mitch, Clyburn was one of the new hires I was back checking. You've covered what I had on him, but now we have three possible murders."

"We do, and we're the only group we know of that thinks the killings are related and focused on the same thing. We're going to be busy tomorrow." She kissed his cheek. "We need a little escape while we can."

They walked toward the couch with their drinks. He whispered in her ear, "We'll be busy tonight, too, and I do like your outfit."

As they curled up on the couch together she kissed his cheek. "I thought you would. I don't think I've ever worn it at home."

"You haven't, trust me. Do I want to know where you've worn it?"

"No." She leaned back. "Something else is on your mind."

"I have some new information about your boss. Nance is her married name. Her adoptive family surname is Autry."

"I didn't know she'd ever been married."

"Well, babe, she was to Taylor Nance for a brief time, four months, when she was in her twenties."

"Why'd they get a divorce?"

He filed for divorce when his family couldn't get a quick annulment after discovering her adoptive father killed her adoptive mother then committed suicide. Bad for the image."

"Murder, suicide; when?"

"About the time Andrea was entering the university. It seems mom was enjoying the comforts of a neighbor and had been for some time. Trouble was, she wasn't putting out very often at home. Dad started an affair with the same neighbor's wife."

"This is beginning to sound like a swap."

"Oh yes, swap and STD's, then suicide. Andrea's mom contracted gonorrhea from the neighbor guy, Andrea's dad picked it up from her mom on one of their rare encounters and gave it to the neighbor's wife. Apparently the neighbor's got things worked out or maybe they were closet swingers, who knows? Obviously they weren't doing each other very often. But Andrea's parents had a difficult time resolving their infidelity issue. Dad kills mom. Dad kills self."

Santiago said, "I'm surprised Taylor and his family didn't find out about the history of her family. The Nance's are prominent people in Washington."

"According to the gossip columns leading up to the wedding Andrea explained her parent's death as the result of a fatal car crash in Italy and no one questioned the story."

"I'm equally surprised she kept the Nance name."

"The family wanted it back but it wasn't their call. I personally think even as a young woman in college Andrea was very shrewd. She wanted to start a public relations firm after graduation and knew the name of a murder suicide attached a budding business would stop it cold in Washington."

"You know, Link, she's smart, shifty, sneaky; maybe even premeditated in getting the Nance name. Andrea knows her business and is very attractive, a deadly combination in Washington."

"You have a point. After graduating she took a position with Benson and Striker Personal Services. They're a big PR firm. Three years later she formed her own company. She was twenty-six. Noble became one of her first clients after shifting away from Benson. Within six months she was under personal contract to Noble, very much the way you are with DataFlex. She's been with Noble for almost twenty years in that role."

"She is the guru of Noble Security and Public Relations. Tell me, did Mario discover her birth name?"

"He did, Andrea Verot. Nothing was known about the birth parents which isn't unusual in an adoption of that time."

"Sounds Cajun."

Andrews sipped his rum. "It does. That's all I've got new on Andrea and work." He slid the chiffon peignoir away from her flat belly revealing the tiny green panty. "Now let's focus on us."

She snuggled closer. "Concentration is good."

They kissed.

He reached the neckline of the peignoir. "There's a string or lint caught up here." He pulled the string holding the garment around her neck. As the peignoir fell away he smiled. "There, now it's gone."

She kissed him. "There's a lot more binding on you," she whispered. "Let's see, this big thing is a belt buckle." As she unfastened it she teased her lips with her tongue. "Oh look, it fell open."

He kissed her. "It's been a long two days."

She slid his polo shirt over his head.

He said, "Babe, I'm more exposed than you."

"I don't think so, but you will be."

She took his hand."

He stood. "Shall we?"

They walked across the living room into the bedroom.

She whispered, "Wait 'til you feel this bed."

"Is it firm? I like firm."

"So do I, but this also massages. Little magic fingers make you feel so good."

He touched her shoulders and arms gently.

She took a deep breath. "Am I feeling little magic fingers?"

"You are and we're not even on the magic bed yet."

She pulled him down on her. "Oh yes we are."
They shared a kiss.

*****

It was late, Francis Dade was in his study watching the late news when his cell phone rang. "Good evening, Andrea. What makes you call at this hour?"

She said, "You know we have the video of Senator DuBois frolicking with Valentine."

"Yes, we are quite pleased." He chuckled. "I don't see this type of video very often but I must admit I look forward to seeing this one."

"You will be surprised."

"I hope so. Miss Valentine is so athletic."

"You know her?"

"Yes, through a special promotional arrangement handled by Ishtar and Carl but nothing that involves you."

Nance paused for a moment. *I've heard rumors for years that Ishtar didn't have sex with you. But she arranges for it? This is strange.* She said, "I'm sure. Keeping track of Noble's Washington connections and lobbying is task enough."

"Yes," he said, "we have many investments in smaller firms outside your purview. But you didn't call at this hour to discuss investments."

"No, the laptop computer used in creating the DuBois sex video was stolen from the hotel room after I left with the flash drive."

"Jesus, somebody has the laptop?"

"Yes."

"Did you delete the material before leaving?"

"Yes, but any expert could retrieve it. Everything we enter stays in the program like a footprint. It never goes away."

"I see. Why was the laptop left in the hotel room?"

"I've never carry obvious incriminating data from monitoring sites other than a flash drive. We've always had the rooms checked out to the individual setting up the equipment and retrieving it afterwards. They use luggage to move the cameras, listening devises and computers – always with complete autonomy. Most important, there is no paper trail from them to us because they use false names, identities, and pay cash."

"If that's the case wouldn't they be picking up the equipment tomorrow?" How do you know of the theft?"

"I had a special pickup of the laptop because it was so sensitive and the appropriations vote is around the corner. The only delay was a false fire alarm which I believe was a cover for the burglary."

"Wasn't your new woman, Santiago, there?"

"Yes, she went to the DuBois room when the alarm went off to make sure he didn't come rambling through the hallway and lobby unless absolutely necessary. The place was full of people, firemen, cops, and press."

"I understand. How long was she on site?"

"Into the evening. She left after our pickup person left my room in disguise. Santiago even described her. She said that was the only person who paid any attention to my room."

He said, "Could Santiago have taken it?"

"I don't think so, and as I said, she was in the senator's room during the alarm."

"Any thoughts on who else it could be?"

"Several, everything from a leak in my own system to a casual burglar that has no clue as to what they've got. Even a member of the hotel staff since the security cameras were off by prearrangement. The theft could be unrelated to us; a media spy, political enemies. I just don't know."

"So you haven't heard anything?"

"Not a word. Tomorrow Santiago goes to Maxwell. I have other people that will investigate this and see who, if anyone, starts flexing muscles on DuBois. If political it won't take long to make a discovery."

"One final question, Andrea. Is Broderick aware of the video?"

"Yes, I shared it with him when he arrived in Washington. He understands how damaging it could be to his future career plans."

"Good. I've never liked the bastard."

"Francis, we both know Ishtar and her father call the shots and they chose DuBois. What you or me or anyone else thinks is secondary. I know if you had your way I wouldn't even be in the company."

Francis swallowed. "Enough said. I'll keep my ears open for anything on this end. I'll also be sharing this with Ishtar in a few minutes."

"Of course. I'm sure she'll be talking with me."

"Good night, Andrea," he said and broke the connection.

Francis walked to the living room and poured a drink. *Maybe now I can persuade Ishtar to remove Andrea from her position of power. I just don't trust her.*

Chapter 12
Friday, July 11

Santiago and Andrews were at the Voodoo Coffee Shop by 8:30 for breakfast. As they ate she checked her watch.

"It's only 6:30 in Chandler. What time do you think Ray will get in?"

"Mitch, I'd bet he's there. This operation is important to him."

"I need background on Yeager and especially Sigmund."

"One thing about you, Mitch, when you're focused on something, nothing distracts you. Ray is the same way."

She smiled. "I thought you did a pretty good job of distracting me last night."

"True, but we worked first then played."

She punched House's burn cell number.

"House."

"Good morning, Ray. I'm calling to see if Mario came up with anything on the project leaders."

"I've been expecting your call. Mario is also here. I'll put this on speaker."

She said, "Okay, but Link will have to lean in and listen on this end. We're in a restaurant."

Mario said, "Mitch, I've been digging deep and found a few interesting things but nothing out of the ordinary."

"Tell me about Sigmund."

"Okay, she's sixty-four, a prodigy, entered university training at fourteen, earned her Ph.D. at MIT by age twenty-three and is a specialist in guidance communication systems. She was part of the teams working several different UAV projects in recent years. Currently she is assigned as leader of a classified project – no data available."

"What about family history?"

"She was married for nine years to Desmond Sigmund, also a scientist and professor of physics. He moved often from one school to another. They divorced over professional differences, whatever that means."

Santiago chuckled. "It means she was she was too equal, probably, so they went their own separate ways."

"Both are highly respected in their fields."

"What about her birth family?"

"I have very little on them. She came from a middle-class family from Boston. She attended public school, took her BA and MA in Physics at Boston College. When she went to MIT she met her husband to be. He was a teaching assistant at the time."

"How did she pay for school?"

"She had a full ride scholarship at every level."

"Smart lady."

"Genius, Mitch, pure genius."

"Any children?"

"None from her marriage. However, we are looking further into relationship she had with a teaching assistant when she was about sixteen."

"What is the surname of her parents?"

"Her foster parents are Alma and Philippe Autry. Acadia's birth name is Acadia Verot."

"You said Verot?"

"Correct."

"Did you explore any further into Acadia's birth family?"

"No, it didn't seem necessary."

"It could be now. Look and see if there is any connection between Andrea Nance and Sigmund. Both have the same Cajun surname."

"Will do. There's something else that might interest Link. Acadia is a golfer, and pretty good from what I've read. She sees the game as the epitome of challenge for any athlete and a defining element of a person's moral fiber. She plays once a week at the Lakewood Golf Club. Her partner for years is a man named Bob Server, an auto mechanic."

"Did you say auto mechanic?"

"Yes."

"Apparently they met some years ago when she went to the course to join some of her workmates for a round and they turned her away. The old 'we're a foursome' routine. Server was a loner that same day and they hooked up. In case you're wondering, they have no other social connection, just golf."

Link got Mitch's attention. "What's her handicap?"

"It says here scratch, whatever that means."

Andrews said, "It means really good."

Santiago chuckled. "That's a good piece of information. What did you find on Alfred Yeager?"

"He comes from a family involved in scientific research and philosophy on both sides. All of his work, undergraduate and graduate was at the California Institute of Technology. And yes, he's another genius caliber scientist. His specialty is nuclear physics. The few notations I've read on him emphasize he's an ego maniac; smart, good at what he does, but ego centric. In each article spread over several years he always mentions he is working at a Nobel caliber and is often held back by the level of his colleagues. However, each article was quick to point out he is an excellent scientist but has very poor social skills."

"In other words, Mario, I do this but I need to be recognized."

"Exactly."

"Do you have anything else?"

"No, but Ray wants to say something."

House said, "We have nothing new on Xavier. He's still missing."

"Ray, I'm sure the police have checked his phone records, but maybe Mario can take an unofficial look. See if he has any calls to New York or Washington. We'll talk again later."

Spears said, "I'm on it when we finish here."

House said, "We'll talk later. Be safe," and broke the connection.

Andrews laughed. "No long goodbye there. I like the golf interest."

"You're thinking of a round with her?"

"Mitch, you never cease to amaze me. I am thinking of a round. I could learn more than a little in the right setting."

"I'll see what I can arrange when I meet her today."

"In the meantime, dear lady, what about your friend the senator? Is he really going to hang around 'til noon?"

"I doubt it," she said and called room 407 at the Augustine Bayou Suites. A soft voice answered. "Good morning, Valentine, Mitch Santiago calling. Is the senator up?"

Valentine laughed. "In more ways than one."

"Would you put him on, please?"

"Good morning pretty lady."

"Same to you, Broderick. You sound chipper. I assume it was a good night?"

"Ah yes, and morning. There's nothing like strawberries dipped in chocolate for breakfast with a beautiful woman."

"Thank you for sharing that tidbit. Andrea had me book a flight for you back to Washington for midday. I've already contacted your security man. He'll be at the back entry and return you to the Cajun Lady Boutique until flight time. He has all of the details and boarding passes for both of you. Valentine will walk you to the back entry, but will leave the hotel by the front door."

"Walk down four flights of stairs?"

"There'll be little or no foot traffic on the stairs. At this hour more than a few folks could be heading to breakfast or checkout on the elevator."

"Stairs it is. I certainly hope we meet in Washington, Mitch."

"One can never tell."

*****

Jerome Xavier sat at the small round table near the window of the Mountain Boy Motel reading the 'Welcome to Branson' tourist guide. He glanced up to see a colorful vehicle drive by full of tourists. A plethora of signs covered the sides of what looked like an old World War II vintage Navy J2F DUCK amphibian advertising music shows, restaurants, and more. He shook his head. "That's a time traveler."

He laughed and looked into the wall mirror. "Here I am stayin' in the Mountain Boy Motel, dumpy at best, on Boxcar Willie Drive. Maybe I'm the throwback in time. I'm sure not anywhere I've been before."

He poured a cup of motel coffee. "I've covered a lot of ground in one day. Hitching to Tucson, fly to Wichita and then Springfield, a bus to here. I'm tired, gotta be, I'm talkin' to myself and not even gettin' good answers."

He looked back at the tourist guide. In the center was a city map. "Now where are the libraries?" He ran a thumb across the map. "Yes, the Miller Branch on East Main by Sycamore, that'll do."

He called his secretary, Linda Drake using a burn cell he had purchased in Wichita. "Good morning, I wasn't even sure you'd be in yet."

Drake said, "Jerome, where are you?"

"Right now I'm out of Arizona. Do you still have the burn cell we use when Canfield or I are doing special things?"

"Yes."

"Is it charged?"

"Yes."

"Hang up, I'll call you right back."

When the cell rang she answered quickly. "The police are looking for you. Canfield is dead."

"I know. He tried to kill me. He has other people who want me dead, too. That's why Thelonious came by, to give me a new ID."

"What are you going to do?"

"I need to find the people trying to kill me. If I don't they'll eventually kill me or the cops will find me. Then I end up in prison for life or get killed on the inside."

"How are you going to find them?"

"I need you to take a look at Canfield's phone log. See who he talked to, where, calls out of the ordinary. You know the people we call regularly. I want the unusual numbers, maybe in a cluster."

"That'll take a few minutes."

"I'll wait. I haven't a thing to do."

A few minutes later Linda Drake came back on the line.

"Jerome, I have three 917 New York City numbers and two 202's, that's Washington D.C. While I think of it he also had me get an Apache Junction number for him, an Eduardo Santiago."

He quickly wrote the numbers down.

"Linda, you know where the wall safe in the reception area behind the kid's picture is located and you have the combination?"

"Yes."

"Have the police looked at it?"

"No, they never looked for it. They searched your office and Canfield's. They've sealed them both."

"But not your area?"

"No, I suspect they have a trace and are waiting for you to call."

"There's a mean looking big guy, a black-white mixture, who was looking for Canfield. He was in just before Thelonious came to see me. Has he been back in?"

"The only people that have been in are a few clients wondering about how their cases will be handled and the police. No strangers."

"He will be. I want you gone. In the safe you'll find $30,000 in hundreds. Take the money, call it severance pay, and leave. I believe that man is dangerous and would not hesitate to hurt or kill you. I know it's just a feeling I have, but I'm in the business and he was easy to spot."

"Will I hear from you again?"

"I hope so. First I need to solve this problem. Linda, go on vacation. Just get out of town. You'll know when all is done. I don't want you to get hurt. I couldn't deal with that. Take the money and get out now."

"I'm on my way, Jerome. If you need me call. I'll keep this cell. I'll miss the good times we had even if

Canfield didn't like it. You're a special man." She kissed the receiver and the call ended.

He looked at the New York numbers and dialed the first one. "Let's see who you were talking to, Canfield."

An automatic operator voice came on the line. "The number you have reached is out of service. Please check the number and dial again."

"Damn."

He dialed the second number in New York. The result was the same. "Damn burn cells."

He dialed the third New York number.

"The Noble Group, how may I direct your call?"

"Sorry, wrong number," he said and hung up. "That's one bingo."

He tried the first D.C. number. "I'm sorry, the number...." He slammed the receiver down. The second D.C. number yielded the same result.

He jotted Noble, New York, and D.C. on the tourist guide. "What is the Noble Group?" The husky voiced woman called me from Washington. Santiago is connected to her."

Xavier dialed the Apache Junction number.

A man with an older sounding voice answered, "Hello."

"Mr. Santiago, I'm Max White, a friend of Michelle's. I'm tryin' to reach her about a job she may be interested in but she isn't answering her phone."

"Did you try her cell?"

"No, I don't have it."

"Well, it's not important. She has a new job."

"Already?"

"She went to work for someone called Noble. She's in New Orleans right now."

"Do you know where she's staying?"

"Nope, but she's got a job."

"I'll try some of her other friends."

"Who'd you say you are?"

"Max White. Would you happen to have her cell number?"

"Son, I don't give that information out. You'll catch up with her eventually. 'Til then goodbye, Mr. White." Eduardo Santiago hung up. "Damn fool, all her friends call her Mitch."

Xavier walked around the motel room then back to the small table. "Santiago is with Noble in New Orleans. Canfield talked with Noble in New York. The Husky voiced woman in Washington ordered the surveillance of Santiago."

He dialed the operator and asked for the number of the Noble Group in Washington. When the operator gave him the number he smiled. "Noble's in Washington, too, along with the husky voiced woman."

Xavier booked a flight from Springfield to New Orleans, ordered a taxi and checked out. He waited patiently for his ride. "You're the answer Santiago. I find you, I find them. First the library for a little research on Noble, then the Big Easy."

*****

Santiago and Andrews arrived at Maxwell Cyber Systems together. Lilith Towne met them at the security entrance.

Santiago said, "Lilith Towne, my special friend Link Andrews, a member of the DataFlex security team but on vacation."

Towne smiled. "Mr. Andrews, a pleasure. It must be a DataFlex moment. Your associate, Mr. Evans arrived a few minutes ago."

He laughed. "Must be, but I'm here to spend a few days with Mitch. We often worked together until a few days ago."

A guard approached. "Mr. Andrews, if you'd accompany this man he'll take you to screening. Then we can provide you a visitor pass allowing you access to the DataFlex area based on their clearance. I'm sure Miss Santiago has told you her other assignment is classified on a need to know basis."

Andrews nodded. "Yes she has." He looked at Santiago. "Maybe I'll see you at lunch. Sam will be surprised to see me."

Santiago said, "Lunch sounds good." She looked back to Towne. "Am I clear to visit the work stations and laboratory?"

"You are," said Towne handing over a top security clearance for Reaper and Barrier with a chuckle. "Some of the crew will be disappointed. They've heard about your leggy outfit yesterday."

"That was for my other assignment."

"You're going to kill some of their enthusiasm, but the skirt is just long enough to conceal the thigh holster and still looks great. I have the same thing."

"I noticed."

"Who would you like to meet first?"

"Doctor Yeager and his team."

After going through the eye-scan the two women went into an observation area. Towne pointed. "There he is shuffling about as always."

"He doesn't leave much time for feedback, does he?"

"No, he's more the directive type. His colleagues joke about him not caring for other opinions or points of view."

"I read something about that in his background review."

"All true. Want to go in?"

"Yes."

"I'll leave you on your own. He's expecting you. I may see you before you go to Reaper. If not, use the same process to get through security. Everyone on Reaper is also expecting you and the project leader, Doctor Sigmund is much more enjoyable."

Santiago said, "I'll keep that in mind," and entered the area.

Yeager peered over his dark brown frame thick glasses. "You are Miss Santiago, the new Noble person?"

"Yes, it is a pleasure to meet you, Doctor Yeager," she said extending a hand. "Please call me Mitch."

"Yes, and you may call me Doctor Yeager. First let's get a lab coat for you. Everyone in my lab must wear a lab coat."

"As you say, Doctor Yeager." *So much for warm and friendly.*

After she put on a lab coat he said, "Now tell me, do you have a background in physics?"

"No, I'm a lobbyist with background in law and media."

"I see, another pretty face for politicians to ogle. Let me give you a two minute physics lesson. My task is to develop the ultimate hacker-proof cyber key. Others are working on similar tasks in various places around the world such as Zurich and Los Alamos."

"I understand."

"I doubt that, but hopefully you'll understand me. A quantum object's energy is discrete, very small, finite if you please. Each object has particle and wave-like behavior but only one or the other is observable at any given moment, never both simultaneously. My team is developing a process designed for use as a hacker-proof password. To do so we are developing a program to create the perfect particle wave-length into a single qubit that cannot be duplicated or hacked. Simply put, if someone tries to enter a different password the gate crashes."

"If I'm understanding you correctly, Doctor Yeager, the key and the lock become one and the same and no other combination can be used to enter the program, and once used the code can't be used again. I also read that entanglement cannot be used meaning the code can never be broken."

"That is very good for a beginner. I appreciate someone who studies before interviewing me. Given the randomness of quantum physics duplication is virtually impossible." He scanned the workstations. "My team is expecting you so feel free to move about and ask questions. However, keep in mind their time is limited."

"Thank you, Doctor Yeager."

Michelle began to circulate. At the first station she approached a woman in her late thirties or early forties studying a printout. She looked up and said, "Hello, I'm Heather Robbins."

"I'm Mitch Santiago. I'm with...."

"Noble, Alfred told us to expect you."

"Is that good or bad?"

"You'll see as you learn your way around his lab and Doctor Sigmund's next door. But welcome."

"Have you been on Barrier since the beginning?"

"Close. I joined the team a month into the initial research when another member left over professional differences. "

"Doctor Yeager noted several different groups are competing for a hacker proof password program."

"That's true. Ours is a commercial venture with government blessing, as are several others. Doctor Yeager believes we'll not only complete our program faster but will have a superior product; highly profitable, and with original research that will bring him a Nobel Prize."

"He's ambitious."

"To say the least." Robbins looked Santiago in the eyes. "You're here as Tony's replacement?"

"No, but I knew him when I worked for DataFlex. Did you know him?"

"Heavens yes, a nice man and bit of a flirt. We all liked him. His death was so senseless."

Santiago said, "He was killed in Washington wasn't he?"

"A mugging. God, and at the Vietnam Memorial."

"We worked together a few times. We were good friends."

Robbins glanced at Santiago and smiled. "I'm sure you were."

"It's been nice meeting you, Heather, but I need to circulate a bit more before upsetting Doctor Yeager."

Robbins laughed. "Don't worry about that. You upset him when you walked in the door. I got the same routine, a lab jacket to cover a skirt he thinks is too short and distracting to the guys." She laughed. "In your case he's probably right."

Santiago smiled and moved on. She approached a very tall black man with longish grey hair. "Hello, Doctor Bayoumi, Mitch Santiago," she said holding out a hand.

"Anwar," he said in a deep voice. "A pleasure. Doctor Yeager said we were having a guest." He took her hand. "It is a pleasure to meet you."

"Actually I work here. I'm the new PR representative for Noble."

"I know. You're replacing Miss Nance and we're also expecting someone to replace Mr. Mercedes."

She said, "It is a time of change. I knew Tony from my time with DataFlex. Did you know him?"

"Not really. He got on well with all of us in a professional sense. He and Robbin often talked. I don't know about what. A man in my position doesn't get too close."

"Your position?"

"I'm a black man from Ghana. I have a Ph.D. in nuclear physics but I'm still an outsider, even in the science community here the United States." He looked her in the eyes. "I see you're multi-cultural. Hopefully you've not experienced that kind of rejection."

"No, I haven't."

Doctor Yeager called out to the Barrier Team, "Listen up people, I have an update due for the directors of Maxwell, Noble and DataFlex tomorrow morning. Today let's do lunch as we work. Remember, when we are successful we'll be rewarded relative to our contribution. I expect great things. Someday you may even get a lead on a sensitive project. For now, let's eat. Those needing to pick-up lunch in the cafeteria go now so you can avoid any line."

Bayoumi smiled. "Mitch, if you want to learn a little about your friend Tony eat lunch in the cafeteria with Heather," he said with a nod. "She had more than a passing interest in him."

"I will when I get the chance, but I guess that won't be today."

"Heather hears her own drummer. She'll be there. She eats with friends from Reaper and Yeager doesn't seem to intimidate her."

"Thank you, Anwar. I look forward to working with you and learning more about Barrier."

He laughed. "I'm sure Doctor Yeager wants all the publicity you can generate for him."

She said, "The titles of PR and lobbyist do have their attractions." She smiled. "Off to lunch."

On her way to the cafeteria she called Andrews. His message file opened. "Link, I'll be working the cafeteria today. See you at dinner. Love you."

*****

Kat Parsons sat in her DataFlex cubicle. She tapped the desk with her fingers and feet, shifted in the chair, and looked at the partition separating her space from what had been Vladimir's area. She scratched a small insect bite on her arm. *How can Vladimir be dead? Mexican Mafia, bull. That had to be Xavier.* She sipped her up to now untouched latte, picked up the phone, and dialed.

"Security, how may I direct your call?"

"I'm Kat Parsons in accounting. I need to talk to Mr. House about Vladimir Clyburn."

"One moment."

"Ray house speaking. What can I do for you, Miss Parsons?"

"Mr. House, I need to talk with you about," she sniffed, "Vladimir Clyburn."

House pulled up her file on his screen as she spoke.

"You sound stressed Miss Parsons. I know you worked with Vladimir. Were you and he good friends?"

"Yes."

"Tell me what you need to share."

"Not on the phone, please. It's private, very private."

"I see you're in accounting. I have some business over there. Could we talk in about fifteen minutes?"

"Yes, but not in my cubicle, please."

"I'll see you then."

House stepped to Jessica Rodriquez's office. "Can you be interrupted?"

She laughed. "I work for you, don't I?"

"I want you to sit in on a meeting I have with Kat Parsons in a few minutes."

Rodriguez said, "Kat Parsons in accounting?"

"You're ahead of me."

"I've been looking at her work because of the leak."

House dialed the business office. "I need a conference room over there in fifteen minutes."

The clerk confirmed the request.

As they walked to the business office Rodriguez talked about Parsons. "I've found inconsistencies in records she has accessed, records outside of her purview."

He said, "Such as."

"Most recently, Mitch's payroll records and insurance. Prior to that, bidding files and information."

They walked into the business office. He asked the receptionist to call Miss Parsons to the conference room. "Keep it private. No interruptions."

A few minutes later Kat Parsons arrived.

"Miss Parsons, this is Jessica Rodriguez, my Administrative Assistant. We are working together on the issue of Vladimir's death."

The three of them sat down at a round table equally spaced from each other. Parsons tapped her nails and began shifting her feet. She looked first at House then Rodriguez.

House said, "Kat, we're here to listen. I can see Vladimir's death has been painful for you."

Rodriguez said, "Take your time, a few deep breaths. We're in no rush."

"Thank you. Vladimir and I would talk sometimes. It was like we always wanted to say things, but couldn't quite decide who was going to escape their shyness first. It's like waiting for a green light but it never seems to come."

Rodriguez glanced at House and said, "I'm sure most of us suffer those tongue tied moments, especially approaching someone we're attracted to on multiple levels. I've been there."

Parsons continued. "Vladimir and I were friends, more than work friends. He was a private man but cared about people."

Parsons's eyes welled. Rodriguez went to a cabinet and retrieved a box of tissues.

Parsons took one. "Thank you. A few days ago he heard me talking to a man on the phone. Our cubicles are beside each other."

Rodriguez started to speak but House shook his head.

Parsons took a deep breath and sniffed again. Her voice dropped. "I was talking about one of the people that worked here."

House said, "What did he want to know?"

"He wanted to know if Michelle Santiago still worked here."

House said, "What did you tell him?"

"That she'd been terminated, dropped from the payroll and her benefits canceled as of the end of the month."

House nodded. "I see. Did you tell him anything else?"

"I told him about the rumors everybody is talking about."

Rodriguez said, "Rumors?"

"You know, about her and Mr. Braun. Everybody knows about them. Most women I work with don't believe she was sleeping with him. A few are envious."

House said, "Who was the man you were giving the information to?"

"The man who is missing. He was on the news, Jerome Xavier. I think he killed Vladimir."

House said, "Why?"

"A few years ago I accessed my sister's credit report and banking records. She was being bothered by a collection service. Mr. Xavier was going to help her. He did make them stop but he began to blackmail me. If I didn't give him information he'd expose me to the police. I'd lose my job and go to jail."

Rodriguez said, "Did Xavier ever indicate where the information was going?"

"No, he never said how he was using it. Sometimes I wouldn't hear from him for months." Parsons began to cry. "Now Vladimir is dead and it's my fault."

House said, "Why do you say you killed him?"

"He wanted to talk to Xavier and make him leave me alone. He promised not to see him until we talked that night. But he didn't come over and now he's dead."

House took Parsons by the hand. "Kat, the people that did this will be caught. I know it won't bring Vladimir back but a least you'll have some closure."

"Mr. House, do you think more than one person is responsible for his death?"

"I don't know for sure, but from what you've told us Xavier was working for somebody."

Rodriguez said, "Kat, I'm going to call the authorities. You need to talk with them."

Parsons lowered her chin and looked at the table. "I know."

House said, "Jessica will help you. I have some other things I must attend to."

He left the building and went to Spears cubicle in security.

"Mario, I need you to check Kat Parsons activities in accounting; what files she accessed, when, are other companies involved, go back two years. Check her banking, too, if you can."

"Anything else?"

"I want to know of anything that involves the Noble Group or any politicians that surface. And Mario, be careful, we have a mole in security."

Chapter 13

Santiago went to the Maxwell cafeteria and walked through the lunch line. She selected a chicken salad, ice tea, and oven baked chips. After paying she walked into the seating area. She spotted a group of three woman including Heather Robbins from Barrier. The other two were new to her. She approached the table and asked, "May I join you? I'm new here."

Robbins looked up. "Of course. Ladies, this is the new member of the Noble Team. She'll be standing in for Andrea who is off to D.C. I believe Andrea said you're Mitch Santiago."

"Yes," she said sitting down.

A lady with long blond curls in her thirties said, "I'm Susan Train from the Reaper Project, and this is my associate Joyce Riggs."

"It's a pleasure, ladies. I'll be spending some time in Reaper after lunch. Doctor Yeager has already made it obvious his team is busy."

Robbins laughed. "We're always busy with his reports. He spends more time advertising himself than he does on the research and development of Barrier."

The other women nodded.

Robbins added, "He isn't known as Doctor Humble for nothing."

Riggs pursed her lips. "Mitch, word is you worked for DataFlex before joining Noble."

"True but company politics got in the way."

Riggs continued, "So you knew Tony Mercedes?"

"Yes, in fact at DataFlex I worked security. We did a couple of assignments together."

"Did you do much socializing on the outside?"

I hear a little concern. "No, ours was a professional relationship." Santiago laughed. "As a matter of fact my social relationship is in town right now to visit for a few days. I just left DataFlex."

Susan Train said, "Did Tony have many lady friends?"

Santiago looked at Train. "A few. He was a handsome man and liked the ladies. I'm sure he hit on you a few times."

Riggs eyes welled. "We were close friends, very close."

Santiago watched Riggs eyes. "That would be Tony, heavy on the casual, but a nicer man you'd never find, just not monogamous, but then how many people are?"

Susan Train smiled. "A minority today."

Santiago laughed. "I know a lot of ladies that wondered how good he was in bed."

Train looked at Riggs. "I hear he was really good."

Santiago changed the subject. "So you both are working Reaper?"

Train said, "Yes, and I see you have clearance for it."

Santiago nodded. "I couldn't visit if I didn't."

Train smiled. "You're in PR and a lobbyist?"

"Yes."

Train continued, "But you did security at Data-Flex?"

"Yes, and before that I was a homicide detective in Seattle. I move around a lot."

Riggs said, "You're from Seattle? I'm from the bay area originally."

Santiago said, "Before Chandler I lived in Seattle. However, my parents spent many years between San Francisco and Big Sur. Obviously my sister and I did, too. We were raised in a very colorful environment."

Riggs said, "It was the time of the Hippies."

Santiago said, "Oh yes."

Riggs nodded. "Me too."

Santiago watched her face. "Joyce, you have a Ph.D. in physics. Did you attend Stanford?"

Riggs laughed. "No, Berkeley, center of the universe." She paused. "You know, I really miss him."

"Obviously you and Tony were more than close. Let me assure you he never played the field while going with someone. Like all of us, he'd notice a good looking woman very much the way we do a guy, but he was a one woman man."

Riggs said, "You mean one at a time."

"Yes. I'm sorry for your loss, Joyce. I didn't believe it when I first heard about it from Andrea. I didn't want to believe it."

Riggs swallowed and checked her watch. "I'll take you in if you like. Acadia, I mean Doctor Sigmund, is a wonderful and smart woman. Shall we?"

*****

Wolfe arrived at the offices of Kohler and Xavier during mid-morning. The outer office door was locked, lights off. After putting on his leather driving gloves he picked the lock. Once inside he saw the private offices of Kohler and Xavier were sealed. *Why only the interior offices sealed? They're probably hoping Xavier will come in. That could mean a stakeout.*

The outer office was closed and no activity was in the hall. He checked the phone call history on the receptionist desk and found several calls to New York, Washington D.C. and one each to Kansas and Missouri. All the others were Phoenix area calls. He copied the out of state numbers. In the old Rolodex file he found the Kansas number again along with a name and address.

Wolfe quickly scanned the office noticing the painting of children was ajar on one wall. Closer inspection revealed a safe behind it, also unlocked. He checked for contents. "Empty." He heard some talking in the hallway and held his breath. In a moment it was gone. *I've got to get out of here.*

At the exit door he listened as sweat began to form on his forehead and cheeks. *Still quiet.* He opened the door just a crack and looked down the hallway, then wider so he could see the opposite direction. *Empty.* He stepped into the hallway and closed the door. A moment later he was in the elevator on his way to the lobby. As the door opened he wiped his face with a handkerchief and stepped out. He removed his gloves, went to the lobby coffee shop, and ordered ice tea. *I'm getting too old for this stuff.*

Wolfe dialed the Wichita number.

"Thank you for calling Beam Photo Studios, Ned speaking."

In a soft voice he said, "Hello, Ned, my name is Wolfe."

"How may I help you, Mr. Wolfe?"

"Jerome Xavier contacted you yesterday."

"I don't recall a Jerome Xavier."

"Now Ned, that's not true. I'm sitting here looking at a record of his phone calls. I don't know if you're aware of it or not but Xavier is wanted for the murder of his partner, Canfield Kohler."

"I run a respectable business."

"Of course you do, Ned."

"You can't just call me up and demand information. You need a warrant."

Good, he thinks I'm the law. "Ned, I wouldn't want you to do anything you find unethical. That's why I called you first. I'm sure you noticed I'm calling from Phoenix."

"What do you mean, first?"

"Well, I have people just down the street from you prepared to wait for a warrant. Of course they will come in your door in a matter of a few minutes and close you down while they wait. The warrant they will serve you with covers many things including false identification papers, false passports, fake credit cards, stolen histories, and all of the records and equipment used to produce same. I would think at best you'll be out of business while your phone records, shipping records, and files are searched."

"Wait, wait a minute. I'd be closed for quite a time."

"Of course you would, even if they found nothing. Rather than spend all that time and money looking for one set of false identification and possibly finding many more I thought, as a good citizen, maybe you could help me. I guess I was wrong."

"You said Xavier, Jerome Xavier?"

"Yes."

"Just a minute. I'm looking."

"Be very careful, Ned. Give him up and you stay in business, otherwise the local boys drop in."

"Xavier, Xavier, ah, now I see he did call. He must have talked with one of my staff."

"Ned, let's cut the bullshit. What name did you give him?"

Beam swallowed. "Sydney Loomis."

"Is that a new name?"

"No, he used it once before about ten years ago. I also updated the credit cards and passport."

"Good, now we're getting someplace. Where was he going?"

"He didn't say. He was in a hurry to catch a flight. We met at the airport. He got the ID and ran to the TSA line."

"I see."

"If it helps the only flight leaving around that time was for Springfield, Missouri. That's all I know." He paused and swallowed. "Are we good?"

"Yes, Ned, we won't be visiting today."

A sigh came over the receiver and Wolfe broke the connection. *Dumb Shit. You and Thelonious would make a great pair.*

Wolfe dialed the Branson number.

"Mountain Boy Motel, the hillbilly heaven of the Ozarks."

Wolfe said, "Mr. Greene's room, please."

"One moment. I'm sorry, we don't have a Mr. Greene staying with us."

Wolfe laughed. "My error, I'm reading business referrals. I meant Sydney Loomis."

Please hold." A moment later the clerk was back on the line. "I'm sorry, your friend checked out about an hour ago."

"Darn, did he say where he was heading next?"

"No sir."

"Thank you."

Wolfe called Nance.

Her first words were, "Did you find Xavier?"

"No, but I'm sure he's tracking somebody. Does he have any association with you or Noble?"

"Mitch Santiago, he was tailing her for me. It was his last assignment."

"Where is she now?"

"Mitch is her nickname. She's working security for me at Maxwell Cyber Systems in New Orleans. I have her listed as PR and lobbyist."

"That's where Xavier is heading and so am I. He's trying to find who put the contract out on him. I suspect he believes it to be the only way he'll survive."

Nance paused for a moment. "I'm her boss. We can't let him get hold of her."

"He won't get that far."

"If it even seems possible, kill her."

"I will if necessary. Xavier will be a statistic in a day or two. He'll look for your lady, Mitch, and she in turn will be my magnet for Xavier. I'll next be calling from New Orleans."

*****

When Michelle Santiago cleared security at Reaper she approached a middle aged woman in a lab coat. "Doctor Sigmund, I'm Mitch Santiago, the new...."

"You're the new kid on the block. Andrea told me you were coming. You're younger than most Noble types. She left out you looked like a model. It's a good thing we're all women in here. I still recall the turmoil when Mr. Mercedes would visit Barrier if any of the girls saw him."

Santiago blushed. "You know what they say Doctor Sigmund, it's PR."

"Honey, I'm Acadia and from New Orleans. What they say here and in DC is sex sells. You'll be in Washington before you get unpacked."

Both women laughed.

Santiago said, "You don't have a noticeable accent."

"I've lived all over the country and parts of Europe for years. You lose it after a spell, but if I'm here long enough it'll be back."

"What can you tell me about the project?"

"You're here so your security is cleared. The Reaper Guidance Modification Program's target is prevent terrorists from taking over the control of a UAV Reaper after launch. If such takeover did occur, we'll be able to reclaim control."

Santiago nodded. "In other words learning how someone takes control of a drone, how to prevent it, and if necessary how to regain control before its mission is altered."

"Correct. Our government is concerned terrorists, drug dealers, human traffickers, foreign governments and more are working feverishly to create an override control program of an airborne UAV."

Santiago shook her head. "They could reprogram and our forces become the target."

"Exactly. In today's world we use UAV's in many ways including overseas and at home. They serve as missile launch platforms, reconnaissance of military targets and our boarders, traffic control, forest fires, farming, an endless list. Obviously not all are armed, but each could be highly destructive in the wrong hands."

"It comes to mind if smugglers had drones on the US-Mexican border drugs and guns would have another avenue."

Sigmund chuckled. "Drones are used for some of that today. They're small and the range is limited. We don't want to make life any easier for the smugglers."

"Then control of drones, armed or not, is the real issue"

"Yes. Let's go into the workstation area."

As they entered Santiago saw a Reaper on display and the work stations surrounded it.

"Does the craft carry a self-destruct component?"

"Yes, but if taken over it may not function. Our access would be terminated. That is one of the reasons we are working to modify the guidance system and all related elements."

"Acadia, are armed drones ever flown in the US?"

"I can't say for sure but I know it has been discussed."

"If armed drones were taken over stateside they could cause incredible damage and fear."

Sigmund nodded. "It would be 9-11 all over again, even worse."

"What are your researchers doing currently?"

"Testing varying approaches to find ways into the guidance system and then ways to prevent each."

"Are all the control programs of current Reapers the same?"

"Somewhat, but not necessarily. Think of what we're doing as similar to safecracking. The object is to open the safe, but safes are not all the same, however once inside it's yours."

"Can we walk through the area of workstations without disrupting Joyce and Susan?"

"Of course. As you can see we have large screens monitoring each station but visible to anyone in the lab. They let us work with each other problem solving, testing, checking outcomes, helping in many aspects of our work without running about."

Santiago watched a screen for moment. "I'll bet the openness and knowledge of what is occurring at each station nurtures collegiality and a relaxed atmosphere."

"It does here. That wouldn't be true everywhere."

As they walked past the mockup Reaper displayed in the lab Santiago said, "Acadia, could someone take-over a UAV, land it at a different site, and rearm or maybe reprogram it?"

"It's been rumored the Iranians got one some years back. It appeared in pristine condition although they said it was shot down. If landed then others already have the ability to take over control of a drone which makes ours and Doctor Yeager's work much more important."

"Where would one locate the technicians or pilots that control the Reaper?"

"They could be anywhere. For example, some drone flights in the Middle East are controlled from Nellis and Creed Air Force Bases in Nevada, others from Fort Huachuca in Arizona. I'm sure if the Iranians have a control center it would be somewhere in their country."

Santiago shook her head. "God, there's big targets all over the US. I'm from the Phoenix area and the first thing that leaps in mind is the Palo Verde Nuclear power plant for total damage, or the big crowds at Chase Field for sheer terror. It's spooky."

"Yes it is and the closer the drone is to the target when taken over the smaller the window to regain control or intercept. The more you think about it the scarier it gets. That's why we must succeed. Let's get a cup of coffee."

At the Maxwell cafeteria they got their coffee. Sigmund selected a table off in a corner. She took a deep breath. "You know, Mitch, sometimes it's nice to just walk away. I never thought I'd be doing this when I was a student."

"What did you foresee?"

"My associates and I changing the world through the technology explosion, improving the quality of life for humanity, not perfecting missile launching platforms."

"You are improving the quality of life in a way."

"I suppose, but not the way I envisioned." She laughed. "I still recall one of my professors telling us the military is the mother of invention. It seems he had a point."

"Acadia, you said you were from New Orleans."

"Yes, I lived on the edge of the Garden District. We could see the rich people and their big houses in all their splendor, but kids in an orphanage don't get to touch them."

"You did something right."

"I had good teachers and the people at the home, if you want to call it that. They were good and cared more about us than outsiders give credit for."

"I read in your profile you have 164 IQ. That can't hurt."

"You've been doing your homework. I've known some smart people that either didn't use what God gave them or nobody helped them develop it when they were kids."

"You were fortunate, especially in your setting."

"We had a custodian that taught me more about people and ethics than anyone. He taught me to play golf at a public course that gave free time the orphanage. Learning to hit the ball correctly didn't seem as hard as it should, probably because I was just a kid. The only golfers I saw were on television and they were pretty good. But the rules of golf are something else. By themselves they are simple. The part that is challenging is to be honest. Do you play?"

"No, but my closest friend does."

"In golf the player calls the penalties on themselves even if nobody else knows you broke the rule. None of this instant replay crap, just mark it on your scorecard and continue. An honest golfer is an ethical and moral person beyond reproach."

"What's your favorite course now days?"

"I play every Saturday at Lakewood Golf Club."

"Are you in a set foursome?"

"No, I have a partner. We've played as a twosome for years. He has Saturday off so we have a standing tee time."

"Ever consider a third player."

Acadia smiled. "I take it your man is here."

"Yes."

"Have him give me a call. It's always enjoyable to meet a new friend. Tell him Lakewood is on General Degaulle Drive. It's easy to find."

"I'll do that."

"Have you met Alfred yet?"

"Yes."

"How would you sum up his project? I ask because if he successfully completes his mission it will no longer be possible to access protected programs, a good thing."

"He explained it as a scientist would, somewhat technical. My layman view is if someone tries to hack into a program and does not have the correct password the first time, there is no second chance. I believe the window crashes closing access."

"You're close enough for a layman and the press."

"Thank you."

"Mitch, if you talk to Joyce and Tony's name comes up please be sensitive. The two of them had a relationship of sorts."

"Thank you for the heads up. She brought Tony up over lunch when she found out we had worked together at DataFlex."

"Well, I best get back to work or there'll be no golf tomorrow."

"I'll have Link call you."

"Link, the perfect name for a golfer."

Santiago finished her coffee. *I need to know everything possible on Joyce Riggs.*

*****

Link Andrews was with Sam Evans at Barrier when Mario Spears called. He listened carefully to the newest discoveries regarding Andrea Nance. "I'll be damned. Thanks Mario."

He called Santiago.

She answered immediately. "What's up?"

"Mario had some new information for you and couldn't get your cell."

"Tell me."

"It's possible Ishtar and Andrea are related."

"You've got to be kidding. I'm already trying to figure out if Andrea and Sigmund are relatives."

"No, for real. Ishtar's family name on her birth certificate is Verot. Andrea's birth name is Verot."

"Jesus, Sigmund's birth name is Verot. This could be bazar as sin."

"It gets better, babe. All of the evidence Mario found indicates Ishtar's mother and Nance's mother were sisters put up for adoption when their parents were killed in a swamp boat accident."

"The scenario fits. Did the sisters know of each other?"

"Not as far as we know. Adoption files were sealed."

"How did Mario get this information?"

"It was something connected to security clearances."

"How old were the sisters when Ishtar was adopted?"

"I can still hear the cop in you," he said with a laugh. "Ishtar was the baby by a few minutes. All either one would know later in life is they had a sibling."

"Was the older sister also adopted?"

"No, she was raised in an orphanage."

"And you're speculating Ishtar's sister is the mother of Andrea?"

"I am now, Mitch. Andrea was also placed in an orphanage and put up for adoption but was raised by a foster family named Autry. The agency, state or orphanage have no record of Andrea probing her origins."

"I'm probing. If they're related Ishtar's sister would probably be Andrea's mother. Now I need to find out who knows what."

"Look at the bright side, Mitch. Maybe Verot is a Cajun version of Smith."

Santiago laughed. "That would be nice. Otherwise we have the potential of three different people being month-daughter-aunt. I don't need more confusion. If everything plays out the way we're speculating Acadia and Ishtar are sisters and one is Nance's mom."

"Well, Mitch, you definitely have a new level of interest."

"I do. This is most intriguing. One other thing while I have your attention. Doctor Sigmund would like you to call about a golf game tomorrow." She gave him Sigmund's number.

"Now we're getting somewhere."

"And Link, she prefers to be called Acadia."

*****

When Jerome Xavier arrived in New Orleans he rented a red Ford Fusion and took a room at the Moss Back Motel. He immediately called Maxwell Cyber Systems. "I'm Jack Tracy, a writer for the Cyber Journal. I would like to speak to a Miss Sanford. I believe she works on site with the Noble Group."

"Mr. Tracy, we do not have a Miss Sanford working on site with any of our associate companies. You probably want Miss Santiago. She is the PR spokesperson for Noble."

"You could be correct but before I contact her I best check my own sources and make sure she is the right person. Lord knows nobody wants to be embarrassed, but thanks for your help."

He found driving directions to Maxwell on a map in the motel office. It was mid-afternoon traffic on Old Gentilly Road all the way to the entrance at Maxwell. He found a parking place with a view of the entry and pulled in.

Now I'll wait. You'll eventually come out or go in. Either way we'll connect, bitch. You'll tell me who the husky voiced woman is. That's all I want from you. I get them out of my life and disappear.

Within an hour of Xavier's arrival in New Orleans, Wolfe landed at Louis Armstrong and took a cab to the Hilton Garden Inn New Orleans French Quarter where he had made a reservation. Once in his room he stepped to the window and watched the city. "It's into rush hour. I best get going."

He unpacked the metal lockbox from his suitcase and checked the Ruger SR9 center fire. He slid it into the waistband at the back of his slacks and checked his watch again. "3:30."

At the Hilton entry he caught a cab and headed for Maxwell Cyber Systems. "Driver, it's on Old Gentilly Road."

"Yes sir," said the driver.

Wolfe could feel the humidity of the city compared to his recent few days in Phoenix. "Pretty sticky here today."

"Every day, sir. We're approaching Maxwell's entry. Where would you like to be let out?"

"Just drop me at the coffee shop coming up on our right. I can always cross when I want, but a bite to eat sounds pretty good."

The cabbie pulled off and dropped Wolfe. "Tony Joe's Coffee Bar is a good place, sir."

Wolfe said, "Thank you," and tipped the driver twenty dollars.

Once inside he scanned the small shop, went to a window seat and ordered a black Café Americano. Several patrons were at small tables working vigorously with laptops, readers, iPads, notebooks, and phones. He took his phone out and checked for messages. The coffee arrived and he sipped it as he watched the street while scanning parked cars, vans, and trucks. *You're here somewhere Xavier. You wait for Santiago and I wait for you, show yourself.*

After an hour he stretched his legs and stood. He left Tony Joe's and walked the sidewalk still on the opposite side of the Old Gentilly Road from Maxwell's. As he passed the entry across from Maxwell's parking lot a truck pulled away from the curb. In the car behind the truck was a man sitting, watching. Wolfe crossed the street at the light. As he stepped on the sidewalk a blue Terrill's Taxi pulled into the entryway. A young attractive woman rushed out of the building and got into the waiting cab which quickly reentered the evening rush. He watched as the red Fusion left the curb. He looked at the driver. "Hello, Xavier."

Wolfe hailed a passing cab. When he got in he told the driver to follow the red Fusion now stopped at a light two cars behind the Terrill's Taxi.

"I'll do my best, sir."

They followed the Fusion to Jackson Square. When the taxi stopped and let the woman out Xavier was stopped on the corner of Chartres waiting to make a free right onto Peter. The woman went into the condominium. Xavier made his turn but there was no available parking and he drove past the building.

Wolfe exited his cab and walked toward the entry of the Frenchman Condominium. *He'll be back.*

As he approached the door the woman and a man came out of the building. The doorman tipped his hat. "Have a pleasant evening Miss Santiago, Mr. Andrews."

Wolfe watched Santiago and Andrews as they walked down Peters toward Bourbon Street. He waited a moment but Xavier did not reappear. He followed Santiago at a distance. When they entered Galatorie's "33" Bar and Steak, Wolfe found a bar on the opposite side of Bourbon Street with a view of Galatorie's entry. He took a seat at the bar and watched. A few minutes after entering Galatorie's, Wolfe could see Santiago and Andrews through a window.

For the next hour he watched as they ate dinner and chatted, held hands, smiled at each other, and took turns touching hands. Wolfe saw every person that entered the restaurant or passed the doorway of the bar he watched from. As Andrews stood and held Santiago's chair Xavier passed the open doorway only feet from Wolfe's barstool.

Wolfe left a fifty on the bar and went to the street. Xavier had disappeared in the crowd. He walked in the direction Xavier had gone. He saw Santiago and Andrews leave their table. He stopped and waited. *If you saw them you're waiting here somewhere.*

Santiago and Andrews came out of Galatorie's. Wolfe watched them for only a few seconds. His attention was diverted when Xavier appeared and began following the couple about thirty feet back.

Wolfe smiled and followed him. *In a few minutes we'll be off Bourbon Street, Xavier. Then we'll end this business.* He picked up a copy of a tourist guide.

Chapter 14

As Santiago and Andrews walked along Bourbon Street his cell phone rang.

Sam Evans spoke first. "Link, can I talk to Mitch?"

"Of course," he said and handed over the cell.

Santiago said, "Yes, Sam."

"I found your Senator DuBois is a porn star. The data on the flash drive is him and a blond participating in sexual activities one could only imagine in their wildest fantasies."

"Is DuBois clearly visible?"

"Oh yes, and much more of him than should meet the eye, or most eyes anyway. And his lady friend is rather interesting. I assume you're familiar with a device called a strap-on?"

"Yes. Does he appear to know he's being filmed?"

"No, not that he's paying attention, but he does like to sport his junk."

Santiago laughed. "That's probably more information than I need."

"Have you made any copies of the video?"

"Yes, three; one for Ray, one for you to review, and one for Shari Stiletto."

"Shari's coming into play?"

"Claude has arranged an invitation for her to an investor's reception in Washington tomorrow night. She's flying in sometime this evening to get her copy of the flash drive. I believe her task is to get DuBois attention and then have a private chat with him."

"I'd love to be there for the chat. She'll definitely succeed in getting his attention."

Evans laughed. "I'll be sending everything with Shari on the plane except your copy. Ray or Claude will determine what to do with the laptop and video, most likely depending on the senator's reaction."

"So Link or I won't see Shari on this trip?"

"No, for her it's a touch and go. However, Ray is sending Dash Varga and Desiree Larsson. They're coming so I may train them for the DataFlex role at Barrier. It's my understanding one of them will fill Tony's slot when all of this other stuff is done. For now they'll be your backup as needed."

Santiago said, "Excellent. Do you know what time they're due in?"

"No. It could be anytime. I'll buzz you when they get here."

"Anything else at this point, Sam?"

"Not now." He broke the connection

Andrews smiled. "That was a busy call. I wonder why on my phone?"

Sam's a very careful man. His calling you wouldn't be out of the ordinary. He could also suspect a bug in my personal cell. He has my burn number but chose not to use it, and my cell is back at the condo getting charged." She smiled. "Anyway, I have a small sexy purse tonight."

They turned on to Peters Street and headed back toward Jackson Square. Santiago nudged Andrews' side. "Let's take a cab to Bywater. It's about a mile from here on the natural levee of the river. There's supposed to be art studios, craft shops, music stores and late-night cafes. It might be fun, maybe a bit on the Bohemian side of things. Keep in mind Andrea could still have someone watching me. If they see us together they'll report our date. And I best check my cell when we get back to the condo for a bug."

"Let's do it babe." He flagged a carriage cab.

Xavier watched Santiago and Andrews until a carriage stopped and they were seated for a ride. Wolfe was still a short distance behind Xavier.

*****

Wolfe approached Xavier from the left rear. He pressed the Ruger into his side. Xavier froze.

"Don't do anything stupid, Jerome. You'll be dead before you can move. All I want is to talk with you. Leave the gun in the waist band at your back. I don't want it out in public view."

Xavier nodded. As he did so he saw Wolfe's gun covered with a newspaper.

"Let's walk to your car."

They walked along the sidewalk down Peters Street and past the Frenchman Condominiums. At the corner they turned and went into a parking lot that was only half full. "Where is your little red car?"

"On the far side of the dumpsters. The lot was full when I got here."

They went to the car.

Wolfe said, "Get in."

When Xavier was seated behind the steering wheel Wolfe fastened his hands to the wheel, one on each side with plastic ties having Xavier pull the first tie tight with his free hand while Wolfe kept the Ruger against his neck and held his wrist in place.

"The second one will be easier. I won't need your help."

Xavier looked around the isolated parking place he'd used. It was hidden from view. He began to sweat. "You said you wanted to talk."

"Well, I lied. I just didn't want to kill you in a crowd. That's always risky but I've gotten away with it in the past. Crowds get scared and confused."

Xavier began to tremble. "How much is Noble paying you to kill me?"

"You're direct, I like that. 50K, and you will be my last hit. I'm retiring."

"People in your business don't retire, they die."

Wolfe laughed. "Perhaps most, but unlike you and your partner, the people at Noble don't even know who I am. To them, I'm Wolfe."

Xavier looked at the gun. "I have a million five in the Caymans. I could transfer that money to you and we could go our own ways, nobody knowing the better."

"You mean we both disappear."

"Yes. You said it yourself. You want out. You're middle-aged. It won't get easier as the years stack up. I was planning on retiring, too, but Noble ordered a hit on me. If they would've let things be I'd be long gone."

Wolfe looked Xavier in the eyes and smiled. "How do you think we could do such a transfer?"

"I have a laptop with me. Do you have a phone that gets the net?"

Wolfe switched his gun to the left hand. "Yes."

"We can make the transfer here, on the hood of the car. Take my gun out of my waist band and empty it. Then empty your gun. We'll have to work together to access my account and I've assumed you have an account somewhere."

Wolfe nodded. *A million five would certainly make my retirement easier. I could kill him afterword.* "Lean forward so I can get your gun."

Xavier leaned into the wheel. "You won't regret this."

Wolfe emptied Xavier's gun and tossed the bullets into the dumpster. He set the weapon on the hood of the car then cut the ties. "Get out, get your laptop and stand at the front."

Xavier did as directed but looked at Wolfe's hand. "Your gun?"

Wolfe took the magazine out and emptied the chamber onto the hood. "If I was a smaller man I don't think I'd do this, but fortunately for me, I was an Army Ranger. I already know your background." He took out his cell phone.

Xavier said, "I'll bring my account up first then I'll need your account number to make the transfer."

"Let me see the screen."

Xavier turned his computer.

Wolfe nodded and brought up his account. "That's good."

Xavier said, "I'll make the transfer first, then you confirm it. First why don't we toss our guns in the dumpster, too? Then we can both disappear without looking over our shoulder. We'll both be alive and just vanish. Oh, one last thing, before we leave here would you call whoever you report to, probably on a burn cell and let them know I'm dead, maybe floating down river or something."

Wolfe pushed his phone over to Xavier. "Make the transfer."

Xavier quickly copied the necessary account number.

When he pushed it back Wolfe reached out to pull it toward him and smiled. "Thank...."

Without warning Xavier hit Wolfe square in the front of his throat crushing his larynx. Wolfe fell to the ground holding his throat, eyes bulged, lips curling, face turning deep red, nostrils flaring. He made a hissing sound. Xavier looked down at Wolfe and stomped on his face. "You'll be dead in a minute. Greed is a killer."

Xavier took the cell phone Wolfe was using. He transferred the money back to his account then crushed the phone on the ground beside Wolfe's head.

He looked at Wolfe twisting, sweating, legs thrashing, hands gripping his throat.

"You know the hard part of this is I still have to get rid of the people that want me dead."

Xavier took Wolfe's wallet. It contained ten one-hundred dollar bills but no identification. He stood as Wolfe's body went limp. Xavier laughed.

"You're dead now you son-of-a-bitch."

He kicked Wolfe several times in the ribs and laughed as the bones snapped. He pocketed Wolfe's gun, got in the Fusion and left.

"Back to work."

*****

As their carriage came to a halt at Bywater, Santiago's DataFlex burn cell rang.

Ray house said, "Hi, Mitch."

"Ray, what's up?"

"We have some good news. Mario believes he's found our other leak"

"Great."

"At first he thought it was Priya Gupta. She is living way beyond her means. Then he found out she's the mistress of a young tech entrepreneur with a wife at home. Does it sound familiar?"

"Yes it does. Small world."

"Next he dug into the financials of our head custodian, Rita Eagles. She's always been efficient and is an excellent supervisor. But Rita has an account containing fifty-one thousand dollars and she is the mother of a twenty-four year old daughter."

"Really? I reviewed her DataFlex file and background when I started some two years ago. I found nothing indicating a stash."

"She didn't have the account and no mention has ever been of the daughter. She was raised under the name Trish Brown by her father. When she was fourteen she ran away from home. For the next few years she lived on the streets, in shelters, and was part of a commune. She broke away from the latter when she was twenty and became part of an escort service."

"Did Rita know where Trish was, what she was doing?"

"No, and that's the key. Rita saw a photo of Trish a few years ago hanging on the arm of Claude at some function – the days before the kidnap of Lindsey."

Santiago chuckled. "And with the change of commitment to his family Claude dumped Trish."

"Yes. As far as Claude was concerned it was just a matter of termination of services rendered. He was through with escorts."

"Ray, we still should have found her when we were doing Rita's review."

"Don't be too hard on our investigators or yourself. Remember what Link said about not going as deep on classified people."

"What was Trish's working name?"

"Alyssa Juice."

"God, I love it. Makes me think of Thomas Grant's escorts, Lisa Comfort and Heidi Feelgood."

House chuckled. "Just another great trade name. But you did make him pay dearly for his sins."

She touched the back of her hand over the scar left by Grant's an ice pick. "That's the second time his name's come up this week."

"Yes, well back to Rita. Apparently Trish and mom were reunited after she was dumped by Claude. Mom decided a little revenge was in order."

"In other words, punish the big man."

"Mitch, you're always so subtle, but yes, get even."

"Is the account offshore?"

"No, but remember, Mitch, Rita's not a criminal. She's an angered parent that broke the law."

"So what's next?"

"Jessica and I are going to interview her at the end of her shift."

"Why does interview sound like interrogate when you say it, Ray?"

"Come on, Mitch, we interview, the cops interrogate. We'll be turning over our stuff on her and Kat Parsons to the FBI."

"You've had a busy day or two. On our end Link is playing golf with Doctor Sigmund tomorrow morning and Sam told me about Shari going to meet DuBois. Hopefully Link will gain some insight, we'll find Tony's killer, and wrap this mess up."

House laughed. "I'll drink to that."

*****

Jessica Rodriguez stepped into House's office as the classified shift changed. "Rita Eagles is waiting. Are you ready?"

"Yes, and Jessica, I'd like you to sit in. We don't want any charges of harassment or threats."

"Of course. We should also tape the chat."

"Do you have a small recorder we can place on the conference table?"

"Yes. As I recall seeing a recorder during an interview always had an intimidating impact on our subjects."

"Always."

"Ray, have you considered she may not talk to us?"

"If she declines we'll simply call it a termination conference and turn our findings over to the FBI. Industrial espionage is serious. If she cooperates with us we could pass that along as well."

They arrived at the conference room and Rita Eagles joined them.

House said, "Thank you for coming in at the end of your shift. You'll be paid overtime of course, and we do want to record our discussion. Are you okay with doing so?"

"Yes."

"Miss Rodriguez and I have some issues needing resolution," he said placing Jessica's recorder on the table.

"What is this about? Has someone filed a grievance against me?"

House said, "No, this is about information changing hands and your daughter, Trish."

Eagles looked at Rodriguez and then House. "I don't have a daughter."

House shook his head. "Yes you do, Rita. We know about the difficult life she's had growing up with her father, leaving home at an early age, and her adult life."

Eagles' eyes welled. She wiped her cheek. "Do you really know what she's been through, how she lived? She was on the streets because it was the only way for young uneducated girl to survive."

Rodriguez said, "Yes I do. Rita, we're not here to judge, but we have reason to believe you've been selling information to other companies."

Rita said nothing.

House watched her closely. "We'd like to know who and why you targeted DataFlex."

Eagles sat up straight, her nostrils flared, breathing becoming harsh. In a firm voice she said, "If you know about my daughter you already know why."

"I know she was an escort with Mr. Braun a few years ago if that is your frame of reference."

"Yes, and he dumped her like garbage when he was done screwing around with her and decided to become a respectable married man."

Rodriguez said, "When Trish was with Mr. Braun was she well paid?"

"Yes, that was part of the problem, too. He paid huge dollars for sex, sometimes kinky sex, the pervert."

"How well did he pay her?"

"Miss Rodriguez, he paid her thousands of dollars; a young girl from a hard life getting fast easy money."

"So she was well paid as an escort?"

"No, as a whore! He corrupted Trish. His money, private planes, five star hotels – she lived like a goddess not as an escort. She was a mistress."

House cut in, "After Mr. Braun no longer had need of her services what did she do?"

"The same thing with other wealthy men. Braun had made a life of luxury so common to her she continued. I tried several times to get her to quit the life and learn to do something productive and ethical."

Rodriguez said, "She does lead a different kind of lifestyle, but she has for a long time. She lived in a commune for a few years, was active in the porn industry, and solicited on the streets all before meeting Mr. Braun as an escort."

"That is true, but I think she would have outgrown her sordid lifestyle if she'd not made the big bucks contact. It's one thing to be a wild child, another to do it your whole life."

House said, "And you hold Mr. Braun responsible for her outcome?"

"Yes, the bastard!"

"Is that the reason you came to DataFlex, to get inside the company and hurt Mr. Braun?"

Her lip curled. "Yes, I wanted to hurt him where it counts, his money making machine. Even if it's not going to bankrupt him he needs to suffer for corrupting my daughter. When I was hired in maintenance and joined the custodial group I had access to every office, conference room and cubicle in security. Nobody pays attention to me when I empty a waste basket and leave, bring in a cart with equipment for a presentation, or clean up a spill. It's business as usual."

"So you began collecting and selling information.

"Yes, every piece of information I heard or found that could impact Braun I sold to my contact."

House tapped the table. "You know you can be prosecuted."

"Don't care. Just the testimony in public would be worth the jail time to me."

"And you daughter?"

"It's too late for her. Miss Rodriguez, what would you do if Trish was your daughter?"

"I'd work my ass to save her, not drop her as a lost cause."

House said, "Who was your contact?"

"A man named Kohler. He recruited me to apply for my position at DataFlex after telling me about my daughter. He said he and his friends in New York could help me even the score for Trish."

Rodriguez looked at House. *She was groomed*.

House said, "What did you sell to Mr. Kohler?"

"Nothing, I dealt with a woman on the phone. I don't know her name. She had a husky voice and sent money to my bank account whenever I provided information." Rita laughed. "She didn't know who I was, either. Kohler told me to try and sound like a man with a high pitched voice."

"And your account is in the states?"

"I don't trust foreigners."

Rodriguez said, "Rita, I feel badly for the pain you've experienced, but I also believe each of us is responsible for the decisions we make, including Trish who is now an adult."

House said, "What do you feel?"

"My only regret is I've accomplished so little and been caught. I know you'll be contacting the FBI."

"Yes, we deal with classified projects and information. What you did on behalf of your daughter may have compromised national security."

Two men in dark suits appeared through the windows standing in the outer office.

Rita glanced toward them. "That didn't take long."

House nodded. "No, sensitive information generally gets an immediate response. But Rita, you have been candid and I will advise these gentlemen of your cooperation. Regarding Mr. Braun, I will neither defend nor condemn him. Just as Trish has now chosen her lifestyle, he has chosen his."

Rita wiped her eyes. "You know, I thought about killing Braun."

*****

While riding a carriage back to Jackson Square Santiago and Andrews passed a parking lot just around the corner from the Frenchman Condominium. Several police cars were parked at the back of the lot with lights flashing. An ambulance was on one side near some dumpsters and yellow security tape was strung around the area.

She said, "Looks like the old days in Seattle."

Andrews smiled. "I suppose it does. Probably a mugging victim. A lot of tourists prowl around the backstreets and alleys."

"Could be."

Andrews's cell rang. "It's late for you to be calling, Sam."

"Just wanted to let you know Dash and Desiree have arrived and Shari is now on her way to DC."

"That was fast."

"One other thing has surfaced. We don't know if it's related or not, but for what it's worth the body of a fellow named Thelonious Jackson was found in a car crash in one of the canyons."

"Who is he?"

"As I said, maybe nothing to us, but he has had dealings in providing false identification, credit cards and passports according to police records. He was also a regular associate of Kohler."

"If he's tied to this it would help explain why nobody can find Xavier."

"Let Mitch know about him and you two keep alert. If Thelonious is connected we could be encountering a cleanup operation and Xavier could be looking for Mitch to lead him to Noble."

"Well, that pretty lady is here beside me in a carriage. We've got the police around the corner working a crime scene and now an alert. Thanks for the heads up. This could get even more serious."

Santiago said, "Well, at least we're at our home away from home. Let's go see if my phone is bugged or the condo tossed. Maybe, just maybe we can find a happy ending to this evening."

"Babe, I love the way you create happy endings, then it's golf tomorrow."

Chapter 15
Saturday, July 12

Jerome Xavier arrived at Jackson Square early in the morning. The vendors, artists, and musicians were just setting up. The smell of the muddy Mississippi was stronger than the night before. He sat on a bench and sipped a cup of coffee as boat horns sounded, men shouted, and the odor of fish hovered. "Is this what retirement is about, to watch the world go by and just enjoy it, no fast paced run, run, run? I may like this after getting everyone off my back."

He watched the entry of the Frenchman and glanced at the latest *Times-Picayune*, published three days a week; Wednesdays, Fridays and Sundays. "Strange not to get a daily newspaper in a big city."

Link Andrews came out the door and went to a waiting cab. Xavier lit a cigarette and continued to watch the entry. After a few minutes he stubbed out his smoke and walked to the entrance.

The doorman said, "Good morning, sir."

"And the same to you my man. I'm here to catch a friend of mine from Phoenix. I just dropped into town for a day or so and her dad told me she's staying here."

"Who would that be?"

"Michelle Santiago."

"Miss Santiago is staying here."

"Great. Her dad didn't know her apartment number but I believe he said it was a Noble Group room."

"Miss Santiago is in condominium 402, sir, a very nice suite."

Xavier took out a twenty dollar bill. "Of course, how easily we little people forget. May I go in and I surprise her?"

The doorman accepted the tip. "I'm sure Miss Santiago would enjoy seeing a friend from home."

"Thank you."

Xavier went to the elevator. *Time to meet this lady for real and play.*

When the elevator door opened he was only a few steps away from 402. The hallway was empty. He took out his Ruger, stepped close to the door, knocked then turned his back to the peephole. Without hesitation he said, "Doorman."

Santiago opened the door. He said, "Remember me?"

"Xavier, yes," she said looking at the Ruger. "Tempe, roof tops, newscasts."

He stepped in the doorway and pointed toward the couch. "I can hurt you badly, kill you, or you can tell me what I want to know."

"Go to hell."

He slapped her face hard. "I don't mind beating you up. I just don't want you out cold, understand?"

She squinted her eyes. "Is that the best you can do big man?"

"Lady, I can do a lot of damage," he said leaning toward her face.

She wrinkled her nose and turned away. *God, the breath of a shit eating dog.* "What do you want?"

"It's simple, who's your boss?"

"Everybody knows that, Andrea Nance of the Noble Group. If you called Maxwell they would've told you. We're PR."

"Okay, but where does this woman Nance live?"

"In Washington, D.C., where I don't know. When she's in New Orleans she stays in one of Noble's condos."

"You don't share this one?"

"Not with her."

He put the Ruger under her chin. "Call Noble and ask them her address."

"They won't give me that information on the phone. Noble has offices in New York and D.C. Why the rough stuff? Everything you're asking is public."

She watched his eyes as he kept looking at her breasts in a powder blue silk blouse. He licked his lips every time he paused.

"You know I'm wanted for murder?"

"The whole country does." She sat up straight arching her back. "What now, are you going to kill me? Or are you going to slap me around some more because you like to bully woman? Real men don't do that."

He smiled. "Real men screw the hell out of 'em and beat 'em up."

"You're a Neanderthal."

He grabbed the blouse and ripped it open. "You've got great tits!"

She laughed. "It's been awhile for you hasn't it, Jerome. You're getting turned on and all you see is a bra."

He tore the bra lose. In a harsh voice and waving the gun he said, "Now I see tits. I wanted to see 'em when you were playing kissy face with your boyfriend in the hot tub. But no, only him and your damn plants got the show."

"Loser."

He slapped her again. "Take off the blouse and bra, now!"

She leaned forward and started to stand. He pushed her back onto the couch then he stood up straight

She looked at his groin. "Now you look a little sexier, big man. Your junk is starting to show."

"Yeah," he said reaching down and touching himself. "Get the skirt off."

"I'll bet you've never made love to a woman."

"Shut up bitch. I'll bet you've never been raped 'til now."

In a soft voice she said, "At least show me what you've got, Jerome. You have the gun."

He unfastened his slacks and let them drop to the floor and then his boxers. "You like what you see don't ya, bitch?"

"Impressive, very impressive." She leaned forward and slid out of her five inch pumps, then the skirt. "A hot woman in hooker heels looks pretty sharp, Jerome.

Too bad you wouldn't let me stand and strip. I was the best." She began to slide the thong off.

His breath became shorter, sweat formed on his upper lip. He waved the Ruger everywhere as he watched Santiago slowly slide the thong down her legs while still sitting on the couch. Xavier stood in front of her, naked from the waist down. His hips were thrust forward. "Rip it off. I wanna enjoy this moment. Who knows, you might like it, too."

"You're wasting my talents, Jerome."

"Yeah, do that, slide 'em off."

She stood and slowly slid the thong down her legs. "Do you like it rough, Jerome?"

"Yeah."

"Me too. We could enjoy this. I'm getting excited."

"I'm gonna ram you."

"I hope so."

"Jesus, you're a crazy bitch."

She reached out to touch him. "Slap me hard, Jerome, hard."

He struck her left cheek with the flat of his hand and grunted. Santiago fell to the floor on her knees.

"Yeah, I want you on your knees. I want your face."

Santiago turned toward Xavier as he reached for the back of her head, grabbed one of the stiletto heeled shoes in her right hand and rammed the heel into in his groin with all her strength. He screamed. His cries were guttural and harsh, saliva covered his lips and chin. His eyes bulged and tears rolled down his cheeks. He dropped the Ruger and grabbed at the stiletto shoe.

Blood poured down his thighs. He gasped for breath as he fell forward.

Santiago dove out from under his falling body grabbing the Ruger from the floor and rolled onto her knees facing him. Xavier fell to the floor in a fetal position holding the bloody shoe between his legs looking at Santiago. "Help me. I'm bleeding like a pig!"

"You are a pig."

She held the Ruger on Xavier as he twisted, cried out in pain, squeezed his knees together. Sweat covered his face and torso. Mucus covered his upper lip. "Please!"

Santiago kept the Ruger on Xavier and dialed 911, gave the necessary information and broke the connection. She slid what was left of the blouse and thong back on. "Cops are going to get a show, too."

"You crazy bitch, I'm bleeding to death!"

She smiled. "You said you liked it rough. I win." She gave him a wet towel. "Hope your balls are ruined. Apply some pressure. They'll love you on the inside."

Xavier pressed the towel to his crotch. His breathing was forced. He swallowed and wet his lips frequently. "I'll spend the rest of my life in prison or on death row being somebody's bitch, all for killing Kohler and that was self-defense. He was trying to kill me."

Santiago watched Xavier squirm. "You caught the hooker heel in your nuts because you were going to rape me, then kill me."

"Shoot me. I killed Vladimir Clyburn, too."

Santiago slid the other stiletto on her foot while Xavier pressed the towel harder against his groin. She placed the shoe on his throat and applied some pressure.

"Talk to me, Jerome. A bullet would be painless, too fast and the police will be here in a few minutes."

"I know, but you'll get to Nance and her people before them. You play by your own rules."

"Why did you kill Clyburn?"

"He heard Kat giving me information."

"Who ordered the hit?"

"Kohler told me the order came from the top. Now the only way to get 'em is through you. The cops could be dirty."

"Were you involved in the killing of Tony Mercedes?"

"Don't know anything about that but a man named Wolfe tried to kill me last night. He was a professional sent by Noble."

"Where is he now?"

"The morgue." Xavier was becoming pale. He raised one of his hands. It was shaking. "Taking him out was the only way I'd ever get away even with a new identity."

She raised her foot and slid the shoe off. "I hope you get life just to experience hell every day."

There was loud pounding on the door, then a crash as it opened. Police rushed in weapons drawn to see Xavier on the floor with a bloody towel pressed between his legs and a near naked Santiago holding a gun. They handcuffed him, then firemen began giving first aid and placed him on a stretcher. One of the firemen handed the stretcher blanket to Santiago without a word.

"Thank you."

The fireman smiled. "Ma'am."

Within a few minutes they removed Xavier. One of the police officers began asking Santiago questions.

She said, "You'll have to wait a minute while I put something on. This is going to take some time." She nodded towards the door. "Xavier shared a lot with me and he'll do the same with your group, but you need to arrange protection for him even in the hospital. Some very big people want him dead."

*****

Susan Train worked at her Reaper station vetting errors in the new program. She hummed softly, "Keep finding the little errors until Sigmund is happy. Then imbed our new piece for outside access. Noble makes big bucks and so do I." Her cell phone sounded. It was Nance.

"Susan, how is it going?"

"It's quiet here. Sigmund hasn't even come in yet, of course it's her golf day in the morning. Maybe she got a date with her playing partner but I doubt it."

"Who did she play with?"

"Link Andrews, Mitch's shack job."

Nance was quiet for a moment. She laughed. "Probably not. More important, how are the modifications of the software coming?"

"Sigmund's been monitoring our work pretty close. I expect that at this stage of development. She's found a few changes, nothing too serious. As you know, our changes won't be embedded until we finish the vetting.

I put it in after Sigmund has cleared the project for implementation."

Nance smiled, "And nobody will know it's there until it gets used."

"Exactly."

"And we're close to complete?"

"Yes, and a good thing, too. I suspect my lab partner Joyce Riggs is a plant for a competitor."

"Why?"

"Just her comments, questions, always wanting to know what Sigmund or I am up to. She's always probing, watching. It's not normal lab chatter."

Nance changed the subject. "Susan, are we good on the money you needed for your mother's transplant?"

"So far, so good. Transplants are expensive."

"Yes they are, and she'll probably need additional care after the surgery. How old is your mom?"

"Fifty-one. I'd like her around for a long time."

"She will be and when this project is completed we'll have the opportunity to work together on other things."

"I hope so, the bills just keep coming in."

Nance went to Noble's security files for a minute. "As I thought, Santiago has already done deep background on Yeager, Sigmund, Train, Riggs and," she laughed, "Nance. She is thorough."

"All of us including you?"

"It's her job."

Susan chuckled. "She won't find much."

"Has she had any contact with you or Joyce?"

"Just a visit one or two times. She seems more interested in Barrier which is fine with me."

"That makes sense, her friend Tony Mercedes was connected to Barrier." *You haven't got a clue who Mitch and I are looking for; one of you is a leak.*

"She's focused on her job. Do you think she'll discover who he was talking to?"

Nance said, "I hope so. We need to end that leak."

"Do you think his killer will be found? If they do the FBI may connect the dots and that would be big trouble."

Nance smiled. "I doubt they'll find him at this stage of the game. We'll talk later but call me when Sigmund gets in."

After breaking the connection Nance went back to her iPad screen. She scanned the information Santiago had found using the Noble people. "Good searches, Mitch. Not too deep." She checked her history. "You know I'm a Cajun girl named Verot making good. I told you that, too." She switched back to Sigmund. "You didn't dig deep enough, Mitch. I see no Verot here."

Her cell rang. It was Santiago.

"Mitch, what can I do for you?"

"Just called to let you know I've had a busy morning. The detective you had following me in Tempe tried to break in here and kill me about an hour ago."

"Xavier?"

"Yes, he said he wanted to know who my boss is. I told him you and that it was public information. He seemed to be thinking someone higher up."

"I'm sorry, are you okay? I should've asked that first. Xavier's showing up just surprises me."

"I'm a little shop worn but good."

"And Xavier left after seeing you?"

"No, he's in police custody at a hospital. You could say I hurt him with a shoe."

"Oh," Nance paused, "in custody? That's good. Did you talk with him?"

"Yes, among other things he admitted killing Kohler and then another man named Wolfe last night right here at Jackson Square."

"Wolfe, what a strange name."

"He was quite dramatic before they took him away. He said he had more information for the cops if he lived. He was bleeding pretty badly and I wasn't very sympathetic since he'd already told me he was going to rape and kill me."

"Where did they take him?"

"East Jefferson General Hospital. Why?"

Nance looked around. "I hope they keep a guard on him."

"I'm sure they will. He's a felon wanted for murder in Arizona plus whatever they have on him here."

"If anything comes up keep me posted, Mitch. I'll try to get back to New Orleans in a day or two for another quick stopover."

*****

Link Andrews and Acadia Sigmund were driving up to the 16th tee at Lakewood Golf Club when his cell phone began vibrating.

"Excuse the call, Acadia. I try to turn it off when I play but there are a few really important things going on right now," he said checking caller ID.

"Not a problem, Link."

"Hello, Mitch."

Santiago said in hurried voice, "Link, Xavier just tried to kill me."

"Are you okay?"

"Better than him."

A smile crept across his face. "Where are you?"

"The condo. The cops and firemen just left with him. He's going to East Jefferson General first, then jail."

Andrews pulled the golf cart to the side of the trail and stopped. Santiago shared the details of Xavier's invasion and how she turned the tables on him using a hooker heel.

He said, "That had to hurt."

"Bad I hope. Then Nance calls. She may be on her way back to town."

"What are you thinking?"

"With Xavier being taken alive she has no clue as to what he does or doesn't know, especially since he admitted killing Kohler and Wolfe. He also implied Wolfe may have killed Tony. I think she's coming back to clean up the left overs."

"Careful, that could be you."

"Me, Xavier, maybe the mole, and surely whoever was talking to Tony if she knows who it is."

"Do you think she knows your cover?"

"She's suspicious, especially now that Xavier is talking. Too bad considering I'd just gotten a little trust. She'll be even more nervous after Shari meets DuBois tonight."

"Get ready to bailout just in case. I'm coming over." He broke the connection.

Sigmund looked at him. "I wasn't prying but I couldn't help but hear. Mitch is still with DataFlex?"

"Yes."

"Someone tried to kill her?"

"Yes."

"Is she hurt?"

"No."

"You need to go to her now, Link. I'll drive you, skip the cab. There is something I must share and until now I didn't know who to go to. It's about Tony and me."

He pulled back onto the cart path. "Let's go."

They left Link's rental equipment and the cart in front of the pro-shop and drove to the Frenchman. On the way Andrews called Evans.

"Link, I thought you'd still be on the course."

"Xavier tried to kill Mitch."

"What! Is she okay?"

"Yes, and not as shook up as one would expect."

"She doesn't get shook up, not after Thomas Grant out in Quartzsite."

"That's true, or Yancey Quarterman at Braun's cabin. She's always in control."

Evans said, "Have they made her?"

"Possibly, but she isn't sure."

"Let's pull her out."

"No, we'll talk to her first. She thinks she knows who killed Tony. She wants to know who ordered the hit."

Acadia Sigmund looked straight at Andrews, gripped the seatbelt tightening a forearm and pressed the gas.

"I'll call you when I get to Mitch's, Sam."

"And I'll see what my old contacts can find out about Wolfe."

Andrews noticed Sigmund's tense posture. "Take it easy, Acadia. We'll get there. I'm just sorry there's a lot going on right now."

"Link, ever since Tony's death I haven't known who I can trust. Tony and I were friends, distant friends. He didn't know me except as the lead in the Reaper Project but we shared other contacts."

"Acadia, were you his contact?"

"Yes, but he didn't know it."

"What is going on at Barrier that had him so interested?"

"Nothing, his focus was on Reaper even though it was out of his arena and clearance. He discovered someone was trying to sabotage the guidance system by imbedding a worm which allows a rogue on the ground to take total control of the Reaper, from flying it to firing its armaments at newly selected targets."

"How did he discover this?"

"I told him anonymously. What he set out to do was discover who on the Reaper Team was doing it,

Joyce, Susan, or me since he didn't know I was his source."

"It could have been someone else with access to the facility as well, or a world class hacker. I know a fellow that could probably imbed a worm even in something as carefully guarded as Reaper and never be detected."

"Link, that's not important now."

"It was important enough Tony was killed."

"I know, I saw his murder."

"What?"

Sigmund weaved into another lane briefly and her eyes welled. "I was there."

"You were also the person he was meeting?"

"Yes."

"Why not meet in New Orleans, you were both here?"

"He believed someone was onto him and he didn't want to neutralize his source of information. He was very cloak and dagger like."

"Spying, sabotage, espionage; they're dangerous business – lethal. Tell me about the shooting."

"Tony was by the Vietnam Veterans Memorial waiting for me. As I came across the grounds of the National Mall a large man in a tattered field jacket approached Tony. They spoke for a moment and Tony gave the man something, maybe two things. The man left. Within a minute or less he came back, shot Tony and leaned him against the wall. He spoke to a woman then walked into the crowd."

"You didn't hear a shot?"

"No."

"Smart, he used a suppressor. When he walked into the crowd what did you do?"

"I was afraid first for my own safety. I didn't want to become a second victim. I thought if they sent someone to kill Tony they knew he was meeting someone and just didn't wait long enough for me to show. In another minute or two we would have been together."

"So you left the mall."

"Yes, taking almost the same pathway as the shooter. I saw him dump the coat in the trash and tried to pick it up. I thought maybe I could get it to the authorities but another street person grabbed it from my hands and ran off with it."

"Damn it."

"Link, I have the gun."

"The gun?"

"Yes, at my home. After the street person ran away with the jacket I saw the gun and a wallet in the trash. I took them."

"How did you pick the gun up?"

"By the butt. I used my index finger and thumb on a rough wood surface. I thought I'd be leaving fewer prints that way."

"Good thinking. Do you think you could recognize the shooter if police showed you some pictures?"

"No, he was too far away. I'd bet we were a hundred feet apart when he shot Tony. I know he was a large man, possibly of mixed color. He looked like any other tourist after he dropped his jacket in the trash, right down to a camera hanging from his neck."

"I don't want to scare you Acadia but in few minutes we'll be at Mitch's place. I believe she'll agree with me you need to go out of circulation until we can get you into the hands of someone connected with Homeland Security and the FBI, and be sure they are trusted."

"You mean you're not going to just call the police."

"No, this is top priority security."

Andrews called Evans.

"Sam, can you meet me at Mitch's?"

"On my way."

"Great, we've had an incident and got a break? I'll be there shortly, after we pick somethings up at Acadia's."

*****

Andrea Nance called Francis Dade at his New York office in the late afternoon. "Francis, I won't be attending the reception tonight. I'm sure Senator DuBois will be co-operative because he has viewed the video."

"I hear urgency in your voice. What has come up?"

"Wolfe was killed in New Orleans last night and Xavier captured this morning, alive."

"That is serious."

"Yes, I believe it's time to cut our losses and start over. You and Ishtar will still get your revenge and you'll have a new item to market to interested parties, but I believe it's more important right now to safeguard your identities than risk it all at this stage. Worst case scenario is we lose a month or two."

"I agree. What do you plan?"

"Since Santiago captured Xavier I feel it is necessary to remove her. She could have knowledge Jerome may have forced from Kohler or Wolfe. We just don't know. Second, I believe we must dispose of Susan Train. We can always replace her with the right money and pressure. She knows who I am."

"Yes, close the funnel."

"And finally, I believe my contact at DataFlex has been found. I've tried contacting her but get no response. Too bad, she had many sources of information."

"Is that the lady that used a high pitched man's voice?"

"Yes."

"She did have good resources, sometimes even House's office. Can we dispose of her?"

"Not if they already have her, but she can't hurt us like Train or Santiago."

"What is your plan?"

"I'm leaving Washington in a few minutes. I'm not telling anyone I'm coming. I'll take a room at a hotel somewhere we've never been under an assumed name, dispose of Susan and Mitch and fly back. It should be a short trip."

"Are you sure you have everything?"

"Yes. I'm also identifying elements for the next effort."

"Good, I'm sure Ishtar's and my objective has not changed."

"Nor has mine, Francis. Our personalities may clash but we are both loyal to the same end – revenge and wealth."

*****

When Acadia Sigmund and Link Andrews arrived at Santiago's condominium Sam Evans was already there. Andrews rushed in and hugged her.

"Mitch, you're alright, you're sure?"

"I'm sure."

He stroked her chin with his fingertips. "You're bruised."

She smiled. "I'm not bleeding. He is. Smart wins."

He chuckled. "I think your new tag line should be 'no fear.'"

She laughed. "I like 'smart wins.'"

Andrews shared Sigmund's witnessing of Tony Mercedes shooting and her role in the conspiracy.

Santiago looked at Sigmund. "We're putting you on ice. Sam has a place to keep you safe until we get you into the hands of the FBI. Any luggage?"

Sigmund said, "First, I'm pleased you're not injured, Mitch. As to baggage, Link said to leave it. If anyone was watching my home they saw us unload golf clubs and come back out empty handed except for my purse."

Evans said, "Good. The odds are nobody was watching your home, but they could be here. We'll be leaving by a back entry."

Sigmund looked confused. "Won't the FBI come and get me?"

Evans said, "They will when we call. We have an associate in Phoenix that will handle it so we don't get any unknown elements involved."

"Mr. Evans, do you mean there could be corrupt FBI agents?"

"No ma'am, just better safe than sorry. We already know this web of deceit goes much deeper than most would anticipate."

Andrews said, "Will we be using your rental, Sam?"

"Yes, I'm, parked on the backside of the building."

Sigmund said, "Where are we going?"

Evans glanced at the door. "A safe house on the other side of the river, a community called Algiers. I have two operatives from DataFlex that will stay with you as long as needed."

Santiago looked at Evans. "Dash and Desiree?"

"Yes."

She took Sigmund's hand. "They are two of the best. Desiree and I shared a really dangerous situation previously, and Dash has proven top of the line when needed."

"Thank you, Mitch. This is a frightening situation. At least I'm familiar with the community of Algiers."

"Link said you had the gun and a wallet."

"Yes, in my purse."

"Good, the FBI will want both ASAP."

Andrews looked at Santiago. "Babe, I'd rather stay here with you."

"No, you need to get going. I can take care of myself. Call me when you get there."

"Will do. Sam, let's get going."

Andrews and Evans put Acadia Sigmund in the back seat and drove down Canal Street to the river crossing for Algiers Ferry Landing, and the safe house on Homer and Brooklyn. When they crossed and reached the location Desiree Larsson let them in while Dash Varga watched the street.

Evans said, "Thank you, Desiree. It's nice to have you and Dash here. I know this isn't what you expected."

Larsson laughed. "We work for Ray, expect the unexpected, right?"

"Right. Doctor Sigmund, these ladies are Desiree and Dash. They'll be your housemates for the next few days."

Sigmund held out a hand. "Ladies, I feel safe just knowing you're here. Link and Mitch have been spectacular and Mr. Evans comes with the highest recommendations from his colleagues."

Dash took her hand. "Let's get you squared away. I hope you don't care for sun too much because we'll be keeping you mostly inside and out of sight. We'll put you in the master suite but Desiree will be sharing it with you. I'm in a different room. One of us will be awake at all times, but you can sleep as normally as possible."

Larsson said, "Except for the river boat horns, obviously."

"Ladies, please call me Acadia. I'm a Cajun woman. Those boats won't bother me." She looked at each. "Link didn't tell me you two were so attractive."

Varga laughed. "In Mitch's company we're all just average."

Andrews smiled. "But appreciated. Let's get Acadia settled in."

Dash said, "There are some toiletries in the main bathroom. Feel free to use them until we do some shopping. And feel free to use some of our night ware if you choose."

Desiree said, "It's a little...," she waved her hand.

Sigmund laughed. "Skimpy? Not a problem. When I was your age I knew those little pieces of translucent fabric were designed to entice and enrich. Truth be known, they still are and work wonderfully."

Dash said, "After you drop off your purse we have fresh coffee."

"I smell it and I'm ready. Besides, I owe you some background on who I am, who you're protecting."

Andrews said, "Well, we have some background information that may surprise you, too."

Evans took the gun and wallet from Acadia and placed them in plastic bags. "I'm ready for coffee."

Sigmund sat down at the kitchen table with Evans, Andrews and Larsson. "Okay, Link, out with it. You make it sound like a mystery."

"Ah, dear lady, it may be, at least part of it."

"Then out with it. A mystery can only last so long."

Andrews reached for his Marlboro's then stopped. "Alright, your maiden name is Verot, correct?"

"Yes. You must know I have a twin sister. She was adopted as a baby, almost at birth. I was overlooked even though I was ten or twenty minutes older – an unusual circumstance. As a result I never had legal parents or a family name."

Andrews said, "How many families did you stay with?"

"Twenty-two in fourteen years. Then I was identified as...smart."

Andrews laughed. "I believe the word is genius, something in the 164 range."

"There are many variables, Link, many."

Evans said, "What happened at fourteen?"

"I was assigned to a special family unit affiliated with a university and began attending regular classes – a little kid in an adult world. I rather liked it. For the first time in my life studies were meaningful to me, not just some rote response so to speak."

Andrews mixed several spoons of sugar into his coffee. "I've read the childhood of a genius is a lonely place."

"It is when you're an adult, too, or can be. Most people you're exposed to seem uncomfortable in your presence. I believe some feel threatened. Many of my colleagues over the years have had similar experiences. We know our world moves much faster, the things we like to do, the games we play are not for the average person. I'm sure some of the many families I spent short amounts of time with felt those things. As I grew older I became more aware I was different, too. Combine their discomfort and my awareness and you have a foster kid on the move."

Evans changed the subject. "Have you ever tried to find your sister?"

"Oh yes. I looked for her all the time. The advent of the internet expanded my searches, but never with success. Sealed records, especially those before computers are much harder to access. Over the years I no longer dwell on it. She could well not know I even exist. She may not know her birth name. After all these years I would think she may have found me if she knew I existed. Eventually it becomes time to move on, something I had to do twice."

Andrews looked her in the eyes. "Twice? Acadia, do you want to know who your sister is?"

"You've found her?"

"We believe your sister in Ishtar Dade."

"Of Noble?"

"Yes, she was adopted at birth and her name changed."

Tears filled Acadia's eyes and she giggled while rubbing her hands together. "Are you sure?"

Evans said, "Ninety-nine percent, a DNA test would verify our findings for sure."

"This is wonderful, after all these years!" Her eyes welled. In a soft voice she said, "Maybe she wouldn't want to meet me. But we need to meet, touch each other and talk. I've lost two people in my life. To find one was beyond hope at this point."

Andrews held out a tissue. "Acadia, is the other person your daughter?"

"Yes." She wiped her eyes. "I gave her up at birth. Her father was a married professor, old enough to be my father. I didn't know what to do, fifteen and pregnant."

"I believe we have found her, too."

"Link, is that possible? Two people I lost; a sister I could never find and a daughter I sent away, and you do this in a few days?"

He nodded. "We have the best team in the business."

She continued, "I'm such a terrible person. All the doubts I grew up with, the confusion, asking myself what is wrong with me, why didn't anybody want me – a terrible life for a terrible person. Then," she burst into tears, "I did the same thing to my child."

Sigmund wiped her face, blew her nose, and sniffed. She tossed her head back. "Do you know I never even looked for her? I knew she'd be better off without me. Who is she?"

"If, and I mean if we are correct, Andrea Nance is your daughter. She was born in Baton Rouge, raised in New Orleans. She is the only illegitimate birth noted for March 7 given up for adoption."

"Good, she had a home."

"No, Acadia, she didn't. She was raised in part much like you. She was a scholar in high school. When she graduated she received a scholarship from the Garden District Foundation to attend LSU."

"I've never heard of that foundation."

Andrews sat up straight. "No, but the Noble Group of New York is one of its biggest donors."

"Link, what you're suggesting is my sister knew about Andrea and me all these years and never said a word. This is so twisted."

He nodded.

She sipped the now cold coffee. "Do you think Andrea knows who I am?"

"It's possible. She's head of Noble security. If our team could find all this out using various means I'm sure she has people that could do the same thing."

Evans said, "One other thing. You're the only MIT graduate student at that time who was born May 2nd in New Orleans."

She took a deep breath. "It's been quite a day. My life could be at risk, my possible daughter and sister could be the perpetrators, I'm hidden away in a Navy neighborhood in Algiers." She shook her head. "May I have a fresh cup of coffee? All of this sounds like a television soap opera."

Sam Evans said, "We do have one more piece of possible family information, and again, it ties into Reaper."

"Jesus, what's left? I'm skipping the coffee and going to gin."

"We have reason to believe your sister, if she's your sister, also gave birth to an illegitimate child, a boy."

Yeager shook her head. "It must run in the family."

"Her adopted father, Nelson Noble, became aware of the pregnancy almost immediately. Rather than embarrass the family he literally hired a husband for Ishtar. She gave birth to what was referred to as an early birth, but in reality was a full term baby. He was raised as Ishtar's and Francis Dade's son. He was a genius just like his aunt. Unfortunately he was killed in Afghanistan while on a National Guard deployment."

"How awful. Do you know who his birth father was?"

"We speculate his father was Broderick DuBois. Your sister had a somewhat casual but intimate relationship with him while they were in college. However, Nelson Noble did not want some 'bumpkin' in his family. Little did he know then DuBois would become one of the most powerful senators today."

"But you're not positive on DuBois?"

"No, all it would take is testing; DNA or blood."

Sigmund sat up straight. "Gentlemen, enough of this sordid family history. I'm a scientist and you're trained in espionage – obviously beyond just the industrial realm. Let's sit back and see why all of these individuals are coming together at this point in time. For example, how did Noble become involved?"

Evans said, "The obvious, a huge government contract. They're investors."

She nodded. "Who selected the team to work on Reaper?"

Andrews said, "Francis Dade and Jim Trainer selected you as the only choice to head the Reaper Project. I believe Dade suggested you."

She wrote notes on a legal pad. "Who selected the technicians? Normally the lead does, but they were already assigned when I arrived in New Orleans. Each had top credentials so I had no objections."

Sam said, "From what we could determine Doctor Train was selected by Francis Dade and Doctor Riggs by Jim Trainer."

Andrews interjected, "Sam, is there any blood relationship between Trainer and Train?"

"None."

Yeager tapped her pencil. "It's obvious to me Ishtar, Andrea, and myself have all been brought together for a reason. Part of it is the Reaper program and my skills. But I doubt they brought me into this for my mind. Others could do my job."

Dash shouted from the living room, "We have company."

Evans said, "It should be the FBI."

Larsson drew a Glock 19 from her belt and stepped behind the door. Varga held her Glock and watched the door from the side.

Evans stood at the door. Andrews and Yeager remained in the kitchen watching the back door.

There was a heavy knock on the door followed by a man calling out, "FBI."

Evans opened the door and checked the identification cards. "Agents Zachery and Everly, come in."

Zachery said, "Agent Paxton from the Phoenix office contacted us."

Evans smiled. "Gentleman, we have a story and a half for you."

Chapter 16

When Santiago finished with the police reports it was close to noon. She took another shower and did her makeup. She used Dermablend to hide some of the bruises left by Xavier. She put on a blue skirt that only went three inches above the knees and a brief slit on the right thigh. Her powder blue blouse had the two top buttons open. She wore a thin gold chain with a gold Glock 19 charm which settled at the top of her cleavage. *I earned the right to wear this today.*

She went to the living room and placed a thigh holster on her right leg, then her Glock 42 and checked her watch. *First order of business is get to Maxwell and discover Sigmund is missing even after her golf game; no calls, emails, or other communication from her and report it to Nance.*

Santiago called Link Andrews on her burn cell.

"Hi, Mitch. You feeling little better?"

"Cleaner."

"I thought we were using your cell?"

"We are, but this call is off the record. I'm going into Maxwell in a few minutes to put on a little more pressure."

"Good. Sam and I brought Acadia up to speed on how the FBI works and the implications of protective custody."

"Getting sticky isn't it?'

"It is. Have you reported Acadia missing yet?"

"I'll do that from Maxwell. That way Andrea can confirm I've been there."

"You could use a Maxwell in-house phone."

"I like that idea."

"The FBI guys Patton arranged have arrived. They agree our safe house courtesy of Sam's agency friends is ideal. They've interviewed Acadia and want us to continue our coverage for her safety because we know the players."

Santiago laughed. "That and we have higher security clearances."

"That too, Sam said higher than the agents."

"We'll talk later, Link. When we do my bruises ought to be standing out like beacons."

"As long as they're your beacons. Later babe."

On her way out of the building Santiago asked the doorman how Xavier got in without her approval.

"Don't know ma'am. He entered before I came on shift."

"Thank you."

She caught a cab and watched out the windows on her way to Maxwell. The bright sun alternating with rapidly passing tree shade created a rhythmic pattern. She closed her eyes for few minutes. *That's almost hypnotic.*

She opened them and it started again. "That shade-sun pattern can make your mind dance."

The female driver said, "Ma'am, you say some-thing?"

"No, just talking to myself."

"I saw the police at your building. Looked pretty busy."

"It was but over now."

"That fella they took away slap you 'round?"

"A little."

"Bruise startin' to show even with your makeup."

"Great way to make an impression on a new job."

"I know what you mean. I've worked Maxwell a time or two, usually a bachelor party."

Santiago looked at the driver's eyes. "Catering, bar-tending?"

"Special catering."

"I think we're in different businesses. I work public relations, today in a battered format."

"Sorry, ma'am. I thought, you know...nothing."

The driver was quiet the remainder of the trip.

God, she thinks I'm a hooker or stripper. Come on girl, these are not stripper threads. This is conservative for me.

She put her sunglasses back on as they pulled into the Maxwell lot. When Santiago got out of the cab she gave the driver a twenty dollar tip. "Don't work those special events too often. It's a rough business in a tough world." She turned and walked into the build-ing, her five inch heels clicking across the brick entry into the terrazzo lobby.

Once in the Noble area Santiago checked the workstation schedules, then went into the Reaper area. She approached Doctor Train and asked, "Where is Acadia?"

"She hasn't come in yet."

"She call?"

"Nothing, it's just Joyce and me so far today."

Santiago looked around the area. "I see," then went to the Noble office area and called Nance.

She answered on the first ring. "Mitch, anything new on Xavier?"

"No. Right now I'm at Maxwell checking on the progress of the teams. Doctor Yeager isn't here yet. She had a golf game with Link this morning but hasn't been heard from since."

"What are you thinking, Mitch?"

"I'm going to run out to the Garden District and stop by her house. With all that has gone on yesterday and today is seems the prudent thing to do."

"Agreed. It's been a scary morning. If you don't find her or hear from her let me know."

"I will. It seems like a lot of things are happening at once."

"It does. I have to go but keep in touch, Mitch, and see a doctor before the day ends."

"Thank you, Andrea. I will if I get the chance."

Nance broke the connection.

Santiago smiled and hung up. "Squirm lady."

*****

A young assistant took Andrea Nance to Reagan National Airport. Just before boarding the Maxwell jet she handed the young woman her personal credit card. Tina, I have a reservation for two at the Patriot Bar and Grill this evening. I won't be able to keep it. Instead, I want you and your hubby to go on me. Just sign my name to the tab. It's a five star no questions asked fabulous restaurant with a view to die for."

Tina took the card. "Thank you. We'd love to go there. It's just so expensive for us."

"As I said, my treat, no limits. You've earned a night out."

Nance boarded for the flight to New Orleans. *Alibi complete.*

She arrived at Louis Armstrong International two hours later and took a cab to Ramparts and Parish after looking up the address of Susan Train. She secured a cash room with a false name and immediately took a different cab to Train's neighborhood.

When she arrived the cab dropped her at a nearby restaurant and she walked. The house was a rebuilt structure in part having been repaired following hurricane Katrina. The yard appeared well maintained in the late afternoon sun. The smell of freshly cut grass added to the embellishments. She went to the door, knocked, and watched Susan Train come to the door through its old fashioned window in the center.

Train opened the door. "Dear me, what a wonderful surprise. Andrea, has Doctor Sigmund been heard from?"

"No, nothing yet. Did the FBI visit Maxwell today?"
Train shook her head. "No."

"They will within the next seventy-two hours if they follow standard missing person protocol. Given Sigmund's assignment and security clearance I would expect something within twenty-four hours if she doesn't surface."

"Andrea, pardon my manners, come in. I have a fresh pot of coffee on."

"I'd love some."

"Let's go to the kitchen."

"It's nice and bright in here."

Train noticed Nance's hands were gloved. "You can't be cold."

"The opposite. I burned my hands today and the gloves protect the bandages. It's not a big deal, just inconvenient."

"Sit down."

"This is very nice. I see you cook with cast iron. I like a true Cajun, and the pans look good hanging there. I use cast iron, too, have most of my adult life. They don't even feel heavy like in the beginning."

"I know what you mean."

Train turned toward the stove on the opposite side of the kitchen and began pouring two cups of coffee. "Do you take cream or sugar?"

"No thank you," said Nance as she stood and took a six inch cast iron pan from its hook.

She turned and struck Train on the back of her head. Susan fell forward toward the stove, then the sink. She slid down the face of the lower cabinets to the floor. She was on her back, eyes blinking, blood pooling under her head, lips moving but never uttering a sound. Nance struck her again on the forehead, the edge of the pan crushing its way into the skull. Train's eyes stared unblinking as more blood pooled around her head.

Another woman's voice came from down the hallway. "Susan, Susan, are you alright? It sounded like you fell."

Nance was quiet for a moment. She looked at Susan Train's body, took a deep breath and watched the dark hallway. "No problem, I dropped a frying pan."

She crept down the dark hallway to the last room on the right and peered around the corner of the door. A woman was propped up in bed, a small lamp on the nightstand provided the only light.

She walked into the room. "Everything is fine. Susan's cleaning up a little mess."

"I'm Susan's mother."

"It's a pleasure."

"Likewise, and you're Andrea Nance. I've seen your picture. Susan speaks highly of you. Come in."

"Here, let me help you with your pillows while we wait."

Nance took a pillow, fluffed it then pressed it over the woman's face. The elderly woman struggled, grabbed at Nance's wrists and hands but could not get the pillow off her face. She wiggled, twisted, and shuddered. A muffled few sounds and breaths escaped as her chest ceased to expand and retract. Nance removed the pillow after a few minutes. The woman was dead.

Nance wiped sweat from her forehead, tossed the pillow on the floor, and returned to the kitchen. The blood from Susan's wounds was congealing. Nance carefully stepped over the blood and body, and went to the living room. She walked to a bookcase and swept a shelf of books onto the floor. Next she pulled the drawer from a desk and scattered the contents, then tossed an open laptop on the floor.

She put on dark glasses, left the house and walked back to the restaurant. After waiting out in front for a few minutes a cab approached. She flagged it down and went to Canal and Bourbon Street then walked to the Frenchman Condominium. She called Santiago on her burn cell while sitting at an outside coffee patio watching the front entry to the building.

"Hello Mitch, anything on Sigmund yet?"

"No, not a clue. It's like she's gone out of circulation or someone has snatched her. She wasn't home either."

"I'll be in New Orleans by tomorrow. If we haven't heard anything by then we call the local police. Right now I'm going to alert Homeland Security and see what their course of action will be. I'd expect them to contact you very soon. Are you going to be in or do you and Link have plans?"

"If we did they would be secondary. Truth is, he and Sam are off working on something dealing with Barrier, probably in a bar. I'll be hanging out here for the next few hours if not staying in all night."

"Good, I'll let them know it's a good time, and make them aware of the incident this morning with Xavier."

"Thank you."

"Have you heard any more about him?"

"No, I probably won't for a day or two, then it'll be expanding on my statement as they prepare evidence to send to the DA."

"Good, try to have a quiet night. I'll be in touch tomorrow."

Nance watched the entry. *How to get in undetected?* She walked around behind the building to a service entrance near the tenant parking. She waited for several minutes. An old pickup truck pulled into the employee section, then a car. She crossed the street as they went to the service door. One of them punched in a code and all three entered. She crossed the parking area but the door swung shut before she could reach it. She stepped back in the shadows. *People come to work, people get off work.*

The door opened and two people in employee uniforms came out. Nance rushed up to the door and said, "Pardon me."

"Sorry ma'am, this is an employee entrance. All guests must enter from the front."

"Oh, the client in 309 said I was to come in the back to avoid, you know, the wife thing, a French Quarter weekend."

One of the departing employees held the door open. "We get many weekend visitors but you probably know that. When you come out just hit the crash bar."

Nance said, "Thank you and rushed in still wearing the dark glasses and gloves. She took the stairs to the second floor avoiding the lobby then the elevator to the fourth. When she knocked on 406 it took Santiago only a moment to answer.

"Andrea, a little early for tomorrow."

Nance held a Beretta M9. "Inside."

"No FBI?"

"Not tonight. Do you know where Sigmund went?"

"You know I don't. What is this? Do you think I'm part of the leak group?"

Nance shook her head. "No, I think you're here looking for the mole just like me, but having your boyfriend show up is just a little too convenient, especially when he's playing golf with Sigmund and then she disappears. My conclusion – you're still working for DataFlex."

"You know better. You did the vetting."

"Call Link. Tell him you need to talk with Sigmund about one of her team members, say Susan Train."

"You're making a serious mistake, Andrea. Why would I tell you about Xavier? If I was with DataFlex the authorities could have kept that situation quiet for several days."

"I know you've been doing deep background on all of us."

"Yes, you said you wanted me to use your sources, do my job. When at DataFlex one of the first people I researched was Claude Braun, and I had met him years earlier when he was dating my best friend."

"Sounds logical." She waved the gun. "Now call Link."

Santiago took her personal cell from the coffee table and punched in Link's number. "Hi, where are you?"

"With Sam. It's a good thing you got your phone charged, Mitch. I've been meaning to call."

Nance said, "Tell him."

"I'm here with Andrea. She wants to talk with Doctor Sigmund and believes you know where she is."

Nance grabbed the cell. "I know you have her. I want her brought here now or your cute sexy playmate is dead meat. Understand?"

Andrews paused. "I understand. Where are you?"

"The Frenchman. Call when you get here. We'll be coming out to join you. Don't come into the building, come alone and keep this to yourself. If I don't get what I want, Mitch dies."

"What is it you want?"

"Right now Doctor Sigmund."

"I'll bring your mother, anything else?"

Nance opened her eyes wide, swallowed, and took a breath. "No."

"It'll take thirty minutes from when I can get the next ferry from Algiers."

Andrews broke the connection.

"Sit on the couch, Mitch. I'll sit over here. And keep in mind, the walls of these units are foot thick concrete; fireproof and soundproof. I'm sure you've noticed no boat whistles or trains when the windows are closed."

"You know we've made the connection between you, Acadia and Ishtar."

"I would expect that."

"Why the intrigue, the deception. Acadia didn't know who you were."

"She didn't look for me either, didn't give a damn."

"So what is the purpose of bringing everybody together? Revenge for a bad childhood?"

"I want to destroy my mother's professional legacy by compromising the most sensitive project she has ever worked on and casting her in the role of traitor. God, sweet revenge."

"And Ishtar goes along with this?"

"No, she doesn't even know of my plan. She has her own scores to settle."

"Ishtar knows who you are."

"Of course. We connected in Washington after my marriage fell apart and I was trying to form my own company."

Santiago shook her head. "No, she has known who you are your entire life. She is the one that made sure you had clothes, were moved often if you had questionable foster homes, and most important the Garden Club scholarship."

"That can't be true. You make it sound like she groomed me."

"Think about it. She and Francis could have adopted you even without telling you who you are. Your mother didn't know where you were and could not unlock sealed records. She didn't have the resources Noble has."

"If that's true I've been deceived."

"Yes."

"Why would they deceive me?"

"You know why. Ishtar has her own agenda. I think you're the instrument to complete a plan she has that will leave her completely in the clear, perhaps above suspicion. I'm sure you know the plan, but keep in mind all the details, dirty work, everything leads to you, maybe Francis, but nothing to Ishtar. You can go to prison for life, even death row. She's going to skate unless you cut a deal."

Nance said nothing.

Someone knocked on the door. Nance checked her watch. "It's too early for Link." She waved the gun at the door. "See who it is."

They crossed the living room. Santiago shouted, "Who is it?"

"Doorman, a package from a Mr. Braun. I need a signature."

Nance nodded and stepped behind the door. Santiago opened the door and crashed it against Nance. Link Andrews and Sam Evans rushed in. Santiago threw Nance to the floor and took the Baretta. "Damn, I had handcuffs in my other life."

Evans stepped over Nance as Santiago got up.

Andrews put his arms around her. "Are you okay?"

"Better than what she had planned. How'd you get here so quick?"

"While we were talking Sam arranged a helicopter from the Naval Supply Center. It was only a mile or two away. I'm surprised you didn't hear us landing on the roof."

Santiago chuckled. "Soundproof."

Evans stood Nance up, pushed Nance against the wall and patted her down. "She's clean."

Nance straightened her cinch belt, spun and slashed Evans on the side of the face with a box cutter. The cut reached from the cheek under his right eye to his throat. Evans fell back into Santiago and Andrews. Nance dashed out the door as Evens fell to the floor with blood covering his face, neck and torso. Andrews caught him. Santiago looked at the empty doorway then rushed to the kitchen and got a wet dishtowel. She gave it to Andrews and called 911.

Andrews shouted, "Oh fuck, this is bad! Hang on, Sam, they'll be here in a minute." He applied pressure. "Mitch, the copter is still on the roof. Take Sam's phone and hit redial, get them to stay. We can fly him faster than an ambulance."

As she did four firemen came through the door way and began first aid on Sam. They strapped him to the stretcher and raised it.

Santiago shouted, "We have a helicopter on the roof. Use it to move him."

One of the firemen said, "Will it hold the stretcher?"

"Andrews said, "Yes, it a transport unit, let's go."

New Orleans police arrived after Evans's was moved. Andrews addressed the officers and filled them in on the events.

Santiago said, "They took Sam to East Jefferson Hospital, same as Xavier."

One of the officers smiled. "It's been a busy day at the Frenchman, not your normal business day."

Andrews said, "Officer, an FBI agent will be in con-tact with you. We need to get to the hospital."

*****

Shari Stiletto entered the Techno Investors reception at the Monroe Savoy on Massachusetts Avenue in Washington, D.C. She was greeted at the door by a gentlemen in a tuxedo, white gloves, and a bulge at the back of his jacket. He took the printed invitation and said, "Welcome, Miss Stiletto, it is a pleasure having you join us this evening."

"The pleasure is mine."

Stiletto walked into the room. She wore an elegant black floor length gown that fit like a glove with a slit up the left leg beyond mid-thigh, a revealing tasteful neckline, five inch heels, and a golden tan. Her dark brown shoulder length curls with a dash of red tint set her off from the standard diamonds and gown set.

Senator DuBois watched her from across the room and nudged his friend. "Now that is arm candy and more."

The president of an investment firm he was chatting with laughed. "She is gorgeous, Broderick. I think you have more than arm candy in mind."

"Hundred bucks says I bed her."

"You're on."

Both men laughed and DuBois began to work his way toward Stiletto.

A waiter passed with a tray of champagne flutes. He took two and continued on his quest. As he neared Stiletto he took a deep breath. *Beautiful eyes, stunning gown, teardrop earrings, middle-aged with the body of a model.*

DuBois stepped in front of Stiletto. "Champagne?"

Stiletto arched an eyebrow. "Thank you, Senator."

"Have we met?"

"We have now. I'm Shari Stiletto," she said in a sultry voice.

"Indeed. It's always a pleasure to meet a beautiful woman for the first time. I wouldn't forget you."

"Thank you."

"Are you meeting someone?"

"You."

"Really?"

"Claude Braun asked that I meet you and present an offer from him to you."

"DataFlex carries a great deal of wait wherever it goes. I'd love to chat with you. Can we wait until after the reception?"

Stiletto took a deep breath not lost on the lustful eyes of the senator. "I'd rather get together now in case we need more time to complete our business."

A Triad executive approached. "Miss Stiletto, it is a pleasure to meet Mr. Braun's personal representative. If you have any needs don't hesitate to call." He handed Stiletto a card then nodded at DuBois. "Senator."

"Shari, I think you're right. Now is better. I can't have all these wealthy business executives drooling all over you all night long. Do you have a room?"

"Will a penthouse cover it?"

DuBois glanced at the slit in her gown. "Claude Braun always shows class in his business dealings."

"It's not Claude nor his business you're focused on."

"True, but business with you will be much more enjoyable."

"Shall we go?"

"Your penthouse sounds wonderful."

He took her arm and they retreated to the elevators.

"I'm surprised Claude didn't contact me first, not that I object, but business can sometimes require lengthy negotiations."

"He believes I'll make the necessary connections and headway this evening. I'm accustomed to success."

The elevator door opened. He smiled and held out a hand. "I'll bet you are."

When they entered Stiletto's suite DuBois slid his dinner jacket off. "I was going to order some champagne but I see you've already set the stage."

Stiletto chuckled and bit the tip of her tongue. "I like to be prepared."

He took the bottle from its bucket and filled two flutes.

She said, "I'm going to get into something a little more comfortable. Do you mind?"

"No, not at all. What is it Claude wants to talk about?"

Stiletto was sliding the zipper down the back of the gown as she went into the bedroom called back, "We'll talk when I come out. Go ahead and get comfortable."

"Works for me."

A moment later Stiletto appeared wearing a black fitted leather jumpsuit with the top two buttons open. The senator looked up. "Kinky, I like this. You do have all the necessary skills for achieving Claude's goals."

"Of course. In my profession it is all about the bottom line and how to make it swell."

He stared at her breasts. "I like your philosophy. Shall we go out on the balcony? The view of the city is spectacular."

"I'd like that," she said stepping outside.

They finished their champagne. She touched his chest lightly with the tips of her fingers. DuBois stepped closer putting an arm around her.

"Senator, I'd like to start negotiations with a video, something a little spicy. Are you game?"

"Oh yes."

They went back inside. Stiletto turned on the television and video player. The flash drive came on the screen and Stiletto sat down on a chair to the senator's side.

"Claude wants you to watch closely."

DuBois focused, then sat up straight as the video of him and Valentine Smith began. He furled his brow, formed fists repeatedly as he watched through squinted eyes. In a harsh voice he shouted, "Where did you get this?"

"We have our sources."

"It's a fake!"

"No it's not. It was made in New Orleans just two days ago at the Augustine Bayou Suites, room 407."

Valentine's body came into focus; nude, beautiful, writhing about and riding a man.

DuBois squirmed, shifted his weight, pressed his knees together. Sweat covered his brow. The camera focused on the groin area of the woman.

Stiletto pointed and said softly, "I've never tried a strap-on. That's kinky."

The camera focused on the man. He was on his knees and pulled away from the woman and the strap-on, sitting up straight on his knees. The camera slowly moved up the torso to the head and face.

"You're hung, Senator, in more ways than one."

Almost in a growl he said, "Turn that off."

Stiletto flicked the control. "You don't like watching yourself perform, Broderick?"

"It's disgusting."

"Especially when you think of it being a U.S. Senator known as the family guy and all those good things."

"What does Braun want?"

"Your cooperation."

"Yes, yes, for what?"

"You resignation, of course."

"Which committee?"

"No, no, your office. He believes you should resign your office."

"You can't be serious."

"This video will be on the internet and around the world in twelve hours beginning now if you don't resign."

"I can't do that. I'm a U. S. Senator."

"Choice is yours."

"Give me the video. You could get hurt. I could make you disappear."

"I'm sure you could but that won't change anything. The video is already scheduled. It will now go on in eleven hours and fifty-eight minutes. What Mr. Braun wants, and what the public needs is your corrupt ass out of government forever. Resign and never become involved in any government activity again either as an office holder, consultant, lobbyist – nothing. If you do the video comes out. If anything happens to me the video plays. Am I making myself and Mr. Braun's position clear?"

"Yes."

"It's time to become that wholesome southern gentlemen involved with his family and plantation."

"Other politicians have been caught in affairs and survived."

"True, a mistress here, an intern there, a model here, and escort there, but none have been seen in public getting screwed with a strap-on. It's your choice."

He shook his head. "I don't know what to do."

"As I see it you have three options, Broderick. Go forward and see what happens when the press and public see the video, suicide, or resign and retire. The choice is yours."

"This is blackmail."

"Of course it is, just like the pressure you've put on so many over the years while getting your way. I believe you once used the term 'hardball' to explain how you gained cooperation from some reluctant party members."

"Yes, but this is extreme."

DuBois sat quietly for over a minute. He looked around the suite, the woman in the black jumpsuit, the blank television screen.

She said, "What's your pleasure?"

"Not you."

"You have eleven hours and ...."

"Shut up, I know what I have."

He took out his cell and punched in a number.

His press secretary answered. "How'd the recep-"

DuBois shouted, "Schedule a press conference for tomorrow morning at 8:00 a.m."

"It's pretty late to-"

"Do it. I don't give a damn how late it is. And have my entire staff report at 7:00 a.m., no exceptions."

"Broderick, what is wrong?"

"Not a damned thing."

"What about the judicial breakfast tomorrow?"

"Screw 'em, screw 'em all. Just do what I say."

He slammed the phone down. "Braun should've called me himself."

"Is it your decision to resign?"

"Yes, damn it, can't you tell?"

"You have a future retired. Claude is trying to give you that opportunity even though you have violated the trust of the people. I think he's protecting your family if you cooperate."

Stiletto punched in Braun's cell number. "Claude, Broderick Dubois would like a word."

"Put him on."

DuBois took the phone. "You bastard."

"Broderick, you best chill a little. I've given you a safe avenue out of a career overflowing with corruption and deceit. You don't have to follow it if you don't want to. I believe you have eleven hours and one minute to decide."

"I have made my decision, 8:00 a.m. tomorrow morning I'll submit my resignation to become effective in two weeks."

Braun laughed. "Not good enough. Immediately or the video plays, and it will go viral."

"There are some bills that need action."

"Some of those bills have been bought and paid for by lobbyists, Broderick. You're not voting on them."

"It's impossible to resign instantly."

"Then you can set a precedent. Call it health, personal, whatever. I'll be watching the news tomorrow morning, your time."

DuBois said, "We're done here," handed Stiletto the cell phone and walked out the door.

She said, "Sorry about the late call but he needed that final push."

"I wouldn't have it any other way."

"Will you notify Ray in the morning? I don't want to bother him at this hour either."

"You may have to tell him yourself. You're leaving now aren't you?"

"Yes."

"Just open your door."

Stiletto went to the door and opened it.

Ray House was standing there. "Surprise, Shari. Just in case you needed a little backup. That and I have a great story to tell you on the way back about Mitch's afternoon."

"She laughed. "I've got the jet, how'd you get here?"

"I flew charter – a day long adventure, but our New Orleans team is very busy, and I have many connections in this town if you had any trouble."

"Ray, do you agency types ever retire?"

"That depends on how you define retire. Jessica and I are still working on that."

"Is she with you?"

"At the plane, shall we?"

"Yes, I travel light but I want these two flutes. Mitch said DuBois's DNA could be critical."

They left the building.

*****

Santiago and Andrews stood by Sam Evans bedside at East Jefferson Hospital.

"Mitch, do you want to wait 'til Sam wakes?"

"No, his wife will be here before he does. She's already on her way. The doctor says it looks worse than it is and he'll recover. I want to move now and nail Nance before she hurts anyone else."

Andrews nodded. "She's a mean bitch."

"Lucky for Sam she missed an artery."

"Lucky for all of us."

She took out her cell. "I'm calling Francis Dade. He may not know about how privy I am to their operation."

"Do it."

She punched in Noble's New York Security office.

"Noble Security, Elmer speaking."

"Good evening, Mitch Santiago calling from New Orleans. We have a very sensitive situation regarding

Adrian Nance. I would like to speak with Francis
Dade."

"Mr. Dade's office is not in security."

"I know, but I do not have a number for him. Being
that it is the weekend I believe a cell or home number
is necessary. Could you contact him and ask that he
contact me back if he so chooses?"

"That's not possible. Mr. Dade has left word not to
be disturbed under any circumstances. He and his wife
are out of town for a few days."

"Oh, a short vacation." She paused. "That's probably good for them. He's been quite busy of late. Did
they get off to Europe this time?"

"Nothing that elaborate, just Palm Springs. Sorry, I
can't help you any further Miss Santiago. I can track
down one of the vice-presidents but it will take some
time since we're into the weekend."

"No, I'll wait 'til he gets back from Palm Springs but
if you hear from Miss Nance tell her I called. She'll
ring me back." Santiago broke the connection.

Andrews answered a call on his cell. "Yes, Agent
Zachery. Thank you."

"Mitch, Zachery has received a report Susan Train
and her mother have been murdered at Train's home."

"That has to be Nance. She came here to kill me after a bit of quizzing. She's trying to clean up loose
ends."

"Why Train?"

"She had to be Noble's eyes and ears inside Reaper.
Her mom was probably collateral damage would be my
bet."

Santiago called Spears cell. "Are you on a date?"

"No, I'm here at the office. Ray went to Washington and assigned me to hang here – everybody else is gone."

"Find out where Ishtar and Francis Dade are staying in Palm Springs. Link and I need to go there."

"Can do. I'll call back."

Santiago brought flight information up on her cell phone and bought three first class seats on the next scheduled flight to Palm Springs. She smiled at Link. "First Class is always the last filled. They had room for all three of us. We leave in an hour and a half."

"Three?"

"Dash is coming with us. Neither the Dade's nor Andrea know who she is. Desiree will stay in New Orleans and fill Sam's slot until Ray assigns a replacement. She may continue working with the FBI as a guardian of Acadia, but I doubt that will last very long. Let's get our stuff and meet Dash at the airport."

"She already knows she's coming with us?"

"No, but she will before we're out of here."

As they walked down the hall from Evans room they passed a police officer standing in front of Xavier's door.

Santiago smiled. "He won't forget me for a while.'

"I'd bet never."

They both laughed. Santiago's cell rang.

"Mitch, the Dade's are staying at the Gold Dust Condominium and Resort."

"Thank you, book two suites for us. One for Link and me, the other for Dash. And let Ray know when you talk to him." She broke the connection and called Dash. Then it was a cab to the condominium, quick change, pack and off to Louis Armstrong International. The privacy window in the cab was closed.

"Mitch, what are you going to use Dash for? She's not backgrounded on this operation."

"The obvious, drive Francis Dade up a wall with her womanly charms. If she finds him willing to play she may turn him."

"Is he a player?"

"He has a little friend at home, a Miss Fawn, who comes from his wife's reward world when he does well on his tasks."

"Really?"

"I don't think Francis created his mess, Link. I think Ishtar did and has a unique control over her husband and created a scenario to get revenge for the death of her son. Francis was a pawn in her plan, Andrea a tool, a sociopath loyal to her auntie so to speak. Right now we don't have enough evidence to get an indictment on Ishtar."

"You mean the Feds?"

"Yes. Unless Andrea or Francis rollover we, they don't have squat."

In other words Ishtar is the brains, the mover. She's used all these other players as pawns."

"Yes, but she probably doesn't know Andrea's plan to gain revenge on her birth mother."

"And the senator?"

"I believe he's Jeffrey's father but doesn't know. I think his use was in getting Noble government contracts and in a position to control the development of the new Reaper guidance program – for her use, a government contract, and as a possible future black market product."

As they boarded their flight Santiago received a call from Noble Security in New York.

"Yes,"

"Miss Santiago, Elmer again. Through a vice-president I did get your message out to Mr. Dade. He will not be calling but did ask I advise you your services are no longer required."

"I see. May I speak with your supervisor?"

"Of course."

The phone clicked twice. "Miss Santiago, I'm Frederick Gilliland. I was Miss Nance's number two, now I'm temporarily filling her position."

"So I should answer to you."

"You would if you were still working for Noble but it has been determined to reorganize both Reaper and Barrier with new teams. We've had some changes in the government, the Noble leadership team, and Reaper. We'll pay you according to the language of your contract but you are, as they say in sports, a free agent." He broke the connection.

She looked at Andrews and laughed as they sat down in their seats across from Dash.

"I've been stalked, beat-up, burgled, had two attempts made on my life and fired twice all in one week. It's a good thing I like working the private sector. Being a cop was high risk but much easier than this week has been."

Andrews smiled. "Palm Springs, here we come."

CHAPTER 17
Sunday, July 13

Dash Varga was asleep across the aisle from Santiago and Andrews as the redeye flight to Palm Springs glided through the night.

Santiago looked out the window. It was dark except for an occasional cluster of light as they flew over a small community. "Big city lights are few and far between."

"It's a big country, Mitch, sometimes we just don't realize how big."

"Think we'll see Quartzite? I still get a chill thinking about Thomas Grant pinning my hand to a table top with an ice pick."

Andrews laughed. "Probably not on this flight, but you definitely got even when you shot his family jewels off at the Quartzite Airport. In fact, you seem to be rather hard on men's groins if you include Xavier and your hooker heel. I'm sure he'll shudder every time he thinks about you."

She kissed his cheek. "Seems to be a good equalizer."

"Just don't ever get mad at me."

"Come on. When Alex had his fling with Desiree, I didn't do anything to him. It was another learning experience for me and my noncommittal world. He had a similar problem."

"True, she didn't hang out very long with him either. He lost both ways; you and her."

She laughed. "He's a better agent now, not as easily distracted. As for me, a girl's gotta move on. I've never been as connected with anyone as I am now."

"I like the sound of that. You probably didn't have much chance to grow roots as a kid in a hippie culture."

"Maybe, but I think working as a dancer taught me most guys are looking for a one-night stand. The hustler's didn't even care what your name was."

"You ever get caught up in that? I did in my Navy days."

"I did a couple of times. It didn't take long to learn."

"Mitch, I want you to think about Hawaii as we finish up in Palm Springs. We ought to take a vacation."

"I could go for Hawaii, sort of like Palm Springs, surrounded by water."

"Possible, Mitch; Palm Springs and golf to me are like string bikinis and sketch pads to you. We could do it all in the islands with no interference."

"When we finish up here I want to check on my cousin John with Doctor Grossman. I also want to see what he's come up with for assisted care living for my parents."

He nodded. "Back on task, do you think Shari will get a DNA sample from DuBois after forcing his resignation?"

"I have no doubt. She'll do whatever is needed."

"Do you think Andrea will show up in Palm Springs?"

"It wouldn't surprise me. She can run. She might try to get even first. We know she would've killed Acadia if she found her."

Andrews shook his head. "If we see her we'll call it in, maybe keep track of her, but no capture unless necessary. You think she'll go after the Dade's?"

"If she turns up here, yes."

"What about Dash?"

"I'm thinking she should make a contact with Francis if possible; hangout in the lounge, pool, gym, whatever. He'll notice her for sure."

"It's a guy thing, Mitch."

The flight attendant approached them. "We'll be landing in about fifteen minutes."

Santiago said, "Thank you." She looked at Link. "It's wonderful to have Claude's name behind us, no 2:00 o'clock check-in time.

Andrews reached across the aisle and nudged Dash. "We're landing."

They fastened their seat belts.

*****

Santiago, Andrews and Varga were checked into the Gold Dust via the executive privileges extended to many corporate groups.

Dash smiled. "It's nice not having to wait until the regular time."

Santiago laughed. "Work these types of assignments often and you'll get spoiled. Claude takes care of his people. You have a suite overlooking the pool and we're two doors down with the same view."

Andrews raised an eyebrow. "Let Francis find you, Dash, and we'll have your back."

Santiago said, "You might discover he's a man looking for more than sex. He could be a guy that wants a friend; someone to talk with and listen. From what we've learned, Ishtar and her father call the shots and Francis is totally under her thumb."

Dash laughed, "Show him the goods but dig deeper."

Santiago nodded. "That about covers it, so to speak."

After checking into her suite Dash Varga opened the slider and went out on the lanai. "Sweet."

She turned and saw the fruit bowl with a note on a table. "Thank you for working with the team on short notice, Claude Braun." Beside the basket was a bottle of Jack Daniel's Sinatra Blend.

She stepped in front of a full length mirror and slid out of her five inch stilettoes and white sheath. "Claude, you do know how to get a girl's attention." She stood in front of the mirror while putting on a bright yellow string bikini and chiffon wraparound. "I need my yellow stilettoes."

After getting dressed she went to the lobby, visited the lounge, made an appointment at the salon, and checked the pool area and gym. She was in the gift shop looking at magazines when she encountered Francis Dade. She rubbed against him and dropped her magazine while he was glancing at the pictorial of a men's edition.

She said, "Excuse me," and bent to retrieve her magazine displaying ample cleavage and her dark form against the yellow fabric.

He said, "Here, let me help you." He bent over with her, picked up the magazine and handed it to her. "Are you staying here?"

No, I always walk around almost naked when I'm shopping. "Yes."

"I see you're interested in fashion."

"A girl's gotta do what she's gotta do."

He smiled and put the men's skin magazine back on the shelf.

Dash nodded at his magazine's cover. "Now those girls are beautiful."

Dade blushed. "Yes, but not as beautiful as you."

She looked down and away.

He scanned her easily visible frame. "Or as fashion conscious."

She wet her lips. "Thank you. Are you staying here, too?"

"Yes, in the penthouse."

"Maybe I'll see you around. After I take care of a few things I'm going to the pool. I overlook it from my second floor suite but nothing like the view you have."

He smiled. "And all those muscular young men. I'm sure they'll enjoy you."

"I enjoy them, too."

"And you should."

She winked. "I do, but sometimes I like the company of a mature man; one who can carry on a conversation, be a friend, knows what he wants and how to treat a woman. The younger men have their obvious benefits, but most are rather narcissistic." She glanced at the magazine cover again. "I bet you know what you want and how to get it."

"I usually do get what I want. Perhaps we'll bump into each other again."

"I'm sure we will Mr...."

"Dade, Francis Dade."

"A pleasure, Francis, I'm Dash Varga. I hope we'll meet again, maybe at the pool."

Dade left the gift shop. Varga remained for a few minutes then headed toward the pool. She found a lounge chair partially in the shade with a view to the top floor railing. She slid the cover off, put on her sunglasses, and stretched out on her back looking up at the penthouse balcony. She waved at a waiter.

"Yes ma'am."

"Diet cola, please."

She leaned into the lounge putting her head on a cushion facing the penthouse. Before the waiter returned with her cola Francis Dade was looking over the railing and smiling.

She smiled back and waved. *God, you're in your sixties, out of shape, rich and horny. Come on down little man. There's a pool full of eye candy here just waiting to be licked.*

The waiter stood beside her. "Your cola, ma'am."

"Thank you, my room number is 204. Who is that staying in the penthouse?"

The waiter smiled. "Another Mr. and Mrs. Smith."

"I thought so. Give yourself a nice tip."

"Thank you."

"And who are they in reality?"

"Mr. and Mrs. Dade of the Noble Group. I believe Mr. Dade is the CEO."

Dash took out her cell and dialed Santiago. "They're in the penthouse using the name Smith. I'd think of something more original. I met him in the magazine section down in the lobby. Old Francis drooled out his real name while checking the skin mags. When asked, the waiter poolside said, 'Another Mr. and Mrs. Smith,' with a nice tip they became Mr. and Mrs. Dade."

Santiago laughed. "I saw Dade waving at you. Nice work."

"Hey, are gift baskets from Mr. Braun a normal routine or is he hitting on me?"

"It's a tradition on special assignments. Claude has a thing for good booze. What do you drink?"

"I'm a Jack Daniels fan."

"I'll bet you received a bottle of the best in the Jack Daniels line."

"Jack Daniels Sinatra Tradition."

"That's Claude, only the best of your favorite brand."

"What do you usually receive?"

"Walker Blue Label, and Link received Captain Morgan Private Stock."

Dash picked up her bottle of sun tan lotion. "I'll talk to you later. I have to get back to work."

She sat up and slowly applied the lotion to her legs, arms, neck, face, then rubbed a little more on her thighs. She finished by lying flat on her back and rubbing lotion on her belly and shoulders. She adjusted the lounge to a partial sitting position and stretched out, feet parted to shoulder width. She glanced toward the penthouse. *See anything you like, Francis? You didn't miss a stroke. Will you be down to do my back or does the wife have an anchor locked to your leg?*

A young man approached Dash with a large toothpaste smile, the torso of a Greek God, and the tan of a lifeguard. "Want some help putting lotion on your back?"

She shaded her eyes and teased her teeth with her tongue. "I love it when someone volunteers to help me out. By all means, but I don't want to be molested."

"I wouldn't think of it."

She rolled over on her belly and pulled the tie to the top loose. "Don't want a tan line."

He nodded. "Never."

He squeezed lotion from the bottle and rubbed it in taking his time. His strong fingertips teased the waistband of her bikini bottom but he didn't probe.

Dash moaned approval. *You're waiting for an invitation I'd give you in a New York minute if I wasn't working.* She turned her head and glanced at her unknown helper.

"Thank you, I think my date is due back and I'm sure he'll be curious how I got my backside oiled."

The young man stood and smiled again. "Maybe another time. You could do me, too. I'm here all week."

"And you're...?"

"Rory Bullet. My friends call me 'Bull.'"

"I'm sure they do. It's nice to meet you. I'm Dash Varga."

"You're the hottest woman I've encountered here."

She laughed. "There are others. Later, Bull, and thank you."

She glanced over her shoulder toward the penthouse patio. "Empty."

She rested her cheek on the pillow and waited. A shadow crossed her body. She turned and looked up at the sun blurred figure of an older man in a Speedo staring down at her.

Dade said, "I thought I'd try the water. It must be fate that we meet twice the same day."

She smiled. *Don't laugh, do not laugh.*

He sat down on a chair and stretched his legs.

"Must be. I was having a soda and catching some rays. Would like to join me?"

He waved his hand and the sun caught a diamond on a pinky ring. "I'd love to."

She watched his eyes but said nothing. *You weren't wearing that a while ago.*

"So, Miss Varga, are you going to try the water?"

She retied the straps of her top and rolled over. "Not right now, I just got oiled, so to speak. I want to take care of my skin."

He laughed. "And beautiful skin it is; beautiful body, full face, cross cultural appearance. Your lips are full, sensual. If I were writing a story, I'd say inviting."

"I've heard that phrase many times, Francis, but nobody's ever told me what it is I'm inviting."

He laughed and ogled her breasts pressed against the triangles. "Use your imagination. I'm sure there are several answers, all good." He swallowed.

"That's one answer."

They both laughed.

He said, "You're quite intelligent and quick. I was thinking we might have a drink together and chat after a quick dip."

"Really? The way you're staring at my boobs suggests another thought or two."

"I'm sorry. I don't mean to make you uncomfortable. It's just you're so...."

She smiled and tilted her head, "Inviting? Don't worry about it. I didn't come here to be ignored. It takes too much work for that."

"You're a very open young woman."

"Most women my age are; a different generation, different mores."

His breathing rate increased. "Yes, modern. Maybe just for this afternoon we could be friends if you don't mind."

"I'd like that. Nothing like a mature gentleman to hold the bulls at bay."

Dash's cell rang. "Yes."

It was Santiago. "Is he cooperating?"

Dash looked at Dade. "Oh yes, I've made a new friend. We'd like to spend some time chatting, I think."

"Good, get him to the lounge; maybe a delay for a private business call and he could join you shortly; you know, wet his appetite."

"I can do that although I think it's already wet. I'll see you shortly."

Dade looked at Dash and frowned. "You have to leave?"

"In a few minutes for a brief business meeting, a working vacation. We could get together in about half an hour if you're free. Maybe the lounge?"

"That would be nice."

She sat up, looked at him, and winked. "Now they're easier to see. You know, Francis, anything beyond a mouthful is a waste."

He blushed. "Yes, you seem to understand me."

"Men are pretty much the same regardless of age, so are women."

He laughed and wiped his chin. "I'll be there."

"I see a wedding ring."

"It's a business arrangement – not unusual in corporate America."

"We'll talk when we get together. It could be good for both of us."

"I'll bring you a special gift."

"I don't expect anything. Not rich and powerful, not sexy and inviting. Just two new friends. We'll see where that takes us; maybe my room, maybe just a pleasant time getting to know each other. Now I must go."

*****

Santiago and Andrews were finishing lunch in the crowded resort coffee shop off the lobby. Her cell rang. Caller ID showed only a number.

"Hello?"

"Mitch?"

Santiago's eyes opened wide. She looked around the coffee shop. "Andrea, where are you?"

"I'm in Palm Springs."

Santiago pressed record. "First you try to kill me, now you call like an old friend. I thought you'd be out of the country by now."

"I thought about it but what you said in New Orleans made sense, except I panicked."

"What I said?"

"Yes, about Ishtar. You were right. I can run, hide, but eventually I'll be found."

"I assumed you'd gone somewhere with no extradition 'til now."

"It wouldn't make any difference. Ishtar would find me. I had Wolfe. She'd find another just like him. He'd find me and she'd be free and proper, as always."

"You don't sound like someone out to kill all the witnesses."

"I'd set up an alibi in Washington, a dinner date where someone else used my credit card and signature. That idea ended when you and Link caught me in New Orleans."

"So what do you want now?"

"I want to talk with you and then turn myself in."

Santiago dropped the sandwich she'd been eating not realizing she hadn't set it down when Andrea called. "Really?"

"Yes."

"That sounded like a lingering yes."

"I want to make a statement. I want it recorded and witnessed; something that some other politician, judge, or official can't bury."

"Are you saying you want to turn states evidence?"

"Yes."

"I've started recording our conversation when I realized it was you. Are you okay with that?"

"Yes. You're good. I'm a dead woman. Her people will find me. It's just a matter of time. Even in jail with protection they'd get me. What I realize now is my obsession to punish my birthmother was nurtured. I was groomed to carry out a vengeful conspiracy for the Dade's, even creating a market for a program that allows a secondary ground station to take complete control of a Reaper in flight."

Andrea, how were...."

"Let me finish. Noble has been investigated but never proven to be an arms supplier to any criminal group. I know along with the government contracts, they never cared who the other groups were. Not as long as the money was upfront."

"Okay, how were they going to demonstrate the effectiveness of the takeover program?"

"By killing General Lube with the first Reaper taken over by their imbedded program. Then it's market time. Think about it; the government spends millions upgrading the guidance system and the people controlling the effort are sabotaging the project from the inside."

"Why General Lube?"

"He could've blocked their son's deployment but refused. As a result Jeffrey was killed."

"What about your mother?"

"I've given a lot of thought to what you said. I believe you're absolutely right about Ishtar grooming me from childhood. In working security I know how difficult it is to open sealed records. My mother didn't stand a chance at doing so. Using foster care, Noble's money and power, Ishtar controlled most of my childhood and education. She knew who my mother and I were but made no effort to bring us together."

"Have you given any thought as to why?"

"The Nobles adopted Ishtar at birth and left my mother behind. I don't know why. Maybe they only wanted one child. As Ishtar grew up, went to the university and graduated with honors, the Nobles were quite pleased. But, just before graduation she ends up pregnant. A prestigious family can't have that kind of dark horse lurking in the background. I'm sure some reference was made about adoptions, how disappointed they were, but how they could solve it – Francis is brought on board almost as an employee."

"Obviously the Nobles still had faith in your aunt. She and her father basically run the company through Francis."

"Yes, my aunt is a shrewd and deadly business woman. Other than tradition, I still don't know why she isn't the CEO."

Santiago sipped her now warm water. "And now you want to tell the story."

"Yes."

"Why did she choose you to groom rather than someone else?"

"When Ishtar discovered the identity of my mother she learned how intelligent Acadia was. That led her to research my test scores from public school. In return, Ishtar discovered my abilities and unique psychological profile. That's when the grooming started. I was a tool, a tool with a possibly useful connection."

"Profile?"

"Sociopathic."

Long conversation but keep her talking.

"I believe what you said in New Orleans, that my bumpy ride through foster care, education, and even my marriage all seemed to have her stamp. I recall how often she said only a terrible parent would abandon their child. Once I worked in security and learned the ropes, I discovered my mother. That's when I determined to punish her for the life I had lived if ever the opportunity presented itself."

"Did Ishtar know about your plan?"

"No, she didn't know that I'd found my mother."

"Tell me, how does Senator DuBois fit into all of this? I know he's a crook, and I believe he's the father of Jeffrey, but I can't prove that nor even if he knows about Jeffrey."

"As far as I know, he's not aware of the link between him and Ishtar other than college sex from time
to time. I doubt he ever gave any thought to his moments with her any more than any other woman he's
banged. He sees sex as a sporting event."

"So he does."

"Think of DuBois as a bought and paid for com-
modity much like Francis. He gets big bucks and does
our bidding, or did until now."

"You've shared a great deal of information with me.
Are you willing to do the same with an FBI agent?"

"I am if you'll attend, along with an attorney not related to the Noble Group."

"The FBI may not allow me to sit in on you interro-
gation, but an attorney of your choice can. I assume
you can afford your own representation."

"Yes."

"Excellent, otherwise you would be sliding into that
court appointed world your aunt may well have a hand
in also."

"One of the things we haven't discussed is Noble's
role in black market arms dealing. The Fed's get everything."

"You do understand they will see your turnaround
as a way of getting some kind of favor as well as being
motivated by a need for revenge against your aunt."

"I do. We'll just have to do the best we can."

"You're sure about this, Andrea?"

"Set it up, Mitch."

"I'll do it right now. Give me a number I can reach
you at."

"No, Noble is just as good at tracking as DataFlex. I'll call you in an hour using a different phone." She broke the connection.

Santiago punched in Alex Patton's Phoenix office.

"Hello, Mitch. Are you still in New Orleans? Our people down there are very impressed with the work you did."

"No, Alex, I'm in Palm Springs, but I have another piece of the puzzle."

"Really, what now?"

"How about Andrea Nance wanting to turn herself in, make a statement, and bring down the Noble leadership and solving some murders?"

"Mitch, are you ever going to give up being a cop? If not, the bureau would love to have your services."

"No, I'll just remain a personal services type and once in a while feed you an anonymous tip."

"What you're talking about now isn't anonymous."

"No its not. But I need you to arrange for a team to come to the Gold Dust Condominium and Resort to take her into custody. She wants her attorney and me with her."

"The attorney part is okay."

"Understand."

"How big is this?"

"Well, you're guarding Doctor Sigmund in New Orleans. There are multiple murders involved, sabotage, espionage, and arms trafficking. Is that big enough for today or would you like me to wait until we have something of greater meaning on our table?"

"This'll do, Mitch. This'll do."

"Call me back when we're ready to move so I can get her here."

"Will do."

*****

Dash Varga joined Francis Dade in the Gold Dust Lounge half an hour after they left the pool. She had changed from a yellow bikini and chiffon cover to fitted blue denim shorts, white blouse, and white running shoes. The top two buttons of the blouse were open, something Dade did not miss.

"Miss Varga, I'm pleased you could make it. One never knows about business calls."

"That is true, Francis. Would you mind if I called you Fran?"

"Not at all. No one has done that in years."

"Good, 'Francis' is just so formal."

The waiter came to their table. It was separated from the room in a corner overlooking the pool. The waiter glanced down her blouse for just moment. "Would the lady like a cocktail?"

"Yes, a JD rocks."

The waiter left. Dade looked at Dash.

"I see you changed."

"Less distracting in a lounge unless you're the waiter."

"He was rather obvious."

"He's rather normal, Fran, not unlike someone else I met earlier this afternoon."

Dade blushed. "Yes, but you certainly put me in my place."

"Well, when the waiter gets back pay him for my drink, but tell him he already got his tip when I ordered. He'll understand only too well."

"That's not necessary, out of the ordinary...."

"It is necessary. Sometime one needs to assert oneself."

A moment later the waiter arrived with Dash's drink. He put the bill on the table; $30.00.

Dade looked at Dash, winked and handed the waiter $30.00.

The waiter paused.

Dade looked at him but said nothing.

She said, "I think you already got your tip when I ordered."

"Yes ma'am." He blushed turned, and left the table.

"You know, Dash, many a time I've wanted to say something to someone, maybe just a no, but I've rarely had the courage to let someone know my feelings, other than at the office. I just choked again. Well done."

They held up their glasses.

Dade said, "Here's to new friends."

"To a new friend, Fran. You said you'd like to talk, get to know each other. I'd like to know you better, too. Why don't you tell me about yourself first?"

"I'm a business man, married. You already know the arrangement. I think when we bumped into each other I was more than a little attracted to one of the most beautiful women I've ever encountered. I discovered you're both intelligent and street smart. You're comfortable with who you are, know what you want, and have great people skills."

"Fran, you left out inviting."

"Yes, most inviting, but I won't say how."

"We both know."

"I do recall something about a mouthful."

They both laughed.

"You're a successful business man. You must be comfortable with who you are, too."

"In business I am successful, in life not so much. We all make choices."

"You're the CEO of Noble, the waiter told me at the pool. That's a pretty good choice."

"I thought so several years ago. Now I think I made a pact with the devil."

"Your marriage?"

"Yes. Have you ever been married, Dash?"

"No, I'm not ready for that. I may never be. I see no reason to get married. Over half the couples in the U.S. living together now aren't married. I can lead a wholesome life and live with someone I love. It's an emotional commitment far beyond any laws or church."

He laughed. "The shack job of the 60's has become the norm of today. My parents are probably turning over in their graves."

"Fifty years, that's even before my parents."

"I imagine it is. Tell me, have you always been so candid?"

"I hope so. I was raised to be true to myself. You?"

"I was raised more in the 'fit in' philosophy of know the right people, don't make waves, network, learn whose ass to kiss."

"Sounds preppy."

"Very. When the opportunity presented itself to marry into the Noble family it was perfect. Now it's a realization of how wrong I was to do so."

"You have wealth, power, and experience. In spite of your marriage arrangement you've accomplished much to be proud of."

"What I've done, Dash, is learn more than I bargained for."

"Really? Tell me, I can learn from you."

"I've already learned from you today, young lady. Your message is loud and clear."

"My father often quoted Socrates. 'Know thyself' was a mantra in our home when I was growing up."

"Even in this brief time we've talked I feel I can be candid with you. That is a far cry from what I wanted when you came into the lounge. You've been refreshing, not trying to get into my wallet. I've been terrible, dreaming about getting into your pants. Yet sitting here now, I can acknowledge to someone I've just met but feel totally comfortable with, that many of the people I've known and worked with in my adult life have been deceptive, manipulative, dishonest, dangerous, and yet no more than me."

He finished his drink and ordered another.

"As the CEO of Noble and the puppet of Ishtar, I've mastered the art of justifying my actions, even when I am the scapegoat being dominated and know better. But enough about me, your turn."

"I'm a researcher. I investigate the background of various individuals for corporations; background checks, personal history, media exposure, banking, criminal records, education, personal references, marriages, family history, hobbies, social life, anything and everything."

"You're a private investigator, a PI."

"In a way, but not a licensed PI. They're more geared to law enforcement and that sort of thing."

"You dig dirt like some of the scandal journals?"

"If there is any, I'll find it. The individuals I do background research on are special people; job applicants for sensitive positions, upper management, security clearances – that sort of thing."

"It sounds interesting."

"Noble does the same thing, I believe in house."

"Yes, we do."

"One of the things I learned early on in my work is everyone has secrets; you, me, everyone."

"I know what you mean. I have a friend who treats me as a confidante. We often talk if only on the phone. I've known him all my life."

She said, "That is a rare friendship."

"Yes. He's now concerned for his personal safety. He's a man with many business contacts on the other side of the law."

"As in illegal."

"Yes, illegal. Right now he is caught between a rock and a hard place. A large project he's been involved with is going south. To make matters worse government contracts are involved, security clearances compromised, crooked politicians, kidnaps, stalking, blackmail, I even suspect murder."

"I'm sure the government is breathing down his neck."

"The government isn't the problem. As it stands right now he could get some prison time. None of the more serious criminal offenses can be proven against him unless one individual comes forward, and she's not likely to do that. No, the problem is someone over him believes he is the weak link. If my friend cuts a deal and talks, they both go to prison. If he's out of the way the other one walks."

"So your friend is caught between what, talk or die?"

"Basically."

"I'd cut a deal and hope for witness protection even if incarcerated. I'd get a lawyer and protect myself as much as possible even going into custody. Many witnesses have been killed inside. Your boyhood friend needs help."

"Yes, yes he does."

She smiled. "I know some people that have contacts. Talk to your friend and ask him if he wants to save his ass. I know it would be a leap of faith to trust someone he's never met but that's his choice. I'd probably do it if I trusted the referral just because I don't have many other options."

"Dash, your point is well taken. If you don't mind I'll call him, see what he thinks."

"Fine. I was thinking of ordering a sandwich. Would you like something?"

"I'd love to but I best get back. I'm expected for cocktails and dinner."

"Understand, but you're welcome to stay if you change your mind."

"No, but I can't tell you how much this has meant to me today. I don't remember a similar experience when someone didn't want something from me; gifts, a contract, money."

They walked to the door of the lounge together.

"Can I give you a hug, Dash?"

"Yes."

They embraced.

"I need some time to think. You've already concluded I'm the friend in the story haven't you?"

"Yes, and I can help you."

"He slid the pinky ring off his finger. "Take this, please."

"No, I'd rather have you come back."

"I shall," he said placing the ring in her palm.

He walked to the elevator alone.

Chapter 18

Santiago called Shari Stiletto late in the afternoon. "How did it go with DuBois?"

"Easy hustle, a little champagne for a saliva sample, thirty seconds of a porn flick starring himself. After that he was easy."

"He didn't threaten you?"

"He did but that was short lived. Once he knew the tape would come out either way, it didn't make any sense to get nasty."

"I knew you'd pull it off."

"Your suggestion about the slit gown certainly worked. I went from that to black leather only to find him half undressed and me ready for a quick exit."

"You know, I love it when we avoid surprises."

Stiletto laughed. "I had one. Ray House was my backup. Right after DuBois left there was Ray at the door."

"Now that's special. Ray's never been in the field with me beyond Braun's house. That's one up for you, Shari."

"I think he was there for the champagne glass. He'd said someone would pick up any sample I could get of DuBois's DNA."

"Those tests usually take several days."

"Ray arranged it privately. When Claude plays, people pay attention."

"So when do we get the results?"

"We have them. Ray just told me they're a match with Jeffrey Dade."

Santiago smirked and looked at Link. "So now we know. Does Ray plan on sharing this with DuBois?"

"I don't know, Mitch. What would be the point?"

"Well put. I'm not sure there is one. Perhaps in dealing with Ishtar. I guess we'll see. Thank you." The connection broke.

*****

Francis and Ishtar Dade were comfortably ensconced in the Presidential Suite. The four-thousand square foot suite had two master bedrooms, a formal dining room, gourmet kitchen, two smaller bedrooms, three baths, plus a private patio with its own pool and spa. Carl, the chauffer-butler and Joseph the cook accompanied them.

At 4:00 p.m. Carl awaited the Dade's dinner call while in the kitchen with Joseph. The Dade's were sipping margaritas and snacking on chips and salsa while chatting under a large umbrella on the patio.

Ishtar said, "We're in a bit of a tailspin. Most of our key people are gone, our project compromised; Broderick resigned, Sigmund has disappeared slowing everything down, Susan Train has been disposed of, and Andrea is nearing arrest if she doesn't get out of the country. Perhaps worst of all, Xavier is alive and in custody."

"That's true, Ishtar. I'm sure Jerome will share what little he knows, meaning nothing substantial about us. However, Andrea could find herself in a bind. Carl, another margarita."

"Yes sir."

She watched over the sprawling golf resort. "Andrea will tell them nothing. She'll have the best lawyers."

Francis fidgeted. "Yes, but it seems our plan to avenge Jeffrey's death has been thwarted, at least temporarily. The big question is can any of this mischief be directly traced to us?"

"That would depend upon Andrea and I trust her. Without her testimony the government would have very little. If the FBI finds her and she gives any testimony it could prove most difficult for you, Francis."

"Me?"

"You and Andrea gave all of the orders and directions for our activities. As I said, she is strong. Noble will take care of her."

Francis shook his head. "Ishtar, she is wanted for murder. She won't get out. She could get death in Arizona. That should make her a target willing to turn states evidence."

Ishtar sipped her drink and said nothing.

Francis continued, "We could relocate her to a country with no extradition. We know people that could then eliminate the threat. This is serious business."

"A possibility, we could relocate Andrea, but what about you? We need to protect you and Noble."

He smiled and sipped his margarita. "Yes, we'll give it some time and then start over. Our need to avenge Jeffrey's senseless death and teach that four-star idiot a lesson will hibernate, but reawaken. We need to guard against our discovery and insure a future product for the government and our black market clients."

"Yes we do, of course. Did the tech gain access, clear the vetting process, and imbed our override before Sigmund disappeared?"

"No, it was part of the final step following the vetting. When complete it will allow access of schedules and programing."

"In other words we lose the ability and market of the software to take control of the Reaper for the time being."

"Yes, until we put together a new team to complete the current task and develop an override of Barrier, if and when it is successfully completed. Time is on our side, Ishtar, and Barrier is years away."

She smiled. "True, and in the meantime other markets will be huge for our program. Once the general is killed our leaders will be humiliated. They'll have no clue as to the origins of a software program that can override their control."

Francis finished his drink. "These are really quite delicious." He licked his lips. "And to think I called them panther piss at one time."

Ishtar laughed. "This is an opportunity for you to exercise your machismo, Francis. Have another. It's just us and no outside interference tonight. We're not even dressed for dinner and no one cares."

They both laughed.

Ishtar called for Carl and waved her glass. "Two more of these and a tad stronger."

"Yes ma'am."

Dade handed Carl his glass. "Ishtar, I wanna go back to Andrea for a moment. I'm depressed over her situation and recent events, but she could be extremely dangerous for me, for us."

"You're serious about killing her."

"It would be beneficial to eliminate the problem after she is out of the country."

Ishtar pursed her lips and shook her head.

He rubbed his hands together. "I can see you disagree."

"She's the most loyal employee we have. Sometimes it is almost like she has her own agenda given the energy she expends serving our goals. I want to protect her."

Dade called out, "Carl, my drink."

"You're getting drunk, Francis."

"Perhaps, but we're up here safe from everything. Why do you want to protect her? She's a sociopath."

"Aren't we all, a little? She's our sociopath."

"You said it yourself, Ishtar. I'm the one at risk. I'm the one that called your shots. I'm the one that goes to prison if she talks, not you. Not the wealthy privileged daughter of Winston Noble. No wonder you and your father insisted I be the voice, the CEO, the...."

She waved a hand. "Enough, Francis, you're making a scene."

Carl brought Dade's fresh drink and left.

"Finish your drink and we'll dine."

"I just got it."

She nodded. "Drink up, darling. Perhaps we'll take a dip later."

"You and me?"

"Fawn isn't here. Don't you need a reward this evening?"

He sipped his drink spilling some on his shirt front. "I always need a reward."

"You take a dip with me after dinner. You won't need a new toy."

He guzzled the margarita. "I'm ready for dinner if you are."

Ishtar softly said, "Carl, we're ready." She stood. "Are you going to escort me to the dining room?"

He stood leaning just a little. "I always do."

He seated her at the dining table pushing her chair in with too much force.

"We may have to help you after dinner, Francis. I haven't seen you this drunk since our wedding night."

Francis called Carl. "I'd like a really good red wine with dinner, maybe some before dinner, too."

Carl looked at Ishtar. She nodded.

"Of course, sir. Would you like...."

Francis shot a glance at Carl. "Jesus, just bring something. We brought five cases with us."

Carl retreated.

"Francis, you're becoming boorish. Keep it up and you won't have a playmate tonight."

He laughed. "If I keep this up I won't get anything up."

She said, "Perhaps, but there are many ways I could help you get it up, and I don't mean a nap after dinner. Or, we can always swim later tonight. I must confess I'm beginning to feel something of a buzz."

"Yes, or maybe tomorrow with a new friend."

*****

FBI Agent Kimo Klein and his partner Clay Zito sat with Michelle Santiago and Link Andrews in the living room of their suite. Andrea Nance and her attorney, Harold Nixon, were also present. After Klein had placed Nance in custody, the six of them discussed how to get Ishtar Dade to incriminate herself.

Klein said, "The Director believes your plan to get Mrs. Dade to incriminate herself is dangerous but sound. My job is to make it happen although I have some reservations because of Miss Nance's role in the operation."

Santiago said, "You and Agent Zito were briefed on all that's taken place leading to this point in time, correct?"

"Yes, by Agent Paxton and Ray House."

Nance said, "Perhaps I can help you understand. Did your briefing include the family structure we are dealing with: the aunt-mother-daughter issue?"

"Yes, but only briefly."

Nance continued, "My motivation is revenge, Agent Klein. It may seem otherwise to you but to me it is essential."

Klein shook his head. "I don't understand. Are you turning states evidence for revenge or are you attempting a patriotic turnaround because of your own pending prosecution – maybe with leniency as a goal?"

"No, no. My revenge has nothing to do with patriotism. I grew up wanting to find my mother; first because I wanted a mom and home, later because I wanted to punish her for abandoning me, and never finding me. A few years ago I discovered Acadia is my mother. I wanted a vehicle that would destroy her prestige in the science world; ruin her career and life. That's why I recommended Acadia to lead Reaper. When Ishtar agreed I believed she was helping me achieve my goal while I helped her and the Noble Group. Then a few days ago I learned Ishtar has known since my childhood that my mother is her sister and I am her niece. She manipulated my entire childhood from foster homes to my education. She made sure I received a scholarship from a foundation I now know was Noble's. When I became a lobbyist Noble was my first contract, and later my only contract. I finally joined the corporation."

Klein said, "And you became head of security."

"Yes, an outgrowth of doing research and background checks on various public figures we wanted to influence. That's also how I discovered my birth mother's identity."

"But you didn't try to contact her."

"No, I was angry and wanted to get even."

"And now you want your pound of flesh from the Dade's."

"Yes."

"Miss Nance, doesn't it strike you as odd that all of a sudden you want revenge on someone with whom you've perpetrated Lord only knows how many crimes with over the years, all without any conscience?"

Nance nodded. "What you're saying is I'm a sociopath. I'm sure you're right, but that doesn't alter the urge to get even. I think you're worried more about what I will do to Ishtar once we're alone."

"Knowing your track record makes that a legitimate concern."

"Agent Klein, if I wanted to physically harm or kill Ishtar it would be rather simple to get into the hotel and their suit. I'm not the only one in this room who could do so."

Klein cleared his throat. "But there is no question you're lethal."

"I understand your concern. I want her and Francis in prison for the rest of their lives. I want them to suffer."

Agent Zito slapped his knees. "You certainly have a family bent on revenge."

Klein said, "I'm surprised you never discovered your aunt's true identity."

Santiago said, "Can we move forward?"

"Klein said, "Yes. What story are you going to use to gain entry into their suite?"

Andrews said, "As far as we know the Dade's believe Andrea is still loyal to Ishtar. She'll go in tomorrow seeking help to get out of the country, preferably someplace without extradition. In so doing she'll discuss many different phases of the Reaper project.

Hopefully she'll draw incriminating feedback from Ishtar."

Klein smiled. "Excellent."

Agent Zito looked at Nance. "Agent Klein and I will be staying here with Miss Nance tonight. It's best she not be out in public for any reason. We don't want a sharp eyed citizen spotting her and calling 911."

Klein said, "We don't want the locals to queer this operation, either."

Andrews said, "Will you use this suite for your listening center?"

Klein said, "Yes. We have another team of agents securing the necessary warrants and equipment. They'll be here early in the morning."

Nance chuckled. "Two agents overnight, interesting. Do I get my own room?"

Zito said, "Yes ma'am."

Santiago took out her cell. "I'll call Ray. He'll get us another room."

Andrews said, "Worst case scenario is we'd move in with Dash because they're booked."

Santiago laughed and whispered in his ear, "In your dreams."

Klein said, "Miss Nance, have you given any thought to the fact this is a dangerous task for you. The Dade's could try to kill you."

"That'd be a first. Francis doesn't have the balls for it and Ishtar always hires someone else to do her dirty work. The other detail in my favor is she doesn't know that I know her relationship to me or Sigmund."

Zito said, "Mr. Andrews, you mentioned a party named Dash."

"Yes, she's in her room waiting on the chance Francis Dade comes by for coffee instead of staying home for dinner. They met informally at the pool earlier."

Klein said, "So Mr. and Mrs. Dade are together at this moment."

Santiago said, "As far as we know."

Nance said, "I wouldn't be surprised if Ishtar asked me to kill Francis. There is no love lost between them and he's always been the weak link in the chain."

Klein shook his head. "This is so twisted."

Santiago changed the focus of the discussion. "Andrea, we know your fate but I for one thank you for helping to bring something so corrupt and deadly to an end."

"Thank you, Mitch. I know everything that has happened I'm responsible for along with Francis and Ishtar. It's time for it to end regardless of the motives each of us may have. I know you, Link, and Sam went to New Orleans mainly to find Tony's killer. What you discovered was beyond anyone's imagination."

Andrews said, "Mitch and I need to brief Dash. If Francis hasn't shown by now he's probably not coming."

Mitch and Link stood.

She said, "Andrea, Link and I will be back tomorrow morning."

Klein said, "We'll be getting ready at 7:00. I'd like an early start. It would be consistent with Andrea coming into the complex before too many folks are up and about."

Santiago and Andrews left for Dash's room first.

As they went down the hall Santiago's cell rang. She nodded and broke the connection. She jabbed Link in the ribs and smiled. "No other rooms are available. You get your latest fantasy and we spend the night with Dash."

Andrews grinned.

"But it is a two master bedroom suite just like the one we left Andrea and the cops in."

They both laughed.

He said, "Of course."

*****

Ishtar and Francis Dade were waiting when Carl arrived with a bottle of Chateau Lafite-Rothschild.

"I have an excellent...."

Francis interrupted, "Ishtar, rather than dinner why don't we go for a dip now? As you said, we're on vacation and we're getting on very well."

"Normally I'd say no but you're right, Francis. Carl, put dinner away. If we want something later we'll call room service."

"Yes madam, as you wish."

She added, "And Carl, you and Joseph take the evening off. I know you both enjoy casinos. Mr. Dade and I will get on very nicely this evening."

Carl went to the kitchen.

Francis said, "That is an excellent idea. I'm feeling quite cheerful."

"I suspect the alcohol has something to do with it."

"Maybe just a little," he said holding his thumb and index finger almost together with only a tiny space.

"On the serious side, Francis, our new man hasn't found Andrea yet. I'll rest easier knowing where she is and out of reach."

"We're both at risk as long as she's on the loose."

Carl and Joseph came to the living room.

Ishtar said, "You boys are looking quite sporty this evening. Have fun."

Joseph said, "Dinner is in the refrigerator as you directed, Mrs. Dade."

"Thank you. Enjoy the evening."

Francis said, "And take the car. We won't be needing it this evening."

Ishtar laughed. "As if you could drive it. You'd be arrested before you left the hotel grounds."

Francis laughed. "Yes, I probably would. And Carl, when you fellows get back, no peeking. We may be skinny dipping."

Carl and Joseph nodded and went out the door.

Ishtar raised an eyebrow. "Skinny dipping? I saw you talking with a young woman at the pool earlier. She must really have put your hormones on the move. I must say she was quite stunning."

"Yes my dear, but tonight I have eyes only for you. This Rothschild is very good. Join me." He knocked a glass over trying to pour and laughed. "Earthquake!"

Ishtar smiled. "I saw she was called away."

"Yes, some kind of business. I went to the lounge."

"In your Speedo?"

"Yes, but I slipped a shirt on. Daring don't you think?"

"That's not what comes to mind, Francis. Careful, a little more wine with your margaritas and you'll be slowed to a crawl."

He laughed. "Nothing I can't solve with a pill. I had some bourbon in the lounge, too."

"Francis, let's undress and try the pool. Our privacy is guarded."

"Yes!" He jumped to his feet and stripped. "Work your mojo, Ishtar. My clock is runnin' and I can't stop now."

She slid out of her clothes and let them fall to the floor.

He laughed. "See, you're beautiful tonight and feeling the freedom, too. Nothing stuffy."

He reached for her and almost fell. He looked up smiling and took her hand. "Another tremor, dear."

She laughed. "Yes, it's that kind of a night."

They walked to their private patio and pool high above any other windows.

He said, "Just think, we're almost done with the crisis. I feel so good."

She laughed, "You're not feeling much of anything."

"True, but I'll feel you."

"I'm going to run inside for a moment. Go ahead and get in."

"I think I will."

He put his wine glass down, stepped to the edge, dove in, swam underwater to the far end, and bumped his head. Ishtar returned to the deck as he turned at the steps and again swam to the far end and back."

"Did you take your pill?"

He stood in the shallow water and leaned back. "Can't you tell? Tonight we'll have senior sex." He reached for his wine. "I'm huge!"

"Indeed."

He laughed and dove backwards.

She watched as he swam rapidly to the far end. *You're drunk, Francis, fatally drunk.*

Again he hit his head on the wall of the pool, groaned then swam back to the shallow end.

He looked up as he stood. "A guy could get a concussion out here."

"You could slow it down a little."

"Never, I can go faster."

"I'll meet you at the other end," she said as she walked down the deck beside the pool.

He pushed off the stairs. "I'll beat ya."

He reached the end first, turned and returned to the stairs. "It's a little pool but feels really good."

"Do another lap."

She looked around. Nothing but blue sky above and the pool area below.

When Francis reached her end he again bumped his head on the side of the pool.

She bent over and got on her knees. "Take it easy, Francis. This wall isn't padded."

"I know."

She reached out a hand as if to touch his head and took hold of his thick grey hair, pulled him quickly to the side of the pool, and banged his forehead hard against the wall. He raised his head as blood began to flow into the water. His eyes rolled upwards and he spit.

"Damn, that hurt."

Ishtar pulled him against the side again. His head struck the side and the blood came faster. He rolled onto to his back and went limp. She pulled him again striking his head, then stretched out on her belly on the deck. She pulled his limp body to the edge of the pool and held his head under water for several minutes as he bled and bubbles escaped his nose and mouth.

She jumped into the five foot deep pool and took hold of him. He had no pulse. She pulled him by the hair to the shallow end, got out, slipped on a robe, and called 911.

Within minutes the sound of a sirens interrupted the quiet evening surrounding the resort. A police car blocked through traffic at the entry. An aid car parked at the hotel entrance. Two firemen rushed through the lobby pushing a stretcher and a kit, and rode the elevator to the top floor. The door to Dade's suite was open. They rushed in, passing Ishtar as she pointed toward the patio. One of the firemen leaped into the pool and pulled Francis out as a policeman arrived at the suite.

The fireman's partner placed Dade's limp body on the deck beside the pool and immediately began CPR. Francis remained limp and unmoving. Some blood dripped from head wounds onto the deck. The first fireman took an oxygen mask from a kit. A second team of firemen arrived and a few minutes later a team from the coroner's office.

Ishtar watched them work on her husband. She rushed back and forth watching over the firemen's shoulders. One of the firemen asked how long Francis had been in the water.

"Fifteen or twenty minutes. We both were going for a swim. I left the pool for a few minutes. When I returned he was floating around, bleeding, and unconscious. I tried to get him out of the water but couldn't lift or drag him. Then I called you. Will he be alright?"

The fireman ignored her question. He looked at the wine glass by the pool. "Had he been drinking?"

Ishtar stood quietly, nodded, then said, "Yes, both of us, Francis quite heavily; margaritas, wine, bourbon. I didn't think he was so drunk he'd go crashing into the bottom or wall of the pool. He did bump his head twice before I went inside but I didn't notice any blood. I told him to take it easy and he answered back, 'Yes, mother,' and kept on swimming laps."

"I see you bruised your knees."

She looked down. "I did, probably when I was trying to get him out of the water. I was on the deck and tried to get his face up."

Another man approached and introduced himself as being from the Riverside County Coroner's Office. "Mrs. Dade, I am very sorry for your loss. We're going to move Mr. Dade to the County Morgue for an autopsy when we're finished here, a requirement for unnatural deaths."

Ishtar's eyes welled and she began to sob. Without speaking she looked around and saw a woman from the Crime Lab photographing the pool, Francis, the wine glass on the edge of the pool, and the entry to the patio. A moment later she was taking pictures of the living room; clothes on the floor, the wine bottle and another wine glass. Then she gathered blood samples, the wine glasses and bottle, took a water sample, collected finger prints from throughout the condo.

The man from the coroner's office asked, "Do you have any family members in the area?"

She dropped her chin and swiped her eyes. "No, our daughter Corley is in New York. I'll contact her." She squeezed her hands together. "The domestics, Carl and Joseph, are out for the evening."

"They'll be back later?"

"Yes, they travel and stay with us."

The technician wrote Ishtar's responses in a notebook.

"I've already told the officers."

"Yes ma'am, but I won't get their report 'til tomorrow or the day after. It would be best to move forward as quickly as possible, especially with someone so well known."

Ishtar looked out at the grounds. "This is a private moment."

"I understand, ma'am, again my condolences."

"Thank you."

The lab technician was the last to leave. Within minutes of her departure Ishtar Dade sat on the couch. She took several deep breaths and stretched her arms.

A smile crept across her face and she began to laugh. She clapped her hands. She glanced at the coffee table. The wine was gone along with her glass.

"I hope they drink it when they're done testing it and checking the bottle."

She went to the bar and poured a tumbler of bourbon and looked out the closed patio doors.

"Good riddance. One down and one to go."

Chapter 19

Monday, July 14

Santiago, Andrews and Dash Varga joined Andrea Nance, Agents Klein and Zito, in their room at 6:45. The warrants were in hand, technicians in place, and Nance was ready with a special smartphone to transmit her conversation with Ishtar. The new arrivals pulled chairs from the dining area to the living room.

After greetings Klein said, "I assume you heard the disturbance last night when the firemen, cops, and the coroner were here."

Santiago said, "Yes. We understand Francis Dade drowned last night. The news didn't have much on it and we thought it best not to be wandering around. Ishtar knows who I am. I assume she's seen photos of Link. Likewise her two employees Carl and Joseph."

Klein said, "My first impression was to arrest Ishtar after the excitement. Dade's death was too convenient, but we'd still have nothing concrete on her except Andrea's testimony, which probably wouldn't stand up without corroboration. So we sat tight and waited."

Zito said, "The good news is Ishtar hasn't left."

Klein said, "I did contact the coroner's office so we would be advised of their findings, noting Dade's involvement in National Security work. Dade had a blood-alcohol level of .029, suffered blunt force trauma and died of drowning. Everything was consistent with what Mrs. Dade reported thus far; diving in a shallow pool, hitting his head on the side of the pool a few times and drinking heavily. She came out and found him."

Santiago nodded. "Makes sense from what Dash said, but very convenient, too."

Andrews said, "Are the two domestics in her suite right now?"

Klein said, "As far as we know. We have some people on the fifth floor. They haven't seen anyone come in or out since the two domestics returned late last night. They were not at the condo when the drowning took place."

Andrews picked up a donut. "Are you ready, Miss Nance?"

"Yes, it was a long night."

Dash said, "In more ways than one. Francis indicated he might come by for a drink and chatter. He was more than a little candid about being unhappy in his marriage and position as CEO of Noble."

Santiago said, "Too bad, if he would've rolled over we'd have two witnesses."

Klein said, "Okay, let's go over the details again. Miss Nance, you're going into Dade's suite seeking help getting out of the country."

"Yes."

"Don't make any comments about last night if you can avoid it. Being off the grid could mean you haven't followed the local news in the last twenty-four hours and have kept a low profile."

"I understand."

Santiago said, "Ishtar could be anything from grieving to euphoric."

Nance smirked. "It would depend on the audience."

Klein said, "Play Mrs. Dade by ear but keep trying to engage her about events and comment on her role, especially about the murders. Once she incriminates herself we come in and make the arrest."

Santiago looked at Klein. "Wouldn't it be best to let them continue to talk as long as there's no confrontation? The more incriminating evidence we get the stronger the case."

Klein looked at Andrea. "Miss Nance is an admitted killer. That makes it risky. But you're correct, the more we get from Mrs. Dade, the better."

Andrews said, "Yes, Andrea is a killer and all we've got right now. Ishtar is also a killer but we can't prove it yet, the death of her husband notwithstanding."

Nance said, "It's not rocket science. I go in. We talk. You get what you want and I get what I want."

Andrews said, "The only thing she's carrying is a smartphone."

Nance stood and stepped to the door. "Let's do it."

Santiago and Andrews joined her. "We'll ride up with you and hang around outside in the hall."

"I wouldn't blame you if you let her kill me, too."

Andrews shook his head. "This is for Tony, not for you."

"I know."

Klein gave earpieces to Andrews and Santiago. "You'll hear everything we do."

Andrews tapped his earpiece. "If Sam was here he'd comment about the old days."

When the three of them arrived at the fifth floor they exited the elevator and Nance walked to the door of the Presidential Suite. Santiago and Andrews watched from a distance.

"You know, Mitch, she could kill Ishtar before we could do anything."

"I know. Do you think she's just using us to get at Ishtar?"

"She said it would be easy to get in. This is easy and we're opening the gates."

"Truth be known they should both get the death penalty."

"Yes they should, but I'll bet on life."

"Link, has it crossed your mind Ishtar might try to cut some kind of a deal?"

"Oh yes. That's something for others to worry about. I'm hoping we can have lunch thinking about a vacation and this all in our past by tomorrow."

"I like your idea. Hawaii sounds good to me."

He smiled. "It does; sun, fun, golf."

She jabbed his ribs. "Sun, skin, sweat and sex."

"I like your plan better."

Santiago held up her hand. "She's at the door."

*****

Ishtar Dade was wearing a bathrobe and having coffee in the living room. The morning paper had nothing about the death of Francis but the early morning television news had a brief comment with an old press photo of him. *Now I have to be the grieving widow for a month or so, but I'll take control of Noble. There is nobody prepared to do as well.*

The doorbell rang. Carl went to answer. Ishtar could hear soft voices but not the conversation. She looked up as Nance walked in.

Ishtar stood. "Andrea, I didn't expect to see you this morning."

"I'm sure you didn't. You know I'm moving about quite a bit right now and I need your help."

"Of course, dear. Let's go to the patio. Have you heard about Francis?"

"I did coming in a few minutes ago. If it was an accident it was certainly timely."

"Yes, he was the weak link in the chain wasn't he?"

The women sat down at a glass topped table overlooking the resort aquatic facility five floors below.

"What happened?"

"Apparently Francis spent a good part of the day imbibing. He told me he met a gorgeous Asian woman. He had been talking with her at the pool, but alas, she was called away. He went to the lounge and had a bit of bourbon."

"Francis?"

"When he got up here he started on margaritas, we both did. He was feeling no pain as dinner hour approached and then he started on wine."

Nance laughed. "I can't even imagine Francis drunk. He's always been such a straight arrow."

"Well, last night his arrow got bent. I went to the bathroom for a moment and when I came back out he was swimming laps in the little pool stark naked."

"Francis, naked in the pool. I don't believe it."

"Believe it, Andrea, stark naked. We both were. We decided to skip dinner, swim, and share an intimate moment."

Andrea laughed. "Naked, intimate? Were you drunk, too?"

"No, but I wasn't totally inhibited either. However, Francis, thinking he's a shark or something began running into the side of the pool hitting his head."

"Then it was an accident."

"So it appears. But you say you need my help. How?"

"You know I'm wanted for murder?"

"Yes, the FBI and the New Orleans police have been in contact because of the Reaper Project. It's been a busy few days for you. The police said the deaths of Susan Trainer and her mother, attempted murder of Santiago, and assault on Sam Evans all took place within a twenty-four hour period."

"It started out as a way of eliminating any trail of evidence linking you, Francis or me to sabotage. I had a perfect alibi set up for a dinner date, but once Santiago turned the tables I was cooked."

"That's why Francis and I came here. We didn't want to be in the spotlight, bothered by press or police. That's what PR is for. I knew you would contact me if needed. You've used this condo to keep us out of the public view before."

Sweat formed on Andrea's brow. "It's warm out here for so early in the day."

"It is, but as you can see, we already have swimmers and water aerobics going."

Andrea rubbed her chin. "They all look healthy from here."

"That they do."

"Well Ishtar, the good news is they still haven't made the connection between Tony Mercedes death and Reaper."

"That's only going to be a matter of time, they will."

"I know." She took a deep breath. "Who would've thought all this would happen when you ordered me to contract a hit on him? And Wolfe did so well making it look like a mugging."

"Yes, I did read about the mugging. Very clever."

Nance looked at Ishtar's cup. "May I have some coffee?"

"Of course. Carl, bring Andrea a cup of coffee and I could use a refill."

A moment later Carl walked onto the patio carrying a serving tray, cup and coffee. The two women sat quietly until he poured and left.

"Andrea, you need my help. How?"

"I want to get to a country that doesn't extradite to the U.S."

"Well, the most glamorous place I can think of is Dubai. The United Arab Emirates doesn't have an extradition agreement with the U.S."

"True, but the UAE has made it clear they're not a haven for criminals on the lamb and work through

Interpol and with many countries including the U.S. even without an agreement."

"Then where? Surely you're not thinking of Cuba, China or Russia."

"No, but I am looking at Nicaragua. The general population is at a disadvantage economically, but the upper class lives well. I certainly have the resources to retire there and enjoy a rich life."

"So what do you need from me?"

"A way out of the country."

"I can't do it using one of Noble's jets. I'm sure we're all being watched to see if you turn up. We could do it outside of the company via charter."

"In return I'd be out of reach and you already know my silence is guaranteed. That is true even if I were to be arrested here."

"I know, I've never questioned your loyalty although Francis had his reservations."

Andrea laughed. "Francis was concerned about his own skin. I'm sure his serving as your spokesman scared him. He was never comfortable calling the shots on the arms deals after the shootout in New York. After the Mercedes hit he was nothing if not tense. You are a leader with balls. Francis was a follower at best."

"Not everyone is a leader."

"I do have a question."

"Ask."

"Why did we hit Mercedes before he met his contact?"

"Mercedes had a CIA background. My sources in the government and DataFlex advised he had shared no information at that point. If they met and for any reason he escaped the hit, he'd have spilled everything he knew to the authorities."

"It would've been nice to know who his contact was at that time. Given twenty-twenty hindsight I'm sure it was Sigmund. Why else would she go under in a safe-house in a of New Orleans suburb?"

"Why else indeed?"

Andrea continued to look at the pool below. "Why the hit on Kohler? He'd been an associate for years."

"Think about it, Andrea, we sent Wolfe to Chandler to deal with Kohler after he assured us Xavier was dead. Kohler was a nervous man. I suspected he would eventually crack if he was ever pressured. I had no idea he initially planned on helping Xavier escape until you told me."

Andrea chuckled. "He apparently changed his mind on that, too. Probably something about the money they were going to split. But as always, I've been cleaning up loose ends."

"Yes, I guess that's what brought about last night. It was a chance presented on a silver platter, and I didn't know if I'd see you to arrange an accident. Poor Francis, but he didn't feel much of anything."

The door flew open. Klein, Zito, Santiago, Andrews and Dash came in and rushed to the patio. Klein stepped in front of Ishtar's chair.

"Ishtar Dade, you are under arrest for the murder of Tony Mercedes."

He gave her the Miranda Rights and cuffed her.

She looked him in the eyes. "Agent Klein, I need to speak with my attorney and then we will talk with your supervisor. I know names, dates, places, countries, politicians and military personnel your higher ups would like to know about. Call you supervisor and tell him I want to deal."

Klein turned to Zito. "Call."

Andrea looked at Ishtar. "Deal? You're going to make a deal?"

"It's called survival, dear. We do what needs to be done."

"You filthy bitch. You ruined my life, I'm going to prison, possibly death row, and you shaped my entire life. Why?"

"Do you know your history?"

"Yes, all of it."

"Then you know you're smart, not a genius, but smart. As a child you demonstrated over and over a lack of conscience, strong independence, and loyalty to certain things. You were perfect. I wanted you to become the perfect tool."

"It sounds to me like you're the one with a conscience problem."

"Perhaps, but I was in an orphanage just like you and your mother, my sister. She was the genius that got left behind, but she still excelled. I couldn't connect with her without subjecting myself to the humiliation of being the other sister – something a Noble doesn't do."

Zito completed his call and nodded at Klein. Then he stepped toward Nance holding out a hand. "Andrea, I need the phone."

Ishtar said, "Are you cutting a deal, too? Agent Klein, my information is better."

Nance trembled. "So you set me up knowing I would find my mother. You fed my anger of abandonment and need for revenge."

"Of course."

Zito took the phone then her left wrist. "Please hold still, Miss Nance."

Santiago moved to a position slightly behind Zito on his left. She bit her lip. *Cuff her. She's getting excited, angry.*

Nance shifted her feet.

Zito cuffed one wrist.

Nance jerked her arm away. "And now you want to make a deal."

"They'll deal. I'll skate one way or the other."

Zito grabbed for Nance's left wrist again.

Nance jerked her arm away.

"You bitch, you'll pay just like me."

Nance grabbed Ishtar. Santiago leaped toward Nance but too late. Both women went over the balcony. Ishtar screamed loudly. Nance never made a sound. When they hit the concrete Ishtar was under Nance.

Zito looked over the edge as a crowd gathered. "Damn."

Klein and Zito ran out the door heading for the elevator. Dash joined Mitch and Link at the railing. They watched the scene below without a word.

Santiago watched and took several deep breathes. She pressed her fingers against her palms and shook her head.

Andrews said, "You did what you could. They were their prisoners."

"I saw her anger, her tension. It's like I let her slip away"

He put an arm around her shoulder. "No Mitch, you didn't let her get away. Today, revenge was a kill-er."

Dash said, "Andrea could still be alive. Ishtar's body may have absorbed enough shock to save her."

Santiago said, "It's possible, not likely."

Dash stepped back from the railing. "I've never seen anything like that."

Santiago said, "I'm sure Agent Klein is disappointed at not getting Ishtar's information. Personally, I'm pleased Tony's killers are dead, all of them."

Andrews lit a cigarette. "It would've been nice to have her information. She'd still have gotten life."

"Maybe, but I can name a few mobster hitmen that walked after rolling over. They got new identities, wit-ness protection, the whole bit."

Andrews stubbed out his smoke. "They're gone now."

Santiago looked at Link and Dash. "While we were getting ready this morning Alex called. He said he didn't want another situation like we had in New Orleans when Sam got hurt. He also told me Klein and Zito spent half the night taking a statement from Andrea about the Noble operations; legit and illegal."

Dash nodded. "So they did get some information."

Andrews said, "A lot I'd think. Andrea knew everything going on at Noble, even Ishtar's secrets."

Santiago watched. "It all started with a program that's buried in quantum mechanics and years away from completion, and the death of a friend. Nine, maybe ten people have died. Let's get out of here. Dash, could we join you for breakfast in your suite? Ours is going to be occupied for some time. They can get our statements after we eat."

Andrews said, "Ladies, let's call and see how Sam is doing."

*****

Agents Klein and Zito came to Dash Varga's second floor suite after finishing their investigation at the site on the cement deck. Dash Varga, Michelle Santiago, and Link Andrews were eating breakfast. The agents joined them out on the lanai. Klein took a seat at the glass topped table shaded by an umbrella, Zito went to a bench overlooking the pool. Link Andrews stood, went to the lanai railing and smoked.

Klein shared the fact that both Nance and Dade were dead.

Andrews said, "Unfortunately you didn't get to interrogate Ishtar."

Klein nodded. "No we didn't, but we collected a lot of information last night from Miss Nance."

Santiago said, "Good."

Klein continued, "We need to get your statements. I'll interview you and Miss Varga. Agent Zito will interview Mr. Andrews." Zito and Andrews went to the second bedroom. Klein and Santiago went to the living room.

Varga said, "I'm going to change and soak up a few rays until one of you is ready to talk with me."

Each interview lasted about an hour. When they finished, everyone gathered in the living room.

Klein said, "Miss Varga, let's go in there and talk. Then we'll be done here."

Varga stood and walked into the second bedroom. Vito watched her saunter across the living room in her yellow bikini.

Andrews looked at Zito and chuckled. "Rank has its privileges."

Zito smiled and glanced at Santiago and nodded. "It does."

For the next thirty minutes Zito, Santiago and Andrews visited, talking about the case and events leading to Palm Springs. When Klein and Varga came back out Zito stood.

Klein said, "We're done here. If we need to contact you we'll be in touch."

Andrews said, "You can always find us through DataFlex Security Chief Ray House's office. We never know our next assignment in advance."

"I understand. Agent Paxton in Phoenix told us working with you folks would be a unique experience; something of a cross between industry, private investigators, and the CIA. After last night and today I'm inclined to agree. Obviously you don't follow our protocols, but you're good."

Zito looked around the group. "I dare say if we'd have been in Mrs. Dade's room she'd still be alive and we learn much more."

Andrews said, "Maybe, but she was a very savvy, guarded woman. She always knew what she was doing until her conversation with Andrea. Without her incriminating comments you had nothing to bargain with."

Klein smiled. "Mrs. Dade wasn't the only skilled operator in this group."

Santiago sipped tea whose ice cubes had long since melted. "On the other hand, gentlemen, consider if you had insisted on going to Ishtar's suite. I think it's a fair assessment to say Andrea wouldn't have been present and she knew the only way to get Ishtar to incriminate herself was through their discussion of activities they planned together. I'm equally sure Ishtar had decided to make sure Andrea was silenced long before their discussion. I suspect she planned Andrea's death taking place outside of the country."

Klein said, "Certainly a possibility, Miss Santiago. On the positive side the Director sends his appreciation to all of you and DataFlex. I also thank you for your assistance, but I would prefer next time, if such an occurrence arises again, just advise us of what we need to know and let us do our job."

Andrews smiled. Santiago said nothing. Dash observed the awkward moment without a word.

"Klein said, "Well, we best be on our way."

Klein and Zito left the suite together.

Santiago said, "We still need to call the hospital and check on Sam. If we can't talk to him, his wife may be about. I'm sure the Palm Springs PD will be up here shortly and we'll be doing statements again."

Santiago entered the number in her cell.

"East Jefferson General Hospital. How may I help you?"

"Mitch Santiago calling for Sam Evan's room, please."

"One moment." After a brief pause the operator came back on the line. "I'm connecting you to the Intensive Care desk."

"Thank you."

"Intensive Care. The operator said you're calling for Sam Evans."

"Yes. Can he receive calls yet?"

"Mr. Evans is receiving no calls but Mrs. Evans said she would like to speak with you."

"Please, put her on."

"Hello, Mitch."

"Martha, how's Sam doing?"

"He's resting, coming along nicely. In fact, they're moving him from ICU to a regular room shortly. He'll be recouping for a few more days, then we'll be heading home. Mr. Braun said he'd send his plane so we don't have to deal with all the airport hassle."

"Good. How are you doing?"

"Tired. I never expected anything like this with him working at DataFlex."

"None of us did. I don't know if he told you, but he and Link saved my life."

"No, but he's said many times since you two worked together on the Lindsey Braun kidnap that you're a special woman." She paused. "I'll have to go in a minute. They're here to move Sam."

Link Andrews took the phone. "Take care of the old guy and yourself, Martha. We'll see you when you get home."

"Thank you, Link. Ray House is also here. He'd like to talk to Mitch."

At that moment somebody knocked on Dash's door. When she opened it two Palm Springs Police officers introduced themselves. She showed them into the living room of the suite. Both officers, one male, one female, immediately noticed Dash in her yellow bikini as she slid on a cover. The young male stared at Dash. His partner whispered something in his ear and smiled.

Santiago watched the interplay and looked at Andrews.

Andrews chuckled and handed her the cell. "It's Ray."

"Mitch, are the bad guys gone?"

"Permanently. I thought you were with Shari Stiletto?"

"I sent her back on the company plane solo and came to see Sam. Does 'permanently' include the woman that slashed Sam's face and neck?"

"Yes, Andrea Nance is dead. I'll give you the details later."

"Okay, we have people moving Sam to another room."

"Fair enough, the Palm Springs PD is here for some statements. Give Sam our best. Bye for now." The connection broke.

First Andrews and then Santiago were interviewed by the lady officer. Dash had a longer interview with the young male officer. Santiago and Andrews waited out on the lanai until he was finished. The female officer worked on her notes in the living room.

"Mitch, I think the yellow bikini distracted the young man even though Dash is wearing a cover."

"I certainly hope so. She's young, beautiful and sporting a little skin while being most professional. When they come out I should give her a towel. I think badge boy was drooling on his way to interview her."

He laughed. "I'm glad you're wearing shorts and a blouse today. It would get really lonely sitting out here waiting for both of you."

"Link, where's your male pride? The young woman who interviewed us is more than jaw-dropping good looking."

"Women with badges scare me."

They both laughed.

When Dash finally came out of the bedroom from the interview the young female officer sitting in the living room walked over to her partner smiling.

"Did you get what you want?"

"Not exactly, but one can never tell about tomorrow. How did you do?"

She leaned to his ear. "I'm good and I can stand straight."

Santiago and Stewart could barely hear the officer's repartee.

She looked at Link and chuckled. "Sounds like when I worked homicide with Chance Stewart in Seattle."

Andrews leaned toward her ear. "Mitch, it's all part of the old 'no babe left behind' philosophy.

They returned to the living room. Andrews told the police officers the same thing he shared with the FBI agents if they needed further contact. Then the officers left the suite.

Andrews said, "Dash, I think you have a fan."

"Maybe, for a day or two unless we have to get back immediately."

Santiago winked at Andrews. "Link and I are staying in Palm Springs for a few days. I know a really nice boutique hotel on South Palm Springs Drive. I could make another reservation if you'd like. Ray always has us take a few days after a major assignment."

"No, I'll stay here if we get few days. I have some other plans in mind."

Andrews snapped his fingers. "I'll bet there's a badge number attached."

Dash's face reddened. "I'll never tell."

Santiago said, "Dash, it was a pleasure working with you on this assignment. I hope we'll get to do another together."

"Thank you."

Andrews took out his cell. "Time to call Ray back to make sure we're okay to stay here a few days."

He punched in the number. "Hello again, Ray."

"Link, your casual beginning tells me two things: you're done with the operation and want a few days off."

"Ray, you're a man of wisdom. Mitch wants to check on her cousin and I thought why not...."

"I know, help her out."

"You're psychic, Ray."

"You guys did a great job and this got much more complicated than I ever anticipated. Does Dash want a few days, too? You've all earned them."

Andrews looked at Dash and smiled. "Yes, she has a few things she'd like to do while we're here."

"I've already heard from the FBI. They are quite happy. Martha got Sam moved into a regular room. We'll be leaving New Orleans in a day or two. Link, share with Mitch and Dash my appreciation. You three can send me your reports email now that the moles are gone. And one last thing, a week from today Claude and Nikki would like to have you, Mitch, and Dash out to their place for dinner."

"Mitch and I will be there." Andrews covered the phone. "Dash, want to go to dinner at the Braun's residence a week from today?"

"Really?"

"Yes."

"I'd love to."

"She's in Ray. Anything else?"

"No, just get a little R and R. This has been bizarre to say the least."

Andrews nodded. "We will." The connection broke.

Santiago said, "Dash, we'll see you in a couple of days in Chandler, but beware of boys with badges. I know only too well they suffer a faithless hormonal disorder."

Dash laughed. "I hope so."

Chapter 20
Tuesday, July 15

It had been late afternoon by the time Santiago and Andrews relocated to the small boutique hotel in Old Palm Springs. Exhausted by the events surrounding the murder-suicide of Ishtar Dade and Andrea Nance, they had a quiet evening and retired early. The following morning each was quiet as they shared coffee by the window of their room overlooking a bustling crowd of people on the street below.

Andrews said, "You didn't rest much last night."

"No, just a lot of twisting and turning. Must be nerves."

"Babe, I saw the balcony over and over in my mind all night, too."

"I've never witnessed a suicide."

"I can't lie to you, it won't go away."

"I know. It'll take time to distance myself from it."

"We both need to, babe."

"Dash will, too. I'm sure she's just as caught up in the deaths as we are."

"Mitch, I went through something like this once. I can't describe accurately what I felt afterwards."

"What happened?"

"We were on patrol in a tiny village. A kid approached us. He couldn't have been older than twelve. One of the guys told him to halt. He took one more step towards us and blew himself up."

"God, how awful."

"It was. The only good thing about the incident – none of our guys were killed. Two were badly wounded but survived. The kid, the enemy, was obviously dead."

"But he was still just a kid."

"Yes, but you don't think about that at the time. I still relive the incident in my mind."

Santiago took a sip of coffee. "I saw hate in Andrea's eyes. They were cold and piercing when Ishtar made her offer to the agents."

Andrews reached for his cigarettes and stopped.

"Go ahead, it's that kind of day."

He lit a Marlboro. "Andrea knew Ishtar would find a way to survive."

"When I was a cop we learned not to personalize events. If we did it could be impossible to deal with the next issue; first a traffic accident with a dead child, and then an hour later a cat caught in a tree. We were taught to be detached. It was a survival skill, always be professional."

"Mitch, I know it's early but would you like a drink?"

"No, I want to go to the pool and swim laps for a couple of hours, just burn all the energy and anger out of my system. I wanted to grab Andrea but couldn't get to her quick enough."

"Don't blame yourself. Zito had a better opportunity than you. It just wasn't meant to be. Everything happened too fast."

"I know, but it just won't go away."

"Try to focus on something else. What about Doctor Grossman?"

"I should call. Mom needs help and dad some relief."

She picked up her phone, glanced at her messages then called Grossman.

"Good morning, Miss Santiago."

"And the same to you. Have you found anything for my mom and dad, yet?"

"I have found a very nice new facility which provides the care your mother requires in East Mesa. I would suggest you visit and make your own evaluation before committing yourself or them to anything."

"An excellent idea. You have my email, can you forward the information so I can study it before I get home in the next day or two?"

"Of course."

"And how is John doing?"

"Miss Santiago, John has checked himself out. He and a young lady who was also here for rehabilitation decided they no longer needed our help. He said he was going to LA when they left."

"Damn! Have you heard from him since?"

"No, and I wouldn't expect to. The odds on him returning on his own are minimal at best."

"I see. Bill me for what is due and terminate the residence. If you have particular forms I need to complete send them to my home address. Did he leave anything behind?"

Grossman laughed. "According to the report some dirty underwear, socks, shirts, and a ripe pair of jeans. Do you want me to send them to you?"

"The dump is a good alternative."

"We shall take care of that and I'll complete the necessary paperwork for John. My secretary will send that and the information for your parents today."

"Thank you. Hopefully I'll get him to return someday."

Grossman said, "Good fortune, Miss Santiago," and rang off.

Andrews said, "Are you ready to swim now?"

"Almost, I missed a call from Jill."

She called her sister.

"Hi traveler, how's the cruise going?"

"It's over. I'm in Honolulu. We landed two days ago. Now we've sorta parted company."

"Sorta?"

Jill's voice cracked. "I'm not with him anymore."

"Ah ha, going to find another fish in the sea."

"First I have to get him off my back. He's following me everywhere. It's kinda creepy."

"I'd think you'd be accustomed to men hanging around by now. Swimsuit models have a way of attracting attention. We both know that."

"We do, but he makes me nervous. He's spooky. I just want to get away without him knowing."

"Jill, if you feel threatened, go to the police. If you're free and want a place to hangout for a while come to Tempe and stay with me. I'm sure we could find a thing or two to do while together."

"I'll come to your place. If I file a report I have to include and address. I'd rather catch a redeye."

"Okay, I'm in Palm Springs for a day or two. When you get to Phoenix go to Ray House's office. He has a key to my place."

"Do I want to know why he has a key?"

"Business, Jill, real business."

"I'm sure."

"Right now let's get you on a plane. I have groceries a in the pantry and freezer. You'll probably need to get some fresh vegetables."

Andrews said, "Can he trace her movement if she uses a credit card?"

Jill said, "I heard Link. Yes, he probably can. He's a high tech CEO of a small company."

Santiago said, "Okay, Jill. I'm booking a flight for you. I'll pay with my card, but it will be in you name. Just pick up the boarding pass and go. I'll text you the flight information when I get the reservation made. Do you have any cash?"

"About a two-hundred dollars."

"Save it for necessary expenses like cabs to the airport and my place. When you get to the loft you'll find $500.00 cash in my nightstand. Use that rather than your card until I get home. More important, stay inside and out of sight as much as possible."

"In other words, stay home."

"Hey, we both know how our social skills get us in trouble once we're out and about."

"Yes, but you have Link."

"True, and I don't have a rich guy stalking me, either."

"You're right, and he frightens me."

"When you leave for the airport go out a freight entrance and catch a cab. Don't use the hotels shuttle service. I'm sure the guys in receiving will let you through."

Jill laughed. "That won't be a problem."

"And sis, from now until you get to my place, leave the booze alone. Better safe than sorry."

"I'm pretty nervous, I'll be here waiting for the flight information."

"I'll call back shortly." Santiago broke the connection then ordered a flight on American for 9:30, direct.

Andrews poured another cup of coffee. "Well, we won't be in Hawaii for a while. How about that two hour lap swim?"

"Yes, yes, yes. Too bad we can't do it naked."

"True, but we'd end up in jail. Mitch, I can help you and Jill if need be. Ray shouldn't have too much in the next few days or we wouldn't be here."

She stood. "Let's go change."

"Let's do it together. We can make up for our empty night."

"I've never thought of making love as part of recovery. I like your concept of therapy."

Epilogue
Thursday, July 17

Tempe, Arizona

When Michelle Santiago returned home her sister Jill was already enjoying the condo. After greeting each other Jill headed for the complex swimming pool and Mitch began unpacking. Her cell phone's ringtone sounded a new tune she had downloaded on the return trip from Palm Springs.

Link was the caller. "Hi, Mitch. First day home and I'm already unpacked. How 'bout you?"

Just getting started. I had to greet Jill and chat a little. Why?"

"I'm heading your way and thought we could do lunch on Mill. Jill is more than welcome, too."

"Right now she's at the pool. We'll ask her when you get here."

"That'll be in about ten minutes."

Santiago chuckled. "You just can't stand missing the company of two hot chicks."

"I'm a typical guy, Mitch, horny and hungry."

"Today you get a sandwich."

Santiago's door bell sounded.

"Hang on, Link, someone's at the door. It'll just take a second. Nobody knows I'm home yet."

Santiago checked the peephole and saw a middle-aged woman.

"Miss Santiago, I'm Linda Drake."

She opened her purse and took out a Smith & Wesson .38 snub nosed revolver.

"What the hell?"

Drake waved the gun. "Step back inside away from the door. I have no qualms about shooting you."

Santiago was still holding the cell phone. *Don't say a word, Link. Just get here.*

Drake said, "Are you done with the phone?"

"Yes."

"Toss it on the couch. Go to the center of the room."

Santiago did as directed.

"Sit."

"What is this about?" We've never met."

"No, you don't know me."

"What do you want?"

"You ruined the life of Jerome Xavier."

Santiago paused for a moment. "Ruined his life? Was he your lover?"

"No, a special friend."

"Your friend wanted to kill me right after he raped me."

"He wouldn't do that. You must have enticed him."

"If you mean by that he forced me to strip at gun-point, yes."

"That's not possible."

Santiago's face became flush. She squinted her eyes. "I was on my knees in front of the couch after he made

me strip and hit me. Then he tried to force my face into his crotch. I turned my head and he hit me again. I
grabbed one of my stiletto heeled pumps and rammed
it into his balls. That's why I'm alive and he's in custody."

"He said you wanted him dead."

Santiago smiled. "It crossed my mind."

Drake circled Santiago.

"Stretch out on your belly."

Santiago did as she was told.

Drake stepped to one side of Santiago and kicked
her in the ribs.

Santiago coughed bile and screeched as the ribs on
her right side cracked.

"Lay flat, bitch, or you're dead."

Santiago began to sweat as she struggled to catch
her breath. Her face became flush. Drake kicked her
ribs again.

Santiago screamed. "I am."

"Not fast enough. Now, flat on your belly."

Santiago gasped as she stretched out on her belly.
Hurry up, Link. "You loved Xavier, didn't you?"

"He was a good man."

Santiago shouted in a hoarse voice, "He was a mon-
ster."

"You took him away from me. I loved him from a
distance."

"No, Linda, he took himself away. Murder is murder."

"Self-defense, Canfield tried to kill him just like that
man, Wolfe."

"What about Clyburn?" Bound and a bullet to the back of his head."

Drake said nothing. She walked around Santiago.

"Keep flat or you'll get a bullet in an elbow or knee."

Santiago watched Drake circling her.

Drake pointed the revolver at the back of Santiago's hand. "Interesting scar."

"Ice pick."

"I bet it hurt."

"Yes."

Drake stomped on the scar.

Santiago screamed and pulled the hand back.

Drake laughed and waved the gun.

Santiago rolled onto a hip and shoulder.

"I'm gonna hurt you bad. You have to pay for Jerome's pain."

As Drake talked, Santiago looked up while trying to catch her breath. Sweat covered her face. *I must have a punctured lung.*

Drake stepped close and pulled back a foot to kick Santiago again. Santiago gasped, made a quick sweep with her legs and kicked the back of Drake's stationary knee. Drake lost her balance and fell. Santiago grabbed for the gun. Drake kicked her in the face.

Santiago's nose began bleeding, but she got hold of the gun hand. They struggled, rolled back and forth while hitting each other with knees and elbows. Santiago shielded her right side as much as possible.

Drake dropped the gun. Santiago hit her in the jaw with an elbow, rolled over and grabbed the gun.

Drake sat up. Her eyes bulged, blood dripped over her lower lip. Both women breathed deeply and started to move.

Santiago aimed the .38 straight at Drake's forehead. "I won't miss from six feet."

Drake's eyes shifted to the door as Link Andrews came crashing through it. He aimed his Glock at Drake. And smiled. "I see you ladies have settled your difference."

Santiago rolled away from Drake. In a raspy voice she said, "Call 911."

"Already did, Mitch. They'll be here in a minute."

Santiago looked at Drake. "Linda, I don't know what you saw in Jerome but he wasn't worth it."

"I loved him."

"He was a bad man."

Two Tempe Police officers came through the door, weapons drawn. One of the officers shouted, "Drop the gun."

Andrews did so and said, "Linda Drake assaulted Mitch. I think she intended to kill her. I'm the one that called you, Link Andrews of DataFlex."

The officers took Drake into custody.

An ambulance crew arrived. While they attended to Mitch, Jill returned from the pool.

Jill looked at her sister and Andrews. "What's goin' on?"

Andrews pointed at Drake. "That woman attacked Mitch."

Jill looked at Mitch, then Drake. "Burn in hell, you bitch."

One of the officers approached Jill. When she looked up from her sister her cover up opened revealing the gold lame bikini.

He said, "I'll need to ask you some questions, ma'am."

Jill looked at him, raised her eyebrows, and shrugged.

Andrews said, "Officer, this is Jill Santiago, Mitch's sister. She just came in from the pool. She wasn't here when the attack took place. More important, Jill is here undercover. She is being hidden from a stalker. If you do a press release her name must be left out of it for her protection."

The officer watched Jill. "I need to ask you a few questions."

Andrews continued, "Stalker."

"We'll guard the young ladies confidentiality from the press."

Andrews said, "Thank you."

The officer looked at Jill. "Miss Santiago, I may be back to ask a few questions later. Right now I'm going to the hospital to get your sister's statement."

The other officer took Linda Drake to their cruiser.

Andrews said, "Do you need a lift since your partner left with Drake?"

"No, I'll go in the ambulance."

Jill said, "Which hospital?"

"Chandler Regional."

The officer winked at Jill and left the condo.

Andrews closed the door after the officer. "Jill, are you staying or coming with me to the hospital?"

"I'm coming. I just need a minute to change."

"No rush, Mitch won't see us for the better part of an hour since she has to talk with the police and get checked in. I just want you to know it's okay for you to stay here out of sight if you choose."

"Link, Mitch is always there for me. I need to be there for her."

An hour later Andrews and Jill stood by Mitch's bed in an emergency room station.

Mitch looked at Andrews. "No more loose ends."

"Not that we know of. You give your statement?"

"Yes."

"How are the ribs?"

"Sore, not broken."

"Your lungs?"

"So far, so good."

He leaned over the bed near her face. Her eyes were bruised, swollen, flesh flush. "It's not pretty."

She smiled. "It just gives you something to look forward to tomorrow or the next day."

She patted his hand and looked at her sister. "Jill, I want Link to stay at my place with you tonight. I'll be out tomorrow and we can look into your seagoing stalker."

"Okay."

Mitch looked at Link. "Tomorrow we could still be in Hawaii, spiritually."

"And so we shall."

"The pills they gave me are beginning to work." She closed her eyes. "What a fitting end to our quantum adventure.

****

From the pages of *Eyes of the Stalker,* the fifth book in the Santiago Mystery Series.

PROLOGUE
Tempe, Arizona

Wednesday, August 12

Swimsuit model Jill Santiago stretched out alone on a lounge five floors up at her sister Michelle's Tempe Town Lake soft loft. Sweat covered her body and soaked her powder blue bikini. She watched the lake and park below while sipping ice tea through a straw. It was not crowded at this hour of late morning.

"You said it was hot out here, Mitch. No kidding."

She ran a hand over her flat belly just as her cell phone rang.

Two heavy breaths greeted her followed by a man with a harsh smokers voice; deep and forced. "Hello, Jill, you're beautiful today; sweaty and sticky looking, just waiting for me."

Jill looked over the railing of the lanai at the lake and park five floors below. "Who is this?"

"Your Number One Fan. I have been for years. I've followed every swim suit shoot you've done since we met at the Alcatraz event."

"Are you with the media?"

"No, the community of lust."

Jill paused. She rubbed the back of her neck and glanced at her door. *It's bolted.*

She said softly, "How did you find me?"

The man laughed. "Sweetheart, you're on line bio told me you have a sister living in Tempe that works for DataFlex. The rest isn't rocket science."

Jill swallowed and her blood surged. "What do you want?"

"That's obvious, you."

Jesus, this guy is in a fantasy world. She coughed. "I'm not available."

"How can you say that? Of course you are. Girls in your business are all whores."

Her blood surged. "Watch your mouth, asshole."

"It's okay, I'm here to save you from that sordid life. Your only passion will be me." He laughed. "We'll lust for each other."

Her hand began to shake. She shouted, "Goodbye." *Where are you, Mitch?*

"Wait, Jill, go to the door. I left a surprise for you." He ended the call.

She sat up and looked around. He's been to the door? *Jesus, a nut case. I left Hawaii to get away from Randy Rhodes. He was bad, this guy's scary.*

She went to the door, rubbed her palms together, and checked the peephole. "Nothing, nobody's out there."

She pressed an ear against the door. "All is quiet."

She touched the door handle. Her hand began to shake. Goosebumps appeared on her arms. She was covered with a cold sweat.

Jill stepped away from the door. Her left knee began to shake. She pressed her back to the wall. "Breathe, Jill. Breathe and relax."

She gasped for breath and rubbed her chin, turned and watched the door then darted across the loft to her purse and returned with a can of pepper spray. She looked at her hands and chuckled. "Phone in one hand, pepper spray in the other, an ex-cop/industrial espionage specialist for a sister – what more could I ask for?" She speed dialed Mitch.

"Hi, Jill, what's up?"

"Crank caller, a very threatening sounding man lost in a fantasy. He says he left a surprise for me at the door."

"Have you looked?'

"Only through the peephole. I didn't see anything but you can't see the floor at the bottom of the door, either."

"Is the door bolted?"

"Yes. I'm now standing here with pepper spray and a cell phone wearing a blue sweat soaked bikini."

Mitch laughed. "You're a girl dressed for action, but this is serious. Did he sound like Randy Rhodes?"

"No. He sounded much older; spooky, harsh, raspy."

"Don't open the door. I'll be there in a few minutes. I'm running across the park now."

A minute later Michelle Santiago boarded the elevator and punched the fifth floor button. No other passengers were on board. She took her Glock 42 from a purse and counted the numbers as the elevator went up. The door opened and she quickly glanced out. The hall was clear. She walked to the door of her condo and tapped.

Jill opened the door. "Thank God. I've had lots of guys call but nothing like this."

Mitch pointed at a wine bottle with a stick-on bow attached, and a plastic freezer bag taped to it. Both women crouched down to view the contents.

Mitch said, "I see, your fan spared no expense. Cheap wine with a screw on top, a plastic bag of goodies."

Jill said, "Let me see what he brought." She began to laugh. "A few packages of condoms, mints, wipes, and, oh, would you believe it, a used condom."

"That's disgusting, but it'll provide a great sample for DNA."

"Mitch, I'm thinking old guy for sure. The short breathe and raspy voice to start with, but I do believe the bottle in the bag contains little blue pills."

Mitch shook her head. "Nothing like a sharp eyed model. Have you called the cops?"

"No, I wasn't sure I should considering my under the radar role I have from Hawaii. You know, public information and all."

Mitch waved her hand. "True, but this is evidence which could provide critical data as to the perpetrator."

"I see your point."

Jill's cell rang again.

"I see big sister is home. She's as attractive as you. It looks like a threesome to me."

Mitch looked into the loft then went and closed the curtains. "Call 911, we'll work it out."

The man said, "You'll have to get rid of the other man's clothes. It's bad form and all."

Mitch and Jill looked at each other.

Mitch said, "Hang up now."

The man laughed. "Have a pleasant night's sleep.

****

Other Books in the Santiago Mystery Series

Book One

Book Two

Book Three

ABOUT THE AUTHOR

Ron Wick is a retired teacher, principal and poet from the Seattle area, now living in Arizona. As an educator he also worked with police and court authorities involving many criminal issues, ranging from juvenile delinquencies to suspected pedophiles. One of his students was alleged to be a Green River murder victim. He is dedicated to improving the quality of life for all humanity and will donate 10% of his royalties to Lions Clubs International Foundation, the charitable arm of the association of which he has been a member and officer for 35 years.

If you enjoyed *Quantum Kill*, be sure to look for the first title in the Santiago mystery series, *Gold Coast Murder*, the second title, *Desert Kill* and the third title, *Killer Disc*. They are available through all major ebook venues and in print at Amazon.

Talk to me at peterputter@juno.com